TIMESKIPPER

Stefano Benni

TIMESKIPPER

*Translated from the Italian
by Antony Shugaar*

Europa
editions

Europa Editions
116 East 16th Street
New York, N.Y. 10003
www.europaeditions.com
info@europaeditions.com

Copyright © Giangiacomo Feltrinelli Editore, Milano
First Publication 2008 by Europa Editions

Translation by Antony Shugaar
Original title: *Saltatempo*
Translation copyright © 2008 by Europa Editions

Library of Congress Cataloging in Publication Data is available
ISBN 978-1-933372-44-0

Benni, Stefano
Timeskipper

Book design by Emanuele Ragnisco
www.mekkanografici.com

Cover photo © Vicky Kasala/Digital Vision/GettyImages

Prepress by Plan.ed – Rome

Printed in Italy
Arti Grafiche La Moderna – Rome

CONTENTS

And I dreamed so hard
That blood came out my nose.

FABRIZIO DE ANDRÉ/MASSIMO BUBBOLA
"Sand Creek

PART ONE

1.

When I was very small, I saw a God. I was hop-hiking toward the Bisacconi school. Hop-hiking is when you sort of bound along as you walk downhill; I lived up on the mountain, and the school was down-slope from there. There's no stopping to catch your breath when you're hop-hiking, because the downhill momentum keeps you moving, a relentless rattling of young testicles, tiny lungs heaving with miniature panting. The Bisacconi is the village elementary school, a vomit-yellow cube surrounded by a garden of barbarously unkempt weeds. The school takes its name from a man called Lutilio Bisacconi, memorialized for dying at his own front door, murdered by his Fascist cousin.

And in fact, on the plaque is written:

To Lutilio Bisacconi, who fell.

At that point, they must have neglected to pay the stone carver, or maybe there was an ideographological dispute of some kind, because that's how it ends: "who fell." They don't say whether he fell in combat, or fell fighting in the Resistance, or fell in the prime of his life. Nothing. He just fell, period.

And whenever we read those words, we couldn't help but think of Tadeo, because back then nobody fell like Tadeo, eight years old and he couldn't see for shit, like a little old man; bowlegged as a cowboy and pigeon-toed, too, but he insisted on riding a bicycle anyway, and his bike looked like it had been chewed over thoroughly by a shark, plus he couldn't tell a guardrail from a cliff, not to mention the recurring tic that twisted his head to one side, so that not a day went by without Tadeo falling, with lumps on his forehead and bandages on his wrist, and Egyptian knees covered with hieroglyphics punched in by the gravel.

So really, they could just as well have named the school after him: *Tadeo, who fell, or is falling, or—you can rest assured—sooner or later, will fall again.*

I even suggested changing the name in a school composition; I got a lecture a mile long for my trouble.

Still, it was such a beautiful late-winter morning that my mind couldn't help wandering off on tangents. The meadows were sugared with frost and the sun was licking it off as I quietly sang that old Michele hit to myself: "If you've gotta leave me, won't you please tell me why." I sang as I ran down toward the school—my character-building destination—with my book bag banging against my legs, my feet aching from the cold, rime frost everywhere and birds soaring high overhead. The valley far below looked like an artist's palette.

I stopped to have a drink at the water trough and, let me tell you, I was ugly. Covered with zits of every shape and form: cusped, cratered, like a squeezed fig, nipple-shaped (let me enumerate the shapes). Then there was my nose, hooked like a chickin's beak, and a tufted thatch of hair that seemed to operate by vertical propulsion: an upward-thrusting toilet brush. Whenever I smiled winningly at a princess, she ran to the nearest dragon for protection. And whenever I went a-roving with my musketeer friends, they concealed me beneath their capes, to keep from unleashing panic among the populace.

About halfway down to school, I stopped hop-hiking at a vineyard to steal a cluster of Geschkwürtztraminer grapes. Every grape in the cluster was the size of my head (I exaggerate), a cluster of heads, eack with my face, every one of them screaming, "Don't eat me!" To add to the enjoyment of my stolen fruit, I reached into my pocket for a crust of perma-bread. In all my life, I have never encountered anything as hard and unyielding as that crust. Not even the teeth of a combine harvester or of a ravenous caiman could so much as scratch its surface. The crust seemed to have been forged of steel. The crumb had the consistency of certain stones, porous but extremely solid.

And so I sat down, since dawn was breaking and the sun was setting fire to the frost, laying down strips of smoldering coals, and the mountain skyline looked like a slumbering giant stretched out on his side. The sound of the running river kept me company, because I knew that in those waters swam creek-fish and pike and barbel and smelts: an array of magnificent creatures, darting and exploring dark depths that we can never hope to see. Not to mention squirrels, the slumbering badger, the tunneling mole, and the hawk soaring straight overhead. And two dappled cows, ruminating under a tree in perfect happiness as horse chestnuts plonked down on their heads.

It was a moment of poetry, but back then I had difficulty telling sad poetic moments from cheerful poetic moments. Whenever I felt a poetry attack coming on it was a little like when the bowels begin to stir, sending signals and tensing prior to the final liberating movement and so whenever the cramp of an eclogue or a sonnet or an unforgettable instant arrived, I'd grab myself a bite to eat.

I unhinged my jaw as if I were about to devour the horizon; I gobbled down Mount Mario, followed by the train station, a section of rural road, and then, with a grinding noise, a piece of bread. It was called perma-bread because you could keep it for a thousand years, and it would still be perfectly good.

Perma-bread could be eaten only by me, my dog Fox who was a hound dog the size of a horse, and the Irontoothed Witch, Strega Berega. Since Strega Berega was an imaginary creature that Selene (my babe) and I had dreamed up, and Fox only ate perma-bread softened with water, milk, and self-produced salivation, I alone could gnaw at a piece of authentic certified perma-bread—they had good reason to call me Lupetto, the little wolf.

So, crack went the authentic certified bread under my canines, woof went Fox in the distance, splurt went the juice of the Geschkwürtztraminer, and I wouldn't know how to ono-matopoeticize the sound of the river, but the sun continued ris-ing and the air was redolent with the scent of a particular and evanescent happiness.

I popped four grapes in my mouth, and three detonated in my trachea, because if a Geschkwürtztraminer grape doesn't get stuck in your throat it means there's something wrong with it. The grape must be swollen and compact with juice and sug-ars and bee-lust, and it should go off like a hand grenade when the tooth pierces it, an ejaculation of flavor, and the *schkwürtz* shoots up your nose and down your bronchi all the way to your pancreas. You choke and cough and writhe with pleasure and choke and writhe and, as you cough, you toss back one more grape for yet another burst of pleasure.

If you've never tried it, you're missing something, as my father used to say, after he caught his foot in a fox trap (I'll tell you the story later).

So there I was sitting on the icy ground, my butt freezing, eating perma-bread and Geschkwürtztraminer, watching a spi-der tatting its web, sunlight flooding the picture, and suddenly it was time for school. I thought I could hear the sound of the school bell faintly wafting up from the valley. I don't actually have a watch, I tell the time from the chill in my feet, and it was a chill that said seven-thirty: my big toe had gone to sleep, lucky thing, and my heel was creaking.

So I got to my feet and suddenly the panorama opened up and spread out, I could see the backs of fish leaping in the river and the village square and Selene sitting on a bench waiting for me, twisting a lock of hair around one finger, and that state-salaried swinish lout, Professor Tortoise, tapping one foot impatiently because I was late, and I could see the bust of Bisacconi (Who Fell) in the school atrium. I was already savoring the fine scholastic aromas that I knew would greet my nostrils—the smell of vomited chicken noodle soup and soft cheese wedges incubated by warm butts and pears boiled in grandma's chamber pot, and I thought to myself: one day, someone will pay for all of this. And at that very instant, I beheld the apparition.

Up out of the garden patch walks a man, lofty as a cloud, with a vast beard the color of a dung heap and an entourage of flies, dressed from head to foot in layers and rags, and a short black cape, patched with shiny swatches of old cloth, around his shoulders. He walks swinging a pearwood cane, and behind him snuffles an old, incredibly old, dog, who must have sniffed at puddles of tyrannosaurus piss in his day; the dog limps and wheezes as if he were full of broth.

The cloud-man smiles at me straight away, and it is clear that only a god could smile like that. Then he squats down on the hillock, silhouetted against the light, surrounded by heliotrope and chicory, and tugs down three or four different varieties of trousers and underpants, and then he starts taking a crap. And not just any old crap, the mother of all dumps: it looks like an anaconda unwinding, or kernels of corn pouring out of a combine harvester, or warm polenta being tipped out of a huge pot; it's a spectacular triumph of lukewarm shit, and when it spreads out on the ground it unleashes an immense and aromatic mist of steam, and the more he craps the more the steam spreads, settling onto the meadow and the trees and fogging up the shells of the snails.

And still he craps, a volume of shit that is just unbelievable, while the dog looks over at me as if to say, ah, this is nothing, and by now you can't even see the man anymore, just a huge cloud of steam with a rainbow running through the center of it. From the mist comes a labored, rapid panting that means he is still shitting, and birds fly around the cloud, chirping festively.

Then the cloud of steam dissipates and there, on the ground, stands a smoking obelisk. By now the earth is warm, and my feet no longer hurt.

And God takes from beneath his cape a fig leaf that can be found only in the gardens of Eden, gleaming, five-lobed, and without any of that butt-scratching fuzz, and he begins to wave the leaf as if he were fanning the sultan, wiping himself down and up and down and up.

Then he launches the biodegradable leaf into the air, and it glides away down into the valley, and I imagine that if it lands, holy and shit-covered, on the square in front of the church, it will become a relic, and people will come from all over to venerate the Leaf of God, and I'll become a latter-day St. Bernadette—leaving aside the chastity.

"This is the life," says God, stretching, and with his divine gaze he spots a royal amanita mushroom, though you'd never expect to find one here; he picks it, gobbles down half, and gives the other half to the dog.

"*Buon appetito*," I say to him.

"Thanks," he says. "It's a magnificent day to go fishing; it's the kind of day on which you might stumble into a chronosynclastic infundibulum and a Fuller-Gauss space might spring into existence, or you might suddenly fall in love and only realize it the next day."

"That's the truth," I say.

"Well then, what's your name, boy who never wants to go to school?"

"They call me Lupetto."

"Little wolf of the woods," says the God, raising heavenward a filthy and magnificent finger, "enjoy your freedom and one day you'll have the honor of assassinating the emperor. Do you happen to have a piece of perma-bread?"

I hand it over.

"You can't imagine how much good eating I'll get out of this," the big man says, "or what I'll give you in exchange. Now then, Lupetto, go over and stand under that hazel tree dripping with dew, and make sure to listen to the sound of the falling dewdrops. All set? Now, let me explain something fundamental. This," he says, "is a clock for the world outside."

And he pulls out a magnificent pocket watch, made of burnished steel with a pattern of stars and fishes. He opens it, and inside is a music box, with twelve spinning ballerinas. As each ballerina goes by she makes a little bow; in the middle is a gnome beating out the seconds on an anvil.

"It's wonderful," I say.

"The devil has even better ones, with incandescent minute and hour hands and a cuckoo bird that pecks at your eyes. But this one isn't bad at all. This is the timepiece that marks the hours of what you might call your normal day: the time involved in being tardy to school; getting up early; the hours that never seem to pass; calendars; the ten days it'll take you to recover when you're sick; or the six months you have left to live. The movements of stars, tides, and soccer games. Now: Pay close attention!"

The Lord God swallows the watch in a single gulp.

"Don't worry," he says, "I swallowed it. It's gone now, but time isn't stopping. Look around you: the magpie hasn't frozen in flight, the dew is still dripping, and you are still getting older. Now listen."

And I stand listening to the patter of dew dripping from the hazel tree.

"Now, that is the sound of your inner clock, inside. It measures a nonlinear time. This time runs back and forth, goes around curves and switchbacks, rolls itself up, invents things, and replays scenes. You can't measure this kind of time, whether you use stopwatches or the most sophisticated astro-mechanism. This is your own time. It measures your life, which is unique, and so it's different from my time or the time of Gabriele, my illustrious dog."

The dog makes a courtly bow to me, and as he does so, I notice he is wearing a watch on his paw.

"Don't be frightened, but you will always live with two clocks, one for outside and one for inside. The one for outside helps keep you from getting to school late; it's for when you're waiting for a bus, and it's for the day you die, to calculate how long you've lived. You swallowed the inside clock when you were little, though you can't remember that now. The inside clock measures and encompasses 176 protological times, ninety eschatological times, and thirty-six forms of chaotic, romanti-cized time. You can call it your second clock, or your duo-clock. Every time you hear ticking, whether it's water dripping, the chirping of a cricket, or any of the world's other rhythms or stammers, your duoclock may just start up as a result. You can't stop it. You'll zip forward or plunge backward, you'll see certain things, and you'll see other things over again."

"What does a duoclock look like?"

"You can't see it. It's made out of lots of different compo-nents, all mixed together so that they become invisible. You want an example? Take your house. You look at it from out-side, and you say to yourself: this is my house. But underneath the house is a cellar, a dark sub-basement with barrels, mold on the walls, and the smell of bygone years and centuries. But in that shadowy past, wines have aged and cheeses have ripened. Overhead is a grain loft, where you store flour, apples, walnuts, and dried tomatoes, with gnawing rats and thieving dormice scurrying everywhere—that's where the provisions for your future are kept. Then there is the house you live in, with its warm fireplace and smoky kitchen, water rushing through the toilet pipes, and the bed that embraces you, readying you for pleasant dreamland and nightmare alike, ice-cold sheets in the winter, and fevers, and hours of nighttime insomnia. And then there are times when everything changes: down the chimney comes night, the blazing sparks of ghosts, or fear of what's just behind the door. In the cellar, wine and darkness make you imagine journeys and sea battles. And in the grain loft, trapped birds bang their heads, like horrible thoughts. You understand this is your house, not the house that you see from outside, with windows, a front door, and ivy growing up the walls."

"It's complicated," I say.

"Nothing's complicated, once you walk around inside it. A forest seen from above is an impenetrable welter of foliage, but you can get to know it tree by tree. A human mind is incomprehensible, unless you stop to listen to it. History, well, okay, let's leave history out of this. And all this chitchat is just a way of telling you that from this day forward, your name will be Timeskipper. Now get going, because I can hear the school bell ringing, Selene is worrying about you, and light is glinting off the backs of the fish."

"Amen," says the dog.

And the God walks away, disappearing among the cypresses and quince trees. There are tears in my eyes, because I have just seen a deity—who can say whether it was a pagan deity, a clerical emanation, or a forest god?—but it's not the kind of thing that happens every day, and only rarely to good people, so think of the odds for a mischief-making, chronically-late scoundrel like me. I hop-hike down as fast as I can, sobbing and sniffling as I go, weeping and hop-hiking, and then I trip and fall and the Geschkwürtztraminer grapes explode in my pocket. As I lie there, flat on the ground, I listen to a chirping cicada as it peeps away rhythmically, *tzick tzick tzick*, and suddenly I feel as if gears are starting to turn in my belly, oh God, it's already happening. I hoist myself up, and I see a louring sky and the whole countryside twisting and deforming as if there is a rubber band inside it, like when you see the images of fish refracted in the water, and an instant later everything is transformed. The rutted path is now a street lined with houses. There is a stink as if the God had left the gas on. Down in the valley, a swath of black smoke wafts up from the town, and the river is just a parched bed, excavated and sucked dry. Running across the riverbed is a long, wide road that plunges into a hole in the side of the mountain. The road is full of cars pouring into the hole at top speed. Let's hope they've drilled another hole on the far side, otherwise there'll be a horrible catastrophe. And these cars aren't little runabouts or station wagons, they're long and streamlined; they look like spaceships out of that book by Jules Verne, and there must be thousands of them. Clearly, though, while autobody design has made great strides in the future, engine performance has slid backward, because they inch along slowly in a long line like fuzzy caterpillars, honking and spouting fumes from their rear ends. In the sky, an enormous and monstrous dragonfly is hovering, emitting a deafening roar. "Mamma mia," I say, "what's happening to me?" Then in a flash everything goes back to normal including the Geschk-würtztraminer juice dripping down my legs and the brutal chills, as well as a wonderful sense of freedom inside me, the sensation that many discoveries still await me, that there are many pages left to read.

I hop-hike and hop-hike and come into town and reach the middle of the little square. The bench is empty, Selene is gone, and I must be about ten minutes late.

2

My classroom was 5B, small and cramped; there was a single map of Europe, with Russia cut in half (no one knew if that was for lack of space or for political considerations), a single stick of chalk for the blackboard, a single large window, and a single giant dickhead at the front of the room: Professor Naselli, also known as Tortoise.

He was a nasty piece of work by birth, by training, and by personal preference, the whole unpleasant concoction rendered even more toxic by hemorrhoids and government manufactured, low-priced Alfa brand cigarettes, which we called stink-nails. He smoked four packs a day: four times twenty, eighty Alfa stink-nails. Each stink-nail meant a minute of loogie-hocking. A long succession of barking, huffing, and general nastiness that wound up archived in a sopping-wet handkerchief tinged the unhealthy green of riverbed slime.

Tortoise had a lopsided mustache, one segment trimmed shorter than the other, for reasons unknown to us. He always wore a dark-brown striped suit and never buttoned up his trousers properly; woolen underpants stuck out, occasionally offering glimpses of the old, slimy slug. Selene said that he did it intentionally, and that he was a sex maniac. The one thing she knew about sex maniacs was that you can never take candy from them; you could have sex with them, if you wanted, but never take candy.

Tortoise had a number of other unpleasant characteristics: he used an aftershave that smelled like a funeral wreath, his fingernails were yellow, and he had a wife who never left their house because she'd had a nervous breakdown; people said she smoked even more Alfa stink-nails than he did. Last of all, Naselli Tortoise Loogie-Hocker Funeral-Wreath-Stench was a political crusader, a follower of Federico Fefelli, nicknamed Fefè, who was running for mayor and was the biggest livestock dealer in the area. Fefè's campaign slogan was: "In a man's life, there's three things that count: family, barn, and church."

My classmates were a fine assortment, like woodland mushrooms: some good, some rotten, some broad and some skinny, variously gray or colorful, manure lovers or log dwellers; there were some who lived in isolated farmhouses high on the mountainside, while others were the privileged offspring of wealthy grocers and vintners. Some were adolescents innocent of real-life experience, others jerked off like Gatling guns. Some were tiny fragile creatures like Grattino, who died when he was just thirteen, his bones riddled with holes like Swiss cheese, others were lanky and goitered like Sterpa, whose mom and dad were first cousins—Sterpa lived in a desolate wasteland where blood relatives had been fucking one another freely for at least a century; he looked like a troll, but he was good-hearted.

Then there was Fulisca, a petite dark-skinned girl. Her father sold coal and cleaned chimneys. She had a faint voice that sounded like a rotary saw, and she knew how to make beautiful acorn necklaces for herself.

My best friends were Osso, who weighed 155 pounds, with fine fat thighs and the neck of a young calf; in fact, his father was the town butcher. He was such a constant font of wisecracks and horseshit that they had assigned him a bench all to himself, at the far end of the classroom, as if he were in quarantine, but you could still hear every word he said because he had a grown-up's booming voice.

Then there was Gancio the Sharp, who was skinny and fast, with almond-shaped eyes. He had been born under a full moon, so he had a head full of shooting stars, and he spent all his time planning pranks. He was an orphan, and lived with his three somewhat grim and surly brothers.

There was Selene, who was a cute little blonde, a bit chunky, and I thought she was beautiful, even if her teeth were a little rabbitish and she tended to whistle her *s*'s.

And there was Valisi Testadiferro and Nico Castagna and Lucianina Banghera and Camillina Figarina and Merlone Secchione (a nickname that dubbed him a "gullible grind"). In the younger classes, third and fourth grades, I'll mention just the special ones.

Grillomartino, because he had fast footwork and was a good soccer player.

Ciccio Mia, because when we played soccer he was always calling for the ball, "Mia! Mia! Mia!!!" He was short, but he was a very determined defense player.

Li'l Viper, altar boy and spy, the son of a wealthy landowner who possessed twenty-six vineyards.

Hilda the Howitzer, whose mysterious and magical larynx allowed her to burp, at the age of seven, louder than any boy in the school. If we filled her up with a carbonated drink, like Chinotto, she sounded like a belching choir of ten ogres.

Last of all, the hall monitor Grazia, who ran a black market in marmalade, twenty lire the schmear.

Now that I have listed them all, I walked into the classroom and Tortoise said:

"Late again, the young gentleman? Any special excuses today?"

Could I have told him that I'd seen God take a shit in a cloud with a rainbow? Could I have described the whole duo-clock-in-the-belly thing? So I gave him a simpler version:

"I was walking, teacher, sir, along the banks of the irrigation canal known as the Wall-o'-Butts, because the village laundrywomen do their washing there, and I was observing a number of specimens of the local flora and fauna with a view to bringing them in to present them as instructive displays for science class in fifth period. When all of a sudden I glimpsed a suspicious and vibratile movement in the stinging nettles that grow in such profusion in that area. Blind to my own personal danger, I ventured into the foliage in search of the reason for that mysterious quivering motion.

"And what did I see, teacher, sir?

"A serpent, bold and brash and particularly venomous, sandy colored, with a small head engorged on either side, just like Osso when he crams half a sandwich into his mouth, and I realized that this swelling of the neck (in the serpent, not Osso) meant that the snake was really pissed off and was about to attack.

"So I grabbed a big forked stick from the ground to defend myself.

"And then I discovered, teacher, sir, that the stick was nothing other than two bold and brash serpents, entwined in an embrace because this is mating season.

"What was I to do?

"I hurled the two bold and brash serpents at the lone serpent, and the unthinkable ensued.

"The lone serpent was the husband of the female serpent entwined around the male serpent, her lover, and so their illicit tryst was discovered, a huge fight ensued, a vicious quarrel with hissing and puffing and a battle to the death and so I delayed my arrival in order to observe the conclusion.

"And how, sir, did it end?

"Badly, sir. All three of the serpents bit one another to death. It was clear to me that there is just no room in the world for love, so I took the little corpses and buried them and erected a little altar with flowers on it, and they're still there if you want to go check whether this sad, sad story is true."

*

Of course, I didn't tell this story. It was too good to waste like that. I just sat there in silence, listening to Tortoise as he hocked loogies and lectured me. He was saying that we were a village full of goiter-ridden dolts, half child half beast, but things would be changing soon, oh how things would change, and that was what he was going to tell us about today.

I sighed. I watched in fascination as Osso dug a booger out of his nose and tucked it into his pocket. He can keep them alive for as long as two or three hours; he knows how to keep them from losing weight and moisture. He really has a green thumb. Fulisca was filling her notebook with black fingerprints. Selene was drawing houses. Since her house is small and cramped—her father's a tailor, her mother's a seamstress— she draws houses with dozens of bedrooms, elevators, escalators; you'd need to pack a lunch to go take a pee. In the meantime, I could see that Gancio was preparing a bumblebee. Gancio is the greatest blowgun sharpshooter on the planet, with the possible exception of the Guatayaba Indians of the Amazon. He makes blowguns out of plastic tubes and duct tape. He makes single blowguns or pan-pipe Gatling guns, and most important, he makes little darts that are faster and more lethal than any stinging insect. He doesn't use curare, only spit and a resin that he gets from cherry trees.

"You all believe that the world is nothing more than this god forsaken little village," said Tortoise between rings of smoke from his Alfa stink-nail, "and your bumpkin parents have never put it into your heads that anything else might exist. But now everything is about to change. A new mayor, whom some of you may know, Doctor Fefelli, is going to win the election, and then they'll build a highway through here. We are going to become an important—a very important—interchange. They'll build gas stations and restaurants and factories, and it's high time that you started studying hard, because when all that comes through here, it's going to belong to whoever grabs it first. This is the New Land of Opportunity—you can all become rich if you try hard. Understood? Do any of you know what a highway is?"

"It's just a bigger road," said Merlone Secchione. "Where you have to pay a toll to get on and off."

"In that case," said Fulisca, "they're going to get rich, not us."

"No, you donkey! Because, first of all, they'll have to exercise eminent domain. Where they're putting the highway through, the Italian government will condemn houses and land and pay top dollar. Then they'll put in infrastructure, and then tourism, big livestock operations, and they'll be hiring, in other words. There'll be construction and jobs and money changing hands."

"And what about the chickins?" asked Sterpa the Troll.

"The chickins?"

"Yeah, even with the road we've got now, there's a whole heap of chickin road kill. If there's an even bigger road, it won't be asphalt, it'll be solid chickin goo."

"Not just chickins," Selene said dramatically, "we'll wind up road kill, too."

"What a classroom full of donkeys you are," Testuggine shouted. "I ought to . . ."

But he never finished his sentence. Gancio's bumblebee hit him right in the thigh, his leg collapsed, and he tumbled to the floor. We were all suspended for the rest of the day. The next day, we had to be accompanied to school by a parent.

My father took me to school and listened to the lecture. But since he was a Communist carpenter, still limping from when his leg was caught in a trap, all forms of authority just pissed him off, and deep down he was on our side.

"For a needle in a teacher's thigh," he said dismissively.

"What should we say, then, after shooting at each other for years?"

But once he was in Tortoise's presence, he passed himself off as a serious, responsible father, and nodded sagely as he listened to the ravings of the stink-nail-puffing teacher, and each time he nodded I could feel him launching a mental pox that struck my teacher in various parts of his body.

"You see," said Tortoise, "your son is an intelligent young man, but he is also distractible. He daydreams, he drifts off, in history he mixes up dates, he does homework for the day after tomorrow, he talks about the future as if he already knows it, he discusses the Babylonians as if he had met them. He scrambles together novels and geography and animals. And, worst of all, when he talks he skips around from one thing to another, one topic to another, he follows tangents, and he never seems to know what time it is or what day it is. At least buy him a watch."

"I'll do that," said my father.

As we went home, he got an expression on his face as if he were about to reprimand me. Then he saw that I was feeling sad, and said:

"There are going to be serious consequences."

I waited, staring at my feet.

"I'm going to have to call you Timeskipper. You're not Lupetto, the little wolf, anymore. Now you're Signor Timeskipper. And today, as a punishment, you're going to have to split an eighth of a cord of firewood."

"Half today, half tomorrow," I said.

After the dressing-down, luckily, it was Saturday, and we went down to the river.

First we hop-hiked down along the riverbank, and then we arrived in the canebrake, and then we made our way across the Desert of Green Horseflies, a stretch of sand that was particularly well suited for a meditative pause for us and all the other little river rats of the village—maybe it was because the sand was soft, or maybe it was the natural haven created by the cane plants, which formed something like a line of shady curtains, but our bowels found inspiration there, and then the flies would descend to check our work. We set up base camp near our favorite water hole, where the river water flowed slow and clear; then the water tumbled over a little waterfall and pushed on, dark and muddy, beneath a large boulder. Under the rock, the river was fifteen feet deep, and immense pikefish lurked there, pikefish with snouts twisted and torn by the hooks they had battled, riven with scars, fighting pikefish that had yet to meet the Fishing Rod of Destiny.

I felt that the Fishing Rod of Destiny lay far from me, too, as I stretched out on the sand, dangling my feet in the flowing water, with a dragonfly hovering over my head. And as I lay watching Osso and Gancio getting ready to fish with the rock-banger method, the sunlight glistening on the napes of their adolescent necks and their muddy legs, I couldn't see a golden hook hovering above their heads, ready to snag them and hook them and then, with the great whirring buzz of the reel, haul them straight up through the clouds, up to the place where the Great Fisherman in the Sky landed squirming, gasping souls in his net. Nearby would be the man wearing a hat and watching, because not even God Almighty is immune to the First Law of Fishing: *whether or not you catch anything, sooner or later a man wearing a hat will show up to watch.* And the river changed color, depth, speed, and even water—the bright and musical water that flowed shallow over the river rocks was not the same as the slow green water that lingered near the tree roots, and the dark and ice-cold water underneath the bridge wasn't the foamy white water that rushed headlong down from the big slabs of rock, turning into a treacherous current, where, reckless kids that we were, we would dare each other to swim closer to the fatal point where the current began to swirl in icy whirlpools. There were many different waters and many different thoughts buzzing between the sun, my head, and the dry mud that served as my pillow. I watched Selene as she made a cane flute, carving it with her sharp little teeth, her slightly cross-eyed blue-green eyes and her buckwheat-colored hair, and I made a devout wish lest a strange fishing line take her away from me, perhaps using a strawberry as a lure—she loved strawberries. She glanced at me out of the corner of her eye, alternating between gnawing at the cane and smiling at me, and I felt strange. I didn't know if that was love, but I wouldn't have wanted to be anywhere else.

And then the first rock crashed down. This is how Osso and Gancio fished: they would find a broad, flat rock barely breaking the surface of the water, probably riddled with underwater fish dens, and then they would lift another massively heavy rock, and drop it onto the first rock. With the impact and the shock wave, all the fish that had taken refuge beneath the rock that had just been bombarded would bob to the surface, dazed and gasping, and Osso and Gancio would rush to gather them up.

I didn't like that way of fishing. It was as if a person were sitting at home having dinner and—*badabam*!—someone dropped a one-ton boulder on your roof and you shot out the window with a napkin still around your neck and a forkful of tagliatelle halfway to your mouth.

But even if I'd said something, they wouldn't have stopped.

In the meanwhile, Selene had hitched up her skirt a little bit, and she was wearing a very roomy pair of white panties. Roomy they might have been, but they were panties nonetheless, and I felt a warm current rush through me, with little fishes in it, leaping and diving.

What's more, I noticed that all the dragonflies were flying in pairs. It was mating season, they were having sex in midair, everywhere you looked there were duo-dragonflies. I tried to take my mind off all that aerial eroticism, but the first thing I noticed when I looked down at the sand was a dung beetle, big, shiny, and black, grabbing his girlfriend from behind; the pair of them were moving along in unison, taking dainty mambo steps and leaving a stripe behind them on the sand—the path of love. After that, I stripped down to my boxer shorts and leapt into the pool thinking, I want to see if they're having submarine sex down here, too. But the water was cold and tasted like mud. I got a knot in my stomach and went back to lie in the sun and dry off.

Badabam!—went Osso's huge rock, and up came four stunned little creekfish.

High above us, on the riverbank, we saw a group of men looking down at us. Then we heard a sound that we were to hear quite frequently from that day on, and high over the canebrake loomed the dragon's gaping maw, baring its teeth. It was a steam shovel.

"The destruction is already starting," sighed Selene, and began playing her flute. "They're going to take away the river, the fish, everything."

"The river is big, the steam shovel's little," I said.

Osso and Gancio rushed off to see the steam shovel. The current carried a little, crushed fish close to my feet. It was still alive. It was thrashing its tail, but it couldn't swim any longer, and the water was dragging it away.

It occurred to me that we were little fish ourselves, and that from one moment to the next a giant rock could come crashing down on our lives. We were of no importance to that rock; we counted for nothing.

For my age, it was a precocious, sad thought, like one of those children who draw nothing but skeletons, and their mother says "Good job!"

So I embraced Selene, and she didn't pull back. She was trembling, and she caressed one of my toes. She was smooth all over and had a good smell of soap.

3

I was standing still in the middle of the dirt track, watching my father. He was sitting on the stone bench on our little hillock-terrace, smoking a cigar stub and looking down at the valley. With him were his three dogs, each in a different pose. Alaska, the hound dog, was looking into his face, asking, "Well, what do we do now?" Fox, the shepherd mix, was sniffing the woods in search of any Cherokee Indians who might be lurking there. Nestor, the sausage mongrel, was slumbering, resting his head on his paws, and foreseeing trouble. The authorities had just told my father that, since the excavations for the viaduct would be running directly beneath our farm, they were planning to condemn the property and demolish the house; in exchange, they'd give us a lot of money. With that money, we could do anything we wanted, we could buy a house wired for electricity, we could start a profitable business venture selling licorice candy or shotgun shells. In short, we could behave just like all the others, who were glad to sell. My father wasn't glad at all, though. He hadn't shaved in three days, and he spent his time wandering the trails with his dogs, all the way out to the prehistoric gullies and the cliffs of Mount Mario. He was coming home late.

What could I say to him, as he sat high atop the rise that resembled the prow of a ship, in that sea of greenery and fog that occasionally made us feel as if we were miles away from the rest of the world? "Time to shave, Dad."

So I hop-hiked down along the dirt path, and in the meanwhile a year went by and the whole valley was a construction site. There were cement mixers ruminating away and excavators digging and pumps sucking and metal sheds and unfamiliar faces in the bars and cafés and glittering late-model cars and shredded chickins and a tremendous hubbub.

I went on through the vineyards: God had not appeared to me again. The only thing I saw, practically every morning, was an elderly fox, half blind, who noticed me only at the last moment.

It was the last day at the Bisacconi (Fallen) elementary school. I decided to take the lane that ran down through the plum trees, down to the Pond of Tree Frogs, which was a shortcut. Halfway along that shortcut was a vegetable patch and a wooden shack that made Robinson Crusoe's hut look like a penthouse apartment. In that shack lived Celsus. Celsus was six hundred and ninety-two years old and had always lived there. His home consisted of four boards nailed together and a sheet-metal roof. Inside was a stone bed, a fire pit, a couple of frying pans, a couple of chickins, and hundreds of empty cigarette packets.

I stopped outside the door and thought to myself: how can a man live for years and years in this dark hovel, what a tattered shred of a life, what a void of thoughts and human faces, what bottomless solitude.

And yet, when I saw him come toward me, hunched over, a basket of potatoes under his arm, carrying his hoe, I felt the warmth of his tattered shred of life, I felt his thoughts, I saw the fire that he lit at night, the blond woman that visited him in his dreams. I felt the hacking cough that interrupted his heartbeat. And the noise of the rain, the icy dawns, the smell of potatoes scrabbled out of the soil, and the taste of the wine that my father gave him.

I couldn't tear at that shred of life, it was made out of the same cloth as mine. Celsus, I felt like asking him, did you used to go down to the river when you were little? Did you see dying fish in the current, too? Who had the right to sweep them away? The world was moving on, and in order to move forward it might just destroy everything that lay in its path: that is, a fragment of our world, not some enemy planet. They were driving tunnels through the mountains, people needed to travel quickly everywhere, it was impossible to be alone, there would be no more huts, no more solitude. So it had been written. But when that vegetable patch had been wiped off the face of the earth, the highway had devoured the mountain, and the boards of that shack had collapsed under the huffing and puffing of the wolf, then where would Celsus go?

And I hoped that either the blond woman or the black cough would carry him off before he was forced to leave this home, because every hovel is a home. Every hole, every nest, every underwater stone is a home, even if it lacks a nameplate with a buzzer, a phone number, and a front door with a security-chain lock.

I couldn't understand why life had been allotted in this way, a vegetable patch for one person and the whole world for another, long days to squander for some and a short time of illness for others, freezing cold for Celsus and Alfa stink-nails for the teacher, dreams for Selene, and for me, freedom and ice cream and a career as a famous soccer player or as the conductor of a symphony orchestra, and the long-distance bus to the big city and, of course, scads and oodles of sex, more than a dragonfly. A brilliant future was awaiting me.

I felt happiness and pity at the same time.

I walked toward Celsus. He was half blind and didn't recognize me till I was just a yard away. He wore a snakeskin dangling from his belt. If snakes see the skin, he said, it scares them and they won't hurt me. Doesn't work with people.

He smiled at me through his two-and-a-half teeth and thrust a bunch of radishes into my hand. A gift. He lolled his head, his way of communicating friendship.

So I gave him two cigarettes I had stolen.

He acted surprised, rolled them in his soil-encrusted hands, and vanished. I thought: I'll never see him again.

Then I ran down the hill; it was the last day of school.

The IllustriousPrincipal (sir) delivered a speech about our future and the future of our little town which would soon became a great metropolis, and Gancio objected under his breath that the term "metropolis" was inadequate, if it's big then it should at least be a kilometropolis, and to shut him up I hit him with a lopez, which is a direct knuckle-first punch to the thigh, which hurts like a mother; he struck back with a salami-slice to the nape of my neck.

Here we should take a moment to run through some of the nasty tricks and forms of aggression commonly used in the schools of Italy in those legendary and admittedly savage times.

The lopez, as described above, is a knuckle-punch to the hard muscle of the upper thigh.

The *sblisgo*, or *scazonte* (untranslatable in any language), consists of a sharp snap of your knee to the back of the victim's knee, resulting in the complete collapse of his leg, as if he had suddenly stepped into a pothole. It's murderous.

The dogbite. You clamp your teeth ferociously onto the victim's calf, snarling like a rabid dog. It's stupid, but it always works.

The wet snap. You take the heavy elastic strap normally used to tie your books together, and you snap the victim's butt cheek with it.

The stretchie. This is a stinging blow to the ear of the guy sitting next to you with a tiny rubber band; stretch it to breaking point, and then snap it with vicious accuracy.

The drop-satchel kick. This is a brutal flat-footed kick, from behind and by surprise, to the book bag of the guy walking ahead of you. It has two-fold consequence: the victim drops his book bag and also suffers a painful sprain to the muscles of the arm holding the bag.

The salami-slice. Open-handed slap to the nape of the neck.

The lopez special. Sharp jab of the elbow to the ribs while running side by side, used in soccer as well.

There is insufficient time to cover a number of other stock attack moves, such as the sticky-booger, the simple arch-stomp, the back-handed smack to the nose, various shots to the balls, the simple trip-up, or the coordinated two-man backward trip, and other nasty attack moves that are rarely seen in action.

Anyway, I responded to the salami-slice with a double lopez, which is a second lopez delivered right on the bruise from the first. Gancio hit back with a jesusgod, and, in so doing, dropped his straight ruler, his triangle ruler, and his lunch box—not that he cared much about the rulers.

Even on the last day of school, sighed the IllustriousPrincipal, even on the last day of school you behave like donkeys. Mr. Tortoise, shrouded in a cloud of Alfa stink-nail smoke, nodded as if to say: these kids, at the very best, have careers ahead of them as panhandlers, and then Gancio puffed a bumblebee at the principal which, luckily, just missed him. The dart thwacked into the wooden frame around the blackboard, just like in the movies about Robin Hood, the guy who used to steal from the rich to give to the poor, which is something you can do if you're already rich yourself. And so the IllustriousPrincipal, unaware that a deadly Guatayaba arrow had just narrowly missed him, talked to us about the highway and the new businesses, like the chickin farms and the cement plants that would be springing up in the area. The Troll, as usual, got excited at the mention of the topic of chickins; he started bobbing his neck and nodding his head, just like a chicken. Fulisca stuck a finger up her nose, adorning it with a cinder-black nimbus, and then emitted a banana-flavored belch (she snacked on antique bananas, as dark as eggplants) and fell asleep at her bench. Flies buzzed over the LustriousPrincipal's fractured grammar; in conclusion he braided together a pair of phrases in Latin and then wished us happy summer holidays while reminding us to study because, he said, a brain is like a garden tool, if you don't use it, it will rust—and we all thought the exact same thing. And at that very moment who should walk in but Fefelli with his wife. It was an odd thing, because there were no other grown-ups in the auditorium except for the LustriousPrincipal and Tortoise, but Fefè was there to campaign—he felt as if he were already mayor, and there was an envelope sticking out of the breast pocket of his shit-colored pinstripe suit. A murmurous buzz of double entendres and lewd comments arose, a rosary of sly budding neighborhood gossips and young satyrs in waiting, because Signora Tiziana Fefelli, also known as Hotlips, was a woman with quite a reputation. An infectious wave of snickering and giggling swept through the room. Even Selene, who pretended indifference, couldn't quite keep a straight face, because she too had heard the legends concerning the lady in question. These legends sprang out of confidences that had been entrusted to Paolo the barber, and by him propagated to the rest of the community. The name Hotlips had to do, perhaps, less with her kissing techniques than with her corporeal structure at a, shall we say, deeper level. The stories that people told about her were a veritable latter-day Odyssey, but one in which it would have been better if Ulysses had never come home. Popular lore, in fact, held that our small town's Penelope tended to unzip men's trousers with her eyes, and that at dinner parties she was a regular and ruthless hidden commando, gifted with prehensile toes, capable of grabbing a man's pretzel under the table while the dinner guest she was targeting choked on his lasagna. Out in the fields, wherever you found flattened patches of alfalfa, there were two possibilities: either a cow had slept there, or Hotlips had screwed someone. People said that in her oral and rhythmic application she was as versatile as a world-class conductor, ranging from an alluring and enveloping *lento* to a majestic and heroic *crescendo*, all the way up to the finale with an impetuous, snarling, lip-smacking flourish. It was also said that she made love in varied callisthenic positions, and that she had practically induced a heart attack in a doctor who had come to treat her for a sore throat and would never have imagined the unprecedented throat therapy in question. She was untamable: her husband had forbidden her to leave the house, but there was a steady procession of plumbers, technicians from the gas company, and carpenters and electricians, because there seemed to be a gnome at work in that house, an especially muscular Cupid, who managed to crack a water pipe every day, damage plaster, gnaw at light bulbs, and shatter chairs, so that the lady of the house could receive professional visits from the local artisans.

But Hotlips, swathed though she was in renown, seemed to take no interest in the gossips, in the LustriousPrincipal, nor in us; she appeared to be lost in some magnificent thought. She batted her eyelashes and smeared her bee-stung lips with enough lipstick to turn a pot of hot pasta bright red. But her face bore a pliant, melancholy expression, as if to say: "Oh, let me have my fun."

At her side was her little husband, restless and excitable, short and fat and sneering, with a three-hundred-dollar check for the school's new gymnasium. Puffed up with conceit, as if to say, "Here, I have so many of these I can't be bothered," he put the check, folded and rumpled as if it were scrap paper, into the LustriousPrincipal's hand. She, meanwhile, engaged in a little by-play. She bent over, making her slip rustle, and picked at a run in her stocking. Our young heads tipped to one side, our rosebud mouths popped open, and she noticed: she gestured, as if to say, you little rascals. In our minds, two golden cuckold's horns garlanded with grapevines protruded from Fefelli's forehead, the tips polished with Brasso. We felt a burst of gratitude to Hotlips.

Still, we'd been there for a while, and we were ready to pee in our pants, when finally the ceremony concluded with the Italian national anthem blaring over the loudspeaker. After that, there was a general exchange of farewells and lopezes, and then, howling like wolves, we ran outside, free at last, in an unforgettable burst of group and individual joy. Some were laughing, others leaping, and a few, like Selene, were weeping. The Troll alone, kept asking if we'd understood the whole thing about chickins, but a book bag to the crotch finally shut him up.

We went out to the village square, and the loudspeaker was playing a polka—polkas aren't Polish, as my uncle the dancer, had once explained to me: "Mazurkas are Polish, and your dead mother, bless her heart, loved mazurkas." I couldn't remember anything about my mamma, except a photograph on my dad's bedside table, or a skinny face watching lard melt in a frying pan. Who can say if she caught a glimpse of how few were the days left to her? But this was not a day for sad thoughts: there were lots of new faces at the market and a line of chrome-bedecked cars with big rounded rear ends—models that we had never seen before. Bortolini the mechanic stood studying the cars, his present and future line of work. We went hunting for cotton candy because everywhere we turned were little kids with gnome goatees, sugar-spangling all the way back to their ears, but by the time we reached the candy stand there was a line. And so we bought liquorice; Fulisca was happy about that because it ensured that we were as sooty-dark as she was. Then we went to watch the cattle trading, where Fefelli was sparring with two red-faced Tuscans, in a hail of numbers and weights and God-Almighties. Gancio bumblebee'd a young city slicker who had pissed him off by courting the mailgirl, who was one of our sex symbols. Then we figured out how much money we all had and decided to go take a ride on the asskicker at the Luna Park. The gypsies had set up their carnival on the town soccer field, and from far off we could already hear shrieks of aerial fright and excitement.

Just then, I saw my father sitting at the tables of the DPC.

The DPC, or Doofuckallian Philosophical Circle, met, depending on meteorological conditions, out front of or inside the café in the village square. Some were members of the proletariat, others a little less so. They assembled to discuss an array of topics: plant blights, like downy mildew; the great historic soccer star Omar Sivori; Mussolini, and the fate of the world.

This seems like the right time to pass in review the various leading characters of our village.

First of all, Baruch, former resistance leader. He had been given his nickname because he was very wise and somebody had once seen a book of philosophy by a certain Baruch Spinoza; Baruch sounded better than Spinoza, so the nickname stuck. He was a skinny, bony, horsey type, invariably wrapped in an overcoat, whether it was sunny or freezing out; he also wore a heavy fustian jacket with patches on patches on patches; the jacket was exponentially patched. He smoked Toscanello cigars that you could smell four miles away. I don't know what treatment was involved—he claimed that he steeped them in grappa, his friends said that he slipped them up a cow's asshole—whichever it was, the aroma was unique. Baruch served as our spiritual guide.

Lavamèl was the town *jazza*, which meant jinx, hoodoo, or bird of ill omen. He dressed in black, with an ample Draculaesque cape, dark glasses, and a fifteen-year-old black cat named Carbuncle that always looked as if it had just been run over. When a car finally did hit it, a week went by before anyone noticed. It was Lavamèl's responsibility to announce misfortunes, diseases, and bus delays.

Luckily for us and unfortunately for him, he was completely incapable of bringing bad luck. And so he was simply our professional pessimist.

Karamazov was spheroidal and mustachioed, with a head of hair like Einstein's. He had spent six years in Russia constructing oil pipelines. Because of the freezing cold, he had lost two fingers and many brain cells. He had become a libertarian Stalinist, which is a pretty spectacular contradiction in terms. According to him, anything you cared to name was better in Russia. His job was to be village ideologue, Kremlinologist, and liar.

Then there was Caprone, professional peasant. He had the face of a boxer, a pair of arms that could move any object necessary, from a 250 pound hog to a tree trunk. He had thumbs that would put any super-endowed macho porn star to shame. He lived downhill from the soccer field, with sheep, hogs, and a dog named Hisssss, because that's how Caprone called him over, with a sibilant whisper. Hisssss was the biggest, dirtiest, friendliest dog on earth. Caprone lived in a hut made of an assortment of building materials; he scorned his own brick house, and he hid a box containing all his money in a different place every day: down the well, under his mattress, in a hole in the floor. Occasionally he forgot where he'd hidden the cash, and he'd go hungry for a week until he found it again. He was our agricultural expert. The only problem was that he almost never said a word—maybe a sonnet a month. So if you wanted information, you had to frame your question as a multiple-choice quiz.

Example: Caprone, what's the best time of year to plant tomatoes?

a) All year round?
b) Spring?
c) Fall?

d) Winter?

"Springtime, consarn it," Caprone would answer.

Don Brusco, our parish priest, saw to the care of the town's souls. He was a rigid, sanctimonious, overly religious pedant. After a couple of glasses of red wine, he became a tolerant, middle-of-the-road moderate. After five glasses, you could make any confession imaginable and obtain full absolution. Balduino claimed that with grappa he'd gotten him to sing "Arise, ye workers from your slumbers, arise ye prisoners of starvation!"

Skipping forward one generation, we have Balduino the barman. Balduino was the head of the local chapter of Alcoholics Homonymous, whose membership consisted of Piero the cheese maker and Piero the barber. Together, they would drink experimentally. That is, they would try to see how many types of cheap but potent high-proof liquors a human being could absorb before dropping to the floor. They loved whisky and fine wines, but their joy and their damnation were Strega yellow liqueur, Cucchi-brand *millefiori* sweet herbal liqueur, Borghetti coffee liqueur, Pezziol Vov eggnog liqueur, Inca Pisco, Marsala wines, and aged Stravecchio brandy with mint. Their motto was: if you can knock it back, it ain't bad. The three of them were liars, visionaries, and—since alcohol offers extraordinary illuminations—solvers of complex problems.

My uncle Nevio was the Expert. There was nothing in the vast catalogue of the world that he did not know. He was an expert on hunting, fishing, tilling the fields, vineyards, automobiles, tractors, ancient and modern history, soccer, and Olympic sports. All that was necessary was to utter (nowadays, we would say "type") a single word, for instance: *hare*. Uncle Nevio would raise a finger to his temple, start his search engine, and out would come the first ten results:

—The biggest hare ever caught in our area weighed six-and-a-half kilos; the hunter was Osso's grandfather, with a first-barrel shot.

—In winter, hares don't turn white, they just grow a softer fur, and don't dig dens.

—The most delicious recipe is jugged hare with black grapes.

—In Yugoslavia, hares are so abundant that hunters catch them with butterfly nets.

—Hares can leap as far as seven meters, but they don't attach any real importance to that; they don't give a fuck about it.

—The *Leprotto*—Italian for little hare—is a model of a 2-cycle 48 cc. scooter; a decent scooter, though the clutch is stiff and the wheels are too small.

—O'Hare was the name of a guy who died when he tried to defuse a land mine on a bet. He said, just before doing it, "You know, it's not like you need the bomb squad," but he was wrong, that's exactly what you needed.

—The iron-bound law of the hare says: if you have a permit to catch only a single hare, and you shoot a big one, while you're putting the dead hare into your game bag, a hare twice the size will inevitably go bounding by.

—The main difference between a hare and a rabbit is temperament.

—A dead hare is one of the most popular subjects for still-life painters.

Press one finger into the nape of the neck for more results.

At café tables in the shade, beneath a linden tree buzzing with bees, sat the Courvoisier group, named for the fact that they were not just old, but VSOP, that is, very special, old, and pale. They were:

Cipolla, who in 1947 hit a land mine while plowing and shattered both eardrums; he was so deaf that, when he hit a second land mine with his plow in 1948, he came home all covered with mud and blood and said: A mine must have gone off down by the river, I heard a roar from that direction.

Arturo Ninety-Six, because he was four years short of a century.

Maria Casinò, who at age eighty would play any game imaginable, from tressette to poker to four-card bestia; she'd even play Go Fish with kids, if nothing better was available.

Among men and women of average levels of education, the most important local institution was Regina, who ran the stationery shop, newsstand, and tobacconist. Born to a family of southern extraction, a former Communist courier in the resistance movement, with the beautiful face of an Apache brave, Regina was an expert in any type of publishing you care to name, from cookbooks to love stories and romance novels, from crime reporting to comic books, from political analysis to gossip magazines. People turned to Regina with all sorts of inquiries. To find out how to roast quail with cognac, to learn how *Gone with the Wind* ends, but also for the name of the current Italian minister of the interior and in what issue Tex, the comic book hero, encounters his nemesis Mephisto for the first time. Moreover, she was an assiduous reader of obituaries. If somebody died who had had even the slightest contact with our town, she told us about it. One morning she appeared before the group of Doofuckallians and announced: "Ettore Glisenti is dead."

"Who's that?" they all asked.

And so she reminded them all that, ten years ago, there had been an invasion of wasps in the village. The wasps had built a nest in the bell tower, and they set out from that base, raiding food sources and stinging like crabs. Luciana's son went into prophylactic shock. He swelled up like a watermelon, and they had to take him to the hospital and give him an antihistaline. At that point, it became clear that something had to be done. From the big city, a yellow truck showed up. On it was written

Rapid Extermination by Ettore Glisenti, Killing Mice and Bugs for the Cognoscenti. True professional that he was, in a single afternoon Ettore solved the problem. The ground was littered with so many dead wasps, it looked like the aftermath of the Little Big Horn. After that, Glisenti was an honorary citizen of our little town, and now Regina was admonishing us to pay him the honor that was due him.

Then there was Luciana: haberdasher, fortune-teller, and fashion expert.

Zoraide, who did needlepoint and was the local beauty queen in 1950.

La Grinza (aka Wrinkles), the single most devout old lady in the village, who prayed while pedaling her bicycle.

Veronica the gas-station attendant, tall and bosomy, who'd heard so many jokes about pumps and nozzles and fill'er up that her hair had turned white before she turned thirty.

Breadlocks the baker, who was unfailingly cheerful. He'd sing opera all night long while mixing and kneading dough. Legend had it that from time to time you'd bite into a doughnut and hear a few notes from *Rigoletto*.

Then there were his sons, Giglio and Loris Arduini, the heartthrobs of the village, their biceps always dusted with flour.

And Favilla, the blacksmith, with cinder-singed whiskers.

And Maghino the electrician, who used to say that if a lightbulb blew it was because it had seen something that upset it.

And Luis the tractor driver, who embroidered the fields with his Landini tractor.

And Bortolini, the mechanic who could fix anything, from a bicycle to a bulldozer; and who more importantly, was the world's greatest fisherman.

I mostly hung out with the group known as the bombardiers, so called because of their overbearing personalities and their tendency to raise their voices, disagree, and argue.

Carburo, who burst into thunderous tirades at the drop of a hat, was a labor organizer and a champion billiards player. Belloni the plumber, the Sherlock Holmes of plumbing, renowned for his skill at finding leaks in walls, and equally famed for the size of his own God-given piping. Ossobuco, butcher, father of Osso, inveterate Fascist, and magician of the barbecue. Edison Rondelli, holier-than-thou grocer, who smelled of detergent, boullion cubes, and various herbs. Dogs followed him everywhere and peed on his trousers. No one knew just why; one of his several aromas just must have set them off. Chicco the coppersmith, decorator, house painter, and caricaturist, as well as a painter of "reclining uncomfortable nude women." Paolo, the barber, beautician, and gossipmonger.

Separately, in the full-time Doofuckallian category, was Slim the Magnificent. Slim had never paid for a drink in human memory; he managed to cadge and freeload all year round. He was one of the first, thirty years at least before the media came up with the term, to develop a signature outfit. Always dressed like a dandy, he would sign purchase orders with tailors, but he'd never pay a cent. The only work he ever did was as a bird-man. He had a unique dental structure, with a space between his two front incisors, and he could imitate to perfection the songs of 120 different bird species—and twenty-six of those species were imaginary. When I say that he imitated them to perfection, I'm not exaggerating. He'd walk behind a cat, twitter, and then watch the cat go crazy. Every so often, he'd go hang around an outdoor trattoria, wait for the busiest time of the night, begin his bird show, and make a little extra money. The hunters tried taking him out in the woods with them, but it didn't work. He could fool cats, but he couldn't fool birds.

And, last but not least, Libero, the village nut who walked with a limp, the world's most skilled carpenter, a man who knew how to make a model cuckoo bird out of toothpicks. And, in case you hadn't guessed, my father.

4

My father stood out even among the bombardiers. He always spoke standing up, his arms outstretched, walking back and forth like a referee, smoking and tossing back glasses of red wine. The others would listen and never managed to get a word in edgewise. He'd see me and wave, but without a smile. His beard had grown long and was speckled with white; he looked like the old fox of the hill.

I heard him say:

"They're giving us a few bucks, but then they'll make all the real money. They'll take everything we ever owned. How can you be so blind?"

"You're just a pessimist," said Uncle Nevio. "There'll be tourism. They'll come here for the hunting. And I'll open a hunting and fishing supply store: shotguns, cartridges, fishing line, waders, nets, all kinds of bait and lures, earthworms, crickets, red wrigglers, and maggots. We'll get rich."

"Sooner or later, there'll be no more hares," said Rondelli, who actually looked exactly like a hare.

"There are currently ten million hares in Italy," said Uncle Nevio authoritatively.

"I sold out, and I'm happy I did," said Ossobuco. "Look, there was no real choice. You want to take on the lawyers working for the highway? They decide what the price is going to be, it's the law of the market place, just like with veal calves."

Slim cawed once like a crow; it was his way of expressing disagreement.

"But it's not just the government condemning land," my father insisted. "There's land that hasn't been condemned, and Fefelli's been buying it up. What's going on?"

"I'm selling," declared Chicco the coppersmith. "I'm going to open a restaurant with a menu embossed in gold. I'm already working on it."

"What about the craft cooperative?" asked my dad, grim and querulous. "We're not doing that anymore, I gather?"

"Oh come on, drink up," said Chicco, and the group of friends seemed less friendly than usual. Maria Casinò showed up, suggested a trick-taking version of *tressette*, and was brusquely invited to go somewhere else and turn a trick.

"What about the river?" put in Baruch. "Why do they want to dig up the whole river?"

"Because they need gravel to make concrete. They're even going to build a plant."

"Then we can go catch fish in the asphalt," said Arturo Ninety-Six, worried about his future like a young person would be.

"You're a bunch of stick-in-the-mud conservatives," sighed Uncle Nevio. "I'm going to watch the new television set at the bar. You can see the game with life-size Omar Sivori, and when they kick the ball toward the screen it knocks you right out of your chair. Cheer up boys, new things, that's what we need in this town, new things."

Then Karamazov spoke up.

"There's new things and then there's new things."

My uncle knew already knew where he was heading.

"Why, how would they do things in Russia?"

"In Russia, when Stalin needs work done, he moves men. He says: you, a million of you, drain the river. And a week later, the river's gone. Then, you, another million, get out of there, you're not doing enough work. Off to Siberia with you, to cultivate vine-yards. And they do it. It won't do you any good to shake your heads. I've seen Siberian grapes, they're red, fat, and lustrous, with a little fur to protect them from the cold. And every Russian has a single bunch of grapes and one bottle of Siberian wine— not two, or you have to pay a fine. Because over there it's all owned by the collective, including land, bicycles, and animals."

"What about cows?" I asked.

"Russian cows produce easily a hundred, or even two hun-dred, liters of milk. Whatever the party orders. And they have little scoops tied to their tails to scoop up their own manure, and they dump it in the cesspit themselves. They make neat, square shit piles, with the red flag flying overhead."

"And the chickins?" asked the Troll, appearing suddenly out of nowhere.

"Russian chickins are as big as falcons, and they lay eggs twice a day, morning and evening. They don't get run over by cars, because in Russia the cars have brakes we can only dream about. I've never seen a Soviet chickin squashed flat on the road and I've never heard of a car crash there. No one has ever even heard of a Russian falling off his bicycle."

"Karamazov," said my father, "you should run for mayor, you have a real gift for lying."

He said it in a loud voice, possibly because he had noticed Fefelli arriving, accompanied by Hotlips and two oversized greaseballs, with the faces of cat killers. They were the Pastori brothers, Licio and Nerio. They worked for Fefelli, as drivers, gophers, and all-purpose hoodlums.

"So, are you all coming to my party tomorrow?" asked Fefelli with a broad smile.

"At Villa Meringue?" replied Balduino, appearing suddenly with a glass of Sheepherder's Special Amaro in hand. Balduino specialized in inappropriate wisecracks, what the French call *gaffes*.

Fefè's villa was, in fact, known as Villa Meringue. It was a blinding white with a profusion of stuccoes, matchboard woodwork, slender columns, sugar-frosted parapets, festoons, and bas-reliefs. There were conjectures as to the identity of the architect. In our opinion, it was the witch from Hansel and Gretel; some believed it was the architect who designed the Fascist Littoriale Stadium, and others thought it was Bread-locks the baker.

"Then we'll see you all in the garden behind my villa. You know where it is," said Fefelli, with a hint of annoyance.

"And what exactly will we be celebrating?" insisted Balduino.

"Why, the start of my campaign for mayor, of course. Wine, grilled sausage, and dancing. And I'll talk about my platform."

"He never stops working," said Hotlips, apologetically, with a downcast expression, her eyelashes lowered.

Slim imitated the cry of a pheasant in heat.

"Well then, I'll expect you all tomorrow night," said Fefelli, and began handing out Muratti Ambassador cigarettes, the flat kind, a real treat. My dad was crazy about them, but he brusquely said he never smoked that brand, turned on his heel and left.

"That guy," said Fefelli, "is a nut; pay no attention to him."

"He's my brother," my uncle said, "he's a little wild, but in the end he always obeys."

"He's not a dog, you know," I said. I was so angry that I felt as if I were about four inches taller.

"And who is this nice little boy?" asked Fefelli.

"The boy who's going to cut your throat," I muttered in reply.

"I beg your pardon?"

"I didn't say a thing. I'm not coming to your party. We're going to catch frogs."

"Excellent," said Fefelli. "Then you can sell them to a restaurant and earn yourselves some pocket money."

"Hey, guys," said Osso as we walked away. "The next mayor is cool. He can make money by farting."

"If that were possible, you'd be Rockefeller," said Gancio.

"Let's get out of here," said Selene, "it's getting crowded."

"The reason you say that," said Osso, "is because of all the babes walking around in plaid skirts and white knee socks. You're just jealous."

"Us town girls can be just as elegant as they are," Selene objected.

Just then, Hilda the Howitzer walked by, a bottle of orangeade with a straw in one hand, and she let out a burp that could spin a merry-go-round. Right behind her was Luciana, scratching her ass.

"So, are we going to the asskicker or not, guys?" yelled Gancio.

"Last one there, the Guatayabas'll cut their head off."

The asskicker was the most wonderful ride imaginable. In the middle was the rotor drum, painted gold with a bunch of Martians that looked like a hybrid between angels and chick-ins with staring eyes. On top of it was a flashing sign that read Magic Flight, and hanging from chains were the chairs, in an array of colors, each with a safety bar. "If you use the safety bar," said Gancio, "you're just a pussy."

"I don't care, I'm using it," I said. "Last year, a little kid was thrown off the ride, flew a hundred yards through the air, and landed in the kitchen of his own house. His mother found him in a pot of minestrone."

Osso and I had dreamed up that one.

At the ticket window was a Gypsy with an earring and a scar on his chin. I immediately guessed that he was the pirate Van

Maxel, there in disguise to rescue the young Contessa Velda who had been kidnapped by the guy running the shooting gallery; she was being held captive, forced to reload carbines.

"Snap out of it, kid," the pirate snarled at me, because I had fallen into a reverie standing in line.

"How much is a ride?"

"Fifty lire a ride, three rides for a hundred lire. It's a bargain."

"Guys, should we get three rides?"

"I don't have enough money for three rides," said the Troll.

"Then you can stay on the ground and watch us," said Osso.

When the siren sounded, the previous shift of riders got off, weaving and stumbling, their brains still spinning. The new shift pushed forward: there were twelve seats for twelve asses, and it was between us and a gang from Castellito, a village on the far side of the river. First, Osso threw a punch and hit a guy in the forehead who had been about to steal his favorite chair, painted silver; then Gancio got into a skirmish with a guy twice his size; with a synchronized move, Selene and Fulisca tripped a bossy fat girl—one shoved while the other bent over to form the "stumbling block." In a gang war, you have to command respect.

The rotor started turning and the centrifugal force was with us. We gained altitude and I felt a tumbling lurch in my stomach and heard Fulisca shrieking as if she were already in the ionosphere. Then there was a sudden yell of pain, Gancio had bumblebee'd one of the guys from the Castellitese gang. I reached forward and grabbed Selene's chair and gave her a shove, then I started to spin round and round, and at the same time I was swinging further out and further up, pitching and yawing, and I saw the piazza below me spinning, the banners in the market square, and the line of the mountains. I thought I saw my father down below, watching, with his hands in his pockets, and the chair kept going higher and higher, and I felt a surge of nausea, I saw a stormy sea and a pirate ship with Van

Maxel handing out tickets "three rides, three rides on the boarding party, a hundred lire," I had a nail in my head and everything went black until I projectile-vomited right onto Osso's head, I heard him swearing in the darkness of space, I flopped over and lost consciousness. The rhythmic creaking of the swing chairs had set off the duoclock. Another planet swung into view.

Now I was spinning through space in slow motion, as if I were on the moon. The village square was full of new buildings, all of them were wired for electricity. There was a bank with black plate glass windows and a big store with televisions and hanging lamps all glowing inside. There was a restaurant: the Foglia d'Oro. In the distance, two twin smokestacks were spewing out bilious fumes. In the middle of the flatlands, toward the big city, a low building had sprung up: it emitted a horrible stench.

Fulisca, dressed as a witch, was riding ahead of me on a swing chair in the shape of a broom; she called back:

"It's a worm farm, they're born in rotting flesh. Nearby they're building a battery farm for chickins."

In the distance, I saw the Troll washing chickins with a disinfectant spray.

And then I saw the riverbed, carved out, torn to ragged shreds; I saw huge piles of gravel, and our little pool, dried out and brackish, trucks going back and forth, and the broad strip of highway pushing relentlessly forward, like a knife blade cutting into the belly of our valley. "And yet," I thought, "it's kind of pretty."

"Anything is pretty, if done with moderation," said the pirate Van Maxel, and began dueling in midair with Gancio, both of them swinging sabers. All of the kids from Castellito were dead on their swing chairs, riddled with blowgun darts, Selene was spinning her chair wide, showing her panties to everyone. Osso was fast asleep, drenched in vomit.

The wind freshened, and I could feel my swing chair going higher still, and it was chilly in the sidereal void. High above the forest, I looked down at the dirt path and it was still there but the mountain was gone, and our house was gone, too. All that was left was the chestnut grove and, beneath it, a steep bare escarpment, as if it had been sliced away with a single slice of a scalpel.

I saw my father on the swing chair behind me; he was ashen-faced, and was drinking directly from a wine bottle.

"Dad," I said, "what are you doing up here?"

"Where else am I supposed to go?" he answered, then leapt straight up, turned a somersault, and plummeted straight down onto the piazza, luckily onto the cows' haystack; there he lay, arms stretched wide, completely sloshed.

At last I noticed the swing chair starting to descend, I saw Selene's skirt folding up again, and her panties disappearing, modestly concealed once more. The pirate Van Maxel shot downward, landing with a leap, and cried "End of the ride!" and all the kids from Castellito pulled out the darts, saying: "It's just a scratch."

The rotor groaned to a halt, and I opened my eyes again. I was stretched out on the ground, surrounded by the smell of almond brittle and chestnut biscuits. My father was looking down at me with concern on his face.

"It's nothing," a woman's voice was saying. "Maybe he ate some junk food, sometimes people get sick on this ride."

"It should be against the law," said Fefelli's voice in the distance, "when I'm elected mayor, I want to see all these gypsies' permits."

A voice speaking Gypsy told him to go fuck himself.

"Feeling better?" asked Selene; she made a move as if to stroke my forehead but then stopped, suddenly shy in my father's presence.

"We wiped them out," said Gancio, twirling his blowgun.

"You are such a fag," said Osso, and I saw that I really had puked on him.

To get over my nausea and shock I had to eat two flat-breads and a huge bag of candy. That night, I couldn't sleep. We'd given our dogs away to a guy who lived in the pine for-est. My father was snoring and calling out to them in his sleep. I felt as if the house were about to fly away, spinning through the air.

5

Two years have gone by on the clock, two cricket-chirps in the duoclock. I'm hop-hiking down from the woods where my house used to be. Under my arm, I have a basket filled with mushrooms. Fat little brother Porcini, patron saint of risotto. Orange-hued boletus, egg-shaped beneath an umbrella. Tiny herds of spreading hats, gossiping in the shade of the verdant grass. Gleaming white meadow-dweller with an undergarment of violet silk. Drum stump, parasol mushroom, tough little wart-covered cock of a fungus. Tiny hobnails driven one by one with the gnome's mallet. Twisted and delicious little hunchback mushroom, wolf-fart puffballs, nasty old oblique fungi squashed onto trees like a disease, even though you might actually be good to eat. Amanita, lovely and treacherous as a vampire. Satan's mushroom, greenish and slobbery—ties up your intestines into knots and makes you sweat bile. I hop-hike along, my basket filled with wholesome mushrooms, though I'll have them double-checked because, as my grandfather used to say, all it takes is one bastard in the basket to ruin everything, just like with people. I stop to watch some green grasshoppers that look like dragons—one time I managed to slip a thread leash onto one, but I hurt its leg, I was very upset, and that night I dreamt of a long-legged fairy who was weeping, she was the queen of the grasshoppers. I walk through the high grass, the swallowtail butterflies are gone, all I see now is the occasional cabbage butterfly. And there aren't as many spider webs as there used to be. My dad says that when a forest is sick, it empties out, from the topmost branch to the life underground. The forest seems pretty much the same to me, only it's not silent anymore, you can hear the sounds of the highway in the distance. I decide to pass by where my house used to stand. I have to break off a branch and swing it as a machete, which is pronounced mah-cheddy. In the course of a year, thorn bushes and ferns and ghost grass have sprung up, the tender mercies of the forest have covered over the wounds of digging. I recognize the stones that walled in the little hillock terrace, a ship's-prow pattern, but I can no longer find the bench where my father used to have his conversations with the dogs.

I wade into a welter of thorns and stinging nettles. Sweaty and red, I burn with vegetal passion until I finally recognize a giant hoary chestnut tree, and I realize that I am standing just about where the house used to be, but there is nothing to be seen, nothing but a dark downward plummet, and at the bottom, the pylons of the viaduct. But if I climb up to where the quince trees stand, I can see the Fanara, the cattle trough where all the animals of the mountain used to drink, a fashionable watering hole if ever there was one. I thrust my way through a wall of thorns, and there it is.

It's all covered with moss, a thin stream of crystal-clear water runs down from a wooden spout, singing as it mingles with the green water below. Everything is moist, dark, cool, this is a holy place, drops of moisture fall from the leaves overhanging the edge, creating circular patterns. Mysterious drips plunge from above. The chalices of the liverworts and the tips of the ferns tremble, quivering with hidden lives, the footsteps of ladybugs, slime-trails of slugs, ambushes laid by spiders. I can hear the various instruments played by the water, snapping, rustling, gurgling. So many different notes, including the murmur of the rivulet at my feet. I slurp up a mouthful of water, and it tastes of bark. Slowly, the darkness and the sound of falling drops cast their spell. The hands of the duoclock move across the dial.

Right away, the gnome shows up.

He is about half my height, with a thick white mustache, a loose green overcoat, and hip boots; he's practically invisible as he moves through the foliage. He is holding a bucket and a basket of mushrooms, much bigger than mine. A sharp axe dangles from his belt. He doesn't bother to say hello. As he fills up his bucket, I look at the axe with some concern. He notices.

"Are you afraid I'll cut off your head, boy?"

"No, no, it's not that," I reply. "It's that I didn't expect to meet anyone here."

"It's true, the forest has emptied out. First come the tape-measuring civil engineers, with their murderous entourage of surveyors. Then come the bulldozers. Then the landslides and avalanches. Then the fumes that waft all the way up here, the stench of those damned battery farms. Did you know that they grow worms in living corpses? When old people get sick, they take them there instead of the hospital."

"Really?" I say. I wish I'd thought that one up myself.

"But if I run into another one of the woodcutters who come up here, I'll chop his head right in half, like a block of wood. What do they do with all these trees? I need only two a year, myself."

"The town is growing. You should see how many houses, each one with a wooden dining nook and a fence around it. I know because my father is a woodworker, even though he's losing all his work to Legnami Capponi, this company that operates out of the big city. They do it all, from sawmill to finished chairs, from chopping down the tree to fine-sanding the egg cup. They have two huge trucks."

"Made of wood?"

"No, the trucks aren't made of wood. Don't you ever come into town?"

"I can't. You know why?"

Of course, I want to say, you are a woodland creature, probably imaginary, like the cheerful god of the hillock, the witch fox, the pinecone man, maybe you are a berry-eating gnome, or else a mossy dwarf, or a chestnut elf.

The gnome gives me a nasty look and is suddenly transformed. His whiskers turn green, his eyes are bloodshot, and he begins to sweat a slimy ooze.

"Don't you think of making fun of me, sweetheart. I have two versions. The nice version with the hearty appetite—that one's kind and goodhearted. But I can turn as green and venomous as a Satan's mushroom, and if I do, you're fucked. Apologize immediately."

"Sorry," I say. You don't want to fool around with a poisonous gnome. He returns to his kindly version, but he is still pissed off.

"I don't go into town because they make fun of the way I dress. They call me the walking mushroom. But in the restaurants they eat my porcini mushrooms, and how! So I decided to become the guardian of the forest. I live way up there, where the hornbeam and silver fir trees grow. And you used to live right there, where that hole filled with thorns is now. And your father didn't used to drink."

"How do you know that?"

A shadow of sadness steals over his face, and at the same time the forest darkens, the sun is hidden. The gnome rinses his whiskers in the trough water, and a tree frog sticks to his mustache.

"I just know. And I know that one day the trees will come down into the valley, bringing mud and rain with them, and they will take their revenge. Did you know that last month someone tried to burn down the chestnut grove?"

"Who?"

"Two squat ugly men, who looked alike. I saw them, and I unleashed the dogs, Henbane and Amanita, on them. They gnawed on them like bones. And if they ever dare to come back . . ." He whirled his axe in the air. I noticed his eyes were different colors, one was dark green and the other was light green; his hands were hairy and three times the size of mine.

"In my opinion—pardon the presumption and please don't transform yourself—you are a gnome," I said, all in a single breath.

"You've found me out," he sighed. "Yes, I'm a Meddlesome Gnome, the one that used to play tricks at your house. Do you remember when the shoe appeared in the polenta? I did that. And when your dog started walking backward, that was my doing as well: I put grappa in his soup. And how about when the cuckoos grunted like pigs? And those mysterious footsteps on the roof? Those weren't dormice—it was me, cleaning the chimney, you lazy slobs, and if I hadn't cleaned it, you would have smoked up the entire forest. But then I shat down the chimney."

"Those green shits with currants in them?"

"Those are the ones. And then I tampered with your father's shells so his shotgun wouldn't fire. And with your mother . . ."

"With my mother what?" I exclaimed, offended.

"Well, if I ran into her in the woodshed . . . with a full moon . . ."

"Liar."

"Maybe I'm confusing her with someone else. But you remember that time it snowed all day and at midnight there was a wall of white outside your front door and you said: 'Oh boy, no school tomorrow'? And do you remember how the next morning it was all shoveled away? Well, that was me. And I buried your ginger cat, when it wandered out into the woods to die. I was the one who always got to the strawberries before you could. The one who dropped pine cones on your head. Who made fake bear prints. And I was well acquainted with your cow."

"You fooled around with my cow, too?"

"No, not like that. But do you remember that sometimes she ran away at night? She came to my parties. She danced like a baby goat, big, fat thing that she was."

"You're not a gnome, you're just a big liar, ten times worse than me."

"Right you are. It must be the effect of the honey I lick off flowers. Or some magical elixir released by moss. Anyone who is born in the woods sees time from two sides, from the roots and from the treetops. It's a madness from which you never recover," said the gnome, as he drew back his axe, letting it fly and centering a tree thirty feet away. "So tell the people from town to stop trying to come up here."

"But what about me?"

"You will forget all this, your roots and mine," said the gnome sternly. He shook his shoulders and disappeared with heavy footsteps, his bucket spilling drops as he went.

At that very moment, a thunderstorm burst down, and before long the splattering of raindrops on the leaves was deafening. Water gushed down from the forest canopy; the big leaves filled like so many dippers. I had nothing to cover myself with, so I ran for a rocky outcropping close to the basin.

I hear the slap of a lightning bolt splitting a tree down below me. The light turns leaden. I see a patch of mud spreading over the trough; I think to myself that maybe there's been a minor landslide and dirt has fallen into the water runnel, but then the water clears right up and I look in to see my reflection. But I can't see clearly, raindrops are pebbling the surface.

I look a little closer, and maybe I'm still the child who saw God on the hillock. Or maybe I've grown older, and I'm about to take the bus down to the lower valley, where I attend middle school. Perhaps there's a fire in the fireplace in my home, I could run there to take shelter, but then again maybe my home is now only a pit filled with thorns and stinging nettles, and in a week or so they're going to start work on the highway. I can't see my own face, the rain is falling straight down, but sometimes it seems as if the wind is gusting the rain upward. Spiders are scurrying to take shelter beneath the leaves, and I can't tell anymore if it's morning or evening. The mushrooms are getting soaked, and I have the impression that a few of them are actually trying to escape from the basket. Now there is a shadow on the bottom of the stone basin; there's something enormous swimming in there, and suddenly it leaps out of the water, it's the biggest pikefish from the pool, long as a sword, its mouth encrusted with hooks, its teeth as sharp as a wolf's. It slaps a mighty blow with its tail, and then falls back, off to one side, half in the water. I realize that the pool is dry now, and the pike has come up here to die, navigating its way uphill through underground rivers, like a salmon. Good luck to you, pike-wolf. It's even raining into my trousers. The noise of falling drops is interrupted by the horn of a passing truck, far below, on the highway. A raven caws. And it suddenly dawns on me.

I understand that there are two kinds of time, or perhaps a thousand kinds of time, within which I live. One runs along slowly and I manage to see it and measure it from head to tail, while the other time moves along in leaps and gales, things change suddenly, destinies and culminations emerge. I would prefer not to know the future, but the future demands my attendance, it admonishes me sternly, telling me that maybe I can change it, telling me that boys born in the forest spend too much time alone, lost in their own imaginings—which is both their miraculous good fortune and their cursed secret. As the gnome says, "You never recover." And so, as I stood looking into the water, I saw my face as an old man, skinny and suffering, and a cross in a country graveyard. I saw Selene leaving for the city, and I wasn't there to bid her farewell. I saw the cloudy waters of a river running through the center of the village, and in those troubled waters were broken branches, dead fish, and greedy hands splitting up a small patch of land. I saw an ashen moon. Still, part of me listened to the noises of that forest and said: this too exists, something that will never be touched or seen by all people. Only by those people who are truly alive.

It stopped raining, and two months later Fefelli was elected mayor with fifty-three percent of the vote, promising boom times to come: in fact, a succession of boom times—boom, boom, boom—in business and real estate. A shiny modern new town would be built on the slopes of the mountain, and (by an amazing coincidence) right on land that he owned, or else on land that had been deeded over to Hotlips or their son Marcello, who people said was studying at "Ossford" (the local pronunciation), but who was instead excelling in idiocy at the Hogarth High School for the Dumb Rich. Construction began on the bank, but even before the bank opened for business, private loan sharks set up shop, among them Osso's dad, who progressed directly from slicing steaks to gutting debtors. Some fell for it right away. "Listen, everyone, get yourselves a mini-mansion and a car, we've had enough of these dreary little houses and broken-down bicycles," said Fefè, handing out Muratti stink-nails and loans, "We're already a metropolis."

And it was true; the road running around the main square blossomed with new offerings. The most spectacular of them all was the boutique selling ladies' underwear, Luciana Lingerie, though everyone wondered: wasn't her last name Carboni? "Maybe Lingerie is her maiden name," someone ventured. It was a very racy little boutique; when the parish priest happened to walk by it one day he had a bilateral colic attack, and it became necessary to negotiate a downgrade of the display window's erotic content. In the front row were great big Sensible Panties and woolen camisoles, in the next row back were high-waisted panties and classic brassieres, and in the back were the killer lace items and body stockings. At first, no one ever went in, but the miracle of the Blessed Lacy Corset changed everything. Zoraide, former regional beauty queen, a florid, strapping over-forty still hungry for fun, was in the dumps because the only time her husband Oscar would screw her anymore was when the Bologna soccer team won, and even then only if Fogli scored a goal. In the previous three years, Fogli had scored twice. Then, one evening, Signora Zoraide came back home with Cupid's own gift-wrapped package under her arm. After dinner that night, her husband was slouched down in his easy chair, reading *Stadium* magazine and emitting belches redolent of stew. Zoraide appeared, wearing a garter belt under her nightgown. Oscar fell to his knees, overcome with emotion and gratitude, eager for a closer look. From that night forward, Fogli began to score virtual goals every Sunday, and sometimes even during midweek training sessions. The Blessed Lacy Corset became the patron garment of the store itself, and went on to help many marriages, though not all, because, in the wise words of Luciana: "Garter belts are like paintings. You have to understand them."

Then there was my uncle, who opened the finest hunting and fishing equipment store in the entire western hemisphere. Over the cash register, a stag's head enjoyed pride of place; it was, of course, nicknamed Fefelli; on the walls were two stuffed pikefish that Bortolini had caught, as well as a Norwegian salmon, which always spruces up a place. And there were hunting rifles of every make, fishing rods as thin and flexible as riding crops, and the full assortment of Rapala lures and treacherous fake lures, ranging from paper grasshoppers to down-feather flies, from the horsehair dragonfly to the plastic female blow fly (and let me tell you, if I were a male blow fly, I would have asked her out, definitely), and there was always an overwhelming smell of chum and other fish-tempting blends, and of course, maggots from the local Escapè maggot farm: *Escapè, the Maggot That Catches More Fish Than You Dare to Say*. Also newly founded were the Ristorante Foglia d'Oro da Chicco and a sixteen-room inn (twelve of the rooms were eminently reputable, while four had rear entrances). A perfume shop, a fruit and vegetable stand with pineapples, and Paolo the hairdresser's new beauty shop, with four ElectricAire hard-hat hair dryers. When the first few women went in for their permanents and came out with unnaturally large heads of hair, Karamazov said:

"Permanent? That's no permanent. The only fertilizer that could make hair grow like that is cow piss, a natural source of potassium, iron, and magnesium."

Paolo denied it, but he still lost a few customers.

Of course, the most widely discussed and visible new development was the gray, turreted cement plant just outside of town, down by the river. It was owned by a company that clearly had Fefelli as a major shareholder; the CEO was a certain Paladini who never said hello to anyone and had a bleached-blond wife and a son who, at the tender age of eight, had already been relegated to wearing Prince of Wales checked jackets. Over near Mount Mario there had sprung up both the Escapè maggot farm of fertile corpses and Pollo Bello, a gulag for chickins where the Troll now had a job. He would tell us that there were six or seven chickins in each cage, that the lights were never turned off, day or night; they ate continuously and just machine-gunned shit. As soon as they bulked up and reached optimum weight, giddy-up, they were slaughtered, steam-plucked, cellophane-wrapped, and shipped off to a supermarket. Many of the chickins, however, came down with avian depression and were given cough syrups and antibiotics and antiparasitics, but they only got worse, so at that point they had a huge bonfire and burned them. You could smell the stink even down in the village. Or else (rumors circulated to this effect) they chopped them up and interred them in tins of KittyMeow, the cat food (as advertised on TV!). And one important thing I almost forgot to mention, there were dozens and dozens of new televisions in all the houses, there were more antennas springing up than daisies, and Fulisca's dad changed work from chimney sweep to antenna installer; he was still in the rooftop business, he made good money, and in fact he was working too much overtime and finally fell off a four-story building. That was the end of the broadcasting day for him, and for poor Fulisca. She'd been happier when she was all black with soot, the poor thing. At the funeral she was sobbing and shivering people said that she wasn't at all well.

But let's not wallow in sadness! There was a boom going on, literally exploding under our asses. There was the highway, with an interchange, and soon there'd be another exit ramp just four miles away, and another elevated viaduct, with the Castagnette tunnel, 2,579 feet long, that ran under Mount Picone; when they were digging the tunnel they found a cave with freshly greased submachine guns and two skeletons of German soldiers. We rode out all the time to watch from the overpass, to see the vast new artery of progress; we watched trucks and cars go sailing by, and then we'd ride our bikes back to race along the gravel lanes of the cement plant, which continually emitted a smoke, white but not too white, that fogged up the air. But Fefelli said it was good smoke, the smoke of money.

Lavamèl said: "There are some who are getting rich while others get tuberculosis. We'll all wind up like the people in the big city, spitting out bits of our lungs onto the asphalt." Slim twittered the song of the nightingale and said: "Let's forget our sadness and drink something." "Sure," said Luis the tractor driver, "red wine for all my friends." We gladly accepted, and when we were done drinking, Balduino asked, "So who's paying?" "Not me," Slim pointed out with a fine attention to detail, "I said 'Let's drink something,' not 'It's my treat.' It was Luis who said, 'Red wine for all my friends.'" Baruch Salomone said that Slim was nothing but a son of a bitch, but in semantic and juridico-enological terms, he was right. Luis paid for the round.

My father and I had moved to a small apartment just outside of town. There was electricity and a water heater, there was a meadow surrounding the house, and the road was pretty far away, but when the wind blew, you could smell dead meat and chickin depression, and dad missed the forest. He kept plying his trade as a carpenter, but there wasn't a lot of work. He drank red wine in tawdry-looking flasks without straw holders; he had a whole cellar full of them. We were rich, but rich only in wine and sawdust. The money that we actually received from the expropriation was half as much as we had been promised at the outset.

Still, I went every day to the middle school down in the lower valley. I was in ninth grade and I had grown taller, a reaction to a bout with diphtheria that had nearly killed me, but that also stretched me out by a solid four inches. Osso calculated that if I'd been sick for another month I would have grown to be eight feet one inch tall. Instead of elongating, Osso had broadened in the beam. He was now also covered with zits, and had become a snazzy dresser, wearing dark-blue jackets with tin buttons and shirts with high collars (always slightly dingy). Gancio looked like a skinny, surly Amazon Indian, he chased after every girl in sight, and his pranks were becoming more and more treacherous. Ever since Fulisca's dad died, she'd been living outside of town; we never saw her any-more. When she did show up, she was pale and very pretty, her curly locks unkempt, like those of a witch. Selene left town; she'd gone to attend middle school in the big city, and she was studying dance now as well. It had hit me pretty hard. The day she left I felt sad and angry, I didn't even go to say good-bye to her. Every night I dreamed that things had gone differently, in one of three ways.

First, that I had gone to see her off at the bus stop with a bouquet of flowers and a gift basket of the strawberries that she liked so well; I had combed my hair with a part on one side. I was incredibly manly, and I said to her: "I'll wait for you forever." And she was gorgeous in a little turquoise outfit, with a dark-blue ribbon in her hair. With a gloved hand (in some of the dreams, she wasn't wearing gloves) she blew me a kiss through the bus window and said: "I'll never forget you."

In the second fantasy, we had been laying out on the cycla-men-covered meadow, and we'd had sex all afternoon, and then I walked her over to the bus, and the bus driver said: "Look at that, you're all covered with grass and weeds and twigs and leaves. What have you been doing all day, counting blades of grass?" And everyone exchanged knowing glances and laughed.

The third reparatory version was that she had left together with the Goretti brothers, three huge slabs of pork who were complete sleazeballs; they drove three huge devastating bull-dozers and a truck that carried I-beams. Bruno Goretti, the swine-in-chief, had said to Selene, "Come sit by me, little strawberry, and we'll have ourselves some fun, all the way into the big city."

And so, while Van Maxel held the bus driver prisoner under threat of machete (pron., *mah-cheddy*), I said: "Listen to me, brothers Goretti—Bruno, Sergio, and Lanfranco—you get out of this bus or I'll smash your shit-eating faces in."

Then came a fight scene, choreographed right down to the smallest details. In the end, punching and kicking, I laid all three of them flat as pancakes, and Selene gazed at me, panting, and thought: "My hero." The conclusion of the scene, of course, is that we kiss, and in the meanwhile, Gancio, in a grand finale not intended for little kids to watch, cuts off the heads of all three Goretti brothers and impales them on a Guatayaba pike.

I dreamed this third version only when I was truly pissed off.

Anyway, that morning I was pretty happy because my dad had shaved and he had gotten an order to carve seven dwarves and a Snow White out of wood to adorn the lawn of Paladini's villa; Paladini was the CEO of the cement plant. My dad had discussed the job with Karamazov, and they'd decided that ideologically, it would be okay, it was nice money and the work had a certain artistic dignity. Who could say? Maybe the dwarves would inspire Paladini to think more liberal thoughts.

One Sunday, my dad was carving Bashful's face and I said: "Dad, I'm going on a field trip to see the ruins and the mosaics of Santa Putilla." "Nice stuff they're taking you to see," he replied and pulled a thousand lire out of his pocket, saying: "You can't go without a little spending money."

That took my breath away, because that was a period when my dad had little or no money, so I had even less; my uncle gave me what he could spare, and I'd sell the occasional frog and baskets of strawberries to Chicco's restaurant. I saw that the banknote was all crumpled, just like the check that Fefelli handed over that day at school, but it was completely different. Money can be transformed, depending on the hand that is holding it, I thought to myself. In certain hands, money is like a brick, in others, like a butterfly. And so, in my new status as holder of wealth, I ran at top speed across the meadow, with the dog barking at my heels, and I made my way to the road, where the bus would stop to pick us up. The group of friends was already there waiting: there was Gancio, Baco, Galileo the intellectual, Osso, and Rospa, a severely bespectacled and ill-tempered young girl; she was the daughter of the grocer, but she only smelled of bleach, never of chocolate or liquorice.

We were equipped for a journey. I was wearing my father's thousand-pocket vest, Gancio had on a fishing jacket that stank of creekfish, while Galileo was weighed down with a World War I trench rucksack. Osso was carrying a picnic bas-ket that could feed Peru and was already breaking off chunks of bread with one hand, while the Rospa was huffing with impatience, muttering, "Well, is that bus coming or not?" while continually cleaning her shoes with a handkerchief, until finally Osso decided to give her a hand; he hocked a huge spit-ball onto her feet and said:

"There, that'll help give them a shine."

Rospa was about to burst into tears when we heard the horn of the Seventh Cavalry and the SITA appeared, a huge dark-blue tour bus, swaying and lurching, with an odorous cloud of rubber and gasoline, and we hopped on hastily and in great excitement.

6

It's hard to believe how idiotically happy people become in a bus. Twenty-six kids of both genders and not one of them seemed able to shut up or stay seated like a normal citizen, everyone turning around to talk to someone in the seat behind them, or sitting crosswise, or with their face pressed to the window, or wandering around from one row of seats to another, and the driver, Angelo aka Fangio, swearing out loud every time.

Our guide on the field trip was one of the teachers, Miss Zaini; she was bony, skinny as a wooden clothespin, and her jaw stuck forward like a figurehead on an old sailing ship; whenever she opened her mouth to talk, it looked like someone was reeling her in with a fishing rod. She whistled whenever a word had an *s* in it, she sprayed spit when she talked, and she did her best to act stern, but really she was just as sweet as a cream puff. She always emitted a scent of lily of the valley, and wore cheap necklaces, three or four strings of beads, which she toyed with whenever she was nervous or lost in thought. Which, quite often, she was—because, sadly, she was an old maid. She sat close to Fangio, the driver, a great big man with a small tango-dancer's mustache; she began to giggle and whisper to him. He responded with nods of the head because in the meantime he had to drive the bus and keep his eye on the road, which twisted and turned and curled back around on itself as it ran up the mountain. As he headed into each curve and switchback, Fangio honked the admonitory bus horn, and the riffraff of ordinary cars squeezed respectfully to the side of the road.

Couples had not yet formed among us field-trippers, and so there was a constant undercurrent of ogling and uncontrollable giggling and sidelong gazes, and even those who were pretending to be indifferent were shooting glances.

It immediately became clear that there were three divas of the field trip.

There were the Sabbia twins, who weren't very twinnish, Olga, with bobbed brunette hair, and Orsola, a redhead with a ponytail, both of them dressed in checked outfits and with a look of foxy cunning on their small faces. Then there was La Venerelli, who at the tender age of fourteen was already wearing a 38D bra. She had on a cute openwork sweater. Even if it hadn't been openwork we would have riddled holes in it with our prying eyes.

All three divas, of course, were sitting close together, causing a traffic jam in the aisle of the bus, while, scattered in various seats and rows, the average and homely girls were riding in relative unconcern; it is, of course, well known that as a field trip proceeds, girls only get prettier by the hour.

The boys were all hot and bothered and each had his own plan, his own technique for seduction. Gancio was already courting with all the confidence of a grown-up. He had taken up a strategic position right behind the trio of divas; he was speaking directly into Orsola's ear, and after every phrase he uttered, she responded: "What are you, stupid?" But then, if he stopped talking for a few minutes, she found some excuse or other to crane her head around, brushing his face with her ponytail, and begging pardon.

Gancio's rival was named Belletti, and he was a slick character with brilliantined hair who talked incredible trash, making up stories like, for instance, that he had driven a bus himself plenty of times, on the grounds of his father's villa, and that he was going to be a famous Formula One racer. Gancio eyed him coldly and calmly readied a Guatayaba ambush for him.

There was a double team courting Olga: Osso and Bruno the scientist, aka Baco. Their technique involved long jokes that broke down halfway through, greasy lewd jokes, and rapid-fire bullshit. They were constantly shoving one another aside to get closer to their lovely, and every so often one of them would let fly with a lopez, or a powerful and virile belch would be emitted, as if it were a mating cry, the guttural bellow of the stag to his doe or of the he-dugong to the she-dugong.

Osso also offered around mint candies that by this point in the trip were quick-setting glue, and Baco, who punched in at about the same weight as Osso, had a death grip on the back of Olga's seat; his butt was sticking out into the aisle. He was receiving kicks in the ass at a rough rate of one per minute, but he would not give up.

There were three of us courting La Venerelli: me, Galileo, and Cavazzuti. Cavazzuti didn't even count: he was maybe knee-high to a married grasshopper, had the monobrow of a cave dweller, and halitosis redolent of the town dump. Still, he kept trying because back then, thank God, none of us realized how ridiculous we were. Galileo, on the other hand, was a worthy and daunting adversary because he was a genuine intellectual, with a melancholy, cerulean eye, and he spoke to La Venerelli as if she were a pure and kindred spirit, without ever looking at her tits, but I knew perfectly well that while he might not be looking at them just now, he had definitely given them the once-over earlier. Galileo was speaking in a somewhat high-pitched voice about two of his three favorite topics: the destiny of man and the meaning of life. The third favorite topic was why you find so many doubles in soccer cards, but that day he decided against fielding that particular line of discussion. He was always capable of finding some profound reason for doubt in anything: for instance, we were going to tour the ruins of the convent of Santa Putilla. But after all, what is a ruin if not something that was once a home, a church, a milk bar? Potentially, the entire world is a ruin, a heap of rubble, nothing more.

"What about the pyramids, then?" I shot back, having realized that either I had to jump into the conversation with a non sequitur or I'd never get a word in edgewise.

"The pyramids," La Venerelli recited, "were made by the pharaohs in order to be remembered."

"But they could have made do with so much less," I pointed out. "I mean, maybe something more than the bust of Bisacconi at the elementary school, but forcing thousands of slaves into hard labor just to be remembered is so selfish, isn't it? I mean, they needed only one pyramid. Or maybe a nice monument, with an inscription underneath: 'Remember Rameses.'"

La Venerelli laughed. One-nothing, my favor.

"The pharaohs wanted their greatness to be commemorated," Galileo declared officiously. "The powerful are different from you and me. And they care nothing for the fate of the masses. In some ways, we artists are not unlike them."

"Are you an artist?" asked La Venerelli, gazing at him all sweet-faced and starry-eyed. Two to one, Galileo's favor.

"Well, yes . . ." (He sighed).

"What do you do?"

"I paint, I sketch, I play the flute, and most important, I write poetry."

"Really," said La Venerelli, bouncing in excitement, "come on, recite one for me."

"No, no," declined Galileo with a theatrical gesture, "I'd be too shy; perhaps later, after we get off the bus."

And he moved away, followed by a ninety-degree swivel of La Venerelli's tits. Three to one; he now held a commanding lead. There was no reason to hang around any longer; by now, she wanted poetry, not bullshit. I got up and trudged down the aisle to the back of the bus. There was a strong smell of fart, and Rospa, white and green in the face, was on the verge of vomiting, while another girl was crying because she had smacked her head against the window. It truly was the misery ward back there. Rounds of "Frere Jacques" started to fill the bus, then such chestnuts as "Cuando calienta el sol" and Mina's catchy hit from 1960, "Tintarella di luna" (a title I'd render as "Moontan," or perhaps "Moonbathing"). Osso started to dance the twist; the bus almost ran off the road.

"That's enough fooling around," said Fangio. "Here's the first stop. The fountain of Santa Putilla. Get out one at a time, if you don't mind."

We burst out the door in clusters of three. Galileo was sailing along on La Venerelli's larboard beam, so I stood aside, and Rospa stepped out of the bus right behind me, her upchuck locked and loaded. She sprayed it all out on the bright-green grass; at a quick glance I would guess stewed chicken and string beans. Then she said in a raucous voice:

"I'm so sorry, everyone."

Poor thing, I thought to myself. She must have sensed my sympathy, and she stuck to me like glue. When we all reached the fountain of Santa Putilla, Miss Zaini stood in the front of the group, we gathered round in a semicircle, and she provided the obligatory background info. Saint Putilla was an unassuming nun in the Order of Our Lady of Little Trollops; she lived simply and was openly critical of the lavish and luxurious indulgence of the church of the time, and especially of the evil bishop Bernardo, who lived in a huge villa, now a fashionable restaurant. The ecclesiastics began to persecute her as an hysterical and disobedient heretic. The grief and pain this triggered unhinged her mind, and she began to gallop through the woods like a young warthog, openly declaring that God visited her every night in her cell in the nunnery. "Gee, I've seen God, too," I was about to say, and I thought to myself that perhaps

God might have gone to call on Santa Putilla because he was looking for a slightly more comfortable place; in other words, he was sick of crapping on the hillock. I could just picture the scene: Enter God, he goes into the bathroom, you hear the thunderous roar of the toilet flushing, he buttons up his trousers and says, "Now then, my dear Putilla, how are things?" "Not bad, My Lord, they're persecuting me." "Chin up, Putilla, follow your own path, pay no attention to those evil ministers," says God, and he leaves. These were daring thoughts, it seemed to me, but hardly blasphemous. To make a long story short, Putilla was placed on trial for erotic visions, nocturnal forest galloping, madness, apostasy, and heresy. She was thereupon sentenced to be imprisoned in the Fortress of Measleton, atop a high mountain. But she said, "No, I refuse to die in that dungeon." As she rode along on horseback, her horse flanked by two mounted men-at-arms, she said: "I am thirsty, I want to drink some water." "There is no water here," responded the uncouth but pragmatic soldiers. "Oh yes there is," said Putilla. She dismounted, touched the earth with a stave, and water gushed forth. Then Putilla joined her hands in pious resignation and died on the spot. In commemoration of the miracle, a stone fountain with an image of the saint was built on the very spot where that blessed water first gushed forth: water that makes women fertile and cures people of a number of complaints, including strep throat and perlèche. Second salient fact, Putilla became the patron saint of dowsers. Third fact, the bishop came down with smallpox and asked to drink some of the holy water from the spring, but it evaporated as soon as he brought the glass to his lips, as if the devil were holding his red-hot tail in the water, and the bishop died horribly with atrocious buboes. This provides a useful lesson: don't mess around with saints.

"All right, girls, who wants a drink? One at a time." said Miss Zaini.

The girls were allowed to drink first, and a chorus of lewd jokes ensued. The faucet was set fairly low, and one girl craned her neck around to drink from the side, another bumped her nose as she nuzzled it from beneath, one girl slurped at it like a cow, and another cupped her hands to drink; in short, it was a spectacular array of erotic references, at least to our eyes.

"The boys can drink, too," Miss Zaini said very democratically. Fangio was the first in line. He had brought an aluminum cup with him. He offered it to Miss Zaini, and she thanked him with a look that was decidedly daring for a schoolteacher.

Then we boys tried to drink, but between spraying water and kicks in the ass and chipped teeth not even half of us managed to get a drop.

I saw Galileo and La Venerelli; they had wandered away from the group and were sitting in the meadow. I walked after them, and spied from behind a rhubarb bush. He recited to her:

My eyes once wept rivers of tears
My mouth seldom laughed in joy
But now that I know you, my dear,
I've become a much happier boy.
Happiness lasts but a fleeting minute
Then all is chilly snow, and a headstone in it.

La Venerelli sighed, captivated; she said she liked the first part best. The two of them sat in silence, twisting and tormenting daisies, a pursuit that historically serves as a prelude to flaming outbursts of passion. In a jealous fury, I madly thought of hiring a hit man, of giving a thousand lire to Gancio to bumblebee Galileo, the infamous bard. But Gancio had stolen a ribbon from one of the twins' hair, and there the two of them were, chasing one another across the meadow: "What'll you give me if I give it back to you?" Jealousy was scorching my heart, I could feel a lump in my chest and a thud in my stomach. Yes, I would commit suicide on the spot, put an end to it all, toss myself over the bridge onto the road below. But it was only about a ten foot drop; at the very most, I would cripple myself.

That was when the Forest Gnome came to my rescue.

I noticed that Galileo was scratching himself and that La Venerelli's lovely ankle was turning purple. They had chosen to nestle comfortably in a bed of stinging nettles, the small and especially vicious variety.

"It's burning," said La Venerelli.

"I think it might be stinging nettles," said Galileo.

I rushed up like an ambulance.

"Oh yes, I'm afraid it's *ortica grisa*," I said, "the very worst kind of stinging nettles." And I added, sternly, "Never sit in a meadow if you aren't an expert on the details of the plants."

"Right," said La Venerelli, with some annoyance. Three all.

"But I know the cure. Mamonia."

"Oh, yes, please," she said.

"I'll find it. I know where to find it," I said. That was a lie, but four to three, my favor, and ball in the middle of the field.

We got back on the bus, ten minutes of sharp curves and switchbacks, and we were at the convent, which had been converted into a hotel with conference halls and a third-rate bordello. La Venerelli was scratching herself and talking to the Sabbia twins; first she pointed at Galileo, the disappointment, and then at me, the new hope. While the big blue bus bellowed along uphill, we looked down, taking in a view of the entire valley; at this point there was still no highway, the river was crystal clear, and there were very deep water holes under the bridges. I saw pikefish leap to the height of a bus window. I saw smoke from a chimney somewhere through the trees, and I felt a pang of longing for my old house. A wave of sadness washed over me, but just then Fangio jammed on the brakes, and Osso collapsed on top of me. He was sweaty, agitated as a wild animal, and he had doughnut crumbs all over him, even up his nose.

"What shall we do first, children, picnic or tour of the convent with ruins?" asked Miss Zaini.

"Picnic! pic! *pic*! nic! *nic*!" we all shouted in unison.

We spread out in a circle in a beautiful meadow without stinging nettles (Miss Zaini had inspected it carefully); we even had a tablecloth. Galileo walked up to La Venerelli with a glass of orangeade, but he was rejected. This was my moment. I ran over to Fangio and asked:

"Sir, do you have any mamonia?"

"Yes," he said. "But it's for emergencies, things like bee stings. I can't just give it to you."

"La Venerelli has a terrible case of stinging nettles. Please, I beg you, I'll pay you a thousand lire, I'll only use a little bit." He winked at me (the way we do, we gigolos . . .) and handed over the precious little bottle, with accompanying cotton ball.

I went back. Everyone was chomping down. There were mini-frittatas and panini with salami and mortadella and, for the more discerning diners, hard-boiled eggs with a pinch of salt twisted into the corner of a paper napkin. The most uncontrollable scarfers were Baco, who was squirting mayonnaise straight into his mouth, and Osso, who had brought with him two cutlets the size of sides of beef, razor-sharp and dangerous to eat, and he wasn't offering any to anyone else. That little slicker, Belletti, had a baguette with tomatoes and lettuce, and the minute he took his first bite, Gancio hit him with a lopez that knocked the whole thing to the ground.

But the one who really made a splash was Rospa, thanks to her dad the grocer. She pulled out twenty single packs of Zuegg extra-rich marmalade, an assortment of almond-flavored chocolates, and—come one, come all—a jar of Nutella.

"Who'd like to try some?" she asked.

Her approval rating hit the roof; her standing quickly soared from toad to princess, and she was so pleased that there was nothing left for her to eat. I snuck over to La Venerelli and whispered:

"I have the mamonia."

"And how does it work?"

"You have to smear it on your legs with a cotton ball."

"Then let's go behind there, because I'd be embarrassed here, in front of everybody."

I could hardly breathe. I hadn't expected anything so spectacular. I had assumed that she would apply the mamonia by herself. Instead, she picked up her panino and I picked up mine, and we went over behind a hedge, where there was a little country lane lined with sour-cherry trees, dappled with sunlight. I started massaging her ankles with the mamonia. She was eating her panino and saying, ah, what a relief, I already feel better, and the smell of salami wafted over me, along with the piss smell of the mamonia, and together they created a celestial aroma and I was happy as a woodpecker, I would gladly have stayed there, rubbing cotton balls on her ankles and chewing mamonia-scented salami for the rest of my life.

Suddenly I thought to myself, what if she rubbed her tits in the stinging nettles? And I choked on my sandwich, crumbs went everywhere, and I was coughing like a diesel engine. She laughed. Gancio showed up and hit me hard in the back. Galileo, warily, watched the scene, looking opportunistically for any fissures that might offer him a point of entry. Finally I drew a deep breath and recovered.

"Thank you," she said.

"Don't mention it," I said.

"You sure know a lot about meadows," she said.

"Well, sure, I was born in the mountains. A person needs

to know their own environment. Some herbs are poisonous, others can cure you. Resin will cure a cough, chicory refreshes, rue cures stomachaches, elderberry is good for rheumatic pain, wild asparagus will improve your mood, you can eat rhubarb boiled or fried, mayberries are very poisonous, as are ivy and peach pits. And then there are mushrooms. Some are good to eat, and others are toxic. That one there, for instance, is a parasol mushroom. They say that it's an aphrodisiac."

"What's that mean?" she asked.

It was an epic moment. La Venerelli was looking intently at me with her remarkable eyes, and her balcony was swaying about two-and-a-half inches away from my chest. I considered some options: maybe I could tell her that "aphrodisiac" meant something that came from Africa or that made you have bowel movements. But then she said to me:

"Silly, I know what aphrodisiac means."

She took my hand, and we broke into a run down the lane lined with sour-cherry trees. She was laughing, I was giddy with ecstasy. We came to a halt and stood there, panting. The moment was right. On the horizon there was nothing but a distant house and a cow—an intrinsically discreet animal that tends to mind its own business.

"Kiss her," said God, buttoning his trousers from high atop a giant cloud.

"Kiss her," said the pikefish, opening its voracious maw.

"Kiss her," said the gnome, grabbing his crotch.

"I'm so inexperienced, alas," I thought. A few kisses with Selene, lips closed. But now the situation demanded controlled respiration, proper tongue rhythm, good saliva management; it was a lot like final exams in high school, like moving up to the major leagues. And while these thoughts went through my head, La Venerelli was looking at me, her breasts heaving up and down as she panted, tracing in their trajectory a cone of shadow over the hillside beneath us. I thought, it's now or never, I reached out and embraced her and felt her soft curves and the little openwork sweater, inhaled a mingled smell of flesh and mamonia, and I was about to sling my tongue when we heard a strange moaning sound, followed by another.

"Is someone feeling unwell?" I wondered.

"There's someone in the hayloft in that house," said La Venerelli.

"Someone who?"

And at that very instant, we heard Miss Zaini's voice. She was whispering but her words rang out like church bells pealing in that afternoon silence: "Oh, yes, Angelo, all the way, all the way."

We both immediately understood all what way. I wanted to move away. But La Venerelli was already heading in the direction of the forbidden. We walked around the back of the house and immediately, in the golden light of the pile of straw, we saw Fangio's big, hairy ass engaged in a rapid and regular motion, though his trousers hanging halfway down his thighs were hindering his movements to some degree. On either side of the big ass projected Miss Zaini's little legs, one shoe on and one shoe off. There was no doubt about it. We were in the presence of an interclass sexual act, love between a college graduate and a teamster.

"Let's go," I said.

"Why?" asked La Venerelli, who wanted to study the subject more closely.

Miss Zaini gasped and Angelo bellowed, then she bit his ear, and he called her a red-hot slut, and their pace quickened, and just then came the roar of a tractor. Where there's a tractor there's usually a farmer driving it, and so we saw Fangio leap to his feet, with a still-avid cock, and Miss Zaini adjusting her hair and clothing in quick order. But she was still covered with pieces of straw, and when she went running past us I couldn't help laughing.

"Kids," said Fangio, red as a lobster, "heaven help you if either one of you says a word." We nodded.

The ruins were just a tumbled assortment of weathered rocks; the convent had been all tarted up with linoleum and modern paintings. But how could I ever forget the drive home in the bus, by moonlight . . . A dream of young lives in the good and steady hands of Fangio, who sat contentedly at the helm of our vehicle, while Miss Zaini gazed adoringly at him. In one corner of the bus, a few solitary excursionists slumbered while others sang softly. But in other rows of seats, bus-bound eros was celebrating in unbridled triumph. Reality and fiction blended in the stories that were later told of that forty-mile journey. It is said that Gancio un-pantied the red-haired twin, and all sorts of things ensued. That the other twin resisted Osso's assaults, but in the end allowed him to place his hand on her thigh, and that Osso sprang a leak. Even Rospa, with the aid of the very last pack of Zuegg extradense marmalade, managed to explore Baco's trousers. Other young couples were smooching away. But La Venerelli and I were drifting, lost on a tossing sea of suction and saliva, endless kisses, darting tongues, for me it was an intensive course that gave me experience and benefits that lasted a lifetime. And as I pressed against her epic breasts and then bounced back, only to fasten myself onto her once again, rejected but not really, I experienced pleasure and astonishment that moves me deeply even as I write this. Then, as the lighted outskirts of the city heaved into view, following a last duel of papillae, I gazed at her silhouette, beautiful, sweaty, overheated, with a stray lock of hair over one eye and her little woolen sweater pulled back to expose one shoulder.

"I love you," I said to her.

"What are you, stupid?" she replied.

7

You might think that once things are going okay, once life seems to be moving in the general direction of happiness, then you can coast along—as you pick up momentum, the fun increases, until you're rocketing along at a dizzying rate, and you just keep getting happier and happier until you hurtle onto the trampoline of good fortune and you bounce straight up into the nirvana of perfect good fortune and contentment.

But things don't work like that.

First thing you know, there are speed bumps, potholes, and rocks in the middle of the road, and you skid out of your lane in the switchback curves. And straight ahead of you, looming upward, the steepest imaginable hill to climb, and you can't even see the top.

That is to say, in the aftermath of that forty-mile-long kiss fest with La Venerelli, things turned a bit sour. My lovely turned her tits and her heart away from me; she turned out to be a merciless collector of ardent young excursionists. She acted as if nothing had happened, and a week later I saw her climb onto the Motom motorcycle of Augusto, a sixteen-year-old bullock with bell-bottom jeans and a topknot of hair that made him look like Woody Woodpecker, who smoked cigarettes and was an all-around hot dog.

As I watched, she vanished from my life. Now she preferred to the aroma of mamonia the smell of two-cycle fuel and the brilliantine of her new heart-throb. I fantasized a terrifying revenge: the motorcycle ran off the road, and the two of them landed not in stinging nettles this time but in the river, where the pikefish tore the flesh from their limbs, and police divers found only a pair of skeletons sitting astride the sunken motorcycle, locked in a last embrace.

Then I put it out of my mind for good.

Far graver events had supervened. Trucks continued to rumble past, piled high with tree trunks; the massacre of the forest continued. One evening, my father had come home with all seven dwarves stacked on the deck of my uncle Nevio's three-wheeler Vespa pickup truck. He had delivered them to the cement executive Paladini, who had decided they weren't sufficiently Disneyesque—they reminded him of peasants, and the last thing he wanted on his greenery were peasants. My father shot back, "I've seen Disney's dwarves, they're fake, these are more authentic, they're based on the old people of the village, and Snow White is inspired by a woman I know who runs a dairy farm." "How horrible, riffraff that smells of ricotta," said Paladini, recoiling. "Do them over, I don't want them looking like this." And my father had to do as he'd been told. He'd already worked on them for two months, and he desperately needed the cash. But he came home swearing like a Cossack, throwing planes and saws and awls onto the floor and at the walls, goddamn Vall Deesnee and all the shitty moneybags who are too stupid to appreciate the woodcarver's art.

"Dad," I encouraged him, "you're good at this, you just have to try again." And he gave me a smack across the nose, which was his way of caressing me, and said: "Well, at least you're doing well in school." I decided not to tell him that on that very day I had gotten a C minus in Italian, because the subject for the essay had been: "Which historical figure most fills you with admiration and do you consider important in the history of our nation?" All the other students had put in Mazzinis and Cavours and Garibaldis and even Romuluses and Remuses and Dantes, and far be it from me to criticize, they were all wonderful people. But I wrote my composition about Commander Ghigna, who had been the most renowned partisan leader in our area. His Resistance group would come down from the caverns of Mount Mario and attack German formations, rifles against machine guns, but the Germans could never catch him. When the war was over, to round out his accounts, he ordered the execution by firing squad of one or two others, those who had killed his brother. So, all things considered, he might not have been perfectly heroic, like people in history books, but the way I see it, considering the fact that in our mountains the Fascists murdered no more than thirty people, not two hundred the way they did in the neighboring valley, credit should go in part to Ghigna and to the fear that he inspired. My teacher said that what I wrote was neither right nor wrong, it just wasn't on the subject that had been requested. Little did I imagine that there would soon come a day when that same paper would have received first an A minus, then a C plus, then F. All I thought was that Ghigna had done his part, at considerable risk, and that once history gives you a grade, that grade should stay the same. A for Dante, B plus for Garibaldi, B minus for Ghigna, maybe, for that wobble with the firing squad in the finale. But no; judgments change. In any event there was my D minus on my permanent transcript, and there it would remain, a blot through all the school years and centuries to come.

I didn't say a thing about it to my dad; he was busy redoing Sneezy's nose, copying from one of my Disney comic books. I went out looking for something constructive to do. First thing, I ran into Gancio and Osso who were busily shooting out the lights on the gas station with a slingshot. It was fun, reckless; maybe not exactly constructive, though. By then Osso had become a bit of a prick, he was always flashing around a walletful of cash. He'd buy twenty packs of soccer cards at a time, and he'd trade them one-for-one, even though with all the cards he owned, he could easily afford to trade ten-for-one. And so I committed one of the lowest and most shameful acts of my life. Once, when he left his soccer-card album out on a bench, I took a match, heated up the school paste, and proceeded to steal the Alcides Ghiggia (ASA Roma) card, one of the rarest cards there was. Nobody had it. By the time Osso realized it had been stolen, I had already traded Ghiggia for twenty cards and a little barbershop calendar with naked ladies wearing garter belts. Then I bartered the calendar (except for June, which I kept under my pillow) for a fishing rod. I was turning into a shrewd businessman just like Fefelli, except that someone stole my fishing rod while I was playing soccer. That would never have happened to Fefè. He never let anyone steal anything from him, and most important, even though he said that everyone could become rich just like him, in reality, if anyone tried, he would have knocked them out cold. Still, the town was rapidly filling up with para-Fefellis and aspiring Fefoids. Who could say how far the toxin had spread, I thought, how much of the river he had poisoned. I looked at Osso and Gancio and it struck me that a certain chill had come between us, a draft of cold cavern air; we remained friends, but we were already living in different worlds. We encountered one another in an intergalactic tri-universal connection point, and then we each returned to our own planet: Gancio to his world of fury, Osso to his swollen wallet, and me to my forest and my confusions.

The slingshot made a bull's-eye, and an overhead lamp exploded in a rain of glass. I saw Osso and Gancio hide behind a car. Uncle Nevio, together with Carburo the union organizer, was arriving, almost at a dead run, across the bay of the gas station. But it wasn't about the shattered overhead light, it was something much worse. Uncle Nevio took Gancio aside, and I could see that his hands were trembling. He told him that his brother Remo had had an accident. Remo was Gancio's nicest brother. In fact, he was Gancio's only nice brother, because the other two ignored Gancio entirely and couldn't care less about him. Remo had been working at the cement plant for barely two months. There was a truckload of I-beams to unload, and suddenly the entire load had collapsed right on top of him. They led Gancio away. I saw him crying, the first and last time ever.

"I tell you, there are some shitty jobs," Osso said angrily. "You'll never get me to work in a factory."

I looked hard at him. Had he really said what I thought he had? Yep, he had, and before I knew what I'd done, my fist had smashed into his nose, and we were locked in a scuffle. His father came over to separate us and said to his son, stay away from that little piece of white trash with his drunk of a father. Those were his exact words.

That day, a real riot broke out. The factory workers demonstrated in front of the cement plant, but the Pastori brothers came out with a bulldozer. There would have been baseball bats swinging and heads breaking if the police hadn't come. Eight armed agents wearing olive drab—we'd never seen anything of the sort in our town. They were especially tough on my dad because he didn't work there. "It's as if I worked there," he said. And Karamazov, who wasn't an employee either, picked up a big old rock and threw it at the bulldozer just when it looked like things had quieted down. So they took him to jail for three days, and he talked about it for three years.

That same evening, the CEO of the cement plant notified my dad that he would no longer be wanting the dwarves. He wouldn't give money to someone who dared to insult him in front of his own factory. My father managed to sell them to Luciana, who owned the lingerie store and who had crushes on, in order of magnitude, Robert Mitchum, my dad, and Uncle Nevio. "Dad," I said, "did she pay you in panties?" He laughed and went on drinking, partly contented and partly pissed off.

At his brother's funeral, Gancio didn't say a word. We were all walking in line, following a gray car, and we climbed up to the cemetery through the fields of broom. Osso came over next to me. He put a packet of soccer cards into my hand. I pushed them back at him and said:

"It's okay, forget about it, let it go."

"Take them," he said.

"That's not the point," I said.

That day I understood something. I saw one of Gancio's brothers, drunk, laughing with a girl. I saw the other brother smoking a cigarette, clearly indifferent. I saw Fefelli, who stopped by to make a point of his presence, escorted by the Pastori brothers. But when he approached the crowd, first one whistle rang out, then another, and the mayor took to his heels, aware that he wasn't wanted. I saw Fulisca, weeping as if her own brother had died, and Regina comforting her. I saw my uncle, my father, and Cipolla, walking arm in arm. I saw Lavamèl, who had taken off his glasses and gazed, blinking, like a lemur. I saw Caprone, off to one side, his shoes covered with mud. I saw Slim; at a certain point, he couldn't restrain a sad mourning-dove cry. "Pardon me," he said, "it just came out like that." And saw the factory workers from Messina, their eyebrows covered with dust, caps in hand, uncomfortable, with no idea where to stand.

I understood that in my life I wanted to avoid becoming like certain people, and I would try as hard as possible to be like certain others.

But that was a horrible week. As Uncle Nevio put it, the devil played his violin every night from the bell tower. Fulisca wound up in the hospital with an uncontrollable tremor; an ambulance came in the middle of the night and took her away, leaving a red wake of taillights in the fog, while we stood gaping as if it was the Giro d'Italia. One morning, the river upstream of the town was filled with dead fish, including several of the warrior pikefish, their bellies swollen with poison. No one could say where the poison was coming from.

One Sunday, Osso, Gancio, Baco, and I were walking toward the overpass. We heard a screech of brakes, a series of thudding impacts, and then screams. There had been a crash, the first one on that stretch of highway. We saw four crumpled automobiles, and people pulling a dead body out of a Fiat 1100; it seemed as if the body no longer had bones. A woman was weeping and walking around in circles. There was an overturned truck, like a turtle on its back, in the field of artichokes. Another car was still burning. It all seemed far away as we looked down on it from above. But if you looked closely, you could see that there were two sheets on the asphalt, and a foot poked out from under one. There were dark stains on the roadway and a crate of apples in the middle of the road; no one would ever eat them.

"Cool," said Gancio. "I've never seen a real car crash."

"There were all going at top speed," said Osso, excitedly.

That night I couldn't sleep. I dreamt of a huge truck roaring into my old house, chasing me through the bedrooms and into the courtyard, knocking down the hayloft and crushing the well, honking its horn and blinding me with its brights. The driver was Fangio.

"Fangio," I cried. "But you're my friend. The mamonia, Miss Zaini, don't you remember?"

He got out of the truck, and I saw that he only had one leg, a stump of an arm, and his face was all scratched up.

"We've all gone crazy," he said, weeping. "We don't drive anything anymore, it's them driving us."

Then, though we had known it was coming for some time, the Escapè maggot farm was shut down. The firemen came, dressed in safety orange, along with a magistrate; who knows what slight technical problem they had discovered. The truth of the matter, though, was that the smell of rotting flesh was wafting toward the plateau where Fefelli wanted to build the Roselle subdivision, a sort of mountain resort community. They took away the rotting meat in shreds and hunks; three or four of the firemen passed out. They dug an enormous pit, tossed everything into it, poured gasoline over it, and lit a match. The smoke and smell lasted for three days, as if they were burning a tyrannosaurus. Then came bulldozers to plow. One bulldozer overturned, and the driver's ribs were crushed, he was at death's door. But just as they were carrying him away, a giant bearded man emerged from the woods, buttoning his trousers. And he shouted out: "No, not him, he had nothing to do with it." "Who was that nut?" everyone asked. But I knew exactly who he was. And the bulldozer driver survived. And the bad period ended.

One evening, Cipolla, Karamazov, and Balduino the barman were wandering around the village square; they were all three hammered on Vov eggnog liqueur. And as they staggered and wobbled in unison, they heard a yell followed by a thud. A little man had fallen off the bell tower; he had horns, a tail, and was wearing a red velvet outfit. He got to his feet, sneezed, and vanished, leaving behind an aroma of safety matches.

The next morning, I was heading into town to get some medicine for my dad. There was a pharmacy in the village now. My dad had come down with a nasty case of bronchitis; he had gone out to gather wood on the mountainside at night, in the rain. He was coughing like a lion, and you could have baked a flatbread on his forehead.

The sun was shining brightly. Doctor Carabelli, who was planning to open a clinic in town in the near future, had assured me that my dad would be better in a week, and as I looked down at the river I noticed that, as a result of some mysterious shift in the riverbed or overflow from upstream, there was once again a pool along the sandy section, perhaps not quite as nice a pool as before, but still pretty deep. And in fact, there were two people fishing. And I thought, well, even though somebody stole my new fishing rod, I still have the old one. And maybe I'll catch something; Dad loves fried fish. First thing I do is I go to the pharmacy to get a bottle of aspirin and a bottle of Coricidin. I walk in and I notice a smell that's a mixture of pasture and graveyard. There is a machine to test your blood pressure; it's as if they've set up a playground for the old folks, with benches. They spend their mornings competing to see who has the highest and who has the lowest blood pressure. And there is a very polite pharmacist who is definitely a little queer, and so I'm very standoffish. Because in our town, the sexual revolution hasn't happened yet and we still have lots of prejudices, so I mistake his courtesy for some sort of come-on, and I get all hostile, and I say, "Well, make up your mind, are you going to give me this medicine, yes or no?" and I immediately regret it. Then he offers me two Fisherman's Friend lozenges, and I'm not sure whether by accepting I turn into a queer or not, but I take them and we smile at each other. Assailed with doubts concerning my own sexuality, I linger in front of the lingerie shop. I look at the photograph of the sweaty boxer wearing briefs, and the other picture of the blonde wearing a body stocking. Nope, it looks like I check out okay. Then I go by my Uncle Nevio's shop, and I asked him to give me some maggots, the last remaining products of the Escapè line, and two brand-new red floats that resemble radishes. I rush home, I deliver the medicine, I grab the fishing rod, and then I hop on my bike and race down to the river, pedaling madly along the gravel lane; I fall twice, but who cares. And I finally reach the fishing hole. One of the two fishermen is wearing hip waders; I only need to see him cast once, and I recognize him: it's Bortolini, with his incomparable swing. The other fisherman is Baco, who fishes only to satisfy his appetite. He's terrible at it, his float hits the water too close in or too far out, his lead weights wobble, and he jams the maggots onto the hooks so fast and so sloppily that all that's left is the goo. And to make things worse, he tangles up his line to an unbelievable degree. In comparison, the minotaur's labyrinth is a straightaway. He tries to untangle the fishing line, he loses his temper, and he finally pulls out his knife and cuts it all away.

"That's it for today," he says, "they just aren't biting."

Just then, Bortolini the Great snaps his rod, the tip flexes and bends, the reel emits a loud whirr, and out of the water shoots a catfish weighing at least a pound. He nets it, unhurriedly. He drops it into his creel, where there's already a moshpit of thrashing fish tails.

I sit down where Baco was fishing before. I tie on a number 28 fishing hook, and I fish close in to the bridge abutment, where there's a good little current. I know that I'm not going to catch anything big there, but I'm happy with small fry. And I land one, then two, then four, and finally ten tail-slapping sand smelts, and I lose some others. In the end, my hands are smeared with maggot goo and I've lost two hooks, but my creel is full and slapping. Bortolini walks past, behind me. In his creel, he has six or seven monster fish, good enough to mount. He smiles at me and says:

"For sand smelts, you're good."

And it's partly a compliment and partly an incitement to dare to try something bigger, but from him I accept it. I'm exhausted, fishing for sand smelts is challenging; not quite like bullfighting, but close. I stretch out on the river rocks and dangle my feet in the stream. I sense that something is happening; the river has resumed its flow, perhaps not like before, but it's doing its best, the fish are coming back, and maybe the bulldozers will stop carving up the riverbed and stealing the river's gravel. Things die: that's the first truth that you can't erase, once you really discover it. Things heal, things start over, things come back. It's a nice thing to keep in mind, but you can't always have it that way; hope dances around like light in the forest, it vanishes, it reappears for a second, then once again, all is shade and darkness. I hear hesitant footsteps on the gravely, exposed riverbed, and a large rock tumbling and then, someone saying "Darn!" I turn in surprise. Which of my savage and foul-mouthed friends would ever say "Darn!"

With one leg in midair, balancing precariously, her shoes in one hand as she wades through a mini-rapids, is Selene. I can't remember how long it's been since I last saw her, but she has changed. I can't say that she's become a woman; she was one before, I mean, she was hardly a cement mixer. But she's taller and more slender, her face is more intense, her cheekbones jut slightly, her hair is long and silky, and her eyes are still that remarkable blue-green. In other words, she is wonderful.

And she asks me, "How are you doing?"

And, as usual, I think of answering in one of the following different ways.

"I'm doing great, I've engaged in lots and lots of sexual activity, especially on tour buses, my brain is packed with new and fundamental concepts and formative experiences, my penis has grown substantially in size, I'm fishing because I'm planning to open an English-style fish-and-chips shop here in the village, my father and I are now living in a chalet up on the mountain and he has become the greatest sculptor of dwarves in all of Europe: one of his Grumpies (in French, *Grincheux*), enjoys pride of place in De Gaulle's office in the Élysée Palace, I'm getting top marks at school and I never digress in my compositions, right now, I may be dressed somewhat informally, with this army-surplus sweater, but at home I have sixteen Ballantyne argyle-patterned sweaters, each one a different color, a series of chrome-plated jackets, and a monogrammed dressing gown. This is the knock-about bicycle I only use to come down to the river, but at home I also have a corpuscle-red Legnano racing bike, with a gear shift, and last of all, I have a book of cashier's checks, I smoke, I drink, and I fight a duel at every full moon."

Or else I could say: "Now that I see you, I suddenly realize how much I've missed you, and just the idea that you might disappear again makes me feel like I'm dying, I love you I love you, and if you say 'What are you, stupid?' I swear that I'll eat all these fish, raw, and five pounds of bread, crust and crumb, and then I'll hurl myself into this ice-cold fishing hole, I'll have a cramp, I'll drown, and you'll spend the rest of your life struggling with your conscience."

But in the end, I just say: "Oh, all right I guess. How about you?"

She tells me that there are things about living in the city that she likes and others that she doesn't.

She sits down, perched on a rock, and I notice that she has nice legs.

"For instance," she says, "the other kids in school in the city are conceited and fashion-crazy, there's lots of traffic, every time you ride the trolley you get crushed, and there's no way to go down to the river or walk in the woods, the tap water tastes of iron, and strawberries are as expensive as diamonds."

And she starts fooling around with her hair.

On the other hand, for instance, she goes to dance school and she likes that a lot, and there are lots of movie theaters so she has her choice of films, she loves going to the movies, and in the new house they live in she has a big comfortable bedroom, with posters of actors on the walls, a record player, and lots and lots of records, about a hundred, she could even have dance parties.

She draws back her arm and skips a rock across the water,

but she only manages to make about three skips. She's out of practice, poor thing.

Because now, she explains, her parents have started a tailoring business that is doing pretty well; it's fashionable, they make tuxedos and cocktail dresses, it's all right, we're not rich but we're well-to-do. And so her father, who misses the village, has bought a parcel of land on the Roselle Hill, and he's going to build a vacation house there; so she'll be spending her summers here now.

And, implicit in her blue-green eyes, we'll be seeing one another.

And I feel like saying, look out, that's not the Roselle Hill anymore, it's the Fefelli Hill now, it's all his property, he's deforested and plowed up and stuffed everything with gravel, and he's moved the river, it's not the way you remember it, there's nothing wild left there, he's going to build a little suburban neighborhood with a little extra greenery, cobblestone streets, and lamp posts, and lots of cars driving back and forth. Not a fox or a squirrel or a porcupine will go near there, only thieves and cats, rummaging through the garbage.

Instead, what I say to her is: "Well, lots of people are building up there."

She seems irritated and she says, "If you're mad at me, just tell me, and I'll leave."

I say, "No, that's not it, but when you left here you were an untamed piratess, covered with blades of straw and with wheatgrass in your hair, just like us, and now you're back, talking about tuxedos and movie theaters and country homes. I can see that you're back here as a tourist, not as a villager, and if you want to know the truth, while you were away, a lot of things happened that weren't very nice, to Gancio and to Fulisca, to the fishes in the river, and in the heads of the people here. Now I live with my father in an ugly yellow house, in my bedroom I can hang whatever I want on the wall, but it's just small, and it won't get any bigger. We don't have a dime, and if Uncle Nevio hadn't given me the float and the lures, I wouldn't even be able to go fishing. Maybe I'm being obnoxious, but you can't just tell me what's happened to you without asking me what's happened to me."

"I'm sorry," she says, in a tiny voice, "please forgive me."

"Don't worry about it," I say.

She sits there in silence for a while, curling a big lock of hair around a finger, so nervous and jittery that I'm afraid she'll rip it out of her head. And so, to make peace, I put my hand under her nose.

"This is the fashionable perfume this year in town," I tell her, "it's called '*amour de vermicel.*'"

She laughs and sticks her tongue out at me. My god, it looks like that has grown too. She examines the contents of my creel, which is soaking in the water.

"Look how many fish you've caught," she says. "Poor things. Some of them are still alive." "If you want, I'll let them go," I say. She offers no comment. So I dump the creel over, freeing them all. Half of them are already half dead, and half will recover. The plate of fried fish goes swimming off, waggling as it heads toward the sea. What a jerk I am.

"So," she says, "I'll only be here for five days."

"Ah," I say, and an icy river rock sinks down into my stomach.

She stands up, tosses a stone along the surface of the water, and manages to skip it only three times.

I laugh at her: "You've really forgotten how it's done." I take her hand and show her how to hold the *giarella*, our word for the flat skipping stone.

She looks at me with her city-girl boldness and says, "You know, you've turned into a handsome boy, you look a little like James Dean."

And I feel a wave of heat sweeping over me, a blast of fire

that makes everything that happened with La Venerelli seem like a heap of warm chestnuts, and I tell her that I don't know who this Jeans Din is, but others have noticed the resemblance. What nonsense; if anything, people say I remind them of a porcupine, or someone who's been sticking pencils in his hair, or a cactus with a full head of prickles.

"What I mean to say," she explains, "is that you'd look like him if you combed your hair."

"Right," I answer.

"And who do I look like?" she asks.

When she was little, I would always say to her, "You look like a biscuit-eating fat girl," but she knows perfectly well, because she's no fool, that she's a real hottie now, and so I think it over carefully, and I want to say, "You look like an actress who is shot and dies in this one movie," but I can't remember the actress's name, so I say: "You're the queen of the pirates, you don't need to compete with anybody, you're prettier than any actress."

I have the impression that I got it right this time because she throws the stone and it doesn't skip even once, her little hand is trembling. So I say to her: "Let's make a bet. I'll throw the skipping stone, and if I can make it skip more than ten times, tomorrow I get to take you to the forest to pick strawberries."

"Okay, come on," she says.

I feel a little like the discus thrower Adolfo Consolini, or Robin Hood as he's about to shoot the deciding arrow in the presence of Maid Marian, or Pelé when it's zero-all and he's about to take a penalty kick, and I could go on with metaphors for another hour, because, modestly speaking, when it comes to metaphors, I am like, well, I won't offer a metaphor or we'll never stop. It was, in short, a historic moment. I choose a likely looking skipping stone, smooth but not too smooth, with the proper curvature, just the right weight. I kiss it, and I say:

"Fly, little bird, fly."

And the stone hurtles through one, two and three and four long, sailing skips and then five, six and seven and eight medium-long ones and then nine and ten and eleven and twelve and thirteen little blurps of skiplets and on the fourteenth it sinks into the water and vanishes.

"Nice," she says, and does a sketchy little dance step. "What's your record?"

"There was this one time," I tell her, "with a single stone-skip, I crossed the entire lake from one bank to the other, and I broke the tooth of a guy who was fishing on the other side."

"You haven't changed a bit," she says.

"Neither have you," I say.

It isn't true, but we pretend that's how it is.

8

That night, I can't sleep. I listen to my father pounding and planing. He's building a wooden statue, I don't know what it's supposed to be, but he meets with Carburo and Karamazov, they have big noisy meetings, and then the pounding resumes. But that isn't why I can't sleep.

In the morning at nine o'clock I have a date with Selene, under a horse chestnut tree that we both know, in a secluded part of the woods. I've borrowed my father's alarm clock—he didn't say a thing but he must have guessed something; he smiled with one eye closed against the smoke of his Nazi stink-nail.

And so at three minutes to nine, I'm there, early, hair neatly brushed.

At nine on the dot, she's not there.

Women never arrive on the dot.

At five past nine, she's not there.

"That little city chick, she's used to making people wait, she acts like she's the center of the universe, she's doing it on purpose to make me suffer. But that won't work with me." But it does work, perfectly, and in fact pretty soon I'm suffering and walking nervously in circles, like a dog on a chain.

At ten past nine, she's not there.

"You nasty piece of work, if you stand me up I'll never speak to you again, you think I'm just going to stand around hoping you'll show up? Why, I can have all the Venerellis I want, I've broken more hearts than cholesterol from animal fats." And I continue to suffer, and I start ruffling up my hair.

At thirteen past nine, she's not there.

"You whore, I hope you get a rash of canker sores, I should have skipped that rock right off the top of your head, oh sure, of course, now that you're a prosperous city dweller, what do you care about going into the woods? 'Pardon me, clerk, how much are the wild strawberries? Ten thousand lire a basket? May I have three baskets, please?'" And the suffering becomes more acute. I start talking out loud.

Nine-fifteen, and nothing.

"I know perfectly well that you're staying at your aunt's house, and I know where it is, I'm coming over there tonight with my slingshot, I'll break all the windows and I'll write on the wall 'Selene sucks Sponda's dick' (Sponda being Fefelli's ass-kissing deputy mayor, the sleaziest, most skirt-chasing scumbag in the village), and then . . ."

And then she arrives, running and out of breath.

"Forgive me," she says, "but my folks kept cross-examining me: where are you going, who are you going into the woods with, you don't know your way around anymore, everything has changed here, it's not like it was when we moved away, and plus now you're a big girl, and you have to be careful. Have you been waiting long?"

"Oh, three or four minutes," I answer. "I was late, too, I couldn't find the strawberry basket; this is a special basket, it brings good luck, the Forest Gnome peed in it once."

"Strawberries, hurray, let's go," she says.

And we start walking up the dirt path, and right away I notice that she has tight-cut jeans, and, right under the Levi's label, what I see is an ass, in fact, a very nice ass indeed, and it occurs to me that I am likely to spend a lot of time dawdling behind her during this walk in the woods. It's a nice cool day, there's a little bit of golden haze and the leaves are damp with dew, but judging from the odor I would say that the sun will be coming out soon. We reach the edge of the forest, and almost without realizing what I'm doing, I change direction, I'm not heading toward the section of woods where my house used to be; she notices it and says nothing. We hike along the entire ridge until we reach the line of poplar trees, then we climb a little further and we emerge in a clearing where a large butternut tree stands.

"Do you still like slightly bitter butternuts?" I ask.

"Yes," she says.

And so I clamber up the trunk of the butternut like a cat, not that it's really necessary, there's all the butternuts on the ground that we could possibly eat, but I like them just a little bit fresher than the windfall nuts, with a hard husk that peels easily.

And we shell the butternuts of their outer husk, and I start having certain thoughts, and then she starts cracking the butternuts with a rock, and those thoughts freeze, and then when we start removing the skin from the butternut we're venturing into a striptease, a little botanical porn, and I start glancing down at her jeans, and I feel a stirring in my trousers. We eat a bunch of butternuts, naked and rough-surfaced, then I say, that's enough, they'll gum up our mouths and bloat our stomachs.

"Just one more," she says.

Then we steal a bunch of black grapes, and as we're crawling on all fours between the rows of grapevines, she trips and falls forward, and I fall on top of her, with my face plunged into her hair; I can smell all her feminine scent and shampoo, and I hope inwardly that my smell is up to scratch.

And as we make our way upward through the forest, the sun comes out, and we pass continually from shadow to light, and her eyes change color each time, she is agile as a roebuck, and as she climbs, the label on her jeans undulates and her dancer's legs flash uphill; she's faster than me, and that's without grabbing at branches, only once do I reach back to take her hand to help her up, she accepts the help, and she feels incredibly light. And then we're there, on the hillock.

"Fucking gnome," I think, "please, please, let me find lots of wild strawberries."

But someone must have beaten us to it, because there are no wild strawberries at all.

But the gnome sees how things stand, and he sets to work in a flash, and puts all the wild strawberries back in place, fastening them on with a little gnome spit for each, gnome spit being notoriously very resinous. Anyway, what Selene doesn't know won't hurt her . . .

And here is the first strawberry patch, bright shining drops of red, three square yards of wild strawberries. She can't resist, she starts popping them into her mouth, and immediately her lips are bright red; she used to do the same thing when she was little, but it has a different effect on me now. Back then, she was just drooling, now she's driving me crazy. And as I gather strawberries, she eats them, and she even starts taking them out of the basket to eat them, and I pretend to be exasperated with her, and move away from her. And then I notice that she has suddenly started dancing. She spins around, twirling on just one leg, and even though the ground is steep, she leaps, she bows, she moves her arms as if she were swimming underwater, sinuously, just like a real ballerina in a tutu.

"God she's beautiful God she's beautiful God she's beautiful, if she rejects me I have to have three ways of dying immediately: either I'll throw myself off the overpass, or else I'll cut my throat with Dad's saw, or else I'll drown myself."

And she dances and says: "This is the life, you can't get this in the city."

And I think to myself that if I jump off the overpass, I might just land on a tarp covering a truck, I'd be crippled and nothing more. As for my dad's saw, that's out, because then Dad would feel as if it had been his fault somehow, and as for drowning, there's the survival instinct, and I'd swim back to the surface even if there was a boulder tied to my neck, and the pikefish would take it badly.

"I'll live, I'll live for you, my love." And then I start dancing too, but I'm a terrible dancer, I look like a grotesque satyr leaping around, and she bursts into laughter.

Then she collapses onto the grass, among the cyclamens, panting, her chest heaving.

I believe that this is the moment—at least, in the movies, when the girl is lying panting on the grass, unless of course there is an arrow sticking out of her back—this would be the moment of erotic tension when anything—a . . . ny . . . thing—can happen.

She puts a blade of grass into her mouth.

I can't figure out if this is good or bad.

Then she says: "You know, there are lots of boys in the city who want to date me."

This is definitely bad, and my thoughts start drifting back to the overpass, the saw, and so on.

"But, they're so boring," she sighs, "they can't tell a linden tree from a pear tree, they've never been down to the river, only to the swimming pool, or maybe to Riccione, on the Adriatic Riviera, and they like to eat those big old stupid strawberries that are mostly water, and they call them strawberries, and I say, no, really, you've got to believe me, the only real strawberries are the ones you find in the woods, those tiny wild strawberries."

"Exactly," I say. "And then they don't recognize stinging nettles when they see them, and they sit right on top of them."

"And then, when I tell them that I was born up here, they call me the small-town girl. But then I let them see me dance, and they fall hopelessly in love."

"Are you saying," I ask, "that you dance to make them fall in love?"

"Yes," she says. "To make them fall in love. But then I tell them no."

"Ah," I say. I want to ask, "In that case, isn't that what you just did to me?" but instead I say nothing.

She chews on her blade of grass. She dazzles me with a blue-green glance and asks: "And what do you do to make girls fall in love with you?"

What should I tell her? That I use mamonia?

"Well, um," I whisper, "I couldn't say. Maybe they come looking for me."

"Badaboom," she says, "don't act all conceited, you big heartbreaker. And when they come looking for you, what do you do?"

"Nothing," I say, "because . . ."

"Why?"

"Because I can only think about one girl," I answer.

She turns glum. A good sign, it strikes me.

"And who is that? One of the new Tuscan girls? Camillina Figarina?"

"Camillina," I wanted to tell her, "now has a pair of fat cheeks and so much hair on her upper lip that she looks like a hamster ."

There follows a silence, a long silence full of the buzzing of bees as they nuzzle the flowers and the cracking of branches and the barking of dogs in the distance, and I think, I have to say something, even if I say it in Cyrillic, because women like to talk and they want someone to talk to them; silence is for later, after you marry them. Gnome, give me an idea.

"Every time I used to come here and see the strawberries," I say suddenly, and all in a rush, "I'd think of you."

If I had been James Din, I would have said, in my bad English: "Whayn-ay-vayr I cowm heer, I t'eenk owv yoo."

"Really?" she says, and she comes close to me, and with the blade of grass in her mouth, she tickles my lips.

And after that, there was no holding me back, or should I say, there was no holding us back.

And then it was three days in the mountain meadows, three days of kisses that put La Venerelli to shame. La Venerelli was strictly a form of jaw exercise, this was something else entirely, something nutty; after each kiss, I was hungrier than before, I had an unquenchable thirst for more, and so did she, and I kissed her sideways, and standing up, and leaning against trees, and hidden in doorways, and with mouthfuls of grapes, and we even kissed after eating a panino with coppa.

Also, I touched.

I got my hands on her tits, of course, and down onto her midriff, and I wore out the buttons on her jeans from all the unbuttoning and rebuttoning and she would say no no, but each time we started over again.

And I never said to her "I love you" out of fear that I'd get another "What are you, stupid?" but we talked and talked and talked. We made plans about when I would attend high school in the city next year and how she would take me everywhere, to discover urban strawberries, that is, the delights of the metropolis, and how she would throw a party to introduce me to her friends, and how she would teach me the twist and the cha-cha-cha, which is so easy.

"But I'll be embarrassed," I would say.

And then we planned to take a trip to America. That is, we'd start in Canada, where we'd see polar bears and Iroquois Indians, and then drive across New York and the Nevada desert in a car like the one James Din drove, then pass through Mexico to eat some mushrooms, because down there the mushrooms are hallucinogenic, even more than grappa, and then we'd go track down Gancio's uncle in the Guatayaba jungle, and then she would dance on a float in the carnival in Rio, but nothing too skimpy, and then we would go and lay a wreath on the tomb of the Green Corsair in Maracaibo, and then to finish off we'd head down to Patagonia, and from there we'd take a ship all the way back to Livorno to go and see the aquarium, and then we'd climb over the Futa Pass on foot, and descend to the village, handing out souvenirs, and then . . .

And then we had to say good-bye.

And that morning I went down to watch her leave, peering out from my hiding place. Her family had a cream-colored Fiat 1500, the whole family was loaded down with suitcases, and she was dressed in navy blue, a genuine young lady. I went back home, I looked at my empty bedroom, with the soccer cards scattered on the floor, the soccer ball, and the tattered used books, and even though I loved them all, they seemed sickly. I thought about my father pounding away at his mysterious statue, stinking of wine. For the past month we'd been taking turns cooking, we'd eat pasta with tomato sauce, pasta with butter, and every so often, a hare that Uncle Nevio gave us. And I had no money to buy snacks, I'd go to school every morning with two or three apricots that got all bunged up in my pocket, turning into a soft mass of fuzzy-sweet goop.

One day I walked into the café. Most of the customers were watching the quiz show on TV, and Lavamèl was saying, "They'll get it wrong, you just wait," and everyone was asking Baruch if he thought the question was easy or hard. At a certain point, there was a question about dinosaurs, and Slim turned to Arturo Ninety-Nine, "Now, you're the only here who's actually seen dinosaurs, what's the answer," and the old man lost his temper.

Over at the political-conspiracy table, Karamazov had his head down; he was sleeping and dreaming of the steppes. Carburo was reading the Communist Party paper, the *Organo*, and Uncle Nevio was drinking *anicione*, his favorite anise liqueur. The blue-collar workers from Messina were listening to my dad, who was raising his voice, and everybody else was shouting at him: "Shut up, we can't hear the quiz show."

And I looked at the clock on the quiz show that was marking the seconds left to guess the answers, and I suddenly had a temporal convulsion. I saw a huge color television set and a person sitting in an easy chair, shooting at it with a little black handheld gun of some kind, and he must have been hitting it, because the screen changed the pictures it was showing, perhaps either trying to placate the man with the gun, or else trying to camouflage itself. Then I had a vision, as if I was watching the explosion of a towering atomic mushroom cloud of idiocy, and the radioactive fallout was showering down on every point in our country, the crowded cities and the desolate wilderness, and the result was an overwhelming wave of stupidity, a cosmic, indescribable transformation. No one had yet understood that this new electric appliance was the balcony from which future Benitoes would be addressing the nation.

That day, a contestant decided to withdraw with the monstrous sum of 1,280,000 lire, saying: "It's too much, I can't run the risk of losing it." And I heard my father in the background, saying: "Why, sure, let's just level the mountain with dynamite, it's crumbling anyway. Let's just pour more cement. Even the Lunini family, the ones who had the tailoring business, they're building a country home on land they bought from Fefelli. They've become 'haves,' too. It's too bad about their daughter, she used to be friends with my son, she was a nice little girl, but now she puts on airs; she's gotten all snooty."

"That's not true, Dad," I wanted to say, "you're not being fair."

Then I thought, "You know, she never gave me her phone number." I don't have a phone but she does. She never said, "Why don't you call me," she never said, "I want to see you again." She only said, once: "I like being with you." But maybe back in the city, she has a boyfriend, not a James Din type, more like the Brazilian soccer player José João Altafini. And I was so stupid that I failed to understand that, the last time we were together, she couldn't say anything because she was upset about us being separated, the same as me. I felt depressed. Not that I was having overpass thoughts, but just about. I grabbed a flask of wine from the cellar and got filthy drunk. I vomited all night long. When I woke up in the morning, I was ashen and pale, and I said: "Dad, let me see the statue."

I looked so weird and upset that he couldn't say no.

He pulled off the sheet. It was beautiful. There were two men, and in their arms they were holding the lifeless body of a third man. They were wearing neckerchiefs. Beneath it was written:

To those who died in the line of work.

ven though I lived obliquely between the rhythms of the sun and the duoclock, I could see a few things clearly. For instance, the fact that in our town and in its little history a great battle was being waged between good deities, bad deities, and odd deities. On one side, the Cheerful God, the Edible Gnome, Santa Putilla, and the Blessed Lacy Corset helped us and protected us. On the other side, the Violin-Playing Devil and the Boletus Gnome brought on small and bizarre misfortunes. The Shadow, reaper of souls, and the Sacra Pilla, the goddess of money who scrambles the brains of the greedy and the poverty-stricken, brought huge and irremediable misfortunes. And so I had no time to brood over the love that I had found and perhaps lost, because the theomachy, or battle of the gods, was raging, and these were days of great events.

One evening, we were all at the bar watching the game against Switzerland, and Lavamèl was sitting with Carbuncle in his lap. Lavamèl said, "No matter what, the game is going to end badly, Switzerland is small but wealthy, and you can be sure it bought off the referees with Swiss francs and kilograms and kilograms of Swiss chocolate." Instead, however, the Italian team took the lead, one to nothing, with a goal by Mazzola. Switzerland tied, and Lavamèl snickered. Then Corso and Rivera scored for Italy. The match ended three to one, and no one noticed that Lavamèl had stopped commenting on the game. One by one, we left the bar, and still Lavamèl sat there, with his dark sunglasses, motionless—maybe he was angry that the Swiss curse hadn't worked out.

At two in the morning, after the last dregs of Cucchi *mille-fiori* liqueur had been drained, Balduino said: "Lavamèl, it's closing time."

No response.

He took off Lavamèl's black sunglasses, and beneath them, his eyes were closed.

He shook him by the shoulder, but nothing happened, or actually, the cigarette butt fell out of his hand. And Carbuncle wasn't moving either.

Lavamèl had gone to the great hunting ground, and old Carbuncle had gone with him, in lockstep with his master.

Thus far, there was nothing especially strange about it. Lavamèl was old, and we were sorry to see him go, because even though he was a bird of ill omen, every small town and village needs a jinx, and now maybe we would get a real one. The real problem was the anomalous manner of Lavamèl's death. Technically, he had died because his ticker gave out. But, as our undertaker Felix pointed out, the problem was his position.

Lavamèl, in fact, always sat on the same chair, a metal chair with armrests. Since he suffered from varicocele, which is to say, he had one testicle the size of a provolone, he had to sit with his legs spread wide. So he slipped them into the armrests, one leg on each side of the chair, as if he were riding a horse. Now, because he had died in that position, and having immediately gone into an astonishing state of rigor mortis, roughly what you might expect to find in an equestrian statue, the possible solutions for his successful funeralization were three.

First, it might be possible to disentangle his legs from the armrests. But it immediately become clear that to do so would involve breaking his legs; they were so stiff that just touching them made a horrible noise, and there had already been one cracking sound.

Second, it might be possible to melt the armrests with a blowtorch. But as soon as Favilla the blacksmith tried that approach, Lavamèl began to melt away, emitting a horrible scorched smell. The risk was that not only would the chair be burnt, but so would Lavamèl, and instead of burying him we would subject him to a Hindu cremation.

The third solution was to bury him as he was, seated, with chair, cat, and all.

We should point out, of course, that Carbuncle was imprisoned in his master's arms, as stiff as an umbrella.

In Italian, the word for coffin is *bara*, so a barista is as equally apt to describe a coffin maker as a barman. But the barista that the whole town looked to that day was the coffin maker, not Balduino. And that barista had to admit, frankly, that he was at his wits' end, and he asked if my father, a well-respected carpenter, could help out. Together they sketched out a plan for a cuboid coffin. Inside the coffin, they fit Lavamèl with his chair and Carbuncle; we said nothing to Don Brusco about the cat, and a regulation funeral ceremony was readied. When the time came for the interment, however, someone pointed out that it would be a nice touch to bury him upright, but no one had written "this side up," or "this side down" on the coffin, so that was hardly a straightforward proposition. Luckily, my father remembered that the bottom board of the cuboid casket had a darker grain. And so the coffin was lowered into the ground, and to the best of my knowledge, it is the only cuboid two-corpse coffin anywhere on earth.

The following day, the new branch office of the Valley Bank opened for business. That was a good sign; money was circulating. That was a bad sign; money was setting up housekeeping, money was all grown-up and ready to live on its own. The president of the bank was a certain Boccoli, as elegant as

Mitchum and a real piece of shit. He came to say hello to everyone and explained to us all that a checkbook is a handy thing to have because once you have one, all you need to do is sign a check and you can use that to pay for things instead of cash. He must have taken us for idiots; his explanation came as news to no one but Caprone, who was fascinated by the novelty.

The following day, Caprone parked Hisssss outside of the bank and went in.

He stamped out in a fury a few minutes later.

"It's a fraud! Sure, they give you a checkbook, but then you have to use your own money. In that case, what do I need the checkbook for?"

Immediately afterward came the controversy over the statue. My father invited everyone over to our house to see it. Everyone agreed that it would be a fine thing to put the statue in the town's main square. And of course, that idea triggered an epic dispute in the town hall. Carburo said that it was a good statue, that it commemorated not only Remo, but also the workers who died in the construction of the highway. The foul whoremonger Sponda said that it was ill-advised, that a monument of this sort would only give the town's children a bad attitude toward work. The mayor cut short the debate: a monument that was so openly political, he said, never. If anything, we'll build a fountain in the town square.

Fefelli had the deciding vote, but the opposition was hanging tough, and secret deliberations got under way.

For several days, it was the sole topic of conversation. Then the situation resolved itself. The statue was loaded onto a flatbed truck and driven all through the village; from there, the truck with the statue proceeded to the cement plant, where an accordion concert was held, with Regina singing the old protest song, "Sciur Padrùn," followed by slogans and doughnuts, in defiance of the CEO Paladini and his paid thugs; clearly, Fefelli had ordered them to behave and let us blow off some steam. From there, the statue was placed in the lobby of the Casa del Popolo, where it immediately took on a dual role: as a commemoration for posterity and a coat rack. I think it's still there.

Fefelli had no choice but to swallow the open mutiny and build the fountain. But the Pastori brothers had sworn to get even with my father, and one evening they followed him in their car as he was returning home on his bicycle; luckily, Fangio happened to be parked with his bus at the bus stop. He saw and immediately understood, and he moved the SITA bus until it blocked the road, turned off the engine, opened the door and stepped out, saying to the Pastori brothers:

"I'm all out of gas, you'll have to take the long way around."

The Pastori brothers were big and muscular, but Fangio had a jack handle in one hand, and my father had a little hatchet.

"We'll see you some other time," they said, and threw their car into reverse, screeching their tires as they roared back up the street.

The cement plant hired a pair of private security guards, and they patrolled the plant with the Pastori brothers, a grim little goon squad.

"I like them," Osso said immediately, "they're tough. It's like those guys at the O.K. Corral."

"When you can't tell the bandits from the sheriffs anymore," said Gancio, "you're really up shit creek."

It was one of the celebrated statements of Gancio's young life. A troubled life. His brothers had both moved into the city and left him alone. Uncle Nevio had taken him in to work in his store, but all Gancio did was smoke cigarettes and steal money out of the cash register, pilfering only small sums, but constantly. At night, he would roam around with grease balls from the lower valley, small-time thieves. One day, I saw him wearing a brand-new leather jacket.

"Where'd you get that?"

"I won it in a poker game," he said, laughing. He no longer carried the Guatayaba blowgun or his slingshot; instead he had a small switchblade knife. He was fourteen but he looked like he was twenty. He had a girlfriend, a half-insane thirty-year-old who looked after the tomatoes in the vegetable patch and tended to the loneliness of the town retirees. Poor Gancio, our local Amazon Indian with an unpromising future. Luckily, Uncle Nevio had developed a fondness for him. He swore that he would send Gancio to school, make sure he got his high school diploma.

"It's all the same to me," said Gancio, smoking Nazi stink-nails. Whenever he laughed or kidded somebody, grown-up wrinkles would crease his adolescent cheek.

One day it started raining. It rained for three days and three nights. The sewers backed up, a porridge of shit engulfed the streets. Fefelli had pocketed the money for sewer improvements. The river turned yellow and teemed with dead fish; a tannery upstream had flooded and there had been a huge spill of toxins and acids, the water was covered with foam, and we dragged out four truckloads of dead fish that were emitting a stench of death. Several of Caprone's sheep died, too, as well as a pair of dogs that had drunk from the river.

Baruch said that there was something odd happening on the mountain, you could hear noises. And one night when I was dreaming, and my father was coughing more than usual, I saw the benevolent version of the gnome appear at my window.

"Sleep on, sleep on, and as you sleep the world is disappearing," he said to me.

"What do you mean?"

"Come to the Fanara basin tomorrow morning. I have to show you something."

The next day was foggy, and I had difficulty making my way through the forest. There was mud everywhere; I slipped and slid and got bogged down. I walked back by the cyclamen meadow, where I first kissed Selene, and saw that there had been a landslide; half of the meadow was just sliced away, as if a giant had swung his sickle, and two uprooted trees displayed their viscera—wet roots swarming with insects.

I went to the stone trough. As always, the sound of water put me into a trance, and I shut my eyes. When I opened them again, the water began to whirl, swirling first in one direction and then in the other. I saw a reflected face emerge from the water, and then a woman stepped out, dripping wet: it was my mother. Just like in the old pictures. She was skinny and pale, with a pained smile, wearing a gray dress. She held a basket full of linen, and in the middle she had laid several yellow apples.

"How you've grown, my little boy," she said.

"Mamma, to me you still look the same, just like the photograph on dad's night table. I can't seem to remember you. I'm sorry."

"It's not your fault. You were too little."

She started to wash the clothing, singing softly to herself. She seemed transparent.

"Mamma," I said, "why are you washing clothes? The house is gone."

"The house is still there, dear. If it wasn't, why would I be washing clothes and picking apples?"

"But Mamma . . ."

"The forest never stops living, whatever you may do to it. Stay close to your father," she whispered. Then she stepped into the water and gently descended, as if there were a staircase in the basin. And she was gone.

Suddenly, the Fanara basin filled and then overflowed with a muddy stream. I also saw that in the century-old stone base of the trough there was a crack, and water poured out there as well. I ran down to the village, slipping in the muck, leaping over toads. I didn't know who to tell—my father, Baruch, who? In the end, I went into Uncle Nevio's shop. He was making shotgun shells by hand and filling them with pellets. He greeted me with a smile.

"What do you want, Timeskipper? Lures? As muddy as the water is these days, you know you can't fish."

I told him what I had seen in the forest. He told me not to say anything to my father. "He's not well and this will just upset him. Tomorrow we'll go up and take a look together."

But then, in a conversation with Baruch, he let slip what I had told him, and Baruch let it slip to Carburo and Carburo told my father, and they decided, tomorrow morning we'll go up there.

That night I woke up, and I heard a noise coming from the workshop, an unbelievable pounding, it sounded as if someone was breaking through the floor. I walked in and there was the gnome, carving a tree trunk with an axe. Splinters of wood were flying everywhere.

"What in the world are you doing?!" I yelled.

"I'm building a canoe," the gnome replied. "There's a river of mud in the forest, and it's only going to get worse."

"You've lost your mind. You're going to paddle a canoe through the trees?"

"That's right," he said, contemplating his creation. "What should I carve on the prow as a figurehead? A naked gnomette? A doe? Selene in jeans?"

"Leave her out of this."

"I saw the two of you, you know, in the woods," said the gnome, dancing and leaping. "If it hadn't been for me, you wouldn't have stood a chance. Who pasted the wild strawberries back on? Who got the little birdies to wake up and sing, after they had fallen asleep? Who fanned the cyclamens so that a sweet scent wafted over the meadow?"

"Oh definitely, all your doing," I sneered.

The gnome's mustache turned green and his eyes turned bloodshot with rage.

"Conceited midget. Beg forgiveness."

"Forgive me, Your Green-ness," I said, bowing. It wasn't smart to fool around when he turned into Satan's mushroom.

He relaxed, and his big mustache turned a snowy white again. I saw that he was wearing my father's work apron.

"Gnome," I asked, "please tell me, where is my dad?"

"Wake up, and you'll find out." I leapt out of bed and ran into his bedroom. My dad wasn't there, and neither were his heavy boots.

He had gone up onto the mountain in the dark, alone, with his flashlight. He couldn't wait.

The next morning my father rushed out into the town square and started making speeches. A crowd gathered—he coughed, he was feverish, but his voice thundered like the voice of the prophet Nabumelech. He said that the mountain was collapsing. That after all the wounds inflicted on it by the construction of the highway, unless they stopped digging on the Roselle Hill and quit deforesting, the whole mountain would come down onto the town. The Fanara basin was cracked, a number of chestnut trees had already toppled over, and water was pouring out everywhere.

Maybe it was the fact that he seemed like a deranged prophet, but he convinced everyone. A delegation of townspeople went to see the mayor. Fefelli said, "All right, I'm going to call the engineers, the planners, and the geologists; everyone relax, we may have to slow down work, but we can't stop now. The contractors need lumber for just a little while longer, and after that, the trees will be untouchable."

He actually seemed concerned, he rode around town on a bicycle, he stopped to talk with Baruch, Carburo, Luciana, who took advantage of the opportunity to sell him four pair of briefs. He said that he cared about everybody's welfare, not the interests of a few. He attacked the foul Sponda, saying that he had failed to supervise the subcontractors adequately. He even came up to talk with me; he stopped me as I was leaving the café. He said, "I know that you're a good kid, very grown-up for your age, so do your best to keep an eye on your father; he's a good man, but he's a little obsessed with politics. Tell him to calm down, and you'll see; soon there'll be plenty of work for him."

"In any case, I'll kill you, Mister Mayor," I thought. And I asked him: "And what kind of fountain are you going to build?"

"What kind would you like?

"Pikefish. Make it with silver pikefish leaping into the air, with clean water pouring out of their mouths."

"I was thinking more of a beautiful woman holding a horn of plenty," he said, "but we'll see."

"Speaking of horns-a-plenty, maybe we should just put up a portrait of your wife," blurted out Balduino, who had heard everything and already had his midmorning drunk going.

Fefelli shrugged. After all, Mrs. Hotlips had grown older, fatter, and more depressed. Mailmen and plumbers now left the house unsampled. And that evening, at Villa Meringue, a gray Lancia coupe pulled up, and several distinguished-looking gentlemen stepped out. They were envoys from the major developers. They stayed for a long time; evidently they had a lot to talk about.

I had gone out to play soccer, and I was walking back to town with Osso and Baco. We were filthy and mud-covered as if we had just run a motocross race. Osso tried hitchhiking, but given his lack of resemblance to Marilyn Monroe, no one stopped to give him a ride. Exhausted, we stopped at the gas station. Osso pulled out *Playboy*, with a big foldout page that featured a square meter of naked female flesh, and Baco sat down next to him. You'd think they were reading *Paradise Lost*, that's how seriously they were perusing the pages. That's not to say that the subject didn't fascinate me, too, but I was feeling edgy. I couldn't understand Fefelli's sudden courtesy, because a serpent may change its skin, but not its fangs. I started dribbling the ball, but it was caked with mud, as heavy as the world, and after three or four kicks, I let it drop.

"Nasty evening," I said to the two of them, rapt in their pornotrance.

I saw a white Alfa Romeo Giulia stop at the gas station. There was another car parked at the far end of the parking area; two men stepped out. They were the private security guards who worked at the cement plant. The Giulia turned on its headlights and pulled out. Licio Pastori was at the wheel. As soon as I saw that, I shouted, and started running home. Neither Osso nor Gancio understood. They just watched me go.

When I got home it was dark. There were tire tracks on the grass. The light was on in the workshop. I went in, but my father wasn't there. He wasn't in the house. I looked for him in the canebrake behind the house, but he wasn't there, either. Then I heard a moan, followed by a curse.

He was lying by the side of the road. His face was swollen, his nose was broken. The little finger on one hand dangled, lifeless.

"You should see two of the other guys," he said, "I fixed them good. Bastards had masks over their faces, but I knew exactly who they were."

Then he fell silent.

It took him only a month to recover, even though it had been quite a beating. The police took the report—a beating administered by unknown attackers. The Pastori brothers and the security guards all had alibis; ten friends had seen them in the city. As for their bruised faces, well, they'd been in a fight over women, you know how these things are. I asked Osso and Gancio to tell the police what they'd seen. Osso wouldn't talk. Gancio said he'd do it: "But what do I tell them? That I saw a car that might have belonged to the Pastori brothers? Listen to me. The Guatayaba Indians always let ten full moons go by; only then do they take their revenge." Uncle Nevio talked to the lawyer, who told him that, unfortunately, these guys are sly, we can't prove a thing. It seemed as if everybody was ready to shrug and forget about it. A few years before that's not what would have happened. I was furious, but one evening my father said he wanted to talk to me. His swollen nose made him look like cycling legend Gino Bartali.

He told me three things.

That this was how it had gone, but he wasn't giving up. But he wanted me to keep cool and not make any stupid moves. He made me swear it.

Then he said, "Do you see this black notebook? I'm going to write everything I know about all the crimes they're committing, everything they're doing. If something happens to me, take it to the city and give it to this gentleman whose name is written right here, he's a lawyer for the union. But don't worry, it won't be necessary.

"Third, if I die, there's a key in the nail box. There's a steel cabinet in the workshop, and inside it is a surprise for everyone."

"Stop talking like this, Dad," I said, in tears. "Stop it."

"These are things that have to be said once in a lifetime, and after this, we'll never mention them again," he said, grabbing one of my arms with a powerful grip. "Now let's talk about your school. Your uncle will help out with the money—you're going to go to high school in the city, you're going to finish college, just like Dr. Carabelli, like that pig, Fefelli. Work hard— I expect good report cards, and I'll show them to the world, like Moses with the tablets."

I studied like crazy for four months. At night, I'd make a pot of espresso with a Moka Express to stay awake, and when I went to sleep, my heart was beating as if I had Selene next to me, without jeans. But instead I was alone, I was sad, and I had a dangerously elevated pulse. But I didn't flunk. I don't remember the Last Day of junior high school. I only remember saying good-bye to my friends, being sad, thinking that the path ahead of me was all uphill, or worse, vertical, a sheer wall straight up, like the cliffs of the gorge of Mount Mario.

Then came summer, and the sunshine healed all our wounds. My father got a good job: the carpentry work for a cafeteria and bingo hall and assembly hall for the Casa del Popolo. In town, everybody loved him, and he was drinking less. The Pastori brothers were building a new house, right behind Villa Meringue. One night, mysteriously, it burned down. One of the security guards found his motorcycle disassembled, piece by piece, without an instruction sheet for reassembling it. Guatayaba justice had been done.

Construction started up again on the Roselle subdivision, but the houses were behind schedule. The house for the Lunini family had foundations, nothing more. I figured that I'd never see Selene again, that my short love affair was over, and that for the rest of my life I'd have nothing but *Playboy*, jacking off, and the occasional passing Venerelli. Instead, a postcard arrived.

It said:

I'm not coming, as you probably know the country house isn't ready. I'm at the beach in Cesenatico. But I hear that you're coming to the city to study. I'll wait for you, I haven't forgotten you. Selene.

(PS: bring strawberries.)

The postcard had a picture of sails and a port. I clipped it to the spokes of my bicycle, so that the sound it made would remind me that I had it, that it was as real and as precious as my quasi-girlfriend named Selene.

It was a long, soupy, horribly hot summer.

And very boring. Anyone who could go to the beach had gone. For instance, Osso had left for the Versilia region on the Tuscan coast with two pounds of condoms; I wondered if they'd last him for the trip. One guy from the village had gone hunting in Yugoslavia—"As if the hares were different there," said Baruch with a sigh. Of those who remained, a few went to try to cool off at Fiumerunco Beach, but the water was muddy and shallow. Women strolled back and forth in front of Luciana's shop to admire the latest models of bikinis, and had their hair colored Chez Piero & Renata: Unisex Beauticians— the term referred to the clientele, not the hairdressers, as Piero pointed out. The men who didn't have to go to work lounged around, observing the construction in progress on the fountain or on the Roselle vacation village. Slim the Magnificent went to work as a birdman in a nightspot; he earned a little money and, one evening, he said to Carburo: let me pay for a bottle. Carburo said, "No thanks, if I let you pay, the mountain really will collapse on the town." Balduino installed a new neon sign. Mosquitoes and moths flocked around from as far away as Mongolia. They'd smack into the neon bulbs and then plummet, fully roasted, into people's drinks; at the café tables outside people had canapés floating in their drinks, the height of modern convenience. Cipolla, who was nearsighted, drank gypsy-moth Camparis and gnat-garnished Crodinos, and all the while the over-the-hill gang loaded up on games of tressette and puffed Nazi stink-nails. Maria Casinò won six thousand lire playing *sbarazzino* and bought herself a lacy corset. "I don't have any real use for it," she said, "but at least I can say that in my lifetime I've owned one." Balduino introduced the fad of the Antarctic Shiver, a repulsive citron juice and Strega liqueur slush that gave whoever drank it the runs quicker than a cobra bite.

We boys spent our time playing endless games of soccer and engaging in extended discussions of sex. Gancio told us everything he did in bed with his cream puff, and sometimes he'd even sketch illustrations to help convey his point. Baco, on the other hand, was a living encyclopedia of autonomous sex, and he criticized us for being overhasty and underappreciative masturbators, explaining at considerable length the varied refinements of the art of Onan. Chief among his techniques was the cadaverous jack off, or how to numb your hand so that it feels as if it belongs to someone else. Or else he'd lecture us on the proper uses of watermelons, apples, sponges, radiators, the difference between pulling off and rubbing off, the pressure jack off as opposed to the two-finger creamer, complete with such orientalist refinements as the rabbit-fur jerk off and the dancing fly spank.

My favorite way of jacking off was to fuck the meadow, and then lie there, exhausted, grassprints on my face, panting, "Selene, Selene where are you?"

After all the talking, though, the boredom remained, and we'd get out our bicycles, two or three of us on the same bike, like carabinieri, and then we'd go out onto the overpass to watch vacation-goers stuck in endless traffic jams and the inevitable little fender benders, but we never saw another spectacular crash like the overturned truck. We invented a summer scandal: Hotlips, in a last fling of sluttery, had seduced Breadlocks the baker on a nuptial bed of flour, and her wedding ring, with name and date, had wound up in a dinner roll, and, finally, jammed between the molars of the cuckolded husband himself. It was all false, of course. Hotlips, fat, depressed, and stuffed with sedatives, roamed stark naked through the manicured grounds of the villa, and finally a team of male nurses came to take her away. Fefelli pretended to be devastated for twenty-four hours, then forgot he had ever married her.

We forgot about her, too. Boredom engulfed us, like the damp heat.

Then came the paw prints.

On the first day of August, with a temperature of close to ninety—and that was in the early morning—Luciana went down to the river to cool off her peach fuzz before opening her panty boutique for business. The scream she let out was heard high on the mountain ledges. Villagers came running by the dozens. On the sand of the riverbank were the tracks of a monstrously huge animal, almost certainly a biped.

Each paw print measured forty centimeters in length, twenty-eight centimeters in width, and sank about three centimeters deep in the sand. The foot that had made the tracks had four toes: one of the toes was bigger than the others, and sprawled off to the side, with a large claw; the other three toes extended forward. There was no sign of webbing, no marks of a dragging tail, no hair, no slimy or scaly material left behind. Only those unsettling, enormous paw prints.

By evening, everyone had their own personal theory concerning the mysterious animal.

In the opinion both of the highly rational Baruch and of Tavarelli, the carabinieri captain down in the lower valley, the animal was a four-toed bear, the last surviving specimen of a species that was quite common in these mountains in ancient times. It stood roughly six foot three inches tall, it weighed 265 pounds, had thick, dark fur, and had come down to the river to drink because its habitat had been ravaged; perhaps it lived in a mountain cave that had collapsed or had been flooded.

In the view of Balduino and the local chapter of Alcoholics Homonymous, this was a manifestation of an "upright panther," an animal that walked on its hind legs in order to deceive the unwary and conceal its quadrupedal nature. Balduino claimed that he had already sighted this faux biped on the outskirts of town, and that it had once even stolen a demijohn of wine from him. It was about five feet high and ten feet long, it weighed 191 pounds, had a long tail, was a man-eater, and had an especially ravenous appetite for teetotalers; it had come down to the river to wash because, like cats of all sizes, it had a keen instinct for cleanliness.

According to Karamazov and the VSOP's (very special, old, and pale), the paw prints belonged to a Russian Gulibiaka, an age-old creature of the Siberian steppes. The animal in question was an outsized, mustachioed humanoid with fangs and claws, whose cry was reminiscent of the bullfrog's roar. It stood ten feet tall, weighed as much as a (Russian) tractor, and subsisted on potatoes, salad, and cabbage. As for why it had arrived on the banks of our local river, that was a question to be directed to our Soviet comrades.

The women of the village believed that it was a gorilla from the Congo. Height: six-and-a-half feet; weight: 290 pounds, and twice as well hung as even Belloni the plumber (this particular detail was not discussed in the presence of children). It had escaped from the zoo and was roaming through our valley because this was mating season and it was searching for a female biped with which to couple.

But to me and the other guys, it was a pikeosaur, a type of reptilian fish that had almost gone extinct, spawned during the Cretaceous Era from mutations triggered by a meteorite (or perhaps a prehistoric tannery). It had the face of a pikefish, the body of a velociraptor, it was an exceedingly fast runner, and it had a special fondness for osso buco. From time to time, it ventured down to the river, to swim and do a little fishing.

Others thought it was a Tampicoceros, others thought it was a Thang, and some said it was a giant porcupine.

Then, to further complicate the hypotheses, new paw prints appeared on the soccer field. This time there were four paw prints, slightly skewed to one side, with a stripe running down the middle.

The explanation for this new phenomenon covered two possibilities: either a large bear with a limp and a dangling dick, or else an enormous short-tailed panther. In any case, the animal was dubbed the Panthabear, and countermeasures were prepared for a creature so designated.

The following measures were put in place.

First, the establishment of a squad of volunteers, armed with rifles and composed of men with valid hunting licenses, as well as bush beaters, torch bearers, and a caterer, as well as Slim, who emitted an assortment of twelve different animal calls, one of which might (or might not) be the cry of a Panthabear in heat. This squad was under the command of Captain Tavarelli and Uncle Nevio.

Second, a network of spotters, observing from balconies, roofs, and various elevated vantage points around town, consisting of women and children equipped with binoculars, as well as a regular village patrol, with three men in each shift, under the supervision of Baruch and Luciana.

Also: a forensic team was deployed to search for such evidence as further paw prints, huge shits, traces of gnawing; it was composed of Dr. Carabelli and the pharmacist. It became clear only later why they were the sole members of the team.

A task force of old Doofuckallians, assigned to read zoological books and publications, selected by Regina and Karamazov.

A flying squad of junior woodchucks armed with slingshots, wooden pikes, and rocks, commanded in two-hour shifts by me, Osso, and Gancio.

A squadron of young hoodlums, up to the age of ten, assigned to raise a tremendous ruckus in the village, in the hope that the noise would keep the animal away.

A Panthabear Emergency Committee in the Town Council, appointed to alert the press and focus as much media attention on the situation as possible.

Sweeps, searches, and false sightings began in earnest. For

the larger dogs in the village, these were tough days. Two days later, the first gawkers arrived. At the outskirts of town, a sign had been set up reading: THIS MARKS THE BOUNDARY OF PAN-THABEAR TERRITORY: USE CAUTION. In the café, Balduino had pinned up a drawing of the beast, taken from the Italian comic book *Tex Willer*, and customers could order a Panthabear Panino, or guzzle high-proof cocktails that helped to diminish the fear of the Panthabear.

Still, despite all the patrols, every morning new paw prints turned up in unexpected places. There was also a hair and a tiny turd, fox-terrier variety, that caused considerable bafflement. A television news crew came to film a report, and Baco managed to get into the shot and wave "ciao" to the whole country.

A university professor came and issued a solemn opinion: "Either it was a big prank or it was a big bear."

"Thanks for nothing," everyone responded.

But it was no prank. One morning they found a sheep torn to bits in the courtyard of Carburo's house, along with new paw prints and signs of a struggle.

A huge search party spread out over the mountains. Fifty men took part, two men accidentally shot one another, another broke his leg, and twenty hares, a wild boar, and a dog named Tom were shot, but no Panthabear.

Fefelli was about to call out the army, no one talked about anything else, and a general psychosis led people to see the monster everywhere: in their headlights, outside their front door, running down the highway, or even emerging from the restrooms at the gas station. At this point, every shadow was a Panthabear lying in ambush.

One evening, I went to ask my father what he thought about this strange situation. I walked into the workshop, and there he was, with Carburo, Baruch, and the Messinese factory workers, and I saw . . .

What did I see?

The following morning, the street cleaner discovered that numerous blood-smeared paw prints ran from the road, crossed the square, and pointed straight at town hall.

And there he found the paws of the monster. That is, four wooden cutouts, skillfully manufactured, a pile of manure with a sign reading: CAUTION: FRESH PANTHABEAR SHIT, and a poster that said: "Instead of being afraid of beasts that don't exist, see if you can't be afraid of the real beasts that you have right here at home.

"PS: the sheep had already died, of ovine pneumonitis."

"Dad," I said, with a great sense of relief, "so that's where I got my twisted chromosomes."

Yes, it was a wonderful end to the summer.

There was also a major cultural discovery. Baruch, rummaging through a crate filled with old books, found nothing less than Commander Ghigna's wartime diary, one hundred hand-written pages. A radical publisher came to look at it and said that he would publish a book, that things like this were history, and they should never be forgotten.

"Sure, for a while we'll remember," Baruch said to me, "but I'm not sure how long. Once, your father got his foot caught in a fox trap. As he lay there in pain he said, 'I swear that if I survive this, I will never shoot another animal.' He managed to extract his leg, though his calf was pretty torn up. He recuperated, the scar faded, and a few years later I saw him come back from a hunting trip with two hares in his game basket. The pain was gone, the oath was forgotten, and your father is not a dishonest man. But memory is made of more than oaths and words and plaques; it consists of actions that we repeat every morning of our lives, every morning of this world. And the world that we want needs to be saved every day, nourished, kept alive. Relax your guard even for an instant, and everything collapses into ruins."

Baruch squinted as he gazed up toward the mountains, as if he were trying to make out the footsteps that he had left behind, footsteps of his fellow partisans.

"They'll be back," he said, in a disconsolate voice. "It'll take twenty years, or thirty, but they'll be back. We may not see tanks rumbling into town, and they may not speak German. They'll smile at us, and they'll drive handsome cars, to the admiration of one and all. They'll wear tailored suits instead of steel-gray uniforms. Maybe there won't be death squads roving the streets, but people will disappear in silence, eliminated in some elegant new fashion. That's how it will be. Or maybe I'm wrong, maybe it's just the scar from the trap that comes back every once in a while and makes me rave like this."

The pendulum of the café clock was tick-tocking back and forth, but it didn't set off my duoclock. I was afraid that Baruch was seeing things all too clearly.

PART TWO

1.

Half awake and half asleep, I was hop-hiking down along the dirt path. It was no longer the rocks in the little lane that made my headlong progress rock from side to side, but the railroad tracks. At the end of the dirt path was Track 8. Now the flocks of starlings swooped under the awnings of the train station, the forest had become a hedge of plants in large terra cotta vases, and my footprints in the snow had turned into the timetable of departures. My Geschkwürtz-traminer was a snack in a cellophane condom.

The train that had been carrying me to the city for the past two years, hop-hiking along with a rumble and roar, rushing through tunnels and skirting the river, was an old-fashioned train, sooty and creaky; and every morning it departed at 6:20 A.M., and pulled into the station forty-two minutes later, and then I caught the Number 7 bus, I managed to squeeze in another short nap standing up, until the bus pulled up at the foot of the century-old, grim, and looming building of the Giosuè Pascoli High School.

Aboard the train, whenever the regular puffing thrust of the steam pistons set off my duoclock, I'd go down to the river to fish. Sometimes, I'd take Giosuè Carducci along with me; he was impatient, he constantly ran his bait-smeared hand through his beard, and he had a ravenous appetite for little raw minnows, all things that you won't learn from the history of literature. Giovanni Pascoli, on the other hand, never fished, but he was very interested in skipping stones. Interested, but without talent: the most he ever managed was six or seven skips. "Poetry, in the final analysis," he used to say, "is a way of launching the weight of the world into flight on the lightness of verse, like a stone over the water." Okay, Giovannino, if you say so, I'd reply. Dante Alighieri would fish with his hands, reaching under heavy stones and swearing furiously if a creek-fish got away. Ugo Foscolo hurled himself fully dressed into the water, shouting: "Like Shelley, I want to die like Shelley." And when it came to Sandro Manzoni, I refused to take him fishing with me; he spoiled my luck, the fish would hide deep in the riverbed whenever he was there. Or else I'd skip into the future, onto a super-express train, with seats like big easy chairs from the parlor, and a hostess would bring me potato chips and newspapers and magazines, and everyone had a telephone in their pocket, I swear it, a phone no bigger than a wafer, and they talked right into it, there were no wires or receivers or dials with numbers, everyone had their own little wafer, and each wafer made a special noise that they recognized instantly, like the wailing of their own baby. It was a full-fledged science-fiction convulsion, and I'd stop the duoclock, wake up and look around me at the outskirts of the city, rushing toward me, with big-box factories and piled heaps of scrap metal and junk, sheets hanging out to dry at the windows and asthmatic geraniums on the balconies. The train stations of Leona, Caverzo, Caverzo Basso, and Modanella would go by, half-slumbering people would get on and off the train. Sometimes I'd reread my lesson, sometimes I'd just read, but mostly I sniffed and smelled. It was a train filled with blue-collar workers going to their factory jobs, and many carried lunch pails with hot meals. As a result, the air was redolent with an olfactory symphony of macaroni, stew, soups, fermented cabbage, beans, and tangerines. Also, with farts that were metabolically tuned to the diets of each individual, and which could be broken down into three types: a) tolerable, b) make you want to open the train window, c) make you want to jump out the train window. Osso's farts belonged to category c). I assumed my own belonged to category a), but not everyone agreed. There was a bricklayer who dozed, snoring and farting, sometimes separately, and sometimes accompanying himself in a giddy duet; he was generally known as the human orchestra. Whenever he woke up, he'd say, "Excuse me, it's my wife." Which didn't mean that he was married to a fart; he meant that his wife cooked fart-engendering foods for him. There were also smells of socks, shoes, sweat, wet woolen overcoats, and exhaustion—the most indefinable odor of them all, the smell of something damp left out to dry, but which never does get dry, and you have to put it back on every day.

And then there were the conversations. We young male students would talk about soccer and girls and school. The factory workers: soccer and women and the factory. The female students: actors and singers and school and whisper whisper giggle. And whenever the factory workers talked to us, it was a constant round of ridicule, sarcasm, and scorn: sometimes harsh and sometimes cheerful. You fine young sophisticates go to school, you don't have any idea what a factory is like, long shifts, bastard foremen, time cards to punch in and punch out. And we'd say: boring subjects, sadistic teachers, school bells. And they'd say: we have accidents on the job and toxic fumes to breathe. And we'd respond: but at least they pay you. And I heard words like direct-action committee, capitalism, and revolution, words I'd heard from my father, but there they proliferated, they seemed to fill every car on the train, as though when the train finally pulled into the station, the doors would open and out would step three hundred men with bandoliers and rifles, determined to seize the *ciudad*. Instead, everybody trooped off down the platform, with book bags and lunch pails, into the fog.

The city wasn't that big, it didn't have the overwhelmingly

bumptious arrogance of the neighboring regional capital, but you could see that it liked its money. As I rode the bus through the streets, I saw nothing but store after store, banks and shoe boutiques, electric-appliance stores, menswear and womenswear stores, and perfumothèques. I walked through a little park populated by mangy trees, where I discovered a heroic band of mushrooms making a last stand, clinging to the foot of a plane tree. "Hang tough," I urged them every morning, "one day the city will be yours." Then I arrived at the Giosuè Pascoli High School, a huge and decrepit old building, surrounded by hundreds of bicycles, Vespas, and mopeds. This was the first distinction in the social ranking: did you come into the city from somewhere else, or did you live there? Did you ride an expensive Morini or an underpowered Lambretta, or did you pedal a bicycle, or did you walk, and if you walked, did you have the right kind of shoes or not? Did you smoke Yankee stink-nails, like Pall Malls, or did you smoke Italian government-produced National stink-nails?

The forest was far away, and in the city it didn't matter if you could recognize stinging nettles, track porcupines, or find fox dens. What counted in the city was a strange mixture of adult desires and childish foolery, a determination to seem youthful while at the same time more grown-up and more ruthless than you might actually be. And I felt a flame of rebelliousness along with an itch of conformity. Sometimes I, too, wished that I had a red Motomorini, a pair of warm vicuna wool trousers, a high-necked button-down oxford shirt. I was ashamed of my bedraggled sweaters, my beat-up satchel, my second-hand books. There was a continual battle between my two clocks. For a long time, I wanted both things: to be different from the others and, at the same time, exactly like the others. In my heart, a voice was guiding me, saying: "You're special, Timeskipper, and one way or another, you will be unique." But the roar of a sky-blue Lambretta kindled my fantasies: I saw myself at the center of a swarm of a hundred kids riding sky-blue Lambrettas, streaking along the beachfront in a procession, each of us with a mutely adoring little blonde Selene behind us, arms wrapped around our chest, each Selene wearing a white tennis sweater. And every day the Sacra Pilla, goddess of money, gleefully tortured the Grande Rana, the great toad that watched over my constant lack of money.

None of my old friends was in the same class as me, Section B. Osso and Gancio were together in Section D. Osso was bigger than ever and swathed in cashmere; Gancio had gotten even crazier and increasingly prone to brawling. Baco and Rospa were in Section E. Baco was pursuing mathematics as his field, because he had fallen in love with a young math teacher named Tania. Rospa now wore contact lenses and had dyed her hair red. But she was still pretty homely. No news from Selene; she was attending a science high school.

I placed the rest of my fellow students in one of four categories: true shits, quasi-shits with redeeming qualities, simpaticoes, and loser simpaticoes. Among the true shits was Gentilini, a wealthy and overbearing junior Fascist, son of the owner of the city basketball team; he was tall and had hawklike features he went everywhere on his oversized black motorcycle with a babe sitting behind him. Then there was Monachesi, city slicker, bootlicker, and informer and yes-man to Gentilini; he wore a different tie every day, and he burned thousand-lire banknotes in class. Another was Liuba, a fifty-year-old contessa in the body of a skinny, resentful, racist girl. Among the quasi-shits was Brian Pontiroli, the playboy. He had been born in London, and this intimidated us greatly. His first name, of course, was Brian, and he looked just like Bryan Ferry, lead singer of Roxy Music, but nobody would even hear of Roxy Music for many years to come, so for the time being, he just looked like nobody. I admired the smooth lank bangs that dangled over his eyes, which he tossed to one side with a skilled and seductive motion; I liked his slightly put-on English accent and his general cheerfulness. He was a tremendous son-of-a-bitch, but at least he liked to laugh. He could have any girl he wanted. Next came Lollo, also known as Aristotle, who may have looked human, but was really just a machine that devoured textbooks, a pedantic grind, a guy who made the sign of the cross before an oral exam, and who would come to school even if he had a fever of 103° and a rapidly developing case of the bubonic plague. Among the simpaticoes were Valerio Verdolin, a tremendous and likable nutcase who did nothing all day but sketch and write comic strips, and described himself as a Vangoghian anarchist; he immediately became my best friend. Then there was Lussu the Sardinian, unsmiling and decisive, a small, wise man. In order to put himself through school he worked nights at a pizzeria; he spoke very little, and was the only person in school that Gentilini was afraid of. There was Serena Schiassi, a little blonde daydreamer that everyone at school wanted to take to bed, but she never even noticed—she really never noticed; she loved Rimbaud, Pontiroli, and three or four others—, in short, everyone but me. Among the loser simpaticoes was Domineddio, who had been a manual laborer in Belgium. He spoke half in Italian and half in French, and he never felt like lifting a finger; his GPA was 0.5, and all he ever wanted to do was go dancing and dress up as a teddy boy. Then there was Comrade Carpaccio, an asthmatic with a neat little mustache who was constantly using his inhaler and quoting Mao from memory; his breath reeked of garlic, and he never seemed to do anything but pull me aside and criticize me because, as he put it, I was a social-climbing peasant with an underlying tendency to bourgeois urbanization. And, last but certainly not least, La Bottoni. She was tall, big-breasted, and naïve; at least three different guys had screwed her and then dropped her; she'd plunge into a state of depression, take Valium in class, and weep bitterly, gripping the radiator as she sobbed. One day, there was a problem with the heating system so the radiator didn't work; she thought the radiator had jilted her, too, so she cried twice as hard.

I don't remember much about any of the other students. Of the teachers, I'll mention just two in particular. My Italian teacher was named Signore Vainich; at first he seemed mean, he was from Istria and had the face of a bulldog, but when he read Dante he lit up from within, he was better than the finest stage actor. And so he won me over, and Italian literature became my favorite subject. For math, we had Signore Piloni, a young male teacher with short hair and a speck of foam in the corner of his mouth. Numbers, he explained to us, explain and organize the world. He sucked up to the rich students and was abusive to the rest of us. I cordially despised him and might have considered murdering him as an appetizer before slaughtering Fefelli.

It was the last quarter of the second year of high school. I was sick of going back and forth each day by train; I wanted to rent a room in the city. But I wasn't comfortable leaving my father alone. I would come back home late in the afternoon, take a nap, study, and wander around the village. In the evening, we were both dead tired, and we didn't say much to each other. My father would go back down into his workshop, and I'd fall asleep with Edgar Allan Poe in my hands. I dreamed of walling up Gentilini and Monachesi alive, luring them into the cellar with a bottle of Amontillado, even though a Campari would have been sufficient. I'd put Fefelli in the pit with the pendulum. I dreamed of the Lady Ligeia, Berenice, and a Selene with raven-black hair. The duoclock had quieted down. Only once, early one morning on the train, a Moroccan sitting near me was chanting in a wailing singsong, and suddenly I saw him flat on the ground, beaten bloody, and then I saw a heap of rubble and a broken wristwatch. I couldn't figure out in what city the vision had taken place, but it made me shiver. It was a rotten day all around. Vainich was out sick, and there was a substitute teacher who read Dante as if she were a news anchor on TV. I skirmished at length with a sadistic parallelepiped under the opaque eyes of Piloni. And at the end of the class Monachesi made fun of me because my socks didn't match. "It's a look, you turd," I said. As I was leaving school, I saw Monachesi and Gentilini talking intently, then they both climbed onto the big black motorcycle. As soon as I got out onto the street, the motorcycle came up behind me, moving slowly, and I could see that Monachesi was stretching out one leg to kick me in the ass. You have to get up pretty early in the morning to pull one over on a Timeskipper. I dodged the kick in the ass and as they went by, gave a sharp jab with my elbow; Gentilini lost control of the motorcycle, it came almost to a standstill, and both they and it fell to the ground. There was a huge noise of clanging metal, and the motorcycle slammed into a newsstand, scattering newspapers and magazines everywhere. Gentilini leapt to his feet in a cold fury, and he pulled out of his pocket an object I had never seen before: a pair of brass knuckles. An instant later, Domineddio, Lussu, and Verdolin were at my side.

"Put it down, or you might hurt yourself," said Lussu with grim determination.

"You gang of Communists," said Gentilini, pointing at us as if he were an actor in an American movie, "sooner or later we'll clean up this school and toss you out."

"I'm a teddy boy, not a Communist," Domineddio clarified.

Liuba had rapidly spread the word, and three or four junior Fascist friends of Gentilini showed up; things were starting to look bad when suddenly, with the strolling step of a dandy, Pontiroli intervened.

"Boys, there's too much tension in this class. Make love, not war. You're all just a little too edgy. Let me make a peace proposal. Everyone come to my house on Sunday, to celebrate my birthday."

"Me, at a party with these peasants? Never," said Gentilini.

"Try to rise to a higher level, Nino," said Pontiroli. "A true gentleman accepts a challenge. Also, Jeanne will be at the party."

Jeanne was a fabulous French girl, twenty-one years old. People said that she wore a garter belt that could cure you of anything, whether viral or bacterial, as well as various forms of depression.

"Well, maybe, if they're willing to pick up the motor bike," said Gentilini, "I might consider it."

I looked over at Lussu: he nodded. The four of us pulled the motorbike back up into an upright position.

"Look, the clutch pedal is chipped. You bastards. This motorcycle is worth more money than all of your houses put together," snarled Gentilini.

"Brian extended an invitation," said Verdolin. "Are you going to accept or are we going to keep arguing?"

"Well, sure, if Jeanne's going to be there, I'll come," said Gentilini. "And it will be a pleasure to see you in polite company. I can just imagine what a nice impression our little woodsman will make."

"I'll make the impression that I make. I'm not going to disguise myself as a gentleman, and when I fight somebody, I don't need to use brass knuckles," I answered.

That last phrase cut Gentilini to the quick. He started his motorcycle, with Monachesi's help. They whispered something to one another. Then Monachesi wriggled his serpentine coils over to Pontiroli, and hissed: "All right, we'll come to the party, but on one condition. Everyone has to bring two girls; otherwise, they can't come." And they roared off on their motorcycle, leaving a wake of snake scales behind them.

We gathered at the café to chew things over. By now, we had become the group of Communists, even though we had a varied array of ideologies. Lenin Carpaccio, Van Gogh Ver-dolin, Elvis Domineddio, Ghigna Timeskipper, and the bandito Sparasaminca "Shoot from the Pelvis" Lussu.

Lussu immediately pointed out that he had a standing date every Sunday with his two favorite girls, Margherita and Capricciosa—that is, he had to work in the pizzeria. And any-way, the only dance he knew how to do was the Sardinian "su ballu tundu."

"How's it go?" asked Domineddio.

"It's like the hully gully, but with a lot of swearing," answered Lussu.

"What shits those two rich boys are," said Domineddio. "But Pontiroli, he's different. He's a real cool cat."

"You allow yourself to be swayed by the worst form of dandyism," said Carpaccio, after a quick gulp from his inhaler, "and by the false indulgence of the big property owners."

"I want to put Monachesi into one of my comic strips," said Verdolin, "as Snake Boy. He's not evil. It's just that dur-ing a laboratory experiment, he was hit by gamma rays that had been beamed through the cobra cage. From that day for-ward . . ."

"Cut it out," I said, "we need to make up our minds. Are we going to try to go or not?"

"I am astonished," said Carpaccio, "are you willing to fall into a bourgeois, high-society trap? Are you willing to bring two girls as emblems of virile power, just to keep up with the others? Are you willing to accept a conformist challenge on the territory of your adversary?"

"Carpaccio," said Domineddio, blowing a smoke ring, "it sounds to me like you don't have two girls to bring."

"That's not the point," said Carpaccio. "You, Timeskipper, since you're almost of proletarian extraction . . ."

"You leave me out of this," I yelled. "I just want to show those shits that we too have the right, the desire, and the ability to have fun on our own, and that not all women are so stupid that they only chase after guys who wear a cardigan and have a motor scooter."

"Well put," said Verdolin. "I know a girl I could call. She lives downstairs, she has nice tits, but she's only thirteen. Maybe if she put on some makeup . . ."

"Boys," said Domineddio, "I can bring three girls. My girlfriend Cindy and her sister. They are a pair of fledgling hooligans of the first water—one of them can ride a motorcycle better than Gentilini, and the other one guzzles beer like there's no tomorrow."

"Who's the third?"

"Their mother. She's forty, but she's a babe."

"Hey, I have an idea," said Verdolin. "I'll ask Serena Schiassi. I'll ask her with a sketch, I'll draw the Sorceress Graal of the Bosky Dell of Glenfiddich. Serena's such a poetic girl, she'll definitely say yes. And if La Schiassi comes, then her deskmate will come too, the one with the crooked nose."

"Shit," I said, "I was thinking about La Schiassi myself."

"Daughters, mothers, deskmates. You're just a bunch of whoremongers," said Carpaccio as he got to his feet. "You disappoint me."

"If we can find two girls for you," I sounded him out, "will you come too?"

"Well, okay," said Carpaccio after a moment of ideological hesitation, "but only to demonstrate the disaster that will ensue and the political error that you are committing." And he left, in search of wrongs to right.

"Maybe that Carpaccio is more with it than all the others, after all," said Domineddio. "I'll bring a couple of girls for him, too. Okay, then, we're agreed, we're going to try to make this work. C'mon, Timeskipper, you can do your part."

Now I was left alone with Verdolin, at the bus stop.

"If you want," said Verdolin, "we could go to the Irish pub

tonight. I do caricatures there to make money. You can be my straight man, and if we find a girl who's willing . . ."

"Thanks," I said, "the thought is very kind, but if you go looking, you never find."

That's exactly what I said, in rhyme, and I felt so lonely, so profoundly lonely, that I felt sorry for myself at the thought. And while Verdolin told me about his idea for a comic strip about a guy who wakes up one morning transformed into two twin girls, I wondered what deity I should attempt to invoke. Should I call upon the Cheerful God or the Forest Gnome, the Blessed Lacy Corset, or the Great Cherokee Chief Lucky Duck.

"This evening," I suddenly thought, "when I go home, I'm going to go over and see Selene's aunt; I'll ask her for Selene's phone number or address, and then I'll invite her to the party, even if she tells me no and breaks my heart. You have to take some risks in life."

I heard a voice behind me.

"Timeskipper!"

I turned around. And there, on a little red Vespa, with a funny Laplandish hat on her head, was Selene. I had clearly inspired the pity of a varied array of deities and moved the spheres of the cosmos.

We went into the café, and she took off her hat. She had long, cascading hair, she was prettier than the last time I'd seen her, and the last time I'd seen her she was beautiful. Everything started up again slowly, cautiously. We weren't in the forest anymore, we were in the city, shy and ill at ease, we sniffed at one another like a pair of dogs. But I didn't feel lonely anymore.

"Will you come to a party with me on Sunday?" I asked.

"In the village?"

"Here, in the city. Deluxe house, a party."

"Well, sure I will," she answered with a laugh.

"Can you bring a cute friend?"

"I'm not enough for you?"

"I'll explain later."

"Okay. I'll bring Lisa. She looks like Liz Taylor in *Lassie Come Home*. I have to go now, they're expecting me at home."

"Me too. They're expecting me on the steppes."

"I'm happy to see you again," she said, with an edge of embarrassment, and slid half of her hair into her hat.

"I'm happier than you are," I said. I gave her a chaste kiss and fled. I couldn't have stood it if that meeting had been spoiled, even for a second. I saw her whiz past my bus on her Vespa, and she waved at me as she did.

2

Brian Pontiroli's house was in a neighborhood of boulevards inflamed by trees with red leaves, and little houses that looked like they were made of sugar, each with a balcony and a garden with a dog, curled up, and a car, neatly parked.

The party was supposed to start at three in the afternoon, but Selene, as usual, was late, and Lisa was even later, and so we didn't arrive until three-thirty, and not out of snobbishness, though they were free to think that if they liked. I'm not going to tell you how my two girls looked; that's a surprise for later. I was nervous, I had a dry mouth and my temples were throbbing. I could tell myself as often as I liked that a courageous boy from the forest had no need to fear the opinions of professional partygoers. Even the pirate captain Henry Morgan, when he went to Maracaibo, shampooed his hair and shined up his sword and boots: that's in the history books. I had put on my best corduroy trousers and a light-blue shirt with a Beatle-neck collar. I bought it on Saturday from Luciana, in her new store, Moda Bella, "Underwear That'll Dazzle Your Fella." Luciana had spent half an hour offering advice and trying different pieces of clothing on me, and then she said: you can't go wrong with this shirt, it goes perfectly with your green eyes, the girls will drop at your feet, you'll have to step over them. I also had a dark-blue V-neck sweater draped over my shoulders, just in case anyone said anything about the shirt. Underneath the shirt, I was wearing a guinea tee; I didn't expect to have to submit it to the collective judgment, but if I did, it was clean.

I drew a deep breath and rang the bell marked Pontiroli-Williamson; the door swung open, and out wafted the notes of "Mr. Tambourine Man" by the Byrds; wow, that was some beginning. Brian came to the front door, with arm firmly wrapped around babe.

He was dressed with consummate elegance: a long green cardigan worn over a turtleneck. The babe was a slim little fox in jeans, with a bit of makeup. But we weren't staring at them, they were staring at us.

I'll never forget that entrance. There was a huge living room. I'd never seen one that big, with a marble floor that looked like the church of Pragallo; on the walls hung enormous paintings with English horses and English hunting dogs, as well as a pair of abstract paintings, maybe Picassos. Along one side of the living room was a long line of soft velvet sofas, and on them were sprawled the partygoers, in an array of languid poses. On the other side of the living room an incredibly long table enjoyed pride of place, piled high with every imaginable delicacy: sweets, savories, cakes, soft drinks, and even a tub of sangria and platters of salmon hors d'oeuvres.

At the far end of the room was a record player, with records scattered around it on the floor, at least one hundred LPs; two girls were sorting through them and choosing disks to play.

And none of the people in that room—the partiers on the sofas, the partiers at the buffet, the girls selecting records to play—not one pretended not to notice when we walked into the room. Because, while I might not have been much to look at, Selene and Lisa swept the table, lit up the stage, dominated the field—in other words, they were three times prettier than any other babes in the room, and everyone saw that in a split second, both babes and dudes.

Selene had on a pair of skintight jeans and a shirt, knotted Gypsy-style over her belly, leaving her midriff partly uncovered.

She had washed her hair, and a cascade of gold and wheat framed her lovely little face.

Lisa was dressed in existentialist black, she was petite and had curly hair, but she had violet cheetah eyes, slightly oriental and tip-tilted, and she wore pointy-toed stiletto-heeled shoes.

Domineddio, at the center of a gang of teddy girls, raised his goblet of sangria in a cheerful gesture of welcome and approval. Gentilini stood, stunned, with a salmon hors d'oeuvre, untasted, in his mouth. Monachesi bit his forked tongue and tore his gaze away. Liuba actually turned on her heel and left the room in annoyance. Carpaccio was incapable of formulating any declarations on the false self-importance of showing off in the company of two girls who were obviously specimens of bourgeois seduction. In fact, he walked up to Selene as if he had seen Che Guevara in person, and said: "Pleasure to meet you, I'm a friend of Timeskipper."

And he said the same thing to Lisa.

We made our way into the center of the living room, issuing haughty greetings as we went. Looming out of the crowd, to our surprise, was Osso, wearing a monstrous amaranthine three-piece suit with a yellow and red regimental tie. Gancio was there too, half-soused, with one arm draped around the neck of a tall piece of confectionery, and his greeting took the form of a ripping belch. We saw Rospa, her garish makeup veering into cheap-trick territory, wearing high heels that clattered like the cloven hooves of a she-goat. Verdolin was there, dancing with La Schiassi. La Bottoni was already well on her way, necking with a tall, sallow boy who looked like the son of Nosferatu. Then in came a tall, sinuous brunette, older than the rest of us, wearing a T-shirt with an illustration of a face that I later realized was that of Jacques Brel.

"Timeskipper," said Pontiroli with his most charming smile, "allow me to introduce you to Jeanne."

"Brian," I said, "allow me to introduce you to Selene and Lisa."

And from the way I looked at Jeanne and the way that he looked at Selene, I understood that the score was Italy 3–France 1.

An hour later, the party had reached its crescendo. Domineddio, bouncing his black-leather-&-studs girlfriend back and forth like a basketball, was teaching every one how to dance to rock 'n' roll, and had already broken two chairs. Comrade Carpaccio had already bored to tears half of the attendees. Liuba and Monachesi had taken refuge in the kitchen, where they were snacking on gall-and-wormwood canapés. The house cat, Teo, had made an appearance, yowled in irritation, "Could you meow it down?" and then turned and stalked off. Osso was shoveling down his seventieth pizza canapé. Verdolin continued to slow dance with La Schiassi, even when rock 'n' roll was playing. La Bottoni was guzzling Nosferatu's blood. Gentilini was dogging Lisa's every move, filling her glass with fresh-squeezed orange juice like an attentive waiter, and laughing at everything she said. I was meeting lots of new people, drinking moderately, and occasionally holding hands with Selene. I understood that I was held in fairly high regard at that party—indeed, a step or two above high regard. The men were all thinking, "Well, if he shows up at the party with a pair of babes like that . . ." And the women were all thinking, "Well, if he shows up at the party with a pair of babes like that . . ." And at the same time, people gave Selene and Lisa all the consideration of a pair of suitcases; feminism still lay six months and nine days in the future.

In short, I was there and I was having fun. I might perfectly well have thought, "What's all this nonsense, before the party I was less than zero, and then I show up with a pair of cute babes, and suddenly they all think I'm a big man, and why should any of that make me happy, this is the heart and soul of utter conformism." Still, that's not at all what I was thinking; there are times in your life when you have no idea of how ridiculous and naïve you are being, and you can't erase them from your CV. Later you'll come to your senses, you'll remember these moments with shame and embarrassment, but that shame is something you've attached afterwards. I was feeling perfectly comfortable, and my quest for uniqueness was taking a break and relaxing for a while in a home of the well-to-do, with paintings of English setters hanging on the walls, floors straight out of a Roman basilica, and velvety sofas, surveying a buffet with smoked salmon canapés and fresh-squeezed orange juice—at least one hundred oranges had been immolated to the Party God—in the midst of the sangria and the puff pastries, in a chic and expensive neighborhood, light-years away from the forest.

And after all, if this was Selene's doing, then what could really be wrong with it? She was not just pretty, she was luminous. And I knew for myself that she was also ironic, intelligent, and spoiled. Let them feast their eyes, I was the only one who knew who she really was. I had no need to be jealous.

Just as I was mulling these thoughts over, I saw Brian Pontiroli making his way toward me across the room, smiling as if we were the oldest and closest of friends. He asked: "Now that's a nice shirt; is it a Benson?"

"It's a Luciana Moda Bella," is what I should have said, but instead I just said that I really didn't know, it had been a gift. I noticed that he was looking at Selene and that Selene was twisting a lock of hair around her finger, but I wasn't worried. Then, a few minutes later, I noticed Jeanne slinking toward me in a cheetahlike slouch, and she curled up next to me on the sofa. I remembered that a few minutes before, I had seen Brian and the little French babe chatting in a conspiratorial manner, as if they were hatching a plan.

"Now, don't be paranoid," whispered a small voice inside me.

"Keep your eyes open, Timeskipper," whispered another small voice.

"Allorha" (I am inserting an extra "h" here and there to convey Jeanne's French accent), she said, crossing one incredibly long leg over the other, "Brhian tells me that you are a poet, that you know all the plants in the forhest. I come frhom the countrhyside myself, in Prhovence, near Arhles."

Her charm was exotic and undeniable; in any other situation, I would have felt flattered. But I noticed that Brian was now sitting very close to Selene and that she was furiously mussing her hair, the way she does when she's nervous or excited, as he asked:

"What about you, queen of the party, where are you from?"

I couldn't hear her answer. Jeanne was overwhelming me with a flood of words with exotic "rh" sounds. The pizza canapés and slaughtered oranges had turned to lead in my stomach, my palms began to sweat, and suddenly I understood the nature of the wild beast of jealousy, the pitiless Panthabear that claws and bites; it was like discovering a brand-new sense—taste, smell, and jealousy—something so unmistakable and unexpected that it took my breath away.

For a few minutes, I was aware of nothing but the gnawing beast at work deep inside, deep in my love-tormented guts. The Rolling Stones were playing furiously, everyone seemed happy as they danced away, but I was locked in an icy chill.

"Hey, you at the record player, that's enough rock and roll," said Brian in Italian, though he pronounced the word rock 'n' roll with a strong English accent. Then he looked over at Selene and said: "Put on some slow music, if you don't mind."

Verdolin and La Schiassi looked as if they were awakening from a dream. Slow music? Then what had they been dancing to until then?

"A slow dance, what a drag," said Domineddio, and collapsed onto the sofa next to me, sweating like a race horse, resting his ankle boots on the armrest. His teddy girl came over and sat on his knees and they French-kissed for thirty seconds.

"This is Cindy, that is, Cinzia," said Domineddio, "you can't beat her on a motorcycle."

"I know how to do lots of things, not just ride a motor-bike," Cinzia protested.

"Tell Timeskipper what else you know how to do," said Domineddio, with a leer.

"I make clothing, leather clothing, I went to London last summer, and I want to be a fashion designer. Have you ever heard of Mary Quant?"

"I have," said Jeanne, "I think she's crhazy."

"Crazy, how?" asked Cinzia.

And they started talking about women's slips, not even *skirts*, but for me they might as well have been chanting in Assyrian. I wasn't listening. In tortured agony, I was staring at the middle of the living room, where Brian and Selene had started dancing to "Crying in the Chapel" (E. Presley), and were now dancing to a second song "Se piangi se ridi" (B. Solo); with one hand he was firmly gripping one hip, and with the other hand, who knew what mischief he was preparing. Gentilini and Lisa were dancing too, and Gentilini winked slyly at Pontiroli. Gang of bastards, they were all in on it.

As if I needed any further evidence of the conspiracy, Monachesi and Liuba had returned to the party, and he unsheathed his finest alligator smile. Finally, I locked eyes with Carpaccio, who was probably trying to tell me with a glance: "You see, the boss takes the choice tidbits for himself, and the factory worker is left to weep." Or else: "The bourgeois tend to go with the bourgeois." Or else—and at this point he started walking toward me, but I shot him a glance that hit him like a knife ka-thunking into his forehead; at that point he grasped my meaning, and backed off until he hit the buffet, plunging one elbow inadvertently into the cake.

In the meantime, Brian wrapped another hand around Selene—now he was holding her with both hands. Although that was unremarkable anatomically speaking, it struck me as symbolically abhorrent.

And so I asked Jeanne: "This is a nice house, how many stories is it?"

"Thrhee, I believe, but why?" she said, expressing Arlesian bewilderment. I didn't even bother to answer. I was rapidly calculating: three stories, at least thirty feet. And I sketched out an array of potential future scenarios:

First, Pontiroli and Selene leave the living room together. I follow them into the kitchen and, having ascertained that they are in fact necking, I run upstairs and throw myself out the third-story window.

Second, Pontiroli and Selene start kissing while they are dancing, in full view of the rest of the partygoers. After slashing my wrists with my orange-juice glass, I rush upstairs to the third story, etc.

Third, Selene walks up to me and says: "I need to talk to you, I hope you can understand, I am so confused, there are things that can happen before you even realize," and I answer, "Sure, no problem, I understand," and then upstairs to the third floor, followed by the wail of ambulance sirens.

Fourth, I confront both of them, saying, "Selene, you have to choose, him or me," and she says, "Him," and I rush out into the night, chased by the squeaking bats of laughter.

Fifth, I confront both of them, saying, "Selene, you have to choose, him or me," and she says, "I can't decide," so I fight a duel with Pontiroli, but he beats me with laughable ease, first at arm wrestling, then at Indian wrestling, and finally with sabers, and I am wounded, though not fatally, and while I am recovering in the hospital, Carpaccio comes to see me every day, and finally I receive an invitation to Brian and Selene's wedding, hand delivered by Monachesi.

I had not even taken into consideration the possibility that Selene might actually choose me; jealousy was blinding me, poisoning me, ravaging me.

I was suffering the pangs of Othello, or the pangs of any jealous asshole.

Another slow song came on, "Georgia" (R. Charles), and the diabolical young lovers didn't separate, if anything it got worse: now she had both her hands wrapped around his neck, the slut. I stumbled to my feet and poured myself another glass of orange juice, but I couldn't swallow, my glottis was paralyzed, I wondered how I could even manage to breathe. I sat down on a chair, all alone, and thought: "Selene, no, please don't do it," but she couldn't hear me, and she smiled up at him, and R. Charles was only helping them.

Just then, Gancio came over to me, pale and puffy from drink, grabbed my hand, and said:

"Don't surrender, Timeskipper. Life sucks, but if you care about something, you can't give up." I would remember these words of his one summer evening a year later, standing outside a discotheque.

So I tried to come up with some possible alternative scenarios to suicide.

First scenario, I yell "Brian, the kitchen's on fire," and I rush over to dance with Selene, and if she doesn't want to dance with me, I knock her out and kidnap her.

Second scenario, I go into the kitchen myself and choke the cat, and when all the others hear the cat's death meows, they hurry in to see what's happening, so Selene and Brian have to stop dancing, but then I remembered that Selene loves cats.

Third scenario, I put on a tango and say to Selene, "Would you dance this tango with me?" but then it occurred to me that

I dance a lousy tango, and who knows, maybe Pontiroli is a tango genius.

Or else: with a swift and adroit kick, I overturn the record player. I confront Pontiroli and tell him, "I'm going to break your jaw." Then I pretend to faint.

A spaceship lands right outside the window, and a green death ray kills Pontiroli and Monachesi, while Carpaccio is struck dumb for life.

Pontiroli dies of a heart attack at age seventeen.

It was unbelievable the way the images continued to proliferate; I felt that I would scream at any second, or I would run out the door and keep on running in a never-ending rainstorm for the rest of my life.

Carpaccio brushed by me, over toward the buffet, and looked at me. He gulped down a puff pastry, said nothing, and narrowly escaped being murdered.

Monachesi and Liuba came over to talk to me. They poured themselves glasses of Coca-Cola.

Liuba looked at me and asked, sardonically:

"Well, you're alone, aren't you? Not having as much fun as before?"

When she said that, the blood boiled in my veins like hot lava, and rage seethed within me like a fever. R. Charles completed his performance. And a moment later, I heard the first notes of the next record. It was "And I Love Her" (Lennon-McCartney).

I covered the few yards that still separated me from the main street of Abilene. I unhooked the strap that held the Colt in its holster, and swung to face the couple, legs akimbo.

"Selene," I said, "will you dance with me for a little while, too?"

The wind whistled over the sun-scorched prairie, through the canyon of the Seminoles, over the raised hackles of the coyotes; everyone in the saloon fell silent.

"Of course," she said.

The beast, with a howl of thwarted fury, vanished in a cloud of ash. J. Lennon slapped me on the back and said, "See, you big girl's blouse?" Actually, I only thought for a second about how stupid I had been, in a flash I forgot about all the pain I had felt, my glottis unstopped, and I was suddenly ravenously hungry, but this wasn't the time for food. Selene and I danced for a long time, and we even kissed in front of everyone. Everything went perfectly. Brian Pontiroli was a sport about it, and started necking with Jeanne. Gentilini got his face slapped by Lisa. Gancio vomited on Monachesi's shoes, and I have a sneaking suspicion it was no accident. Liuba stood, back to the wall, buttonholed by Carpaccio without the slightest chance of escape. La Bottoni slipped a hand into Nosferatu's pocket and vampirized him then and there. Domineddio showed off his skill at the limbo, dancing under a food trolley. Pontiroli's Anglo-Italian parents appeared at the door just as Osso, drunk on sangria, had pulled down his trousers and was miming an act of sodomy with Rospa. The house cat Teo lost his shyness, and gobbled up the last of the salmon hors d'oeuvres. There was a collective hully gully with animalesque shrieks and howls. Then, in drips and drabs, the party ended and the guests left. Brian and Jeanne had vanished. A housekeeper appeared and began tidying up, even helping Osso out from under the table. Selene and I left, in the growing darkness, walking past the flame-red trees and myrtle bushes. Lisa sailed by, riding behind Gentilini on his motorcycle. It was suddenly a little chilly, and Selene asked me for my sweater to cover her alluring belly button. I kissed her and said:

"I love you."

There was a brief silence.

"So do I, I think," she said. There was an extra verb in there, but it was still better than, "What are you, stupid?"

It had been one of the best days of my life. I had suffered

and rejoiced over things that, many years later, strike me as a little silly. But the duoclock didn't see things that way. I had suffered profoundly, and I had experienced true joy. On many other days, I was rebellious, solitary, and a loner, but that one time, everything went perfectly, in the living room of a respectable and prosperous home, where everyone managed to get along, in their treacherous and generous youthfulness. None of us was yet lost; we would only be lost later. A powerful voice inside me continued to say: "Timeskipper, you will be unique." But that evening was unique, and I will never forget it.

3

School resumed, and the effects of the magical party did not last long. Gentilini, beaten back with heavy losses by Lisa, became as surly and arrogant as before. Worst of all, he was a disastrously bad student, and he missed class increasingly often. Monachesi and Liuba lurked in their den, battening off each other's perfidy; it would have been a relief if they could actually mate and produce a wriggling nestful of savage little vipers, but they couldn't even bestir themselves to that point. Verdolin and La Schiassi were sickeningly besotted with one another; they even lived together—she owned a little apartment, with a small terrace and a German shepherd. Verdolin had started work on a graphic novel—though we called them comic strips back then—entitled *Mickey Marx*, in which Mickey Mouse went underground and became an urban guerrilla, attempting to destroy Hollywood with a million remote-controlled rats. It was pretty good, but it was ahead of its time. Moreover, he never had enough artist's pencils, and so he wound up using anything imaginable in his artwork: coffee grounds, crushed brick, Nutella, grass, and even La Schiassi's lipstick; she was willing to renounce her moderate indulgence in vanity to encourage her beloved in his artistic endeavors.

Domineddio was depressed. There was no avoiding the fact that he was flunking out of school. We'd let him copy our work and did everything we could to help him, but he floundered, bouncing from Ds to Es and Fs. He started smoking in class and openly reading sports magazines. In the last semester of school, he found a job in an auto repair shop, and he came by to bid us farewell. He was choking up, his quiff was dangling sadly over his forehead. "Let's stay in touch," he said. He went back to Belgium, and we would never see him again.

The only one who remained more or less as he had been at the party was Brian. He actually seemed to have become my friend. "You know," he'd say, "your girlfriend is a knockout, but I wasn't really trying to make it with her. It's just that court-ing is instinctive for me, just like painting is for Verdolin, or telling weird stories for you, or, for Monachesi, being an informer."

Sometimes he'd give me a ride over to the train station on his motorcycle. He'd say, "I'll come to the village to see you," but I wasn't sure how much fun that would be. I alternately found Brian fascinating and frightening. There was something in him that had grown old prematurely, a painting in which all of the colors had faded to gray. I told him, "If you're really such a dandy, you ought to at least read some Oscar Wilde, or good old Edgar Allan."

"The only reading I do is the racing sheets," he replied with a grin. He bet and lost regularly, and he still had plenty of money to spend and a steady supply of new sweaters. And the girls were crazy about him. Once, outside of school, I saw Jeanne slumped against the wall, weeping. When he walked out the door, he pretended not to notice her.

"It's all just theatrics, Timeskipper," he said. "Women are just actresses; you'll find out."

I kept my head down and studied, on the train, at home at night; whenever I saw Selene I was filled with renewed energy. We had a genuine passion that filled our words and our senses. We had no place to go for the sacrosanct, eagerly awaited, richly deserved, and longed-for consummation of our love. We hid out at the upstairs lounge of a little café, the Bar Tomoka, a small dark room with a reddish cast, furnished with four small

sofas and adjoining tables. We'd order a couple of hot chocolates and then start feeling around and touching. I'd get her
panties half off, she'd pull my dick partway out, I'd lie down
on top of her, she'd climb on top of me and straddle me, it was
a Kama Sutra of the unattainable, the uncomfortable, and of
sweet and exhausting interruption. One time, we had managed
to find a position that brought us tantalizingly close to the final
objective, when another young couple walked into the lounge.
"Don't stop on our account," they said, and she gave him a
blow job between handfuls of salted nuts and aperitifs. We
weren't alone in our logistical quandary. But we weren't as
audacious as that couple. Then, one evening, as we necked and
felt each other up, a mug of hot chocolate somehow wound up
on both our trousers. Selene said: "That's it, my love, you have
to find us a place to go, we can't go on like this. I don't expect
a room at the Hilton, but I really don't want to lose my virgin-
ity at the Bar Tomoka."

She was right, of course. I planned to go home and talk to
my dad about it. I was going to find a room to rent, and I was
willing to work nights, or else on Sundays for Uncle Nevio. In
the meanwhile, Verdolin and I started buying tickets for the
soccer lottery, the same lineup of scores and teams every week.
Yes, I was through with catching trains at sunrise, sick of empty
pockets, eating bad, cheap meals. I was done with plastic-
wrapped pizza slices and orange soda. I wanted goblets, steins,
boot glasses of beer, and real pizzas, with salmon, with sangria,
with mozzarella made from the milk of savannah-raised virgin
water buffalo. I needed to deal with the situation and become
a millionaire, but for the moment, becoming a thousandaire
would be quite sufficient.

But first, one Friday, I was going to have attend my first significant political meeting. There was a certain unrest among
the young people of the time, and before long it would explode
into open rebellion, commonly dubbed with the last two num-

bers of the current calendar year, a six followed by an eight. Carpaccio had decided that Verdolin and I—even if we were profoundly and irremediably bourgeois, ideologically unreliable, and helpless under the onslaught of our uncontrollable lust for pussy—were, all things considered, potential comrades, and that he would therefore present us to his collective, La Guantanamera, which met in a parking garage.

We entered. There were thirty or so people sitting on the ground; only three were sitting in chairs. Those endowed with chairs were the leaders, the Trimurti or triad: Riccardo, the ideological leader, Paolo Lingua, the operative commander, and Tamara, the Pasionaria. Ranking just below them were the three deputy leaders: Lionello the learned, Cinzia the pragmatist, and Carpaccio the ballbuster.

We were subjected to neither examinations nor blood initiations nor unnatural sexual practices, but we did feel we were being closely scrutinized. A book of poetry that I brought with me was examined with suspicion. One girl, after a brief introduction, asked Verdolin whether he believed that comics were potentially revolutionary. Verdolin said nothing in reply, but simply sketched for her on a notebook Mickey Marx, with a big, dangling, black dick. Carpaccio in the meanwhile explained to everyone our gifts and assets, few in number and limited in scope, and our highly bourgeois shortcomings. Suddenly, the Trimurti gave voice.

First, in the person of Riccardo, the ideologue. He was haughty and long haired, and was two years older than the rest of us. He claimed that he had spent those two years in South America, though some in the school whispered of a spectacular double flunking, from which he had recovered by attaining summits of ideological and cultural solidity unthinkable for us. Riccardo said that this group had done a great deal of theorizing but had accomplished very little, that we needed to compare our bourgeois inertia with the activity being carried on by the French, with the battles waged in South America, or with what was going on in Berkeley. And so I learned in that garage that we had responsibilities on a worldwide scale; I had not expected anything so overwhelming. Then Riccardo went on to say that on a personal level we were also unacceptably constrained, and that we should live life in a new shared and liberated way—and as he said this, he seemed to be addressing with special emphasis two girls sitting in the front row—therefore, at the earliest possible opportunity, we should either engage in an experiment with communal living in a house, or else plan and implement the occupation of a school. Then he quoted from Marcuse, whom I had never heard of, and Sartre, whom I had seen in photographs but had never read. He said that if anyone was there to have fun, they misunderstood the situation, that this was the beginning of a period of new battles that would change the world, and each of us needed to abandon everything we had believed up till then. He concluded with a phrase in French, I think it might have been "Cour ton patron t'attend." It had nothing to do with anything he had said, but it was a nice effect, like a burst of drum riffs at the end of a rock song. There was a brief round of applause, and he sternly rebuked us for that—we're not here to put on a show—but you could see that he had inwardly squirmed with swinish pleasure.

Paolo Lingua was short and stout, and he too was older than us and a university student; he was studying poli-sci in the regional capital, but he had decided that his realm of political endeavor was here, with us. Between puffs on a truly stench-emitting cigarillo, he said that it was crucial to escape our shell of political theory and that, before the month was out, we needed to move from words to deeds. I understood that he wasn't talking about the sort of deeds that boy scouts do. This deed, or operation, said Paolo Lingua, should strike a specific target and sabotage a major ganglion of the capitalist apparatus in such a way as to throw it into disarray; the operation, therefore, should be conceived and planned as an integral part of an overall movement, it should take into account a variety of guerrilla experiences, initiatives undertaken in the past, and future scenarios of struggle, and, finally, that we should all be involved in the operation because only in that way would it be truly effective.

"Could you give us a concrete example of an operation?" said a stern voice. It was Lussu. I hadn't realized that he was there too.

Paolo Lingua said that in this specific context, the question was premature, inasmuch as operations were never decided upon without a prior theoretical elaboration, but, for instance, writing slogans on the walls of a school was an initial operation that might be undertaken, or burning the school's front door, or better yet burning the schoolrooms with scabs inside them when a strike was underway; now that, he said, could be a very nice operation.

"Shit," commented Lussu.

Then Tamara spoke. She said some fairly straightforward things and spoke with a certain warmth; she talked about the life she had led in a small village in the south of Italy, and said, "I wouldn't want anyone else to have to live the way my parents did. We're all a little scattered and lost in this city, and I believe that if we stick together, we can do some effective and positive political activity; for instance, the first thing that we ought to do is take up a collection for a girl who needs to have an abortion."

All of this disturbed me profoundly; I'd never really thought about any of these things. But I immediately trusted Tamara implicitly. I gave her all the money I had with me. Verdolin gave her a caricature he had sketched on the spot. The other two members of the Trimurti looked daggers at him.

Then the floor was thrown open for individual statements.

Carpaccio talked for fifteen minutes, and his little speech had to do with the proper attitude to adopt toward the rival group, Red Power, and how to discuss the problem of the Soviet Union without slipping into the pitfall of oversimplification, the way Red Power did, and how to develop a critical awareness within our group that was also applicable to the world outside, while the revolutionaries in Red Power, in contrast, did the reverse.

Then a girl stood up and asked whether anyone knew if there was a book on how to withstand torture.

Another boy with glasses read a poem titled "My Solitude."

A girl with Indian-style braids delivered a very nice statement, in which she explained that all the books that she loved? she couldn't read them in school. Because at school they forced her to read other books? And she didn't love those books at all. And she wondered why she had to waste all this time, when she certainly had a great love of reading.

I screwed up my courage and spoke. I said: I agree with the comrade in braids, the same thing happens to me, the books that I love are never on the recommended reading list.

"And what books do you love?" asked Riccardo, with a chill in his voice.

I mentioned some names at random: Edgar Allan Poe, Raymond Chandler, Franz Kafka, Ernest Hemingway, science fiction, Flaubert, T. S. Eliot, and books about trees, just as an afterthought.

"Hemingway is a right-wing male chauvinist pig," said Riccardo. "Science fiction is part of American cultural imperialism, and books about trees are of no use. We live in the city; what would blue collar workers do with trees?"

"Well, actually, my father is a carpenter," I said, and everyone laughed, except Riccardo.

"Well, actually, T. S. Eliot is excessively Catholic," said Tamara, with an air of complicity.

"And moreover," said Riccardo, and by now he was clearly angry, "it strikes me that you don't read much political theory."

"But do you know anything about Chandler's life?" I shot back.

A huge and stormy discussion ensued. Carpaccio was using his inhaler furiously; we were there at his introduction. Luckily, Cinzia the pragmatist said it was time to stop talking about books, that the topic on the agenda was the list of things we needed for the headquarters, i.e., the garage. I stood apart from the crowd, leaning against the wall. I hadn't thought that politics was so complicated; in the village it was all much simpler. Behind me, inside the wall, water was running in pipes with a repetitive rhythm. The duoclock started up, and I saw them all thirty years later.

Riccardo had become a university professor. He loved to flunk students whenever he had a chance, he published extremely expensive textbooks, and whenever it looked like he was about to be pinned down to a specific political position, he turned and ran, so he had established a reputation for himself as a thoughtful and moderate intellectual.

Paolo Lingua had become the most rabidly right-wing journalist on a right-wing television network, and every Wednesday, he defamed all his former comrades in a very popular opinion piece.

Tamara had become a labor organizer. She was married and had three children, one of whom was very politically engaged, while the other two cared less than nothing about politics. She lived by the beach.

Then I saw something that I wish I hadn't: Lussu, behind bars in an Italian courtroom, with the usual stern expression on his face. He was just a little heavier, and he had a long beard. There were two codefendants. And the chief judge was reading his sentence: twenty years in prison for armed conspiracy. Then I saw him on the day he got out of prison and took the ferry back to the most beautiful island on earth.

There were three of us accompanying him down to the wharf: me, his brother, and a woman with grey hair.

"Comrades," a voice thundered, "we'll see you all back here next Friday, and if you can, read the book that Riccardo recommended."

I opened my eyes. Standing next to me was the girl with Indian braids.

"What are you doing this evening?" she asked me.

Sexual liberation had officially begun.

I didn't go out with the temptress. First of all, because I was faithful, and second, because she wasn't much to look at—oh, let's be honest, and reverse the order of importance. After the meeting, I took a train back to the village. My first political meeting had lasted longer than expected, and it was almost midnight when I got there. There was still a light on at home, and when I opened the front door, I heard a moan. I shivered at the thought that someone might have attacked my father again. But then I listened more carefully, and I realized that was not a moan of pain. It was a moan that I had heard before: from Selene, from Miss Zaini, and while watching the movie *The Warm Flesh of Susy*. When Susy is in bed, fantasizing about making love with the gardener, her hand slides down between her legs, she starts to squirm and thrash, then suddenly there is a jump cut to another scene, and she's driving in a car the next day, for fuck's sake.

I tiptoed over to my father's bedroom. I heard the moan again, bedsprings creaking, and the sound of panting. I spied through the door. There was my father. It was definitely him, even if his face was completely hidden from view by a snowy-white ass of considerable bulk. That large ass was rising and falling, massaging my dad's dong, and then a voice cried out, "Oh, I love it, I love it," and I recognized Regina, the town stationer, news vendor, and tobacconist, and a number of details fell into place in my mind.

The fact that the house had been full of newspapers and magazines lately, even though my dad never read anything but the party organ, called, appropriately, the *Organo*, and that in the last few months he had changed his brand of cigarette: he was smoking Astors, which were much more expensive than the Nazi stinknails. What's more, once, on the floor in the woodshop, I had found a condom packet, but I hadn't given it a second thought, what with all the people that came and went through there.

I walked out the door in a fury. Why hadn't my dad said anything to me? Though I had to admit to myself that I was being pretty self-centered. How could I expect my father to live without a woman for all these years? What was he supposed to become, a vintage masturbator? Didn't he have hormonal forest fires, just like I did with Selene? But the idea of a woman in the house, taking my mother's place, the idea that somehow I was being pushed aside, was upsetting. I walked all the way to the piazza, and I noticed that the light was on in Uncle Nevio's shop. I knocked at the door and called his name.

"The door's open," said Uncle Nevio.

He was sitting at the counter, loading shotgun shells as usual. There was a smell of gunpowder in the air, and pellets were scattered on the floor.

"Timeskipper, what are you doing here at this hour?" he asked, with concern in his voice.

"I couldn't sleep."

"Problems?" asked Uncle Nevio.

"Yes, but first tell me about your problems," I said. I was having a hard time getting started.

"You already know my problem; it's your friend Gancio. He's a good kid, but there's something dark deep down inside him, and it's ruining him. Like blight on the potatoes. Do you see him much in the city?"

"Not often," I answered. And I kept to myself the fact that when I did, he was usually drunk and in a brawl.

"You should spend a little more time with him. He's running off the rails; he's doing badly at school, and his teachers say he's arrogant. I don't know what to do."

I looked at my uncle, hunched over in the dim light of a desk lamp. His temples were graying, he had started to develop a double chin—in short, he was getting old. But he still had the same simple, unspoken generosity. It was his destiny to help everyone else without receiving much, if anything, in return. How long could he keep it up?

"Uncle," I said suddenly, "Dad has a lover."

My uncle burst into loud laughter.

"Well, I know that," he said.

"Why didn't either of you say anything?"

"Because your father doesn't want you to know. You know how he is. This is a town where words are like bullets. Don't you have any secrets? Don't you have a girlfriend?"

"Well, yes," I admitted.

"And so do I," said Uncle Nevio, stretching his arms.

I swayed on my chair.

"For the past two years," he declared in mock seriousness, one hand on his heart, "I have been sharing, three evenings every week, both Luciana's bed and her excellent tortellini. As you can see for yourself, this village is a den of iniquity. Your father and the news vendor. Me and the queen of lacy corsets. Dr. Carabelli and Nicola, the pharmacist. Maghino the electrician and the wife of . . . well, that's for me to know. Karamazov and a cow."

"Don't pull my leg," I said.

"Timeskipper," said my uncle, running his hand through his hair, "it's hard being alone when you're old. It's hard when you're young, too, but it's really tough when you're old. Go to your father, tell him that you understand. After all, what's so bad about it?"

"Nothing," I said, and I believed it; in fact, I was happy about it now. "Thanks, Uncle, you're a wise man."

"My wisdom is much renowned, and I think it's time to put it to good use," my uncle replied. "By the way, allow me to inform you officially of two major pieces of news."

They really were major.

The first piece of news was that our village would finally have a soccer team all its own, competing in the rookie league. The name of the team was the Dynamo Polysport, and the players wore red jerseys, black shorts, and red socks. For the time being, there were nine active players: three workers from Messina, the school gym teacher, the two Arduini brothers, Grillomartino, Ciccio Mia, and yours truly. For the other players, he was exploring the down-valley market. He might be able to recruit a center forward, a native Tuscan. And, I almost forgot, team president and coach: none other than Uncle Nevio.

Second piece of news. The soccer team was just the first step in Uncle Nevio's campaign for mayor; he would be campaigning in a race against the foul yes-man, Sponda. Fefelli was running for parliament, and he would almost certainly be elected, but this time, in the village, ¡No pasarán!

"Uncle, this is great stuff," I said excitedly. "I'll support your campaign. I'll make goals like there's no tomorrow. Starting tomorrow, I'll train hard, even in the city. I'll go everywhere on foot, at a dead run."

"And no sex," my uncle added with a laugh.

"Well, as far as that goes," I said, "it won't make much of a difference. My girlfriend and I don't have a place to be alone in blessed peace. I wish I could rent a room; I wanted to talk to Dad about it; I know it would be a sacrifice, but I'm a big boy now . . ."

My uncle loaded a shell with a dreamy look in his eyes.

"You know, when I was about your age I had a girlfriend. We

went out in the meadows, we made do, but she used to say, 'You think we could ever have a real bed?' And, when we finally managed to be alone in her parents' house, we got in bed together and fell fast asleep. We had been waiting for a mattress for so long."

"That wouldn't happen to me," I said, haughtily.

"Of course not, you're just a sex machine, you heroic cocksman," said my uncle. "As for the room, we'll talk about it. In the meantime, take this. You can take her out to dinner, and to the movies. But don't take her to a hotel, you're both too young. Be patient."

He put a banknote in my hand.

"Thanks, Uncle. I won't say a thing to anybody about Luciana. Now I understand why you've been wearing all those poplin shirts for the last few months."

"Yes, and enough underpants to outfit a regiment," my uncle confided. "C'mon, it's time to lock up and go home."

We parted ways at the corner of the piazza. I watched him vanish into the night, with his gangly gait. He walked just like my father, but he was a little shorter; his shoulders were a little broader. By the light of the moon, I looked carefully at the banknote; I was suddenly struck breathless. He had given me ten thousand lire. I'd never had so much money in my life. I ran home. Every shadow could be Robin Hood; now I was rich, and Robin Hood was a potential enemy.

Right in front of our house I ran into my father, dressed in pajamas, walking arm-in-arm with Regina.

"So," said my father, "you've found out our secret."

"I heard you, you know," said Regina, "you were spying on us through the door. That's not right."

"You were making as much noise as a combine harvester," I said.

"If you can keep quiet about this," said Regina with a conspiratorial air, "you'll have comic books and novels free of charge for the rest of your life. And maybe cigarettes in a few years. No, I take that back; you'd wind up with lungs in worse shape than your father's."

I looked closely at her. Her hair was gray and she had an Apache-brave's crease in her forehead, but her eyes were youthful and lovely. I thought of my mother. Crickets sang in the meadow and the three of us sat in silence, as if someone were looking at us.

"I'm going home, good night," said Regina, and she climbed onto her bike with considerable agility and disappeared around the curve.

"Come," said my father, taking me by the arm, "tell me about Selene."

I set out to look for a job and a place to live. But it was tough; city folk were mistrustful, and a tall, skinny young man with the face of a madman wasn't likely to be taken for a highly qualified professional. All I could find was a job as a dishwasher at Lussu's pizzeria, two nights a week. I said nothing to Selene about it. But I was saving up for a big night, hoarding my capital in my pocket; actually, sometimes in my pocket and other times in my right shoe.

I approached Verdolin with determination. I said, "Verdolin, it is your great good fortune to be able to make love with Serena Schiassi in complete privacy whenever you feel like it." "Whenever she feels like it," Verdolin corrected me. "All right," I said, "here is my proposal: your job is to take her out and stay out all night long, until three in the morning, and leave the apartment free for my use." "That's not going to be possible," said Verdolin, "by midnight Serena is always sawing logs." "The other day, in an art-supply store, I noticed a box of twenty-four Stabilo pastels," I replied. "Okay, I can make that happen," said Verdolin. "Twenty-four colors, three nights," I specified. "No, for three nights I want a box of thirty-six." "You have a deal," I said, "but let's be clear, from ten at night until three in the morning." "Even if I have to lash her to a lamppost," he assured me, "but there's just one problem, I have to warn you: the dog, Leopoldo." "Does he bite?" I asked. "No," said Verdolin, "he likes to watch. Just ignore him."

And so, one Wednesday evening I went to pick up Selene, and I surprised her by taking her out to a Chinese restaurant. It was really Chinese, with Chinese owners, Chinese waiters, Chinese paper lanterns, and a tank filled with fish that had at least a Chinese-oid appearance. She was delighted and thrilled. She asked, "Did you win the lottery?" We ate rice with chopsticks and scattered grains in all the directions of the compass. I tried to pass myself off as an expert, and I ordered a dish with a strange name; the waiter brought a plate of greasy fritters instead of the chicken we were expecting. But then there was also veal and pineapple, which you might think wouldn't go together, but it was delicious. Then we had two pieces of fruit that looked like glistening Panthabear eyes, and, last of all, sake. We walked out of the restaurant, we kissed, and it was as if a pair of doughnuts were kissing, we smelled of fried dough from a hundred yards away.

"And now," I said, "I have a surprise for you."

I opened the door to the Schiassi-Verdolin apartment with trembling hands. I managed to find the light switch—Verdolin had taught me exactly how to do it, reaching up to the left, one foot up just to the left of the door. Leopoldo came to the door, tail wagging. He was an overweight, cross-eyed German shepherd. He yelped with pleasure and sniffed at Selene with interest. The suite consisted of a kitchenette, a bathroom, and a bedroom, filled with La Schiassi's dolls and Verdolin's drawings. On the floor were drinking glasses full of colored water, pencils, and notebooks; it was a huge mess. But the bed was neatly made, with a nice light-blue quilt.

I sat on the bed, and Leopoldo jumped up next to me.

"Oh, no, three's a crowd," said Selene. We put the dog in the bathroom and shut the door. He started to howl like a coyote. I gave him some bread. It was no good. He wanted to join the party.

Selene felt a little uneasy. I kissed her carefully, with exhaustive gentleness. Leopoldo watched, with nonchalance. It was as if he were thinking, "Okay, this'll do as a beginning, but let's hope there's a little more action soon."

We had both dreamt of this moment for so long, and now here we were, both shy and a little awkward, surrounded by La Schiassi's oversized dolls, Verdolin's oeuvre, and a voyeuristic dog. But Selene was so beautiful, so close. I kissed her, and I could feel her lips giving in, relaxing and surrendering. I gently pulled her sweater down onto her shoulder and kissed her neck.

She sighed. I worked her skirt up her legs.

And then it was like we exploded into the air.

It seemed as if all I'd ever done in my life was hold Selene's nude body in my arms. Maybe because of our preliminary exercises on the meadows and at the Bar Tomoka, we weren't shy of one another in the least. At this point, the only thing left to be determined was the terminology. The word "fuck" may not meet with the approval of the puritanical, but then the puritanical would be unlikely to approve of any of the things we began doing with great alacrity. "Making love" may be a gentler term, but it also sounds vaguely abstract, almost academic. And so, the first time, I fucked her while making love, holding onto her so tight I could hear her bones crack. The only thing she said was "take it easy." Then she went into the bathroom for a few minutes, and when she came out, she climbed on top of me and made love while fucking me. I went into the bathroom and drank a quart of water directly from the faucet; Leopoldo took advantage to stick his cold nose up my butt. Excited again, not because of the dog's nose but at the sight of Selene naked beneath the sheets, I came back to bed and tried a position that I had seen in a book, failed miserably, and we went back to fucking in the classic position. Once again, she took the initiative, and with a series of little shrieks she fucked me lovingly. I discovered, to my astonishment, that women like it just as much as men, and that they have greater endurance. At 2:50 in the morning, we were still rolling around in the bed. I said: time to go. But the following Wednesday, it was show time again. Leopoldo was waiting for us, with a bag of popcorn. I managed to do everything I had dreamed about during the week; I almost hurt myself.

The Wednesday after that, I had terrible indigestion and it was the first major embarrassment in my youthful career as a porn star. I felt better at two in the morning, and we made up for lost time.

Now, I'm not going to say that I've never had anything better than those porno-Cinderella Wednesdays with a deadline, but I can still remember them, instant by instant, gesture by gesture, all the sweetness and all the swinishness. We signed a contract with Verdolin for every other Wednesday, and even though La Schiassi was duly informed of the agreement, she never could quite accept that one blessed day every other week she had to go out to watch two movies in a row, have dinner, and then wander through the city streets. I have to admit she was very understanding. The only thing she said was: "Be nice to the dog." "The dog," I answered, "is a perverted voyeur, and he's having the time of his life."

Dolls, sketches, Selene's blond hair covering the pillow and my sweaters, her perfect ass illuminated by candlelight, the kisses that could never quench our thirst, no matter how many, the scents, and even the little light-blue box of condoms that gazed out at us reassuringly from the bedside table. All this, and much more. And most of all, old fat Leopoldo. For a while, whenever a German shepherd looked at me, I'd get an erection. Just kidding.

4

Then summer vacation came. I had managed to make it through another year of school and into the next class, and I was in love; when I went back to the village, I started putting on airs. My hair was fairly long, and I wore a flower-print shirt and a pair of used light-blue jeans with an authentic patch from Massachusetts.

"Have we gone gay?" asked Balduino when he saw me, revealing all his small-town prejudices on fashion and gender.

"Send your sister to find out," I responded, as they like to say in Berkeley.

"Oh, I'll send her to find out, but then she's yours to keep," Balduino shot back, with a sigh. He treated me to an espresso laced with grappa and told me the latest news of the village. The book about Commander Ghigna had been published, and it had sold reasonably well and had attracted attention, but the publisher had changed the manuscript in many ways. In real life, Ghigna spoke a hybrid mountain dialect of Italian, glued together semantically by obscene oaths. In the book, on the other hand, he wrote like a university professor and issued sentences like these: "At that point, it became clear to us that our strategy was being undermined by the lack of motivation on the part of certain components of our structure." Translated into Ghigna's patois, it would have run something like: "Boys, if any of you are likely to be pants-shitters, then get the fuck out of our way." The publisher had also cut out several pages, the most controversial ones.

Another stale piece of news: work on the fountain in the piazza had stalled. There were twelve different proposals, all with high-level support, which featured mermaids, unicorns, Venuses, and Poseidons, but Fefelli was afraid of alienating the other eleven by picking one, so he kept postponing the decision. Also, apparently, Fefelli was under investigation for fraud in connection with the land of the Roselle subdivision, malfeasance, and several other peccadilloes. The local magistrates had also brought charges against the cement plant for safety violations, and there had been a two-day strike, with brawls between strikers and scabs.

Neither of Balduino's updates struck me as earth-shattering; I'd gotten used to much worse in the city. I tried to find some of my old friends. The first one I saw was Baco. He was carrying a briefcase full of notes, he buttonholed me and sat me down on a bench. He said that, thanks to his teacher, Tania (sigh), he had discovered the future, and the future was cybernetics. "Let me try to put this into terms you can understand," he explained. "The way our brains work is with little boxes; you open one and inside there are others, and inside those are important thoughts. But our brains work slowly, they chug along and they misfire, they open the wrong boxes." I certainly knew something about that. "Now, let's say that I manage to put these thoughts inside little mechanical boxes, so small that you can't see them, and we call those boxes 'chips.' Then I put these thousands of little boxes into a larger box that coordinates them. Then all you have to do is push the buttons and you find the box you want—'sad boy' for you, for example. Or one called 'like Baco,' which would do you a world of good, ha ha . . . And so on, right up to the box containing everything you need to know about Patty Pravo, all of her songs, and a photo of her naked."

"That's a fucking stupid idea," I said. "What is it good for?"

"It's faster, Timeskipper. Say you have a mushroom, and you want to know if it's poisonous. So you start the little boxes, and out comes a picture of the mushroom, stamped 'toxic,' in just thirty seconds."

"Karamazov can tell you that in three seconds."

"Sure, but you can't keep Karamazov on your bedside table."

"If it's a big bedside table you can."

Baco sighed with exasperation. He had clearly run into this lack of comprehension before.

"Timeskipper, you're one of the people in this village of donkeys with a fully functioning brain. Let's work together, you, me, and maybe my math teacher (sigh). I'll show you some American magazines, I'll explain what a chip is. We'll found a company; I already have a trademark. Look at this."

He held up a sheet of paper with a sketch of an apple, and the name Baco Cybernetics, Inc.

"Why an apple?"

"Because it's like the world. You can gather the entire world and then eat it with these new technologies."

"A bunch of grapes would be better," I said.

"You're right. Each of the individual grapes is a component of the larger cluster. I'll change it to grapes."

Many years later, when Bill Gates's competitors went to the slogan office to copyright the Apple logo, they didn't even bother to thank me.

I saw the usual heroes. Slim the Magnificent greeted me with a new creation, his cry of the horny toucan. Maria Casinò and Cipolla were arguing over points in their game of scopa. Arturo One Hundred had finally made it to a full century, and there had been an article in the newspaper, but he modestly warned that we shouldn't count on him making it to two hundred. Caprone had learned to drive a tractor with lessons from Luis, and now he spent the nights driving and singing. Don Brusco had installed a new church bell that could be heard all the way to Switzerland. Karamazov and Carburo had raised enough money with the lotteries at the Casa del Popolo to organize a bus trip to Moscow—four days on the road, so that when they got to Moscow there was only time to turn around in Red Square. The first hunting-dog show had been held as well, and there had been a village scandal: Hisssss had screwed the first-prize winner, an Irish setter of distinguished lineage. But by now the fast-paced life of the big city had become addictive; village life struck me as sluggish and monotonous. I was bored. I talked to my father about it, and he said, "Oh, you're quite the city slicker now, Timeskipper, but you'll get used to things here again. And, after all, you'll be going back to the city soon enough."

"Dad," I said, "why don't you come to the city yourself sometime?"

"When I go to the city," he said, "Charon will be driving me." Charon, also known as Remo Casatelli, was the ambulance driver in the lower valley.

Luckily, to stave off the boredom, the official presentation of the Dynamo soccer team was scheduled for the next day. The appointment was at the town soccer field at three in the afternoon.

Half the village was there, even supporters of Sponda and the Fefellian right wing. Uncle Nevio had dressed up as a proper soccer club owner, with a gigantic Luciana Moda Bella foulard scarf that vaguely resembled a camisole. People kept asking him, how many years until we get into first division? "Not long, not long," he answered. "What about the away games, are all eleven of you going to travel in the three-wheeled Vespa pickup truck?" "We already have a rented van," he explained, clearly giddy with enjoyment.

The field had been renovated. There was no grass, because Caprone's sheep would only have eaten it. But the most insidious potholes, craters, and depressions had been leveled out. Stripes had been painted on the field and—a detail that won universal admiration—the goals had new netting, without holes or rips. The cement bleachers, built in record time by the factory workers from Messina, also displayed the first examples of the corrupting influence of advertising. There were three billboards: Luciana Moda Bella Apparel, Ristorante da Chicco Foglia d'Oro, and Lebboroni Animal Feeds. Fiat and Motta Panettone would come later.

The dressing rooms were in an old tool shed; we changed out of our clothes amidst disc harrows and pitchforks. In the winter it was freezing cold. There were only two showerheads, and if you turned on one full flow, the other one produced only a feeble trickle, and vice versa. There were no lockers, only cardboard boxes. The first division was far in the future.

We were terribly excited as we stood there in our underpants and Karamazov handed out the jerseys. This was when the first problem emerged. They were nice, bright-red jerseys, true enough, but on the left side was printed a face of Stalin, small but distinct.

"I just thought that plain red was a little ordinary," lied Karamazov.

My uncle flew into a rage. He said that sports and politics shouldn't mix, and moreover, he was against Stalin; even if it cost him votes, he preferred Antonio Gramsci. He ordered us all to turn the jerseys inside out; you couldn't tell the difference anyway. The next problem was that all the jerseys were the same size. Mine fit me perfectly, but the players from Messina had jerseys dangling down below their knees, and they looked like so many Dopeys from *Snow White*. And the Arduini twins, who were each as big as a refrigerator, had jerseys that left their midriffs uncovered, Saint-Tropez style. And there was a side of beef, 6′3″ tall, swearing furiously in Tuscan. His name was Roda, and judging from the girth of his calves, we understood that he was champion material. He had cost Uncle Nevio a hunting rifle, a hundred cartridges, and a position as salesclerk at Luciana Moda Bella. We jogged onto the soccer field, and were presented to the cheering audience.

"Ladies and gentlemen, allow me to present the Dynamo team," said my uncle, standing in the middle of the field with a megaphone in front of his mouth. "It is a team made up of young soccer enthusiasts; just like the spirit of youth and enthusiasm that I will bring to the job when I am elected mayor of this town. The victories of the Dynamo will help to pave the way for my own victory in the upcoming election. Tomorrow, we will be debuting when we play a friendly match against Troppiano, a team with a noble tradition, battling away in third division, just like us. And now, here is the lineup; please give a hearty round of applause to each player as I announce the name."

To start with, there were the powerful fullbacks, the sexy baking brothers Giglio Arduini and Loris Arduini (a round of applause, especially from the women). Playing center mid-fielder, or sweeper, as we call it nowadays, was our gym teacher Pieroni (a typhoon of cheers from the students). And playing defending center back was Ciccio Mia, a young and rising soccer talent, the son of Bortolini, and if he can play soccer anything like the way his father fishes . . . (a wave of murmurs, with hesitant applause; Ciccio was just a little over three feet tall). The midfielders and halfbacks were Sciarrillo, Schillaci, and Riggio (a burst of applause from the southern Italians, a few derisive whistles from the Northern Italian soc-cer hoodlums). Right winger, my nephew Timeskipper (a round of applause that brought tears to my eyes). Left winger, Grillomartino, the son of Maghino (a weak round of applause, but then Martino dribbled the ball thirty times in a row without missing once, and the clapping grew stronger and louder). And, saving the best for last, ladies and gentle-men, with twenty-six goals under his belt last year, in the Tuscan third division, the first striker of the future, Attilio Roda (a hurricane of clapping, with fluttering handkerchiefs). And last but certainly not least, the reserve players Baco and Carburo's son, Taddeo, thirteen years old, but with more than enough talent between them. Let's have a nice round of applause for Team Dynamo!

"Hold on a second," a thunderous voice broke in. It was Ossobuco, a soccer fan, but also a Fefelli supporter. "There's something wrong here."

"What?"

"There's no goalie," chimed in Osso, calling on the audience and God as his witnesses. Uncle Nevio seemed slightly taken aback.

"There's a goalie, of course there is, but he's late, it was his shift at the cement plant. He'll be here tomorrow."

"No no, we want to see him today," said Ossobuco. "What kind of mayor would you be? You promise us a soccer team and there's no goalie? It's as if you said, I'll build houses without doors, and roads without guardrails."

There was a roar of approval, from the left as well. At that point, Uncle Nevio looked toward the dressing rooms and called, in a somewhat hesitant voice:

"Come on out, Philippe."

And he appeared.

There was a moment of prehistoric silence.

In the center of the field a very tall, very skinny black man had appeared, sheathed in a spandex suit that was even blacker than he was, wearing goalie's gloves and a dazzling smile.

"Allow me to introduce to you Philippe M'Bukunda, former goalkeeper of the Senegal junior national team, as well as a factory worker at the cement plant."

There was a smattering of applause, scattered whistles, some howls. Almost six-and-a-half feet of coal-black negro was too much for our rural imaginations to absorb.

"Is this the Dynamo team or the colonial national team?" shouted Rondelli.

"We don't want a negro," roared someone from the edge of the field.

"Shut up, you animals," shouted Luciana. "Leave the poor man alone!"

"That's right, you all shut up, and he's not a poor man," Regina corrected her.

"How can we see him during a night game?" asked Boccoli the banker.

There was a burst of laughter, a round of shrill whistles, and even some shoving.

The unfortunate Philippe, standing in center field, understood that he needed to do something. And so he raised both hands in the air. They were huge, a pair of snow shovels. Then, with just one hand, like the dangling crane that picks up teddy bears at the amusement park, he picked up the soccer ball from the ground.

"Well, now," the crowd murmured.

Luciana and Zoraide immediately started whispering and giggling. They were certainly speculating about symmetrical correspondences with Philippe's other appendages.

"Please," said Philippe in a slightly halting voice, "I really want to play, but I understand that you're not used to the idea of an African goalkeeper. Give me a chance. If I play well tomorrow, then let me stay; if not, hire someone else."

This time there was a pretty heartfelt burst of applause. Good manners, and he spoke proper Italian, though he was definitely black, not mocha, not gray—black as pitch.

Of course, that's all anyone talked about that evening. And I understood that in our little town an innate racism would take a long time to defuse. A racism that was cunningly recycled in a number of different forms.

My father put it in technical terms: "Sure, let's let him play, why not, but Senegal is about as strong in soccer as the Scafatese team."

Chicco immediately said: "What if he likes it here, and more of them show up?"

Balduino gravely pronounced: "Well, if he was any good, he'd be playing in his own country."

"Too skinny," said Favilla the blacksmith. "The structure isn't sound."

But the workers from Messina swore that on the job he was as strong as a bull. And finally Baruch came up with the solution, with a skillful rhetorical dodge rooted in semantics.

"I believe," he said, "that the real problem is the name. You can't start a soccer team with a lineup that goes: M'Bukunda, Pieroni, Arduini. It's laughable. We have to find the right nickname."

"I would suggest a Brazilian name," said Uncle Nevio. "They're black and they can play—man, can they play."

In the end, the choice came down to one of three nicknames: Didí, Vavá, and Pelé, the trio of Carioca strikers; none of the three had been a goalie, but they were very nice nicknames. Pelé would be going too far; Pelé was a legend, and there is only one Pelé. Vavá was dangerous because Italian audiences might easily transform it into a chorus of *Vavaffanculo* or *Vavavavoom*. Didí was perfect.

"All right then," concluded Baruch, "tomorrow Didí will be our new goalkeeper."

And everyone was pleased.

It was a triumphant success. We won three to one. It was one to nothing when Roda scored the first goal, a stratospheric head shot; he hovered in midair like a Tuscan falcon and then, bang, the ball went straight into the bottom corner. Roda, on his own, unnerved the opposing team's entire defense. Then came two spectacular saves by Didí, who stretched from one goal post to the other, and he was immediately dubbed Didí

Plasticman. Then, if I do say so myself, I did some excellent dribbling, followed by a cross to Roda, who then unleashed a powerful lofting kick and slipped the ball just under the goal-posts. The bleachers erupted in cheers, and we saw Rondelli leap into the air and hug the first person he could reach—if that person was a Communist, too bad. End of the first half. Midway through the second half, our team began to flag. Ciccio Mia was panting too hard to call "Mia, Mia." For ten minutes they besieged us, and Plasticman made save after heroic save. But in the thirty-sixth minute of the second half of the match, the center forward on the opposing team managed to break free, and Giglio Arduini, panting, seized him by his jersey, just outside the penalty area.

But the referee claimed that the foul had taken place within the penalty area and called a free kick. The indignant fans insulted the referee with the traditional Italian index-and-pinky-finger symbol of the cuckold's horns, and on the spot the unfortunate referee sprouted more horns than a reindeer herd.

Plasticman Didí leapt high and managed to touch the ball, but not enough to prevent the goal.

"Boys," shouted Uncle Nevio, "just three more minutes; you can hold out a little longer."

Actually, it was nine more minutes, but he was pretty crafty. We did everything we could think of to keep possession of the ball, pretending we had lost shoes or that our socks were drooping down around our ankles. Somebody tripped Grillomartino as he was running, it was nothing serious, but he turned it into a scene worthy of the nineteenth-century Italian stage legend Ermete Zacconi, rolling around on the grass as if he'd taken a direct hit from a mortar shell. The referee fell for it and another precious minute crept by. The opposing wing-back started off a second too soon, and the referee's whistle stopped him. Slim the Magnificent had added the cry of the referee-bird to his repertoire of tweets and shrills, and he saved the day for us. We were panting, exhausted, but we toughed it out. We went on the attack, and Roda took kicks to the shins and ankles, battling like a lion; when we were playing defense, Pieroni and Ciccio Mia knocked shots back with feet, ankles, knees, shoulders, even with their teeth. With just two minutes left to go before we finally heard the game-ending whistle, I got control of the ball in midfield and shot off toward the enemy goal. My feet were on fire, my heart was pounding in my gullet, but the first division was within my grasp. I dodged the center midfielder, delivered a mighty kick, and watched as the ball lofted, sank, and ricocheted off the goalpost. "No-o-o-o!" I shouted. But it landed right at Schillaci's feet, and he scored. Three to one, our favor. Schillaci burst into tears, and so did his mother, up in the bleachers. When the final whistle finally sounded, I dropped to the ground, looked up at the sky, and said to myself, "Timeskipper, you're a lucky, lucky boy."

"We earned at least a hundred votes today," said Uncle Nevio in the dressing room. "Thanks, boys."

"Is that all, just 'Thanks, boys?'"

"Here's five thousand lire for each of you," he sighed, reaching for his wallet.

What more could I ask for? In October I would play in a real soccer-championship game, and the next day Selene was arriving with her parents. I saw them get out of their car, a new Lancia Fulvia, with a flood of suitcases, and walk into their country house, filled with the fresh smell of new cement. It was an ugly little chalet, half wood and half stone, with an armor-plated front door, and out front, a field of English clover and a narrow driveway made of compacted gravel. There wasn't even a gnome in the front yard.

I knew that her parents didn't much like me. And so I waited for her to give me a call. She didn't do that until the next day.

She had cut her hair, she was very fashionable. We kissed, the usual kiss but something was missing. Maybe it was a shock to her to be back in the village, maybe I was tired from the game, anyway, we said good-bye at midnight.

An hour later, a huge rainstorm began to lash the village, rain peppering the roofs in a burst of flamenco heel clattering. My duoclock went off. I saw the Roselle vacation village, shuttered and overgrown with weeds, with a sign out front: CONDEMNED, ILLEGAL CONSTRUCTIONS. I saw the trial for illegal construction; everyone else acquitted, but Sponda alone serving a few months in prison. I saw a ranking of the teams in Series A ten years later; Cagliari was there, but not Dynamo. I saw Jim Morrison die. I saw a huge discotheque under a muggy summer sky; there was someone lying in a field, and an ambulance. I saw the basin of the Fanara with another large crack running through it, and red water was pouring out onto the ground. I saw Fangio driving a truck at night; he was yawning and listening to Duke Ellington on the radio. I couldn't sleep, the weather seemed to be warning me, speaking to me in the voice of the cloudburst, asking: "Are your roots strong and solid, Timeskipper? How much wind can the tree of your courage withstand?" Around four in the morning, the rain stopped falling, and I fell asleep. A little later, though, my father woke me up and made me step outside in my pajamas. There was the slightest tinge of a pink dawn in the sky, over the line of the slumbering mountains. Dad was ashen. He said:

"You hear it?"

I heard it. It was a noise as if something huge were moving, trembling, shaking. Then roaring cracks, and then silence.

"It's the mountain, above the Roselle Hill," Dad said. "I told them it would happen."

An hour later, we were all up there. A slab of earth, half a mile uphill of the new holiday village, had collapsed. It was a vast, sagging tongue of soil and uprooted trees. Luckily, the land-slide had been halted by a detachment of stout chestnut trees.

"There was no stopping them, they had to chop down trees, dig up dirt, and now they've done it," said Baruch sadly. My father said nothing. He looked at the roots, touching them as if they were old friends. The tree's viscera, torn open.

The carabinieri said it was the rainstorm last night, it's a fairly natural occurrence. Uncle Nevio said, if I'm elected mayor, you'll see a hail of indictments. The phrase made the rounds of the village. He alienated ten potential voters, but he won over a great many more. Fefelli summoned a trusted geol-ogist from the city. He looked at the landslide and couldn't pass it off as a minor problem.

"That's not good," he said grimly, shaking his head.

That afternoon, Selene and I went down to the river to take a swim. She was wearing a dark-blue Olympic swimsuit, and it drove me out of my head: this time we kissed for real. I said, "Come on, let's go hide in the canebrake." "Later," she said, "when it's cooled down a little."

She laid her head on my knees.

"Aren't you afraid, up there in the chalet?" I asked.

"Why should I be?"

"Well, that mountain could collapse, and the chalet's right underneath it."

"My dad says that's all nonsense, campaign propaganda, that if you listen to them we should just give up building houses entirely and go live in caves again."

"Your father's an asshole," I blurted out.

This time she really got mad. She threw her towel at my head and went for a swim. I could see her head cutting back and forth in the water hole. I swam out to her.

"I'm sorry, I shouldn't have said that."

"You're always the same. You and your father do nothing

but predict disaster, it's almost as if you enjoy it. I have ideas of my own, I certainly don't agree with Fefelli, but politics doesn't turn me into a raving fanatic, there's lots of other things I care about in life. How can I be happy with you if you judge everything I do?"

"We all judge other people," I said. "You're judging me right now. But you have a point. I'll be more careful about the things I say."

"My father's not a complicated man," she said, and she was still angry. "He's worked all his life to buy this little vacation villa. Okay, he's not coming back to the village as a villager, he wanted to show that he's done well in life, that he has some money now. He wanted to prove that he's made it. He worked hard for me, too. And I like this chalet. True, there's the lane for cars, but a car makes things easy. And we weren't the ones who cut down the chestnut grove. Half of me is a spoiled city girl, but half of me still belongs to the forest. Or not?"

"You'll always be the queen of the pirates," I said, kissing her. "You ought to have a nice house. And, after all, the Black Corsair was a count."

"Tell me all about the soccer match yesterday. But tell the truth."

"All right. And you tell me about going to the beach at Cesenatico. How many guys did you seduce?"

She blushed, pretended she was angry, and ran back into the water. Then she stretched out in the sun. What a lovely lizard she is, I thought. I loved her and I would always love her, I'd love every half of her, her wheat-colored hair, her incomparable ass, and her straightforward way. I even loved the fact that she was almost touchier than I was.

She'd left her purse lying open on her towel. I don't even know how it happened, but I saw a postcard in the purse, and I pulled it out.

It was a postcard from London. On it was written:

"To my impossible love. Brian."

I felt as if someone was holding my head under water, suffocating me. The sun really did darken, sliding behind a cloud. I couldn't stand up, I couldn't speak. She came out of the water and looked at me in concern.

"What's the matter?" she said. "Are you okay?"

Then she saw the postcard.

"Why did you rummage through my purse?" she said, trembling.

"I'm sorry. I wasn't rummaging through the purse, I just looked over at it. I didn't want to, and it would have been better if I hadn't." She put her arms around me, but I might as well have been a statue carved in ice.

"Timeskipper, please, don't think of it as anything serious. I only saw him three times. There were a couple of kisses, once, and then I said, stop. I don't even know why I did it, maybe it was my strange half. Nothing happened, and I love you, Timeskipper."

I started sobbing like a child. I remembered every nice thing that Brian had done and said, and I remembered his phrase: "Women are just actresses; you'll find out." I felt as if I had been betrayed, betrayed a thousand times. I thought, "If I break up with her now I'm unfair, cruel—what kind of love is this if you can't get over something this minor—she cares for you, don't throw away everything out of pride, don't hurt yourself, don't hurt her."

"I don't ever want to see you again," I said. "Go away."

I held my face in my hands. She tried to pull my hands away and open them, she kissed me on the temples, then she gave up. I heard her walking away along the rocky riverbed. The duo-clock started up. I saw Brian, fat, grown ugly over time, with a flashy scarf around his neck, standing in front of his auto dealership. He still posed as a playboy, but he had become ridiculous. He walked toward me and said, "Timeskipper, forget about that old affair; you can't still be thinking about her. You want to see the new-model Maserati? This evening, I'll introduce you to a pair of Ukrainian girls. In comparison, Selene is just cool water."

But cool water was exactly what I wanted. And now everything was tainted. I had cried so hard that my throat hurt. I wished I had a picture of Selene in that dark-blue swimsuit as a last reminder of her. I stayed by the river until night fell. The summer was over, before it had even begun.

Maybe the summer was over for me, but not for the village. In fact, it looked like it would be a long, hot summer, with the advent of the Triveneto Trifecta. In the generic modernization and growing appetite of Italy's homegrown capitalism, the cement plant had also become a manufacturer of chemicals, and it spewed forth fumes and smoke that were far more brightly colored and odoriferous. Business must have been good, because the company made twenty new hires. Of those new hires, half, that is, ten, were women. Of them, seven were nothing to speak of, but three were from the Triveneto area, one prettier than the next, starting with the first. I should clarify: she *was* pretty. After all it could have gone differently: the first really horribly ugly, the second ugly in the ordinary way, and the third unsightly but not really ugly. But all three were eminently seductive. And they were different ages, so as to disturb the dreams of every generation still capable of desire in the village. They quickly received three nicknames: Sashay, Birdie, and Cee-cee.

Sashay was an over-forty blonde who moved with a pronounced sway to her walk, swinging everything she had, hence the name. She was a big hit with all the kids aged fifty to one hundred, and Baruch, in a pheromone-driven frenzy, stated that for a woman like her, he'd be willing to move to Rovigo, a city that is notoriously clericalist.

Birdie was in her thirties, and had the legs of a pink flamingo, brown hair, and an ultrasonic laugh, capable of shattering wineglasses. She was unfailingly good humored and, if you paid her a compliment, she'd burst into a refrain of high-pitched giggles, eerily reminiscent of the cry of the tufted chickadee, or of Slim the Magnificent. She was popular with the middle generation, and especially with Uncle Nevio, who once sat staring at her as she strolled past, his gaze glued to her legs like a postage stamp. Luciana noticed what was happening through the front window of Luciana Moda Bella; she calmly walked out of her shop, over to my uncle's table, and poured his Campari into his trousers. He said, "What are you doing?" but continued to stare at Birdie's legs until they vanished over the horizon.

Cee-cee got her nickname because the first time that Balduino walked up to her, she had courteously replied, " Si', si'," and so the barman, who was unfamiliar with the Venetian accent, reported that her name was Cee-cee, that she liked espresso with grappa, and that he loved her, and no one else better get in his way. Cee-cee was well liked by everybody, especially by young men, since she was twenty-three. She was of average height, had tawny hair, green eyes, and a mouth to faint for. Battling for her affections were, in order, Roda the center forward, the gym teacher, and both of the Arduini brothers: practically the entire Dynamo team. Trailing by a minute and a half was Balduino, galloping furiously. And nine minutes behind the pack was Karamazov, who had decided that Cee-cee had a distinctively Russian beauty—Siberian, actually; he immediately asked whether her mother came from Vladivostok.

The popularity of the Triveneto girls, of course, triggered the righteous indignation of the local beauties, who slid from feverishly sought after to merely insistently sought after. They all adopted countermeasures, and there was a proliferation of unusual shades of lipstick and the sort of eyelashes you might expect to see on a streetwalker. A campaign was undertaken to promote the consumption of local products, specifically the more seasoned ones, Luciana and Regina, Rospa's sister, nick-named *Raganella*, or tree frog, and the younger varieties, Nuc-cia and Dolores, from Messina, dark-haired girls with plenty of vim and brio, and Hilda the Howitzer, who had added new weapons of mass seduction to her superbelch. In this compet-itive climate, the town's erotic tension rose to new heights; there was even a running book being offered by Maria Casinò. Caprone had especially long odds: 300,000 to 1. I put down a thousand lire on him.

Even my father was caught up in the spirit, and he said, "Go on, see if you have any luck with Cee-cee." He could tell that for some reason things had turned sour with Selene. The Luni-ni family wasn't fitting in in the village. People said that they put on airs. Selene's mother, Clara, boasted that she had been invited to dinner at Villa Meringue and that there had been eight utensils with every dish. Balduino said, "If that's what you're interested in, come to my house for dinner. I can put out as many as twenty forks, if it'll make you happy." Karamazov said that eight utensils was barely above average in Russia.

Selene was no longer in circulation. People said that in the evenings a group of older kids drove by to pick her up; they'd go dancing at the new discotheque, Marilyn, a low-slung bunker structure that looked like a chickin battery, with green and red lights outside. One evening, Mr. Lunini, the father, confided to Uncle Nevio that he no longer felt comfortable in town, that it had fallen behind the times and was now just a hick village; he was even sorry that he had bought the chalet, the walls were thin, you could hear the neighbors' toilet flush, and he was no longer accustomed to all the nocturnal cries of pheasants and owls and the dogs barking. And so he was thinking of selling.

One morning they packed their bags and left. I hoped that Selene might at least have left me a note, but there was noth-ing. And what did I expect, anyway? I had pushed her out of my life, fairly or unfairly I couldn't say, as I dangled between love and pride. I had been incapable of forgiveness.

I was wounded, bleeding, even if I understood that all this was within the secret of clocks, just part of the time of learning. In the meanwhile, I was doing my best to hurt myself, and even at age sixteen, you can do plenty of damage. I started drinking red wine, like my dad; Gancio had let me try some marijuana, and it wasn't bad at all. "Slightly stunned" was my default setting. In the evening, I often stayed home and read, or else I'd walk in the woods with Uncle Nevio's dog Rufus, the only living creature willing to tolerate my mood swings.

One night, at about one in the morning, I was coming home and I saw that the lights were still on. I heard music. Regina, who loved to sing and dance, had given my father a record player. It was jazz piano. I didn't know it at the time, but it was *Misterioso* by Thelonious Monk. Suddenly the world seemed much bigger to me, I still felt the same pain, but it was a speck of dust, a pebble worn smooth, and it was skipping across the immense sea of other people's feelings. There were two other occasions when music astonished me and made me aware of a much larger world. Once was *Revolver* by the Beatles, the other was when I saw a performance of *The Magic Flute*. But *Misterioso* was the first and biggest temblor. I didn't enter the house; I turned on my heels and went back to town. There was a new bar, the Mephisto, where a group of fairly out-of-their-head young people hung out. Gancio was there, with the sexy Messinese girls, Nuccia and Dolores, and a pale girl with a mournful air. I sat down with them, flirted briefly, and then said: "Gancio, on Sunday I want to go to the discotheque."

"No," said the white-faced girl, who was Gancio's steady date, "you can't bring him, or else . . ."

"Or else what?" Gancio broke in angrily "Mind your own fucking business, Nora."

The girl shut her mouth. We went on drinking, and I spent half the money I had on me. Then Gancio said: "Let's steal a car." Ever since we were both twelve, when Gancio had showed me how, we'd been breaking into cars and getting them running, but we'd never gone beyond that, we'd never actually driven the cars. But this time we got in, started the motor, and took off. He was driving fast, accelerating in the straightaways, and I said: "That's enough, Gancio, don't go too fast."

"It's like when we go swimming in the river, you always turn back before we go over the rapids," said Gancio.

"I'm a lot more scared here than on the river," I said. "Stop the car! If you want to kill yourself, don't take me with you."

I regretted saying that. Maybe that was exactly what he had been doing, in the hidden folds of his own dark night. I wanted him to forgive me, so I took his arm and we walked along side by side. He seemed astonished, as if I had done something that neither he nor anyone else expected.

We had parked the car right in the middle of the big gas station. We were half drunk. As we were walking back to the village, I tried to kiss Dolores, she let me do it, mostly out of politeness. Her mouth was dry and tasted of liquor; she was very different from Selene.

"Sorry," I said, "I just don't feel like it tonight."

"You don't feel like what?" she said.

I understood that I was smashed. When I got home, I saw my father enjoying the cool night air, in a chair on the lawn. He took one look at me and said, "One drunkard in this house is all we need. Either you stop drinking or one of these evenings I'm going to do something I've never done before, I'm going to hit you." He was conveniently overlooking two or three times he'd hit me as a child, but I understood that he was angry and worried. For an instant, I hated him.

On Sunday evening, the expedition for the Marilyn discotheque set out; there were six of us in a Fiat 1300; that worked out to about 200 cc's of engine displacement apiece. At the wheel was Teseo, aka Tex, an eighteen-year-old with the wrinkles of a thirty-year-old and slicked-back hair. Then there was me, and Gancio, and Osso wearing an Elvis-style shirt and white shoes, a hybrid between a whoremonger and a musician in a small-town polka combo. There was Nora, still silent and brooding, and Dolores, whom I had dubbed Medusa because of her unkempt curly hair and her deranged expression. I sat in front, in the back Osso was dogging Medusa and Gancio was distractedly necking with Nora.

It was a very hot night, and there were swarms of gnats buzzing around the lights of the Marilyn, and they were biting, too. I noticed that the kids were dressed more or less like kids in the city. There were necks that looked a little thicker, indicative of field work, the girls had the stout calves of cyclists, but everyone wore miniskirts and flowered shirts, and in the parking lot it looked like a rally for Fiat 500s. At the entrance to the disco there was a bouncer with a potbelly, wearing a badge that said "Staff." Staff? This was Italy, and we all were speaking dialect, not even Italian. In our dialect, "staff" sounds roughly like "*stufo*," or "exhausted," and so I made a joke: "*St'i staff, va ban a cà,*" that is, "If you're tired, then why don't you just go home?" He had the sense of humor of a creekfish, and replied, "If you're going to be an asshole even while you're outside, then I'm definitely not going to let you in." Then he saw Gancio, who was a regular customer, and calmed down. There was electricity in the air, but the charge wasn't particularly pleasant. It was more like a thunderstorm was about to hit.

We walked in. The place was horrible and airless, submersed in a light of reddish molasses, there were shapeless sofas, deflated easy chairs, and crippled café tables, the music was pounding at high volume, people were crowding onto the dance floor, you couldn't even talk. A waiter arrived at a dead run, asked me for my drinks coupon and what did I want to drink? "Can't I have something to drink later?" I asked, and he said, "No, I have to take care of this right away, there's so many of you." So I ordered a Cuba Libre, I emptied it at a gulp and thought, from here on in, it might be better not to be thirsty. Everyone else went to dance and I sat there alone, sinking into the mushy sofa. Next to me, a couple had been glued together in a kiss since we walked in. I wondered why they had come, wouldn't it be nicer in a parked car or under a nice big walnut tree in the moonlight? Maybe he read my mind, because he popped the suction cup off his girlfriend and turned to say:

"What the fuck you looking at?"

"Nothing, nothing at all," I said. And I understood that in this discotheque there was plenty of music and collective sweat, but not much of a sense of fellow feeling. In fact, a few minutes later two guys got into a fistfight at the bar. A girl was screaming as if they were killing each other; I felt like saying, "Miss, don't exaggerate, it's just the normal display behavior of a pair of rutting males." Mister Staff plunged into the fight and resolved the situation with belly-checks and open-handed slaps. Everything went back to normal. "(I Can't Get No) Satisfaction" started to play, and the bass notes rattled around between my ribs. Osso returned from the dance floor, wobbling uncertainly as he navigated the lines of tables; he bumped into a big guy wearing a leather jacket.

"What the fuck you think you doing?" the big guy said.

Osso didn't even hear him, and he collapsed next to me on the sofa. He handed me a ten-thousand-lire banknote and said: "Go get a couple of Cuba Libres."

I found that pretty offensive, but I was dying of thirst. On my way to the bar, I saw Gancio talking to a strange character, elegantly garbed in a lavender-colored suit; he looked like he'd wandered out of a cartoon. They walked together into the bathroom.

At the bar there was a sexy blonde in a miniskirt; she seemed lonely and forlorn.

"Hello," I said, while waiting for the two Cuba Libres.

"What the fuck you want?" she said. It dawned on me that in a discotheque, even if you are alone and depressed, you may not necessarily be interested in modifying your situation. I was learning lots of new things. First and foremost, that this is how they make a Cuba Libre in a discotheque: a finger of rum, two fingers of Coke, and approximately two pounds of ice cubes.

"Maybe you should call this an Alaska Libre," I told the bartender.

He didn't get it; maybe that was preferable. The sexy blonde changed her mind and said:

"So, you want to buy one for me?"

I was about to say, it's not my money, it belongs to the Elvis lookalike at the far end of the room, then I thought, well, that's his problem.

"Sure," I answered; and, to the bartender: "And one for the signorina."

"For Deborah," she specified, with a somewhat ghoulish smile.

I went back to the table. Gancio was stretched out on the sofa and seemed to be in a state of euphoria; he was embracing Nora and saying, very loudly:

"You guys, ain't it great to hang out with your friends in a discotheque, and not give a fuck about the rest of the world?"

"You sure know how to live," said Tex in an adulatory tone. "But Osso is a total loser."

"What the fuck you saying?" snarled Osso.

"Hey, Osso," said Gancio, "when's the last time you got laid?"

"Yesterday," said Osso.

Gancio started laughing in an unnatural, high-pitched voice, and rolled on the cigarette -butt-strewn floor. Nora tried to pull him to his feet.

"When are you two going to stop acting like asses?" sighed Medusa. "Is anyone going to ask me to dance?"

Just then, Deborah came over, unsteady on her feet, with the Cuba Libre in her hand.

"Can I sit with you guys?" she said to me.

"Hey!" said Tex. "Fresh pussy! How about that Timeskipper, he acts all indifferent, but then he picks up girls like a pro."

"I met the young lady just now, at the bar," I found myself explaining.

Osso moved over by Deborah with a leer and a grin. But then he vanished from sight, obscured by the bulk of the guy in the leather jacket.

"What the fuck you doing there?" he said to Deborah.

"I'm just talking with some friends," answered the blonde. I could see she was trembling in fear.

"Get back to our table or I'll beat you silly."

"Actually, we were just . . ." said Tex.

"And you shut your mouth, or I'll have to beat you, too."

Deborah stumbled to her feet, swaying, and he grabbed her roughly by one arm. I felt awful for her.

"Hey," said Gancio, watching as they walked away, "what's the matter with all of you? Are you going to just let him come over and insult you like that?"

"The Guatayabas are patient in their vendettas," I said.

"Don't be ridiculous, what kind of cowards have you become?" It wasn't Gancio talking anymore; he seemed like a stranger: his hair was plastered to his forehead, his mouth was tense and twisted. He rose to his feet.

"Hey, Deborah," he yelled, "come on back here, don't waste your time with that asshole."

It took only a second. Suddenly I was in the middle of a

brawl, kicks and shoves flying in all directions, and no referee; café tables were rolling, glasses were shattering. I couldn't even tell who was fighting on my side or who was against me. I felt like saying, "We should at least have jerseys on." I saw Osso take a tremendous punch to the face from a guy half his size, and Medusa scratching another girl's face. And I saw a knife blade gleaming in Gancio's hand.

"No," I shouted, "Gancio, no!"

The bouncer grabbed me from behind and twisted my wrist.

"I'm not doing anything," I said.

"I'll break your arm, you jerk," the huge linebacker said. "If you want to have a fight, do it outside."

I don't even know how it happened, but stumbling and shoving, we wound up outdoors, surrounded by clouds of biting gnats. Gancio pulled out the knife again, and the guy in the leather jacket warily edged away, along with the rest of his friends.

"See you later, you junkie," said the side-of-beef bouncer.

Gancio was about to start up again.

"That's enough, Gancio, let it go," I said, holding on to him tightly. He spat on the ground, swore, and kicked at a parked car. He couldn't seem to get himself under control. We sized up the damages. Medusa had broken a nail. Tex had taken a hard kick to his shin. But Osso was in the worst shape: his nose was bleeding, and his Elvis shirt looked like something out of a horror movie.

"We showed them," said Osso, and spat out part of a tooth. Gancio emitted a Guatayaba war cry and started leaping up and down in a frenzy. Then he bent over and puked.

I tried to hold his head up. He collapsed to the ground. His eyes were rolling up into his head, his neck muscles were so taut that his mouth was gaping open, his legs were thrashing in spasms. He looked like a fish gasping in poisoned water.

"Something's wrong with him," said Tex, taking a couple of

steps away from him to make it clear that he, for one, was washing his hands of the matter.

"Call an ambulance," said Nora.

"Maybe he'll feel better in a minute."

"No, he's not, he's not going to feel better in a minute. What's the matter with all of you, are you idiots? He shot up again!"

In a flash, I understood everything. Gancio's euphoric states and sudden collapses, all the weight he'd lost in the past year, the man in the lavender suit. How could I have missed it, how could I have failed to notice what was happening, not in a newspaper or a movie, but to a friend of mine?

"Call an ambulance," I said to the people at the door of the discotheque.

"Oh, come on, you get drunk and the next thing you want is an ambulance," said the usual bouncer.

I walked over and stood six inches away from his fat belly and his stupid face and his *Staff* badge.

"Listen, you sack of shit. My dad is Fefelli, the mayor, and if you don't get on the phone and call an ambulance immediately, there will be so many safety inspections and permit reviews that you'll be looking for a new job in a week. And come to think of it, why do you let pushers sell drugs in there, anyway?"

The bouncer ran over to make the phone call as if he had been shot out of a cannon.

We waited for what seemed like a very long time, suspended between the two clocks. I was holding Gancio's hand. That pile of bones in a dirty T-shirt, that young man crucified on the grass, was Gancio from the river, Gancio who rode bikes with me. There was nothing strange about it; he had broken in two, part of him had flown away, just like when your hat flies off in the wind, and maybe we'd never find it again. I thought of Uncle Nevio, I imagined him loading shotgun shells in the light of the little desk lamp.

"Try to live, Gancio," I said into his ear. "A Guatayaba

wouldn't die like this, like a pathetic loser, outside of a two-bit discotheque. At least try to die on the Orinoco, with a funeral worthy of a chieftain."

He opened his eyes, for an instant.

"I feel like shit," he said.

Gancio survived, but the doctor said that his body was in terrible shape, and that if he started doing drugs again it would be catastrophic. Only Uncle Nevio and Luciana were informed of what had happened; we didn't even tell my father. Luciana took Gancio home to live with her for a while. Gancio said nothing, just stared out the window. She cooked him frittatas and plates of tortellini, but he barely tasted them.

One evening, he left a note on the table—"Thank you for everything, from the heart"—and left. Then he came by my house and whistled until I heard him and came outside.

"Timeskipper," he said. "I'm going to the beach with Nora. Don't worry about me, I'm giving up drugs."

"I hope you do," I said.

"You have the word of a Guatayaba. Listen, can you give me some money? I swear it's not for drugs, it's for the train tickets."

I believed him and gave him all the money I had.

That evening, I was out strolling with Baco and Osso, and we saw Fulisca. Impulsively, I hugged her. She was pretty tall now and rather pretty, though her face was still ashen and wan. She told me that she was working in a nearby town, for a clock-maker who was teaching her the trade. She had recovered from her illness, though she never said what it was. She asked for news about everyone.

"Well," I said, "I'm studying and I'm going to be in Series A with the Dynamo soccer team soon."

"I'm studying cybernetics," said Baco. "If you're interested, I can tell you more."

"I'm learning how to make money," said Osso.

"What about Gancio?" asked Fulisca.

"Gancio is completely wasted," said Osso. "He's just a junkie loser."

"Osso," I said, "you're an asshole. Get lost or I'll punch you."

"Try it," said Osso.

We grappled and shoved once again; maybe we weren't even trying to hurt each other, but he fell on top of me and crushed one of my ribs.

"You Fascist," I yelled at him, "you're no friend of mine anymore. You're not anybody's friend anymore."

"And you're a Communist, with a drunk for a father," he shot back.

I understood that this time it would take a lot of soccer cards to forget. Baco walked away with Fulisca. I sat there alone, my rib throbbing in pain. I heard the wail of an ambulance siren. "But I'm not hurt that bad," I thought. The ambulance raced past me, followed by another, and finally a fire truck. They were all heading for the highway. Someone stood up over at the bar and asked what was happening. A highway policeman on a motorcycle stopped and said something. I got into my uncle's car and we drove away.

The highway was a scene of carnage and mayhem. A truck had swerved out of its lane, mowing down about twenty automobiles. Another truck had run off the road. The cars were crushed, some of them were smashed together. They looked like a pile of auto carcasses at the junkyard. Some of the cars were still burning, and there were lines of stopped cars waiting in both directions; traffic was completely halted.

The blue lights on the police cars were pulsating; we heard voices screaming, calling for help from inside an overturned car.

"There," said Uncle Nevio, "that's a scene from hell."

There were lots of us on the overpass, caught between fear

and morbid curiosity. Favilla the blacksmith said, I have a blowtorch and tools in my truck; let's go see if we can help. We walked down along the embankment and climbed over the guardrail. A policeman walked toward us.

"You can't come down here," he said.

"I'm a blacksmith," said Favilla. "I have a blowtorch and crowbars. We want to help out."

"But you need to get off the roadway. Go see if you can lend a hand with the overturned truck."

In the field, the red leviathan lay belly up; one wheel was still spinning. The truck's cab was crushed to half its original size; inside it you could see an arm and a white shirt, a pennant of a soccer team, a coral red horn.

Favilla put on his goggles, lit his blowtorch, and started cutting; a fireman with another blowtorch did the same thing on the other side of the truck. Every so often they exchanged glances. Then Uncle Nevio, Chicco, and Roda started trying to pry the door open with crowbars. Finally, it gave way.

"Now, let the emergency medical team do the rest," said the exhausted fireman. He wasn't much older than me.

The EMT guys came down the slope. They extracted a body, as if they were pulling a shellfish from its shell. And just as they were laying the body on the stretcher, I saw the face. It was Fangio.

He had died, without even knowing what had happened. When he saw the other truck hurtling straight at him, he'd swerved instinctively and had flown over the guardrail. He died on impact. At his funeral, all his truck-driver friends were there, along with his old colleagues from the coach lines. Miss Zaini was there; she had aged terribly, and she didn't recognize me at all. Fangio was buried in a new section of the cemetery— not as pretty, and without broom plants. The cemetery had doubled in size in just a few years.

"The dead need space, too," said Karamazov, and laid a bouquet of red carnations on the grave.

That evening in the town square, the Pastori brothers were celebrating, staggering drunk. Fefelli had been acquitted on all charges; they could keep their jobs.

Licio, the older brother, looked at Fangio's death notice, pasted up on the wall. He thought it over for a while and it dawned on him that Fangio was the one who had pulled the bus in front of them, that time they were chasing my father.

He said loudly: "Well, that's one Communist out of the way . . ."

My father heard him. He went straight for him. Balduino came running up carrying a shovel, and I heard a sharp crack. Licio dropped like a tree. Then Carburo showed up. I wrapped myself around Nerio's legs; he hit me in the head and shoved me away; I went spinning. Carburo punched him square in the chin and knocked him to the ground; my father started kicking him furiously. Baruch came running as fast as he could.

"That's enough," he said, "there's three-and-a-half of you against two of them."

"Yeah, but look at the size of them," said Balduino, leaning his shovel against the wall, as if he were reholstering a Colt .45.

"You'll pay for this," said Licio, staggering away with a deep gash on his forehead. "It doesn't end here."

I felt an anger unlike anything I'd ever experienced, an anger that dug its claws into me.

"It does end here, you're wrong, it has to end! Enough!" By now I was screaming: "Enough, get out, you need to leave this village for good. Go try to boss people around somewhere else. Enough!"

My father had an arm around my neck, holding me tight, but I kept on shouting.

"Don't become one of them," he said to me.

I started sobbing.

"Baruch," I said, "tell me that it ends here."

Baruch patted me on the shoulder. But he didn't answer.

Then it was the last day of summer vacation, time to go back to the city, to the first day of high school, new teachers, and maybe some new classmates. I was stretched out in the field in front of my house. Rufus had come to say hello. I saw Roda and Cee-cee on their way back from a stroll—and a roll—in the countryside. The Triveneto girls were all nicely matched up, Cee-cee with the super center-forward, Birdie with Loris Arduini, and now Sashay had become a partner in Balduino's bar, but she was going steady with an orchestra musician. "Couldn't she have played music with him and made love with me?" Balduino complained.

Roda and Cee-cee were vibrant, beautiful, their hair mussed, their clothes awry; love is a wonderful cosmetic.

"Remember," said Roda, the Tuscan, "play starts in two weeks. Don't let yourself run to seed."

"And you take it easy," I answered. "Those Venetian players will take it out of you."

I saw them laugh and walk off, arm in arm; he loomed over her, twice her size. I felt a pang of envy. I thought of Selene, and pain surged into my stomach, as sharp as if we'd broken up yesterday. I walked up to the walnut tree. The duoclock went off. I saw her on the back of a motorcycle, racing along the beachfront, her arms wrapped around a young man with long hair: it wasn't Brian. I saw Fangio, laughing in a truckstop and raising a glass. I saw my ugly high school and the custodians sweeping the floors and dusting the desks. Rufus barked at two squirrels that were leaping from one tree to another, and he chased after them, head held high, until they vanished into the woods. I waited for someone to show up, the gnome or the Cheerful

God or the Violin-Playing Devil or even a rookie-league witch, just like my soccer team, Dynamo, but nothing happened. My father and Regina were listening to the soccer match on the radio. Even the stars seemed to be paying attention.

With a sigh, I thought, it's time to pack my bags.

I saw a shadow coming toward me. It was Osso. "I'm sorry," he said, head down. I saw that he already had a small double chin.

"Ah, that's all right, it doesn't matter," I answered, but I knew it wasn't true. Something chilly and unforgiving had come to live with me that summer. I could only hope that it would go as quickly as it had come.

"Didn't you bring any stickers?" I asked.

He didn't even remember what I was talking about. He listened to the distant radio.

"What's the score?"

"I think our team is winning, one to nothing. I heard Regina yelling 'Goal!' "

"Now that is good news," said Osso. "I bet twenty thousand lire on them."

"Good for you," I said.

"Well, I'm going home. I'll see you on the train. Good night. You know, I'm going to have an apartment all for myself this year. Downtown."

"Maybe I will, too," I said.

I sat there, alone once more. I heard Regina yell again. I couldn't tell if she was shouting for joy or disappointment.

"What's happening?" I yelled.

"Two to nothing, our favor," answered my dad. "Screw the Milanese."

"Two to nothing," I whispered into the darkness. "Did you hear that, Selene? Happy? Shall we go to sleep?"

6

On one of the first days of school, I took the train and fell asleep. I dreamed about a soldier loading a rifle and Captain Guzano Rodriguez saying, "Don't shoot him in the head, it has to look like he died in combat." When I got to the station, I saw the newspaper headline: Che Guevara was dead.

I had a book in my pocket that talked about him. I don't know why, but in a burst of anger I tossed the book into a trash can. I wanted a living man to admire, not a paper hero to mourn. I couldn't imagine how Che's memory would be celebrated, even by those who had betrayed him. The next day, passing through the station again, I stuck my hand into the trash can; the book was still there. I pulled it out, and went to school.

The Giosuè Pascoli High School was still the same, the only thing that had changed was the assortment of mopeds and scooters. My new classroom had a window overlooking the roofs; we studied under the baleful glares of sickly looking pigeons. Nearly all of my classmates were new faces. Of my old friends, there were only the perfect couple, Schiassi-Verdolin, Lussu, and Carpaccio in a Taras Bulba version, with long hair and mustache. Surprisingly, Baco was there, too, sad about his separation from Miss Tania, the math teacher, but thrilled over the latest developments of Californian cybernetics. Two of my old enemies, unfortunately, were still there: Monachesi and Liuba, dragging on their asplike existences.

Gentilini had flunked out of school entirely, and as a reward had been given a job in his father's company. Brian was gone, too; people said that he'd gone back to London to live. That solved a number of problems for me. Among the new students we immediately identified Gentilini's successors. They were three overgrown cashmere-wearing, pimply boys; all of them had Corsarino 50s, the fashionable scooter at the time. They were named Checco, Fede, and Bobo, all names worthy of genuine real-life corsairs. Then there was La Desoli, also known as La Duse, after the immortal stage actress Eleonora Duse. She introduced herself by saying that she was studying here but also attending theater school. She dressed in black, and every gesture she made was contrived; she waved her hands in circles and stared affectedly as if she were treading the boards; if she sneezed, it was something straight out of *Macbeth*, "Oh, Lord, do I still have a nose?" On a daily basis, she unfurled lines such as: "Oh, yesterday Vittorio came to dinner at our house." Vittorio, as in Gassman. Once she asked me how I came in to the city from my village every day, and I answered, "Oh, I ride my bike with Fausto." Fausto, as in Coppi. Right then and there she didn't get it; they explained the joke to her, and she hated me from then on. Among the simpaticoes, we immediately identified Fred and Tremolina. Fred the maniac had short hair and a Fu Manchu mustache, and he was a complete motorcycle fanatic. He enjoyed the immense privilege of having been left back twice—he was therefore eighteen years old—and he owned a chopped, souped-up Settebello Morini 250 motorcycle, with perform-ance cams and modified carburetors and no mufflers, with a top speed of 92 mph. You could hear him coming for a full minute before he got to school. He described himself as an anarcho-biker, and he led the pack in cornering and joke telling. Tremolina was petite, attractive, and nervous as a cat; she always spoke at a frantic pace, like this: Ihavetotellyou somethingmajordon'tgoaway, and when she had something important to say, since she eschewed the wearing of brassieres, her tits—which were substantial—tended to jiggle and bounce. I have to admit that the first time I spoke to her, they made more of an impression on me than anything she said. Then I found out that she was a voracious reader, that she had read everything from de Sade to the Symbolists, and that she wanted to be a writer when she grew up. In fact, she had already written a book titled *Diary of a Secret*, but since it was a diary and a secret one, she had never shown it to a soul, except for maybe fifty or so trusted confidants ("ifyouwantIcanlety oureadit, too").

Of the teachers, I still remember the Sadist, a bald dwarf who taught Italian. He'd say: "As long as I hear someone coughing, I'm not starting the lesson." In winter, his lessons usually lasted a total of ten minutes, partly because we all had hacking coughs for real, and in part because we took turns clearing our throats as loudly and irritatingly as possible. Then there was Neuros, who taught ancient Greek; he'd surge out of his customary state of complete apathy and leap to the podium, acting out the duel between Achilles and Hector. And last but not least, Dearly Departed, the elderly woman who taught philosophy; she'd say one word every ten seconds and would occasionally say, excuse me, and leave the room because she had a weak bladder. She had only two years till retirement, and she wanted to go the distance. I liked her best of all.

Tamara and Riccardo the ideologue had wound up in the adjoining classroom, so the school already had its political leadership. As for me, my favorite reading matter was no longer the works of Edgar Allan Poe but the collected writings of the classified ads; I read them for hours, and then I'd walk all around the city in my search for a room to rent. Actually, I asked Fred to give me a ride on his motorcycle once, but the first car he passed, I had the distinct impression that I left a slice of my right butt cheek on the door handle, and so I went back to pedestrianism.

I went to see as many as five potential rentals a day, but the rooms were all too expensive. The city had begun to realize that students from out of town were an excellent investment. I made ends meet by doing odd jobs. Occasionally, I washed dishes in the pizzeria where Lussu worked. On some nights, I unloaded crates at the greenmarket; I slept on a cot there, surrounded by the scents of cabbages and lemons, as well as Senegalese, Greeks, and various other nationalities. For me, it was a useful antidote to racism; at least it was until someone stole my shoes and a sweater, and I swore furiously: "Fuck them all, and their respective countries." The following evening, however, the shoes were returned, with a note inside: "I have to keep the sweater, it's just too cold."

Which explained why—although it provided no justification in the eyes of the worldwide proletariat—I couldn't bring myself to continue attending the political meetings at the garage. But one day, they held the first political meeting in school, during school hours; that, I could not miss.

In the main auditorium, there were already a hundred or so students, while lessons continued in the classrooms. Seated at the podium were Riccardo, Tamara, and Carpaccio, who had been promoted to the role of Vishnu in the Trimurti.

First order of business: decide when and how to occupy the school. Next item on the agenda: how best to implement a thoroughgoing critique of the educational platform and approaches, and how to institute a communal management of the lessons, or perhaps even a student-operated scholastic system. Further points: a major demonstration protesting the authoritarian abuses carried out by the teaching staff, and especially the dictatorial regimes of three teachers, specifically, the Sadist and other teachers in Section F. Last item: warmer radiators.

The first speech was by Riccardo who said, as usual, that

the student bodies at two high schools in the city had already occupied their buildings as had many others elsewhere in Italy, not to mention France, Berkeley, and South America. Still no reports on what was going on in the Australian preschools.

Tamara said, "For the moment, we are relatively few in number; we have to persuade the rest of the students that we are not working against them that it will help everyone. We have undertaken, here and in the larger world outside, a great debate on freedom that will one day prove helpful even to those who disagree with us."

Carpaccio spoke for eight full minutes, the maximum time allowed, about the relationship between Lenin and Marx, and concluded his talk by saying: "We must not commit the same error." Nobody could say what error he was talking about.

A tall boy with stereoscopic eyeglasses and a pile of curly hair three times the size of Jimi Hendrix's afro, a real buzzard's nest, stood up. His name was Giandomenico Maria, but you called him that at risk of life and limb. His *nom de guerre* was Giap, just like the Vietnamese general.

Giap said that Riccardo's discourse was basically right wing in orientation because you shouldn't do something just to imitate others, it was necessary to be in the vanguard in every instance. He said that Tamara's discourse also was rightist, because it failed to take on in a decisive manner the scabs who were helping to shore up the crumbling capitalist educational model, and that Carpaccio's discourse was infected with pernicious right-wing fallacies because evoking historic leaders is nothing more than a trick designed to strip the base of its right to debate matters.

Riccardo answered tersely, referring to an author whose name nobody understood.

Tremolina said that she wasinfavorofestablishingcontacts thatwerenotonlypoliticalbutalsopersonal and that she wanted todebatenotonlythequestionofoccupyingtheschoolsbutalso whatwashappeningoutsidetheschools, and then took a deep breath and somewhat more calmly proposed a regular discussion group on interpersonal relationships and a student-organized seminar on de Sade.

A boy wearing a poncho said that he was in favor of greater human warmth and that it seemed to him that everything was too rigidly political and organizational, and wouldn't it be a good idea for everyone to go and eat together at a pizzeria— maybe it'd be better if we did it in shifts.

A blond boy with one earring said that, in any case, the starting point for any rational discussion had to be Frank Zappa.

A slightly cross-eyed girl said that she needed to say what she felt deep down, and that is, that there was some male-chauvinist prejudice at play in the way that this political meeting was being run, because whenever a woman addressed the meeting, everyone chattered away, but if it was a man speaking, everyone listened in silence. There was a buzz of discussion about the point she was making, and she lost her temper.

Giap said that Tremolina had made a basically right-wing point because we needed to study Mao, not de Sade, that if the boy with the poncho wanted personal warmth, he should just buy a space heater because revolutionaries had to deal with the cold, that Frank Zappa had left-wing lyrics but right-wing tunes, and that the cross-eyed girl was super right wing because she had imposed a gender-based prejudice as an obstacle to true political debate.

Lussu said, let's decide who's going to be in charge of the seminars, and let's submit some written demands to the teachers, and also let's discuss the prices of textbooks, because they're too high.

A boy said, "I'm in agreement with the comrade from

Sicily," and Lussu said: "I'm from Sardinia, bloody slutty Virgin Mary."

A fairly attractive brunette said that, as a woman, she was doing her best to overcome her complaints about prejudices, but that, in actual fact, it was harder for a woman to speak in front of an audience. She talked for her full eight minutes, and then went on for another eight.

Baco said exactly what I was afraid he'd say: that cybernetics was conspicuously absent from the political platform, and that there could be no revolution without cybernetics.

Verdolin proposed painting a mural on the school walls.

La Schiassi said, "Yes, but the paint would be way too expensive."

Giap asked if this was a political movement or a billboard service.

Tamara said that it seemed to her that Giap was destructive, not constructive.

Giap said that that was a typically right-wing observation.

Fred said that he hadn't understood fuck-all of the things he'd heard so far, but that a motorcycle only runs if there's gas in the tank, and that the gas that he knew about was, yes, engaging in politics, but also having fun while doing it.

I said that I agreed with Fred, that I'd been born and brought up in a small town where we not only talked about politics, but where politics fell on your head every day, and everything that surrounds you is political. It was a good idea for us to plan the future, but we needed to be ready for surprises as well; we shouldn't be trying to find reassurances, political lines, and parties, it was only important to understand when it was useful to debate matters and when it was time to act. I suggested we hold student-organized seminars to discuss books that weren't taught in class, produce an internal mimeographed newsletter with political reporting but also news of general interest, and, last of all, appoint a committee to examine the exorbitant rents being demanded of students from out of town.

Giap said that I was a good speaker but that he had seen me reading Ezra Pound in the bathroom, and that therefore everything I had said was rightist.

Lussu said that Giap's comments were right wing, without explaining why; the effect of Lussu's attack was devastating.

The blond boy asked if anyone had any rolling papers.

A guy wearing a soccer neckerchief asked what the comrades thought about rooting for soccer teams and going to see soccer matches at the stadium, because he liked doing those things.

Tamara said: "Two hours is up. We'll all meet at the garage on Friday, and in the meantime, I'm in favor of getting started immediately on the mimeographed newsletter. Let's take up a collection and elect a three-man editorial staff to write it."

Giap said: "Three people is a right-wing oligarchic structure: you need at least five people."

Riccardo said, "I'm available, but I don't want to be editor in chief. In this way, he immediately appointed himself to the editorial committee.

Furious debate ensued, there was an attempt at voting, and then the following names surfaced, mysteriously.

Tamara, editor in chief, and Riccardo, Giorgia the cross-eyed girl, Baco, and Giap.

"Three men and only two women," said the attractive brunette.

"Yeah, but Baco's a fag," shouted someone from the back of the room.

"This is ridiculous, what are we, in nursery school?" said Tamara, but everyone was laughing loudly and Baco was denying everything, with a series of macho pumping motions.

We were already starting to file out of the auditorium when Lussu shouted:

"So, before we go, are we going to decide whether or not to occupy the school?"

Shit, we'd completely forgotten! But there was no more time for debate. And so, in the last thirty seconds, we hastily resolved that, in the meanwhile, we'd take part in the occupation of another high school, the Guglielmo Volta Vocational High School.

On the way out, the attractive brunette, who, I now saw, was wearing boots, said that she'd really liked my speech, that her name was Marella, she was Umbrian, and where was I from? "From a village nearby," I answered, "but I am looking for an apartment in the city." "So am I," she said. We made a date to go apartment hunting on Saturday, to go looking together for a place to live, a room to rent, a bed. And then, maybe, once we'd found it . . .

I really needed a relationship of some kind. I had no idea what had become of Selene; once, I thought I saw her walking down the street. I ran after her, she turned around, and she was an ordinary horse-faced blonde with a fatuous smile. It wasn't her. Whenever I thought about her, I felt as if I was smashing the duoclock with a hammer; "Stop," I said to the duoclock. "Don't start up with your visionary cinemascope, don't make me suffer." I was leading a fairly barren life; I was studying, washing dishes at the pizzeria, unloading crates of cabbages. I was always running from one place to another, to stay in shape for the soccer team. I had found a street vendor who sold used copies of *Playboy*, and whenever I couldn't get Selene out of my mind, I'd jerk off till I was exhausted. I was sleeping at home less and less; I made do with sleeping on a couch at Verdolin and Schiassi's house, or at the "Hotel Zucchini," that is, on a bench at the fruit and vegetable market, or in some occupied school or other. Whenever the climate of political tension heated up, it was a twofold pleasure for me: the battle is hard and the sleeping bag is soft.

*

On Sundays, I played soccer for Dynamo. It proved to be a better team than anyone expected. We won our first match two to zero, and then we went to play an away game on the soccer field of Montovolo, a town high in the Himalayas, eighty-six hairpin curves in succession, the twelve of us crammed into a baker's van—we puked our souls out, but Philippe Plasticman blocked everything that came his way, even the sparrows in flight, and even though we were weak from oxygen deprivation, we managed to battle them to a tie game, two-all. Then we beat the Libertas Riovado team five to one. They had played with just nine men because they were as ill equipped for away games as we were; they had traveled in a half-ton open-bed truck through the rain, and two players had practically frozen to death. Then, playing on a field of slippery mud where every fall turned into a jolly sleigh ride, we outplayed the yellow devils of the Castellanese team. In other words, we were now the second-ranked team, just one point behind the front runners—the Libertas San Rocco—a very well funded and religiously affiliated team, owned by a leading capitalist in the sugar-beet sector.

Uncle Nevio had promised he'd give us a little bonus, but then he got in trouble with a bad investment. He bought three hundred decoy ducks; as soon as a real duck saw one, it would flap furiously up into the ionosphere and vanish. "The problem is they're the wrong color," said Anselmo, the most respected expert duck hunter in the valley. Whatever the problem, my uncle said, "For now, no bonus, but I promise I'll give you something midway through the championship games."

And so I was pretty much broke, and I had to budget my skimpy funds carefully. I had a date with Marella on Saturday. I was just figuring that if I only had two thousand lire I ought to be able to afford it, when Verdolin told me that he might know about a little work for me. In the city, they were producing a provincial edition of the newspaper published in our regional capital—*La Gazzetta delle Valli*. It was a two-page supplement, and half of it was obituaries. The supplement was written and edited in the city and then sent by train with a superexpress courier package to the main newsroom, where editors and linotypists transmuted those pages into mass media. It may not have been a left-wing paper, but it was the only paper there was. Verdolin had managed to sell them a few illustrations and some cartoons. They were looking for someone who could write and were offering a good, old-fashioned editorial apprenticeship.

I decided to stand up Marella and go in for an interview. The newsroom was in a venerable old palazzo, with a garden and a pond complete with fountain and carp, but it was pretty tawdry nonetheless. A big, smoke-filled room, packed with tables stacked high with papers, photographs, and typewriters. In a closet-sized room to one side, the ANSA news agency teletype was spitting out news at Gatling-gun velocity. At the far end of the room was the office of the supplement editor, Bedisco, a former city councilman who had given up a chance to become a member of the Italian parliament (he said) to fight in the trenches of truth. They hadn't even hired him; he had a terribly ungenerous freelance contract, but It felt like I was talking with Hemingway. He told me that the newsroom, provincial though it might be, was a linchpin in the economic health of *La Gazzetta delle Valli*; moreover, it had been a hotbed of talents, producing such bylines as Farigari, now a Vaticanologist, Billi, who covered first-division basketball, and Baccarini, now the editor in chief of the monthly, *Trees and Flowers*. They couldn't afford to pay much, but I would learn the business, and little by little I'd come to appreciate the undeniable allure of this profession. To start out, I would be given two responsibilities in keeping with my literary studies. Every Sunday night, I'd compile a ranking of all the provincial soccer championships, getting the final scores of the various matches from correspondents, from the ANSA news agency, or by making phone calls myself. On Wednesdays, I could make myself useful by carrying the courier bag with the finished and composed pages to the station, and I could get my feet wet by doing a little reporting.

He introduced me to the newsroom staff.

Scandoli, sports reporter, three packs of Nazi stink-nails a day, merciless critic of the city soccer team, frequently the target of a crossfire of threats from, respectively, the owners and management of the soccer team and from the fan base.

"It's a great profession, but it's dangerous," he said.

Tirinnanzi, crime reporter. His beat was hospitals and police headquarters; he was an expert on all sorts of misfortunes and mishaps, from first-degree murders to moped spills. His moment in the spotlight had come a few years earlier, with the case of the headless body; he immediately pulled out a picture of that, as well as photographs of a man who had been castrated and two suicides dangling from their respective nooses.

"It's a great profession, but you've got to have a strong stomach," he said.

Giason, known as Gagà. His hair was dyed in an intricate stratigraphy of black tar with flame-shaped highlights in a light Doberman shade; he wore an assortment of bowties that looked like beanie propellers. He had been a school teacher as well as a principal; now he covered the political beat, meaning city-council meetings, local controversies, and elections; on the side, he wrote stinging opinion pieces under the pen name of Yanez. He had already outlived—and covered the funerals of—seven mayors.

"It's a completely shitty profession. Why don't you go get laid instead of wasting your time in here?" he said courteously.

Last of all was Fast Nino, society chronicler and feature reporter, an expert on town sausage festivals and local beauty contests, as well as a photographer covering sports, charity balls, and car crashes.

"It's a great profession, but it's exhausting," he said.

And he looked at me as if to say, "You'd never be able to do it."

There was also an array of freelancers, starting with the Illustrious Professor Lavareti Finzi, who submitted fifty typewritten pages once a week on the mosaics in the church of Santa Marta al Colle and then phoned the newsroom every day for the rest of the week, asking why they hadn't been published. There was Signora Virginia, the kept lover of a bigwig politician; she had been awarded a column on astrology, fashion, and local society events. And so on, down the list, a swarm of aspiring writers who'd bring in fifty words on a soccer match, or low-level party hacks bearing press releases, WRP (With Request for Publication).

Every Sunday, I played my heart out on the soccer field, proudly wearing the jersey of the glorious Team Dynamo, then Uncle Nevio would drive me over to my office, where I presided over the weekly sports rankings with the dizzying power of a demiurge. It was a tough job, demanding a clear head and a sense of responsibility. If you overlooked a point or a goal, on Monday morning they'd be on the phone from tiny Roccacannella: "You bastards, print a correction immediately." They tended to be bit less abrasive if you gave them an extra point by mistake. If the final score of a late-night game hadn't come in, then it was my job to make a phone call; I had all the necessary phone numbers for each team: the home number for the owner or the coach, but most important, the town café. Sometimes they answered politely, but other times, especially if they'd lost, they'd tell me to go fuck myself, or occasionally a woman's voice would respond, with embarrassment: "Oh, um, I think our team won, one to nothing, or maybe we lost, six to one. Could you call back when my husband gets home?" If I wasn't certain of my information, I'd have to do some further checking. Otherwise, I'd write: "Final score not available." But an unavailable final score, Scandoli admonished me sternly, means surrendering the public's right to know.

They paid very little, and yet I grew to love that smoky, neurotic world; I had gotten over my dreams of being an American-style journalist who single-handedly defeated the city's over-lords, and I was learning lots of interesting and little-known facts. That in the Fourth Division, the Maturanese team had won every match it had played, earning sixteen points in eight matches, and that there was a certain Brandoli on the team who had already scored ten goals, two more than Roda. That in Vigneto, there was a nine-year-old girl who was Italy's great hope in roller skating. That a treacherous pothole at the corner of Via Oberdan had already felled three bicyclists and several pedestrians, and in the meantime, why was the city government doing nothing? That the sixtieth Festival of the Legume had been a spectacular success with the election of Miss Cannellini Bean, photo to follow. That the mayor of Pontello had been forced to resign in the wake of a scandal over ten demijohns of wine that had been ordered for the celebration of the feast day of the town's patron saint, only to wind up in the mayor's personal wine cellar. Once, I saw a photograph of Fefelli come in, accompanied by an interview: he talked about his campaign for parliament and his tenure as mayor of our little town; under his leadership, the town had modernized, growing from a population of two thousand to three thousand. He talked about the landslide, now safely under control, and the fountain, which would be completed in a few months. The article's lead sentence was: "The long-awaited fountain may be about to arrive." The byline was Nestori. There was no one named Nestori in town, so we had a reporter working undercover. To my astonishment, it turned out to be Tortoise. I had been educated by a spy.

With a thunderous piece of good luck, I found a place to rent. I read an ad in the classifieds: "Room for Rent, via Tognoli 28. Students only." I rushed over and walked up to the door of a house in a neighborhood by the river, a little village of low, one-story houses and narrow lanes. I liked it immediately. Number 28 was a white house, with a little garden and seven wonderful plaster dwarfs. The air was filled with a tantalizing scent of bread and vanilla. I rang the bell next to a label marked "Bacci." The door opened, and I saw a tall woman with a nice, friendly face and zebra-striped hair, white on black. This was Signora Elide.

We talked. The rent was affordable. She said: "You seem like a very nice young man, and what's most important to me is that you're from a small town; we're from a small town, too. We've lived here for ten years. My husband was a woodworker, just like your father. We own and run a pastry shop right behind the house; did you notice the wonderful smell? Your room looks out over the river, there's even a small bathroom; it's tiny but it would be just for you. It doesn't have a shower, but you could shower in our bathroom, as long as you warn us first (*lilting laughter*). The only thing I have to ask, please, no girls in your room. We are three women, the neighbors snoop and gossip, the city is even worse than a small town. I mean, who can imagine what they'll see when they see you, a handsome young man, coming in and out of the house."

"Handsome young man? Three women?" I thought in a daze. "Am I dreaming?"

A door opened, as if in response. The Bacci girls walked into the room. One girl was tall, with a classical profile and long, very long, legs. Her name was Berta; she said hello with composure. The other daughter was petite, rotund, and blond. She looked like a porcelain doll and greeted me warmly; she practically wagged her tail. Her name was Vanina.

"Here are my two precious jewels," said Elide. "You may

notice that they don't look a bit alike. Berta is the daughter of my first husband, the carpenter, while Vanina is the fruit of another relationship, which ended recently."

"A real asshole," said Vanina.

"Don't talk about your father like that. Signor Timeskipper is going to be renting the spare bedroom. He's a hard-working young man; he's studying and working. Both of you, do everything you can to make him feel welcome."

All three of them looked at me with friendly smiles. I don't know why, but I heard a distinctly odd sound, a mixture of purring and the gnashing of teeth. I walked out of the house and, in my imagination, composed three headlines:

LA GAZZETTA DELLE VALLI
Young Man Brutally Murdered and Baked in a Bun
The mystery of the young student who vanished ten days ago has been solved. The carabinieri were given a tip by a woman who recognized the young man from the photograph published in this newspaper; she remembered seeing him enter the house at Number 28 in the Via Tognoli. And there the carabinieri made a gruesome discovery. In the back room of the pastry shop behind the house they found dismembered human limbs, dusted with flour, as well as finely minced flesh mixed with dough, to be sold as sausage focaccia. Personal effects identified as belonging to three different students, one of them a Greek exchange student, were found in an armoire. The three satanic pastry chefs, a mother and two daughters, were arraigned . . .

LA GAZZETTA DELLE VALLI
UFO Lands in a Backyard. Three Women Kidnapped
It's not true, claims a student who was renting an apartment from them, they were three Nevorians and they returned to their home planet. They always treated me well, aside from the slobber on my clothing . . .

LA GAZZETTA DELLE VALLI
Police Raid a Bordello Being Operated by a Seventeen-Year-Old Student

Then my feverish imagination gradually lost its hard-on. It was late, and I had missed the last train. Where could I sleep? It was cold in the train station, Verdolin didn't have a telephone, and the "Hotel Eggplant" was far away. Just then, I remembered that the Guglielmo Volta High School was being occupied. I went straight there; there was a brand-new mural on the wall; I recognized Verdolin's style. Someone had painted a slogan on the wall: BERKELEY IS HERE. Underneath: AND SO IS SASSARI. An exchange of political views between Riccardo and Lussu.

I knocked at the main door. Carpaccio, dressed as a sentry, ushered me in.

"Timeskipper, good man, we need reinforcements, tonight we're afraid the Fascists are going to attack the school."

"Really? Are you sure?"

"You never know," he said with a speculative air.

There were about thirty people occupying the school. There were some familiar faces. I saw Baco, who was cyber-educating the Marxist-FrankZappista boy. Giap was filthy drunk, and I saw Marella, the brunette whom I'd stood up for our Saturday date. She smiled at me. "See?" I thought to myself. "Sometimes it's a good idea to play hard to get."

"I found a place to live," I told everyone. "I'm really happy about it. But I can't move in until Monday."

"So let's celebrate," said Carpaccio. "I'll play for your delectation a song by Crosby Stills Nash and Young."

"I thought you said we were celebrating, not being tortured," said Baco. Carpaccio, in a solo performance, massacred all four American musicians, in what could have passed for a genuine Viet Cong punitive execution.

Then a debate started up on whose turn it was to wash the dishes. Baco sidled over to me; he seemed very upset.

"Timeskipper, I have to talk to you right away; it's something personal."

"Not right now, please. I'm so sleepy I could fall over."

"Okay, not tonight, but remember, I absolutely have to talk to somebody."

I swayed to and fro for a while, and then I declared:

"I'm not trying to be a factionalist, but I need to get some sleep."

"Do you have a sleeping bag?" asked the brunette.

"No."

"I do."

I followed her up the huge staircase; this high school was even older and grimmer than ours, with busts of venerated teachers set in niches in the wall, and a bust of Guglielmo Marconi that had been given a bleached-blond hairdo by Verdolin. Marella led me to a room that must have been an administration office; there were copying machines and desks, and on the wall-to-wall carpeting, scraps of sandwiches and two pairs of panties, in plain view.

"This is one of the warmest rooms in the building," she said. "Here's the sleeping bag."

"Thanks a lot," I said. I hopped in and pulled up the zipper.

"Excuse me," laughed Marella, "but where am I supposed to sleep?"

"Oh," I said, and understood that I hadn't understood.

She turned off the light, undressed, and in the half light I caught a glimpse of an athletic physique; I was duly intrigued. Marella climbed into the sleeping bag, but head first.

"Hey, maybe it's because of the dark, but you're getting in the sleeping bag backwards," I said. "Your head doesn't go in first, your feet go in first."

"And maybe it's you that's getting it backwards," she said lazily. She slipped into the sleeping bag, and this time I understood that it wasn't a position for going to sleep, or at least not right away.

I thought about Selene for only the first six seconds. "You're a swine without any sense of restraint or remorse," I thought to myself. "At last."

7

This marked the beginning of a period of Dionysian abandon. Marella taught me that every part of the body, if properly employed, could procure delights and spasms. It did bother me some that from time to time other guys slipped into that sleeping bag, as she openly confessed, and once I said to her: "You think we should wipe it down?" She shot me an angry glare.

A series of amazing events followed. I felt right at home in my rented room. I finally had a place to live, and the Bacci mother and daughters proved to be quite hospitable. They often asked me to have dinner with them. The meals were banquets, culinary cornucopias of steaming tortellini, savory pies, and cannoli; I immediately gained five or six pounds. If it turned out that they were satanic cannibals and sorceresses, well, I'd deal with that. We became a jolly little family, the four of us and the cat, Teofilo, a feline giant that had been fed on sardines and baked ham. But just as in any happy and respectable family, the disrespectable was lurking just around the corner.

The three pastry chefs worked at night, and took shifts. Two would knead and bake while the third one rested. One night, as I was about to fall asleep, my door swung open and in walked Berta.

"Shut up," she said, rapidly stripping off her clothes.

"Who's talking?" I thought to myself.

In spite of her stern appearance, Berta was a real she-devil in bed. She spread-eagled those long long legs until it seemed as if they filled up the whole room, and then she started muttering under her breath. Gradually, I came to understand that she wasn't talking dirty, she was indulging in a sort of free-form, bawdy poetry, with lines like "Come on, give me your dongalong and sauté my dingaling, oh yes, gallop gallop my fine young colt, your mare is hot, burning hot." But after a while, all this dingalinging made me feel like laughing, and I thought, if she likes background noise, I can do some talking, too, and I said, "You great big slut, I'm going to let you feel my big whole-wheat breadstick."

I don't know if it was because I called her a slut or because I told her I had a whole-wheat breadstick, but she started up and let loose like a locomotive, howling so loud I had to clap my hand over her mouth, and from that night on, her vocabulary got steadily worse. She said things that made de Sade look like an altar boy; in short, we fucked like bunnies and reviewed the dictionary as we went.

The following week, while Berta had the night shift making fruit tarts, my door opened and in walked Vanina, already half naked. She slipped under the sheets, got situated on top of me, inserted the appropriate utensil, and started moving back and forth. The odd thing was that she looked at me and said nothing. She rocked and swayed, back and forth, and never said a word, smiling slightly. I asked her, "Do you like it, or not?" Silence—rocking, swaying, and me on my back, letting her use me as a jungle gym. When I was just about to say, "Listen, doll-baby, are you real or are you plastic?" she suddenly let out a scream like a coyote, and she came in three seconds, biting one of my ears so hard it bled.

"I'm sorry," she said, "I know I'm a little strange; my ex-boyfriend always said I went into a kind of trance."

Trance or no trance, once I figured out how it worked, it was great. I only needed to figure out more or less when she'd start barking like a coyote and trying to rip off my ear. The tell was pretty straightforward: about a minute before the explosion, she always broke out in a sweat. As soon as I saw beads of perspiration on her upper lip, it meant the coyote was starting to circle. I'd cover my ears and enjoy myself.

With three women, I thought to myself, I could consider myself the most satisfied of lady-killers, and after all, did I really miss Selene?

Oh, I missed her, terribly.

But that was another matter, and what's more, there were still surprises to come.

Fred and I had become close friends. He was nice, always cheerful and full of fun, and, aside from his unfortunate habit of zipping between buses at 60 mph, he was a smart boy.

"I know that I go a little crazy when I ride my motorcycle," he said, "but in life you need to do a couple of things recklessly, flat out, without giving it a second thought. At our age, we need to be able to put the pedal to the metal, nail the needle to the far end of the speedometer, floor it and forget about it. There'll be time later on to drive carefully."

He told me that his mother was paralyzed, and that he'd been taking care of her for years. Gradually, the story of his life came out—the two years he'd been unable to study, the slow and painful return to laughter and fun. The one thing that stumped me was why I never saw him with a woman, even though girls flocked after him in clusters.

One morning, we both skipped school. It was a sunny day, and we decided to ride his motorcycle up into the hills. Three minutes and six seconds later, we were walking across a meadow. We stretched out and gobbled brioches made by the Bacci Mother&Daughters Bakery; by now I was a gluttonous pimp of the worst kind.

"You know, Fred," I said, "I have to admit something. I haven't really had many girlfriends, until recently, that is. Only one, and maybe I still love her. Though this month I managed three at once. How many girlfriends have you had?"

"Girlfriends, just two," he answered.

"Huh, I would have guessed more than that," I said.

"Boyfriends, though, plenty more."

I gulped down a two-pound ball of sweet dough. I sat there, frozen, my ass glued to the meadow, prejudices swarming around me like an angry hive of hornets. Sure, I was in favor of sexual liberation. But it's one thing to make a speech at a political rally or read a book by Oscar Wilde, it's another thing to have a faggot friend sitting next to you, a friend I'd had my arms wrapped around as we rode up to the meadow. I felt like I needed to say something.

"Boys . . . in the sense that, um, boys, you mean, like, men?"

It wasn't one of those decisive phrases that shatters taboos and serves to further global sexual liberation.

"Right," said Fred, laughing, "hadn't you figured that out?"

"Uh, no, not really."

"Well, to tell the truth, I'd like to be able to tell everybody, but it isn't easy. Maybe things are starting to change, maybe I can afford to be a little less secretive. But it's a long way from here to living openly, without worries. And so I try to toss out distractions, I crack jokes, I act funny. Don't worry if you're feeling uncomfortable, that's something that happens."

Now he was reassuring me.

"Forgive me, Fred. I was born in a small town. Even my dad and my uncle used to refer to 'that fag the pharmacist.' Then, gradually, they became friends. It takes time to understand things. Now they refer to him by his first name, they call him 'that fag, Nicola.'"

"Sure, you need to know about these things to understand them," said Fred. "For example, there's this place I know, La Gang. We're all bikers, and a lot of us are gay, or fags, whichever you prefer. Even truckers go there, and the odd curious femosexual, like yourself. You want me to take you there?"

"No, I'm not ready for that yet," I admitted, honestly.

We talked for a long time. He told me how he'd figured it out about himself, and that for a week after that he'd stayed in bed, as if he were physically sick. And how happy he was now.

"And do you have a true love?" I asked.

"Sure, but we broke up," he said. "It's been months since I last saw him."

Great. A vision appeared before my eyes. Selene sitting on the back of a motorcycle, arms wrapped around the bare chest of a macho gay guy.

"So . . . what's he like?"

"Handsome, fair-haired, part Norwegian, conceited, a little bit mean-spirited, but sweet as sugar when he wants to be."

"Mine is pretty, blond, half-countrified, a little bit spoiled, and sweet as sugar when she wants to be."

There was a moment of silence.

"And so we're both all alone," I said with a sigh.

"True, but you're not my type," said Fred. "I like tall, strong men." It almost hurt my feelings.

I was learning a lot of important new things working for the newspaper. For instance, that even a little old man on a motor-cycle is still a biker. That if a city-council meeting actually degenerated into a fistfight, then you have to report that there was "a vigorous debate during yesterday's city-council session." That if a poor person with no influential connections is indict-ed, then you report that "he is facing serious charges," and you don't interview him. If, on the other hand, the person being indicted is powerful, you report that "investigations are under-way," and you interview him immediately to give him a chance to provide his side of the story. During that period, Fefelli faced trial on three separate sets of charges, but he managed to slip from one to the next, asking for continuances, claiming that the prosecuting magistrates were conspiring against him. He had no idea that one day in the future, he would be considered a guru and his tactics would be copied faithfully. I discovered that he was the actual owner of the Roselle Holiday Village Development Company, Ltd., in partnership with a certain Arcari, an ambitious and successful financier. Not to mention the fact that Fefelli and Arcari were also partners in the company that had excavated and deforested the mountain. I wondered if these facts were written down in my father's black notebook. But, as Bedisco used to say, "You can't say someone's guilty without evidence; in twenty years as a working journalist, no one's ever sued me for libel."

"Well, of course not," Giason hissed, "he spends all his time shitting his pants, from dawn to dark." Giason seemed to have taken a shine to me; maybe he was curious. He couldn't understand how my love of Edgar Allan Poe fit in with my fanatical soccer activity in Team Dynamo. One day, he pulled a prank. He listed me as one of the top-ranked scorers in the division, with seventy-nine goals; if I hadn't caught it, it would have been a catastrophic blooper. Then he taught me how to concoct filler news items. It often happened that there was no news to report from our little city, and our insert was half empty. When that happened, the solution was to stick in the puff piece by Professor Lavareti Finzi about the mosaics in the church of Santa Marta al Colle, or else widen the photograph of the new deputy police chief, so that it ran over four columns instead of two. But there were times when we needed short news items to fill in a gap at the bottom of a column. When that happened, and we had used up all the reports of people falling off their bicycles or hitting their thumbs with hammers, we had to concoct a filler news item. For example:

Signore Remo Camola, in his home located in the Via Erliobnz (invented, incomprehensible name)*, was moving an armoire when a framed painting fell out of the tall piece of furniture and hit him on the head. He was taken to the hospital for treatment, and subsequently released.*

It was important to make sure he was released immediately, to make sure that none of our readers might check to see if Signore Camola was really in a hospital ward undergoing treatment. Or else:

Bumblebee stings bicyclist, fortunately without serious consequences, etc.

I invented the following spot news item:

Terrifying adventure with a happy ending for little Arturo Bonciarini, eight years of age. While hurtling down the twists and turns of the Via Largo on his go-cart, he suddenly came face to face with the wheels of a large truck heading straight toward him. Luckily, the boy passed right under the truck, and was completely unhurt. For his parents, nothing worse than a bad scare, and a sense of relief at the narrow escape.

"Not bad," said Giason.
The following week, he asked me to dream up another news item, and I wrote:

Terrifying adventure for little Arturo Bonciarini, eight years of age. As he was riding his bicycle along the banks of the Runco river, he suddenly lost control and tumbled down the bank. Luckily, he landed in a waterhole just a few feet deep, which was deep enough to cushion the fall, but sufficiently shallow that he ran no risk of drowning. For his parents, nothing more serious than a bad fright, and a profound sense of relief at the narrow escape.

Two days later, the newsroom received this letter:

Please tell the parents of Arturo Bonciarini not to let him leave the house, or at the very least, to lock up his go-cart, bicycle, and any other means of transportation he might possess. Sincerely, A Concerned Reader.

Luckily, Bedisco didn't notice a thing.

That evening, just to amuse myself, I wrote a piece in which Arturo Bonciarini left his house, got on his bike, and narrowly escaped a dozen different perils: a swarm of bees, a puddle of vanilla ice cream on the street, a lunging bulldog that snapped at his ankles, a soccer ball in the face, a sudden case of diarrhaea while riding up a hill at top speed, a tree branch in the eye, and finally, the culminating incident when his bicycle split in two, and he managed to stop on just the rear wheel, like a circus performer.

I don't even know how it happened, but Giason happened to read the piece, and he said: "Come here, Timeskipper."

I was expecting a finger-wagging lecture, but I got a surprise.

"What I see in your article," he sighed, "is, to my extreme consternation, talent. Authentic, pure, crystalline talent. Something that I never had, do not possess, and can never hope for. When I quit teaching, I was sure that I could write better than anyone else. Unfortunately, I now have to admit that I am a technically proficient writer, but a mediocre one. To see your talent breaks my heart, but it is so evident that I have to say to you: keep at it. Don't squander this gift."

It took many years before I wrote anything of the sort again, but Giason's words lodged somewhere deep inside me. We went out together to get an espresso, and he paid for my cup of coffee at the bar. He told me about his dreams and his books. And I understood that the man I had dismissed with such facile scorn and pity had the same interests and dreams as I did. I felt a wave of shame come over me. From that time forward, Giason was always on my side, and I discovered that behind a flashy bow tie and a ridiculous dye job a poet may be hiding, while behind a poet dressed as a poet, a great emptiness may lie concealed. He gave me several of his short stories to read. They were really good. "Why don't you try getting them published?" I asked him. "It's too late," he said, running a hand over his Doberman-colored hair. "My dear Timeskipper, in the lifetime that lies before you, do your best never to have to say that cursed phrase: 'It's too late.'"

And when I went back to the newsroom, I learned what he meant. There was a spot news headline: "Bicyclist Hit by Car and Killed on the Via Valligiana." Underneath it was a short article: *A local retiree, Mercurio Lollini, 72, better known by his nickname, Karamazov . . .* and then the final words *. . . it was a hit-and-run accident; no one came to his assistance.*

I had meant to go home that Saturday, but I just hadn't done it. The funeral had already taken place. And now it was too late to say farewell to Comrade Karamazov, who was finally going to discover which was better: Russia or heaven.

I phoned my father the next morning; he sounded very sad, and I said, I'll come straight up. My train pulled in on Track 8, ready to pull out again, heading back up to the village. Just as I was about to board the train, I noticed Schillaci, Riggio, and a number of other factory workers from the cement plant stepping down. "Hey," Riggio called out to me, "where are you going? Aren't you coming to the demonstration?" "Demonstration? What demonstration?" I called back. "Well, look what a shitty student you turn out to be; there's a unity protest march today, factory workers in favor of the summit meeting on piecework and high school students protesting the twelve arrests in Turin at

an occupied school. What are you doing, trying to run away?"
And as I looked around, I saw a flood of people pouring out of
the train, carrying red flags. And so I went to my first major
protest march. There were thousands of us. I saw long lines of
factory workers with drums and banners, highly organized; I
saw people watching as we marched by, some looking sup-
portive, others angry and hostile, and others still with the
expression of cows gazing at a passing train. I saw the authorities turn tail, walking away with their heads down, as the
crowd unleashed a hail of derisive whistles. We broke up into
different sections. There were the super-hard-liners, the organized hard-liners, the creative hard-liners, and the chaotic hard-
liners. The group I was in kept to itself; we were generally
known as the anarchic intimists, or as some put it, the fucking
anarchic intimists. For the first time in my life, I caught a whiff
of tear gas. One tear-gas canister landed just a few yards away
from us. Carpaccio gave Verdolin a lemon and told him to
squeeze out some juice and use it to treat his eyes. Verdolin ate
it. I was shouting slogans in a rhythmic chorus with everyone
else; I was already hoarse. I wondered what Karamazov would
have said, I wondered what my father was doing at that very
moment. I wondered whether Selene had heard about the
demonstration, whether she was there, watching from a window above me, if she was worried, upset, or apathetic. I saw
some of the marchers in the long procession throwing punches
and heard a factory worker shout: "Are you with us or against
us?" I heard the crash of breaking glass. Verdolin said to me,
with a gleam in his eye, "There's an art-supply store just up
ahead." "Forget it," I said. I saw Tamara facing down a wall of
police body shields. She stood, eye to eye with a young police
officer, and said: "Let us through, we have every right to
protest in the public square." We gathered around her. The
shield pulled back, a billy club swung down on my shoulder, I
fell to the ground, and I was suddenly afraid. When I got back

to my feet, they were loading Tamara into a paddy wagon; she managed to break free and run away. I saw an overturned car, and inside a shop, a wedding gown in flames. It was a surreal sight; I stopped to stare at it, fascinated, and suddenly we were cut off from the main procession. "Run! Run!" Verdolin suddenly started yelling. "Here come the Fascists." Pouring down a side street and heading right for us were fifty or so kids with handkerchiefs over their faces, armed with crowbars and heavy chains. The police seemed not to see them; one police officer actually turned his back, pretending he was using his walkie-talkie. I hurried into the only shop that was open, a tiny haberdashery. Inside was a little old lady, who was calmly straightening up and arranging her merchandise.

"Please," I said, "don't kick me out of here."

"Why on earth," she said, "do you think I'm keeping the shop open? There're ten other protesters in the back of the shop." And she went on putting buttons away.

Halfway through the school year, I went back to the village for two crucially important events: the showdown between Dynamo and Libertas San Rocco for the division leadership, and the showdown between Uncle Nevio and Sponda for the office of mayor.

Libertas was in first place with seventeen points; we were second, with sixteen points. If we won this match, we had a real shot at winning the championship.

The big game brought more than a thousand spectators to the soccer field; about a hundred, waving cowbells and horns, had come from San Rocco, led by their parish priest. The Libertas team pulled up in a big tour bus. They carried yellow gym bags with San Rocco embroidered on them; they were spectacular. They wore soccer shoes with white stripes. Their jerseys were golden, like the jerseys worn by the Brazilian national team. Our jerseys, faded from repeated wash cycles, looked like bricklayer's T-shirts. But when the whistle signaled the start of play, it became clear that, even though they might have beautiful gym bags and incredible shoes, we were much more pissed off and motivated. We hit a goalpost at ten minutes and another at twenty. At thirty minutes, a wingback knocked a header of mine out of the net with his ass. Then we scored an own goal, a freak shot that involved three unbelievable ricochets. Immediately after that, Roda confidently attempted what looked like an easy goal, but the ball first hit the crossbar and then the goalpost. It was obvious that God was firmly on the side of San Rocco, in the most shameless and openly partisan manner. Their parish priest was watching the match, both hands joined in prayer. There was a direct uplink. The first half of the match ended with Pieroni limping off the field.

"Guys," said Roda, "playing here is like firing a pistol to clean your ass; there's no way. That team has some kind of an unholy bargain with their patron saint," and then he launched into an array of bloodcurdlingly diverse oaths and curses.

We were expecting Uncle Nevio to drop by and say a few words of encouragement, but he never showed.

When we took the field for the second half, we understood why he hadn't been there. He was sitting by the side of the field, and next to him on the bench was our parish priest and the two most spectacularly pious old ladies in town. Uncle Nevio was clearly showing the Great Referee in the Sky that we had influential connections of our own.

The spell was broken. Grillomartino evened the score with a flying overhead kick. Then, on Schillaci's cross, Roda flew into the heavens accompanied by a choir of angels, and with a header, put us into the lead, two to one.

We had snatched triumph from the jaws of defeat. Don Brusco came into the locker room to bless the team. Uncle Nevio gestured for us to quiet down. Then he explained:

"I made a nice little offering for the church, and I also made a promise: that none of you would swear on the soccer field until the end of the championship. Do me a favor, boys, and help me keep my promise."

Uncle Nevio was elected mayor with 58 percent of the vote. Shotguns were fired into the air all night long, the village got collectively smashed, sausage smoke plumed into the air as if Mount Etna were returning to life, the townsfolk sang in chorus, and there was an emotional eulogy for Karamazov.

The first events of Uncle Nevio's administration were a wrenching mixture of bad news and good. The first nasty surprise was that Dynamo was expelled from the championship finals. We received a terse letter from the soccer federation, listing our violations: Plasticman Didí was not allowed to compete because he was not an Italian citizen, Ciccio Mia and Grillomartino had already enrolled in a junior team, neither the soccer field nor the locker room were in compliance with regulations, and the deadline for paying the enrollment fee had already passed. Dynamo vanished from the team rankings, but not from soccer history. Roda was traded to a fourth-division team for one million lire and a new Vespa three-wheeler pickup. Uncle Nevio shared out the million lire among the team members, and he gave the Vespa pickup truck to Plasticman as a gift. Plasticman started a cleaning service in the city, and, to the scandalized astonishment of many, he became one of the first blacks in town to open a bank account.

The second piece of bad, though totally unsurprising, news was that Fefelli was elected to the Italian parliament; he immediately announced that he would be building a new and enormous subdivision with an adjoining golf course next to the Roselle subdivision, with a hydroelectric dam and power station on the river to bring more electric power to the valley. And that meant factories.

Then came the good news. Uncle Nevio checked the

regional laws, and issued an order forbidding any further deforestation on Mount Mario; he swore that he would put a rapid halt to any plans to build a hydroelectric power station, and then he'd send warthogs to root for truffles on the golf course and order the demolition of Villa Meringue for saccharine defacement of the viewshed. Actually, he didn't mention the last two measures in the town-council meeting, he only talked about them in private, with us. Moreover, he announced officially that all the old proposals for the fountain had been rejected, and that a new fountain would be built. The fountain would be an artistic homage to the river, and Chicco and my father would work on the preliminary models, under the supervision of the renowned sculptor of ichthyo-epic fountains, De Pirris, whose family originally came from our village.

We had all been promoted to the next grade, and the summer began. It was racing by far too quickly, lazy times, moonlit nights. We spent time at the café, in the woods, down at the river, and fantasized about Dynamo vs. Milan in a night game. Gancio came back from the beach; he was tanned and had a dragon tattooed on one arm. Everyone else thought he looked great, but I knew the old Gancio, and I could see the difference. The perfect couple, Schiassi-Verdolin, came to the village to visit for a few days. Verdolin, working from an old photograph, sketched a large portrait of Karamazov as a Cossack on horseback to hang over the bar, as well as a nude Sophia Loren, just for Balduino. Tamara came to see me, and we spent the day together. It was weird for me to see her in the water hole, playing and splashing. For some reason, I thought of her as a much more serious person. I respected her, and so I'd made her older in my imagination. But after all, she was only seventeen.

"Timeskipper," she said to me, stretched out on a towel, "you'll never fall in love with me, because I'm not pretty enough, isn't that right?"

"Tamara," I answered, "I'm afraid that's probably true, but I'm sure that lots of other guys will fall in love with you."

"Well, I appreciate your honesty and your kind wishes," said Tamara.

"Let's just hope that Riccardo isn't one of them," I added.

That same evening, there was an open-air town dance and, to my astonishment, I saw Tamara locked in a passionate kiss with Loris Arduini.

I felt like a prophet. But as I watched the dancing couples—Roda and Cee-cee, my father and Regina, Verdolin and La Schiassi, Tamara and the right wingback, Sashay and her violin-playing boyfriend, and Balduino with his mother—I felt an aching surge of anxiety, a knot in my stomach. The rhythm of the accordion triggered the duoclock and it catapulted me back in time, remembering every walnut I ate with Selene, every kiss, every time we made love, every fight we had. I thought: I have to talk about this with someone or my head will explode. I saw Baco and I leapt straight at him.

"Timeskipper," he said to me, "I'm glad you're here. I have to talk to with someone or my head will explode." He'd said it first.

"Look," he started out, in a very serious tone of voice. "This year, my life has changed completely. Unbelievable things have happened to me. You know that I was in love with, or thought I was in love with, Tania, my math teacher. Well, one evening she invited me over to her house. Everything was perfect, white wine, the lights were dimmed, and we started talking about chips and the things that the Americans are doing in Silicon Valley and the future of information technology. She had on a tartan skirt, she's not as young as she once was but she's always had nice legs, so it stands to reason that she had nice legs that evening, as well, and she had had a bit to drink and so . . ."

"And so?"

"And so nothing. Everything was perfect, but I didn't lift a

finger, at midnight I said goodnight and left; there was something that wasn't functioning properly in my emotional chip.
And then I finally figured it out during the occupation of the science high school. You remember that I was talking with a blond
boy, the one with the earring? Well, I looked into his eyes, and I
started sweating, I talked to him and he was listening to me, and
I had a funny feeling, it took me awhile to admit it to myself. The
next day, I wanted to see him again, and one evening . . ."

"Make a long story short, Baco. You like boys," I said, with
the confidence of a man who'd been out in the world.

"Well, I think so. In fact, that's right. But that evening, we
went out, and I realized that he was normal, or I should say,
heterosexual, in other words, there was nothing to be done, or
anyway, I was afraid to try. Does all this freak you out? Will you
still be my friend? What should I do?"

"Baco," I sighed, "you're ahead of the rest of us in cybernetics, but way behind the curve in emotional physics. You just
have to find someone you like to have your first experiences
with, that's all."

"I don't know how to begin," said Baco. "I'm stumped, I'm
confused. What do you think? Do you find me, well, how to
say, decent, moderately manly?"

"You look like Clark Kent," I said assuredly. "You're tall,
strong, you wear glasses . . ." It wasn't quite true, but the main
thing was to build up his confidence.

"Clark Kent, you mean Superboy?" he said, eyes wide
open. "Really? C'mon, you're just making fun of me."

"Baco," I asked, "in your opinion, who are the best-looking
boys in our class?"

"Bobo, but he's a dreary little neo-Fascist, you because
you're here in the flesh, and Fred."

"You have depraved tastes," I said. "Show up tomorrow
evening at the Mephisto Bar. Don't ask me why. Hush. And go
ask a woman to dance, this might be the last time you do."

The next morning I phoned Fred and said:

"You like tall, strong men?"

"Of course I do."

"With glasses?"

"I think glasses are sexy."

"And if they're shy?"

"Nothing better."

"Well, get on your motorcycle and come up to my village, ask where the Mephisto Bar is—there's going to be a party."

"I'll leave at eight o'clock this evening."

That evening, we were all at the Mephisto Bar: me, Baco, Gancio, Nora, and the dark-haired live wires from Messina. I immediately said to Baco, "Fred's coming up to see us, I think he'll be here about ten o'clock." As we were talking, we heard the roar of a motorcycle negotiating the three curves leading into town, then gearing up as it tore along the length of the Roselle straightaway, downshifting as it came into the piazza, stopping to ask directions, and then roaring off at full throttle again, down the hill to the soccer field, and then a right turn toward the Mephisto Bar.

The doors to the saloon swung open, and Fred appeared, in a heavy leather jacket, policeman's hat, and mirrored aviator sunglasses.

"Forty minutes, average speed of just over sixty miles per hour, pretty good, wouldn't you say?"

He'd taken the situation in at a glance. He sat down next to Baco and said to him:

"You know, you look just like that comic-book character."

"Clark Kent?" said Baco.

"No, Richie Rich is the one I mean. The one with the little white dog."

A great deal of beer was consumed, there were joke-telling competitions and imitation contests. I managed to play footsie successfully with Nuccia. Gancio, for once, didn't throw up.

And at the end of the evening, Baco and Fred left together on Fred's motorcycle. I had done my good turn, with nothing in it for me.

I went home, I kneeled in the grass, and I shouted to the heavens:

"God, God, can't you see how good I've been, how lonely I am, how generous I can be? Give Selene back to me." And suddenly I felt a tongue on the back of my neck. It was Rufus. I can interpret divine signs as well as anyone else. So I went to bed and fell sound asleep.

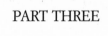

PART THREE

1.

A year was drawing nigh that would go down in the history of the twentieth century, but also in the personal history of Timeskipper. During this coming year, things happening right around me would at times seem much more important than the events that were changing the world as far as the eye could see. It was only later, looking back, that I realized that I was living in the center of a vast galaxy of transformations and discoveries, and that an equal number of surprising new discoveries were being made on my tiny planet at the same time. Signals came down to me from the stars, and I sent other signals back to the stars in response. I understood only one thing: the fundamental force at work in that universe was the attraction to liberty, a force that was sucking everyone in its direction at mind-boggling velocity. There were those who held out, clinging to the dead weight of old ideas or the chains of fear, but others, in the thousands, were flying freely through this new space, some of them traveling comfortably in well-outfitted spaceships, others straddling bucking comets and hallucinations, and others still on wartime missions against the aliens of the System. My two clocks worked hard that year, sometimes in concert, at other times one jabbing its sharp hands into the dial of the other, in a running duel between my personal earthquakes and the temblors shaking the world at large. If that year lasted for many years to come in history, it lasted just as long in my own world of griefs and pains and passions.

After my summer in the village, I went back to my little room in the city, hoping to resume my bigamous consortium. I found a pleasant surprise: a shower in my little bathroom. But I also realized that something had changed. Berta and Vanina were suspicious, they watched every move I made. Only Mamma Elide was as relaxed and sunny as always; she allayed tensions with sesame buns and apricot tarts.

One night, I had just completed an amorous trance with Vanina; she was in the new shower, singing "Quando dico che ti amo credi a me" (T. Renis). The door flew open, and Berta walked in.

"My love," she said, "I couldn't stand to stay downstairs. Mamma went to buy some candied fruit, I closed up the shop. Let's do it, and quickly, I'm dying for you."

As usual, I thought of three possible ways out of the situation.

One: I contracted a venereal disease this summer, you can catch it just from breathing the same air as me. Run, and save yourself.

Two: I hear noises in the pastry shop, I happen to know that a dangerous gang of cream-puff thieves is operating in the neighborhood, let's hurry down and take a look.

Three: I'm not an earthling, I'm a Nevorian, and this is the one day of the week in which I have no functioning sexual organs.

But there was no time: Vanina strolled naked out of the shower. Berta screamed, Vanina ran after her, and I thought: "Starting tomorrow, I'm going back to my cot at the Hotel Melanzana."

But nothing happened.

Our little ménage à trois went on as nonchalantly as before. I don't know what sort of agreement the diabolical sisters had come to; neither one would talk about it, and I continued to be shared property.

One night at the fruit and vegetable market, I was unloading crates from a flat-bed truck, and there was a cloudburst, and I was working in shirtsleeves. The next day I had a fever of 102 degrees. I hadn't had a fever like that since my bout with growth-inducing diphtheria. I climbed under the covers. I was lavished with loving care and nourishing broths; even the cat came to see how I was doing, and slept on the bed. What more could I ask?

After a week, the fever dropped. I decided that I would laze around for one more day, then I would return to school. It was a quiet afternoon, an aroma of cream beignet wafted me into a peaceful intermittent slumber. Signora Elide entered the room with a cup of tea and an assortment of bite-sized pastries.

"Our Timeskipper is all better," she said. "Such a fine strong boy," and she started to stroke my hair in a not entirely appropriate manner.

"Yes, I feel better," I answered, drawing back.

"Well," she said, with her hands on her hips, "now that I've nursed you back to health, don't I deserve a little reward?"

I didn't answer. It couldn't be true. Signora Elide was still appetizing, but as it is customary to point out in cases of this sort, she was old enough to be my mother.

"Oh, come on," said Elide, impatiently, "are you going to tell me that only my daughters get to have any fun, and I have to say down in the shop and work all day?"

"Fun, pardon me, ma'am, but what do you mean by fun?"

"Oh, young man," said Elide, grabbing me confidently in an area that had recently been occupied only by the thermometer. "I know perfectly well that you've been making love to both of my daughters. I knew it from the beginning. But now it's my turn."

I closed my eyes. I put up no resistance. My performance struck me as unexceptional at best, but it must have satisfied Signora Elide, because she said: "Now we're even," and she left the room, adjusting her bra strap as she went.

An incestuous convalescent, I tiptoed away from that house. I understood that I could never go back. Two I could deal with, three would be too many, and after all, there was always the danger that a grandmother might turn up. Tamara lived in a commune; I asked her if I could stay with them for awhile. They set up a cot for me in the kitchen; all night long people stepped over me on their way to consult with the refrigerator, but I got used to it.

As for Number 28, Via Tognoli, I had left a note with the last month's rent and I had fled like a thief in the night. But I couldn't abandon them without a farewell, so I went back one last time.

Berta met me at the door, with a grim expression on her face.

"And so you took advantage of us, had your fun, and left without a word," she said.

"Well, actually, you started it," I defended myself. "But recently, the situation was becoming a little too complicated."

"I'm pregnant," Berta blurted out.

I gaped like a fish.

"That's impossible," I said, "we always used a condom."

"I tore a hole in it. I knew you would leave sooner or later. I love you too much to let that happen."

She threw her arms around my neck.

And I understood what a catastrophe I had triggered. Those few nights of embraces had been a minor pleasure for me, but for this girl they had perhaps been the dream of her life. I had been blind and selfish. But I was too young to climb so steep a mountain. And so I said: "I need some time to think this over," and for the second time I fled like a thief into the night.

For the next week, I practically lapsed into a wordless coma. My friends asked me if I was on drugs. They tried everything they could think of to snap me out of it. Fred and Baco took me to Club La Gang and I danced the samba with a transvestite who looked like the Madonna of San Luca. Marella performed a series of acrobatic stunts that nearly snapped us in half, and I just stared at the ceiling. I had discovered a very simple fact of life: that there are responsibilities that you accept with courage and determination, and there are others that fall on you from the sky, incomprehensible and weighty, and you have to face the ones you didn't ask for just like you do the others.

I decided to talk about it with Tamara. She seemed like the only person I knew who could understand. Or maybe Regina would, too, but I felt a little shy of her, and I was afraid of what my father would say.

Tamara was at home, in bed.

I walked in; her face betrayed suffering. It looked like she had been crying, sobbing, actually.

"Timeskipper," she said to me, "I feel awful. I have to tell you something. I went to Switzerland for an abortion. I took a train in the morning and I was back by evening, it was all organized for me by women I know who are involved in this sort of thing. They helped me, and I think I did the right thing. But I feel horrible just the same, and my head is filled with black thoughts."

I stayed with her all night. We talked until dawn.

The next morning, outside of my school, I saw Berta. She thrust a note into my hand, turned, and fled.

"Forgive me," the note said. "I'm not pregnant, it was a lie I told to punish you, my revenge because you left me. I was suffering. I really did love you. I wish you all the best, Berta."

And so I discovered how many other intimate and painful deities I had summoned in my Dionysian period. I thought of Selene, about the possibility that she might have suffered over me. I had never really thought about it before, the only thing that had mattered to me was the pain that I felt. I threw myself into my studies and books, I read all night long, I devoured Melville and Gadda, Satanik and Foucault, the South Americans and Pasolini, and I listened to the Beatles and the Doors on a compact Gelosino tape player. Even through the static and crackling, sounding far away, every song was a new discovery. Then I moved on to Mozart and jazz and Celtic folk music; I was omnivorous and insomniac. Tamara's commune had emptied out, and now I had a room of my own. Marella was going steady with Riccardo. I was alone, and I was spending more time in *La Gazzetta delle Valli* newsroom. Now I had a friend there, good old Giason, who was about to have some of his short stories published by a small independent publisher. But the rest of the staff hated me, or at least that's what I thought; maybe a rumor was spreading that I was a subversive, infiltrating the newspaper to sabotage the typewriters and replace the old keys with new keys in Cyrillic.

One evening, I was sorting through the ANSA wire service news items when I saw a news flash that took my breath away. A certain Signorina Federica Cinti, none other than my old friend Fulisca, had reported a clockmaker to the police for rape. He denied everything; he was married, with children. Soon two photographs came over the wires. She looked even younger than I remembered her, and he was a pudgy little man.

"With this story," Bedisco said immediately, "we're going to cook up a nice scandal. We've got all the spicy ingredients: a pretty young girl, a rape, a respectable citizen, and a smoldering doubt. It'll split the city in two."

"Doubt? What doubt?" I said. "I know this girl, she's a friend of mine, she'd never tell a lie."

"We'll see about that, or rather, the judges will see about that," said Bedisco. Just then, the phone rang. A special correspondent was arriving from the main newsroom, a certain Milio, an ambitious thirty-year-old reporter who had already nabbed two or three scoops: the murder of the blind contessa, the December-May same-sex orgies along the riverbanks, the anarchist cell in the florists' union.

I went to the hospital to visit Fulisca, but I wasn't allowed to see her. A nice doctor told me that she was in pretty bad shape. "She's an epileptic," he added. "What happened to her has aggravated her condition."

Now I knew the name of Fulisca's disease. I left some flowers and a book for her. I went back to the newsroom. Milio had arrived, beautifully dressed in a sky-blue double-breasted suit, with scented hair that didn't look real, and a yachtsman's tan.

"So, then, young man, you're a friend of the alleged rape victim," he said. "What do you say to a little chat? What was she like in your home town, did she have a lot of boyfriends, what did people say about her . . . In exchange, I'll teach you how to put together a front-page scoop."

"She's a friend of mine, she's not well," I answered. "She's not a front-page scoop."

"Of course," he said, "I'm very familiar with the code of professional ethics. I'd never write anything disrespectful about your friend. But the man has to have a chance to defend his reputation. He's sixty years old, he's worked all his life, he has two children."

"And he's the archbishop's brother," Giason pointed out.

"No one asked you," Milio said brusquely. "So, you say your friend is sick?"

"She is epileptic," I said.

"Very interesting, a human-interest story," said Milio. "Scandoli, you go to the hospital. Nino, you go get pictures of his family, especially the younger son, if you can. Tirinnanzi, draw up a list of rapes in recent years. Giason, you . . ."

"I'm going to the movies," said Giason. "I know exactly what you're going to write." He put on his overcoat and walked out of the newsroom.

Two days later, the newspaper published Milio's professionally ethical article. Fulisca was depicted as a hysterical nut. It reported that while she was in the throes of her epileptic fits, she had no idea of what she was doing, and that afterwards she couldn't remember a thing. The clockmaker was described as a weak but good-hearted man.

Of course (the article concluded) *it's up to the jurors to hand down a verdict. But there a few things we can say. We should not make judgments based on a hasty, instinctive reaction, or allow ourselves to be led astray by this new aggressive and frustrated feminism. On the one hand, we must preserve our necessary respect for a troubled and diseased girl who may not be responsible for her own actions. On the other hand, we must consider a man whose life is being ruined by an inflammatory accusation. I repeat, we are not the judges. But we can say that it is easy to make an accusation of rape, and that relations between a man and woman are often a sphere of ambiguity, in which pleasure and violence can coexist. I believe that the city should observe the progress of this trial in an objective and calm spirit; that is how our newspaper will cover it, without any partisan favor or hypocritical poses.*

I was trembling with fury when I walked into the newsroom. Milio was talking on the phone; the editor in chief was praising him for the piece. Bedisco was gazing at him with adulation and envy.

"Hey there," said Milio, "here's our subversive."

"Nice article, Milio," I said, "nicely balanced and very engaging." He swelled up like an inner tube.

"Watch and learn," he said.

"I have a clock," I said, "that works in a rather unusual way. You and I will meet again. I don't know what I'll be when we do, but I know what you'll be. A sack of shit, a Fascist, and a bootlicker."

"Get out of this newsroom, you little bastard," shouted Bedisco, and he threw a ream of paper at me. Milio hadn't blinked an eye.

"It may interest you to know," he said, "that I have a pistol in my jacket pocket."

"Then you can stick that pistol up your ass," I said.

And that was when I had my second surprise. Scandoli, the sports reporter with an inflated pigskin brain, the one who was basically indifferent to everybody and everything, said: "Milio, you disgust me, too. You didn't use any of the quotes from the doctors at the hospital. If the clockmaker hadn't been the brother of the archbishop, and if she hadn't been a poor country girl with no connections or influence, would you have written that piece? You're just like the referees who cater to the big, rich teams. You don't play fair, and if I had anything to say about it, you wouldn't be playing for any newspaper in the league."

"You get out of here, too," said Bedisco.

"Oh, I already have another job," said Scandoli, "as a publicist for *Giro delle Valli*. Both of you can go fuck yourselves. Timeskipper, you damn Communist, let's get out of here; you can buy me a drink."

That was the end of my adventure at *La Gazzetta delle Valli*, and there was a personnel shuffle in the newsroom. The clockmaker was acquitted on all charges, Fulisca wound up in a clinic. She didn't recover until many years later. The battle for the public's right to know had ended in defeat.

The year burst into flames. More and more schools were being occupied. It happened at our high school, too. The first day we blocked the front door. Dearly Departed tried to get in; she didn't understand what was going on. She asked someone, and they threw a notebook at her.

"You assholes," I said. "She's my philosophy teacher; she's a good person."

"There's no such thing as a good teacher," said Paolo Lingua. "They're all cogs in the system."

"That's not what you're going to say twenty years from now on your television news show," I said.

"What the fuck are you talking about?"

I walked Dearly Departed to the bus stop. She asked me what was going on.

"We're all a little worked up, Signora."

"Read Seneca, Timeskipper. You'll calm down."

I went back and stood outside the school. Somebody whistled at me in derision. Fred and Tamara came to my defense, some punches were thrown, and while we were shouting slogans at one another, fifty or so policemen dressed for combat duty in Vietnam assembled in half a minute. They charged into the school and pulled us out, one after another, dragging us by our ankles and then beating us with clinical precision. They clubbed me on the knees, they broke Paolo Lingua's nose. I couldn't take much pleasure from that; I wished I had been able to do it myself. "While we bicker, they measure us for a cell, or a coffin," said Fred, supporting me as I limped along. One of my ribs hurt like hell. I could barely walk. The cops kept on beating students.

"Look at that," shouted Fred at the top of his lungs, "that blond policeboy sure has a nice ass."

The blond police officer came running straight at us, his face a study in fury. He caught up with us in an alley crowded with bicycles. He raised his billy club, but Baco, who had run after us, got him in a half nelson from behind. The two of us held him captive while Fred gave him a passionate kiss on the mouth, pressing in under the visor of his helmet. It was the most unusual and effective street-guerrilla operation it was ever my privilege to witness. The policeman took to his heels as if we had doused him with napalm.

2

A pril turned to May. Reports were arriving of vast civil unrest in France. One Sunday, we were sitting around in the commune watching television—there was an interview with Sartre—when Verdolin came running in, his eyes wide with excitement.

"Comrades, a request. I wonder if you'd let me take a look at the latest soccer scores."

The motion was denied, six votes to three, and Sartre was allowed to continue his interview.

"The radio," shouted Verdolin, "your transistor radio!"

He ran headlong into my bedroom, turned on the radio; we sat there for a few minutes, waiting. I didn't understand what was going on. Then the voice of the news announcer read the soccer scores. He sounded more or less like the cheerful God.

Verdolin shouted for joy and wrapped me in a bear hug.

We'd hit a small jackpot in that week's soccer lottery. For years, we had always played the same combination of teams and scores, and we'd never matched more than ten. This time, we'd matched twelve, not an astonishing achievement in statistical terms, but it was astonishing for us. We would be receiving almost two million lire, well over a thousand dollars, to split three ways—for me, him, and Fred.

We immediately started making plans.

Fred said he'd spend three hundred dollars to soup up his motorcycle the way he wanted it, a hundred on gifts for friends and relatives, and a holiday in Amsterdam.

Verdolin was going to buy a loden overcoat for La Schiassi, who had been pining after one for the past year; he was going to splurge on paints, and he was going to take a trip.

I said: four hundred dollars in savings, and a week in Paris.

"Paris," Verdolin said, "Good idea, you and me."

"You and me and La Schiassi," I thought to myself.

Instead, La Schiassi gladly accepted the loden, and said: "I can't go to Paris, I have to study, I'm failing two subjects, you go with Timeskipper."

Verdolin almost had a mental breakdown: for the past four years, they had been taking turns breathing, one of them had the systolic heartbeats, the other had the diastolic heartbeats, they were practically joined at the hip. And now an entire week apart was looming ahead.

"It'll do you good to get out on your own," I said.

"Certainly, Valerio, it'll do you good," she agreed.

"Are you two having a secret affair?" asked Verdolin.

"If we were lovers," I said, "we'd be sending you off to Paris by yourself."

"Oh, right," said Verdolin. For three nights, he couldn't sleep a wink, then he finally made up his mind to go, and we left aboard a night train, the first real trip I had ever taken.

I was on the top couchette, he was on the bottom, and we had all the energy of our youthful years, eight panini with mortadella made by La Schiassi with her sainted little hands and two bottles of bubbly mineral water, with the blessings of Saint Pellegrino.

I was happy, thrilled, weighed down with books by Hemingway, Rimbaud, Baudelaire, and Aragon, as well as maps and bilingual dictionaries. Verdolin had a box of colored pencils and twenty or so photographs of La Schiassi, including one from when she was just six.

During the train trip, he had his first attack of Schiassitis. Gasping for air, he said: "Why did she let me go? If she's sick of me, she could at least have said so to my face. Women are treacherous, evidently she just couldn't take having me around anymore, she was eager to get rid of me, she packed my suitcase herself, when I get back she'll have had the locks changed and my belongings will be out on the landing with a note: 'I hate you, you and all your shitty drawings . . .'"

"Verdolin, cut it out," I said, "or else I'll start farting until you lose consciousness."

"You're right, maybe I'm taking it a little too far," he said, and tossed and turned all night long.

We pulled into the Gare de Lyon and headed for the Hôtel des Beaux Arts on foot. We had no idea how far it was, and it was quite a hike, as it turned out, but we were in Paris. I drank in every piece of writing my eyes encountered, every shop sign, every oyster, every bookstore. Everything I saw seemed prettier and more colorful, from the newspapers in the newsstands to the baguettes sticking out of the shopping bags like magic wands. The dog shit on the sidewalks seemed to be so many Impressionist brushstrokes. Verdolin completely ignored all those exquisite Parisianitudes and kept walking faster and faster; he had happened to notice a blond pseudo-Schiassi and now he absolutely had to call back to the homeland. We stopped at a phone booth, he pulled out a handful of Italian phone tokens and suddenly realized, with dawning horror, that they wouldn't work here. I managed to drag him, resisting, all the way to our small hotel, located on a narrow street redolent with aromas of roast meats, spices, and a fragrant tossed salad of humanity. There were people of all races; I drank in the features of every face.

"Verdolin," I said, "here you have the whole world in front of you, waiting to be sketched."

"First, I have to make that phone call," he said.

I dialed the number for him, the phone rang, he spoke to her. I reckoned that this would give him roughly six hours of oxygen.

And so, after the call, we went out walking, tipsy with Paris. I immediately saw that a famous person had lived in every house we passed, a poet had sat musing in every bar, an important person had died in every hotel. I went to take a pee and thought to myself that, at the very least, I was retracing the drops of Picasso. Verdolin vanished into a comic-book emporium in the Boulevard Saint-Michel, I wandered all through the Latin Quarter and then climbed up as far as Place de la Contrescarpe, looking for literary sites and references. The pages I had read became houses, squares, churches. The sky was a book cover.

That night we dined on shish kebab, and then we selected a bar with a fine view of the passing *jeunes filles*, and ordered a couple of *bières*. There was such an endless procession of certified Parisian babes that it made my head spin. But Verdolin had run out of Schiassixygen. He had providently stocked up on French coins and now he began a duel with a French phone booth. I sat there trying to imagine which bar tables Verlaine or Kopa had sat at, I looked for traces, like a hair or a poem scribbled on a napkin. In the sky, clouds were scudding past, dragged by the north wind, two young boys with guitars were singing "Blowing in the Wind" (R. Zimmerman), and I thought to myself, what more could a small-town boy ask for, now that he has reached the world's capital of literature and enchantment?

Then Françoise appeared.

She had long, silky hair, faded jeans that clung to her hips, and a narrow wasp waist. She wore a pink T-shirt with a red rose and the phrase: *Parlez-moi d'amour*.

She was with a mulatto girlfriend, with a big, beautiful nose and a big, beautiful physique. They sat down at the table next to mine and ordered *pommes de terre à l'huile* with an enchanting French accent (actually, now that I think about it, it wasn't a French accent, they were just speaking French). The waiter served them immediately, though he had ignored us for ten minutes. I saw Verdolin furiously trying to damage the receiver in the phone booth.

"*Stai calmo*," I shouted at him.

"Italiano?" said Françoise, with a perceptive deduction.

"Picked up in Paris," I thought to myself: what could be better?

"Oui," I replied.

"De Roma?"

"Further north," I said. "*Village très bello avec bocu des arbres. Châtaignes. Beau fium.*" I knew that if I just talked fast some of my mistakes would go unnoticed, "*Et vous conoscez bien l'Italie?*"

"Oh yes," she said, "the last year, I was one month in Venice, Florence, and Rome."

"My name is Timeskipper," I said, "and the guy kicking that French phone booth is my friend Valerio."

"I am called Françoise, she is Lorette. She is from Martinique. Ever been in Martinique?"

"I've never even been to Cesenatico," I felt like replying.

"No," I said, "but I've heard good things about it."

"What is wrong with *ton ami*?" asked Lorette, as she watched Verdolin swear and gesticulate *chez la cabine*.

"He is terribly in love with his girlfriend. If he can't phone her, he goes into *una crisi*, he *devien fou, tu comprend*, out of his *tête*."

"Oh, you Italians," said Françoise languidly, "always in love."

Her big French mouth was twice the size of any Italian mouth, or at least that's how it looked to me. She was seventeen years old, and she was studying music, *violon*, or violin, to be precise. Lorette was eighteen, and she was studying *pianò*. And what about me? I was finishing school and working as a journalist, minor *reportages*, and I was in Paris on a scholarship from the state soccer lottery.

Verdolin came back to the table.

"She's not at home," he said, and it looked like he was about to faint.

"What number did you call?"

"This one." And he showed me a slip of paper.

"What about the country code?"

"Country code?"

In the end, Lorette helped Verdolin to phone Serena, and the conversation went: "Valerio, I love you, I miss you, what are you two doing, are you alone?" and if he had been honest with her, he would have said, "No, I'm with a mulatto girl with a spectacular ass, but that doesn't matter because I love you," but instead he said: "Well, you know, Timeskipper is pretty depressed, he'd dreamed for years of bringing Selene to Paris, so now he's feeling kind of blue, but I'm cheering him up, sleep tight my love, and the dog, how is the dog? Fine, and are you thinking about me? Every minute, me, too, I'll talk to you tomorrow. What was that noise? Oh, the dog knocked over the saucepans? All right my love, good night, till tomorrow."

After this telephone communication, Verdolin calmed down, he drew a magnificent caricature of Lorette and a group of Italian tourists stopped to watch, clamoring, "Draw us, too, draw us." He said, "Well, actually, I'm not a professional artist," but in the end he sketched a big, horsey woman from Milan and pocketed a hundred francs, the sly dog.

"Shall we go dancing?" asked Françoise, stretching and arching her back, her breasts in magnificent display.

"If possible, in a club with a phone," said Verdolin.

We went dancing in a club near the Place de la Bastille, and there I saw Françoise moving her body in ways that I thought I'd only see in movies or at the Crazy Horse, and everyone made a point of *not* watching her, because, in contrast with the way things are done in Italy, when a Frenchman is excited or horny, he pretends he is indifferent; on the other hand, if he pays attention to someone or looks at someone, it means he isn't interested. Which, now that I thought about it, meant that Françoise didn't like me, because she bothered to speak to me at the bar in the first place.

We left the club, walked off, all four arm in arm, into the night, and finally fetched up at the Pont Neuf, which is actually a very old bridge, though it's called the "New Bridge." Beneath its expansive archways flowed the Seine, lit up that evening by a silvery moon. Françoise asked:

"Who will sing me a *canzone italiana?*" Verdolin looked at me as if to say, "No, don't ask me to betray La Schiassi."

So I sang her "'Na sera 'e maggio," Regina's favorite, then I sang "Bella Ciao" (political folklore), and then "Una lacrima sul viso," because I could really hit the deep notes, like that Elvis imitator, Bobby Solo.

Françoise's eyes were glittering like little fish, and she stared straight at me; evidently she liked me less and less. We made a date for the next day in her neighborhood, Ménilmontant, a short distance outside central Paris. "Not so many tourists, more authentic," she said. When we said goodnight, she gave me a close-lipped kiss.

"Then it's true, she hates me," I thought. But I still dared to hope.

I couldn't sleep at all that night. Françoise's mouth was tormenting me. Verdolin had brought a Minnie Mouse alarm clock, a gift from Serena. The tick-tock triggered my duoclock, in a cultural variant. Picasso knocked at the door of our hotel room, shouting: "Leave my model Françoise alone, you *Italien de merde*, if she's in love she can't pose properly." And I said, "Monsieur Picasso, just focus on your abstract work for a few days and quit busting my balls, okay?" Next I saw Rimbaud riding behind Fred on his motorcycle, tearing along the Boulevard Saint-Germain at 110 mph. Fred was saying, "Arthur, why worry? You're going to die young in any case." And I saw a bookshop with two books in the window. One was *Contes* by Giason, and the other was *Les aventures de Mickey Marx*, illustrations by Verdolin, text by Timeskipper. Then my fellow artist woke up, writhing in an unprecedented agony of Schiassitis. He turned on the little lamp on the bedside table.

"That noise," he said.

"What noise?"

"While I was talking to her, in the phone booth, I heard a noise, and she said the dog knocked over the saucepans. But she never lets the dog get near the saucepans."

"But she was on the phone, and the dog took advantage of the fact that she was distracted."

"But she didn't say, 'Bad dog, get away from the saucepans.' So it wasn't the dog, it was somebody else, cooking something."

Verdolin's eyes glittered in the half-darkness; his face no longer looked quite human. "So who could it have been?"

"Verdolin, go fuck yourself, you're ruining our holiday."

"Someone was there with her, in the apartment. I have to go back. I can't stay here, I'm dying."

"Another famous artist dies in another Parisian hotel," I said, and turned my back to him.

He laughed a throttled little laugh. He muttered and wheezed for a few minutes more, then dropped off to sleep. At six-thirty the next morning, he woke Serena up, and the phone call reassured him. We drank a watery French espresso and ate some exquisite croissants, we saw two or three museums, where Verdolin explained to me that it might seem easy to sketch poppies in a wheat field, but actually it isn't. We bought a copy of *Libération* (foreshadowing) and the headline said: "Tomorrow, Major Protest March, *Camarades*, Everyone Make Sure to Attend."

"Just think," I said, "an authentic, major, French protest march. Riccardo would die of envy."

"Serena would have loved to see this," sighed Verdolin.

We took the Metro and got off at Ménilmontant. It really was old Paris, there were *clochards* and faces that were almost too Parisian; I assumed they were bit actors with walk-on roles. Françoise's house was tiny, it had miniature radiators and a mini-toilet that seemed made for gnomes, but when you looked out the windows you saw the roofs of Paris. She played her *violon*, and as she played her hair draped over her arm, swinging sensuously back and forth as she bowed. Her mouth had gotten bigger since the night before. Then Lorette showed up. We went out to have some spicy couscous, and Verdolin got drunk on beer. Serena had never tasted couscous, he was sure of it, and eating it alone made him feel horribly guilty.

Then we went back into the house to decide where to go next. But I saw Lorette take Verdolin by the hand; she was saying to him, "Come over here, I want you to sketch a nice *chaton* for me," *chaton* being French for a cat, and so I was left alone with Françoise, and she turned the lights down low.

Then she put on a record called "Et je entend siffler le train" (A. Barrière, the French version of "Five Hundred Miles"). Then we kissed, and her mouth, let me say it again, was twice the size of a normal Italian girl's mouth, so it had to be kissed starting from either side and working in toward the middle; it was quite a production.

Then she took off her clothes, and it was almost more than I could take.

Selene had quite a nice little body, but she wore what you might call standard-issue lingerie, white bra and panties. Instead, Françoise had a bra made of peach-pink lace and skimpy matching panties, so skimpy that my heart started racing, and I said: "Ah, *attend un moment, trop de couscous.*"

She seemed disappointed, perhaps heartburn wasn't what she'd been expecting from her Latin lover, and when I say, Latin, I don't mean like Cicero, more like Mastroianni.

She turned to light an interlocutory cigarette, and as she did so, I saw her ass gleam in the shadows.

The Italian national anthem resounded throughout the *quartier,* followed by "Bella ciao" and "'Na sera 'e maggio," and I leapt onto her like a wild beast with a ravening hunger for peach-pink.

The Italy vs. France match was a heart-stopper; both sides played their hardest all night long, stopping only for a drink to bank the fires of the couscous, and then back to *baiser,* that is, screwing, and *allez* again, a drink, and *allons* counter to nature, and back to the bathroom and *allez* fuck me one more time, and I was almost running out of steam, but I thought to myself: if I die, all the better, maybe they'll bury me at Père Lachaise near Jim Morrison (premonition); back in Italy, the very best I could hope for would be for a grave plot next to the drummer for the Maccarons. Meanwhile, Verdolin was talking to Lorette about Serena and then Lorette finally fell asleep, as is customary back in Martinique when you're bored out of your skull.

The next day, Verdolin took the first train back to Italy. I didn't go to the demonstration. I spent the next three days and nights fucking with Françoise, leaving the house only to gulp down a quick croque-monsieur and to take a look at the used-book stands and replenish our supply of beer and condoms, both of which we were consuming at quite a clip.

And that was the beginning of the French May of 1968, which I missed completely, lying locked in the arms of some ordinary Françoise who was actually not ordinary at all.

On the train, returning home, I felt strange. Françoise and Selene were dancing in my head, changing places as if in a minuet, billing and cooing, one blond and the other brunette. The difference was that I was terribly saddened by the idea that I'd never see Françoise again, even though we had exchanged addresses and sworn that we'd meet again. But what hurt me even more—in fact, made me feel like I was dying—was the idea that I'd never see Selene again for the rest of my life. I was lovesick, not as bad as Verdolin, but nearly.

I returned to the homeland.

Back at school, everyone asked me: "Hey, how about that, you were right in the middle of the big mess in Paris, tell us what it was like."

"Comrades, could I have your attention for a moment. Comrade Timeskipper, who took part in the Paris demonstrations, will now provide us with a political report on his experiences."

No one knew it, but on the train coming back from Paris, I had carefully read all the newspapers, both Italian and transalpine, and I had cribbed quite thoroughly.

"The French have bigger mouths than the Italians," I began, "and the noise was deafening. At the head of the procession was a long, red banner, somewhat faded from the many battles it had survived. The red had become a sort of pinkish peach, and on it was written: *PARLEZ-MOI D'AMOUR.*"

A murmur arose from the audience.

"Just kidding. The banner said: *CE N'EST QU'UN DÉBUT.*"

And so I told them all about the French May of 1968, and they all listened happily, and by the time I was done, I had almost convinced myself that I really had taken part. After all, as Che Guevara put it, *"El revolucionario verdadero está guiado por grandes sentimientos de amor."* No one ever found out my secret. Only Giap asked a few probing questions, and wanted to know what Sartre was like.

"He looks just like a frog," I answered.

The school year ended with a huge political falling out. Tamara's group and Riccardo's group broke apart, with reciprocal accusations of childish behavior, opportunism, and book stealing. I shifted my identity and was seen, variously, as the guy who read Eliot, or the one who had seen the French May of 1968, or an unaligned anarchist, or the kid with the Communist dad. This cocktail of affiliations and identities allowed me to argue with everyone, but also to converse with them. The ones with whom I preferred talking politics were Tamara or Lussu. I hated taking part in political meetings, I much preferred to feel that I was part of something that flowed and shifted and you never knew what might happen, and then, gradually, incrementally, it became clear who really was at your side, who really had the strength of their convictions. What I wanted from politics, and not just from politics, could be summed up in a phrase: "You need to resemble the words that you say." Maybe not word for word, but I think we both understand what I'm trying to say here. There were some who spoke beautifully, but for some reason, I didn't believe them; my duoclock told me: "In a year, or two, or ten, this guy will give up; if things go well, he'll just hang up his shoes, but in the worst case, he'll go over to the enemy team entirely." There were others who never said much, like Lussu or Tamara, or who spoke naïvely, like Fred or La Schiassi, but I could tell that behind their words was something that they would do, one day or another. This sensation stuck with me for the rest of my life.

School ended, and I managed to pass and move up to the next grade by the skin of my teeth. I went back to my little town with half my winnings from the soccer lottery and a bundle of lies about Paris. It was already July. My father was busily absorbed in carving a bunch of beautiful pikefish for the fountain, Uncle Nevio was obsessed with trout fishing and spent his days making lures, fashioning fake flies out of the ass fur of wild hares. Gancio and Osso were at the beach. In those days, mass vacationing was experiencing a boom in Italy. Balduino and Sashay's bar was filling up with postcards wishing us "Greetings from the Adriatic Riviera!" with sails, sunsets, and girls' asses; postcards arrived even from as far away as Positano to the south and the Matterhorn to the north. The highway was a solid line of cars. Nowadays, nobody went down to the river except for little kids I'd never met. I considered going on another trip, maybe on my own this time. Once I called Françoise, but a voice answered that she was in St. Tropez. Well, lucky her. A muggy loneliness surrounded me and wore me down. And so I climbed up to the basin of the Fanara.

I looked out over the valley, and I noticed that the sky had changed color. It was gray, the smoke from the factories and the indigestion of the cars had smudged the sky. You could no longer see the peaks of the Monti Alti, the high mountains. To the east, two huge cranes were working on a new holiday subdivision. To the west, a television relay tower was going up. But up where I was, nothing had changed, moss was flourishing, water burbled downhill undisturbed, worms were scaling the flower stems, and ladybugs were candifying themselves blissfully in the trumpet flowers. A hawk was on guard high above. I closed my eyes and waited for my mother.

She arrived. She had come to wash glass mason jars. She looked a little sun-bleached, but she was still skinny.

"Timeskipper," she said, "tell me what Paris is like."

"Big and beautiful, full of places where everywhere you look a poet gave up the ghost, or a painter, or an artist."

"Your father and I had our honeymoon in Paris," she said.

"That's right," I said. I had completely forgotten. I remembered my father's theories about the Eiffel Tower; he insisted that you could make one out of wood, and with Belloni and Baruch he had worked up a rough calculation that it would take six years, you'd need a metric ton of rose-head nails and thousands of board feet of lumber, but it could be done.

"The thing I remember most," said my mother, "was Nôtre Dame cathedral. It was September; the cathedral was so cold and huge. I thought when I saw it: every church in the valley would fit inside it. It frightened me, it fascinated me, it seemed to want to keep you for itself. 'That's what death is like,' I said."

"Mamma," I said, "how is our house now? Is it the same as it used to be? Are there still dormice in the grain loft?"

There was no answer. Just like the other time, she slowly vanished into the water. And then the Boletus Gnome arrived.

"So now we're fucking in foreign countries," he said, with a grinning leer.

"Some of us have that privilege," I replied.

"You think I've never traveled?" he said. "When I was a winged gnome, I traveled all over America. And Canada. Thousands of polar bears, walruses, and mushrooms. I never saw such huge mushrooms, a man could lie down on top of one of those mushrooms and take a nap."

"And were there forests?"

"Forests that stretched from here to the sea. And maybe they're clear-cutting those forests, too," said the gnome, "but by now there's no point thinking about it."

"Uncle Nevio said that no one will cut down any more trees here."

"The world has started spinning out of control," said the gnome. "Humans have given it a good hard shove; now it will be difficult to stop it. The coming years will be sad ones for the mountain and the valley, Timeskipper. Do something about it, listen to the duoclock, boy."

"No, that's enough," I said. "I'm grown up now, I want to live in the present."

The gnome smiled. He took the dipper that had lain on the basin for a hundred years so that people could drink the water. He dipped it in, filled it with water, and pretended to sip. Instead, though, he poured the water slowly onto the ground, drop by drop.

The duoclock went off. I saw a forest fire, a hundred times bigger than our forest, with animals running in all directions. I saw a hundred other forest fires. I saw the river, dry as a bone, and a dense black sea, like tar. I saw people begging for help, standing on a roof surrounded by a vast yellow swamp. I saw, through the fogged glass, a child lost in the winter, with a bear on a leash. Then I saw my father, running and shouting, holding a shovel, and the air was filled with a dense cloud of dust. I saw a house splitting in two, chopped in half by a hatchet. And a white building, many stories tall, and a parking lot filled with countless parked ambulances. I smelled a harsh aroma, something like ether.

"That's enough," I said, totally exhausted. I hop-hiked down along the dirt track. I stopped at the big walnut tree. I bent down to pick up a few walnuts. I put them in my pocket, but then when I reached into my pocket for one of them, they were gone. A hole in my pocket or a little walnut-eating spirit? Suddenly, I had a thought, and I started running. I ran all the way to the Roselle subdivision. There was a car parked in front of Selene's chalet. I saw her father, another short man, and Nando, the realtor. I remembered that someone had said that the Luninis were selling their house. There was a round of handshakes, and then the three men laughed loudly.

Behind me, I heard the rustle of a pheasant's wings as it flew off. I turned around. I knew that she was there.

"And now I have no house," said Selene.

"There are plenty of hollow trees in the forest," I said.

For two days, we walked together from morning to night, without touching, without kissing. It was like bringing blood back into a cold body, bringing new growth to a charred forest. But with each hour that passed, we became closer, we couldn't help it, it was like a magnet.

One evening, we were stretched out in a meadow, like the first time we kissed. She said: "I'm leaving tomorrow."

"I know," I said, though it wasn't true.

She jumped to her feet, her face flame-red.

"Don't pretend nothing's happening. You know what's

going on. Call it magic, call it enchantment or a curse. Whenever I see you, it all starts up again."

I didn't know what to say. I was afraid.

"I had a boyfriend," she said.

"You went everywhere on his motorcycle; you rode along the waterfront. He was as handsome as a movie star and so elegant; he always used aftershave, even when he didn't shave."

"How could you know that?"

"Then one night you happened to wind up in a pizzeria, and he was talking about fast cars and high-performance engines and you thought to yourself: what am I doing with this idiot. You told him, 'I'm going out to look at the sea,' and you were gone."

"You're a damned sorcerer," she said.

"And what do you think I did?"

"You kissed and necked and made love with every girl you met, I'd guess."

"I was always faithful to you, almost," I answered.

"I'm not jealous," she said, with the grimace that always accompanied one of her lies.

I answered: "I am. Terribly jealous."

I ran my fingers through her hair. It was a short, soft kiss. Then she gently pushed me away.

"No, it's not fair, you have the advantage over me here. This is your territory, you're a forest boy, and I've become a defenseless city girl. Here, everyone and everything is on your side, the crickets, the sunsets, the butterflies. Obviously, I can't resist you. This time, I challenge you. Come to the beach, where I'm on my own territory. It's not bad there. We'll spend two days together. If you can win me over there, I'll be yours for . . . let's say, for two years."

"How about fifty?" I said.

"We can negotiate," she said.

We agreed on fifteen.

3

So I took the train and got off at Rivamarina, where I had reserved a 75-square-foot suite at the Pensione Edelweiss, with a view of the sea—if you climbed onto the roof, that is. In preparation for my short but crucial vacation, I had purchased the following luxury items.

A cream-colored Lacoste shirt, with a brand-new tiny crocodile.

A pair of light-blue linen trousers, that look nice even when they're rumpled.

A pair of white Superga canvas deck shoes (to go with the Lacoste shirt).

Two bathing suits, one of them boxer-style with a seahorse pattern, the other a dark-blue Speedo brief, to be worn cautiously, in case of unannounced erections.

A spray deodorant, Gentleman brand.

A red beach towel, with a big cartoon of Goofy about to dive into a pool. Admittedly, I had been cost conscious in this purchase.

A mosquito-repellent citronella stick.

Selene came to the pensione to pick me up, wearing a pair of white tennis shorts, her legs somewhere between sunburnt and tanned. She brought her girlfriend Giusi with her. Giusi was the first challenge to overcome, because she had a voice like an electric sander and she stopped to look in every shop window she saw, shrilling: "That's so cute, that's so sweet, when Ettore gets here I'll tell him to buy one for me!"

I guessed that Ettore must be the head of the Pirelli tire company, but then I found out that he was an accountant; evidently it was a line of work that paid well.

Then we went to the beach.

I was used to the river, where you could lie down wherever you wanted, pee freely, throw rocks, and go fishing.

This was different.

Here, you had to get under a big beach umbrella, set up your folding chair, and all the sand that was covered by the shade of the umbrella belonged, in a sense, to you. But if you happened to set foot in the shade of someone else's umbrella, there was hell to pay.

So I positioned my folding chair half in the shade and half in direct sunlight.

"Not there, you'll get sunburned!" said Giusi.

"No I won't, because in ten minutes the sun'll move around and I'll be back in the shade."

Giusi made a face like a pre-Galilean scientist.

We went swimming, and I have to admit that it was better than the river; you could swim wherever you wanted, without worrying about whirlpools. There were crabs, clams, and little flounders darting away in the clear water, and best of all was a raft in the deep water, out where your feet couldn't reach the sand, where you could lie down in the hot sun.

This was the second ordeal.

"Come on, let's swim to the raft," said Selene, and she and Giusi shot off like young dolphinettes. I gulped in fear: I wasn't much of a swimmer, but I was still a veteran athlete and former Dynamo soccer star. I started out in a careful, leisurely breaststroke.

By the time I heaved myself panting onto the raft, Selene and Giusi were already surrounded by a herd of young mandrills in red Speedos; there were at least six or seven of them. The most enterprising was a very muscular young native of

that strip of beach, with a Speedo visibly stuffed with sub-
stance.

"Hey blondie," he was saying, "why don't you come to the
Bluemoon Disco tonight, there's going to be a dance contest."

"You want to go?" Selene asked me.

"Who's this, your steady?" asked muscle-boy.

"No," said Selene.

"You slut," I thought to myself.

"Then there's no problem. You just ask for Vanes's table.
Everybody knows me, or let's just say all the girls know me."
And he winked with one eye while the other remained closed
in a display of immense ocular dexterity. Then he perched at
the edge of the raft, sucked his stomach in, and showed off a
dive with a front somersault.

The girls burst into cheers. He swam to the surface to
receive his applause. Unfortunately, a huge booger was stream-
ing from his nostril. He snorted it into the water and butter-
flied away into the distance.

The third ordeal consisted of an afternoon stroll along the
boardwalk, through a teeming crowd of beachgoers, to be followed by a gelato. At the seaside, a gelato wasn't a simple matter, the way it was at Balduino's bar: either a Drumstick, or a
Dixie Cup, or just go fuck yourself. Even in the city I'd never
seen an assortment like this. There were ice cream cups called
the Antarctic, the Glutton, the Blue Shiver, the Coffee-Flavored
Temptation, the Tropicana, the Too-Yummy, and the Eiffel
Tower. Every one of them cost as much as two plates of tagliatelle, two chicken entrees, dessert, fruit, and espresso.

We sat down at a bar with a view of the strolling crowd. We
had been joined by Ettore, a bespectacled young man who
never said a word; he didn't need to, since Giusi did all the
necessary talking. In a burst of excitement, the girls said:
"Come on, let's get a really good gelato."

"But it's five o'clock," I said. "We won't be hungry for dinner."

They gave me a look that clearly conveyed their scorn for my forest-boy objections. Giusi and Selene each ordered a Blue Shiver, Ettore decided on a Tropicana, and, since I had been to Paris, I went for an Eiffel Tower.

I expected one of three possible concoctions.

A gelato in a wide goblet, for large mouths, peach-colored and peach-flavored, topped by a tiny pink-lace parasol.

Or else, a gelato kebab, covered with whipped cream.

Or, possibly, a sugar-wafer Eiffel Tower, with a different flavor of gelato on each level.

Instead, what they brought me was a bowl of vanilla and chocolate gelato with four tiny parasols and an obelisk of whipped cream—and maybe that was the Eiffel Tower.

We started gulping and slurping. I stopped when I'd eaten only half.

"Don't you like it?" asked Ettore.

"No, no, it's good, but I don't understand why it's called an Eiffel Tower."

"Maybe because it has a French liqueur in it," said Selene.

"Because vanilla ice cream is a French specialty," Giusi declared.

"If you don't want, I'll eat it," pointed out Ettore.

And that's when I discovered Ettore's second calling in life: garbage disposal. Of course, I paid, because no one else offered.

The fourth harrowing ordeal was the pizzeria. We ordered our pizzas at eight-thirty, and by nine-fifteen we'd consumed everything on the table: bread, breadsticks, and even some soft candy that Giusi had in her purse. From time to time, the waiter walked by our table and said: "Your pizzas are almost done."

And so it dawned on me that it's different at the beach; it's not like in the village, where a person goes into a pizzeria and they make a pizza for him. The pizzerias at the beach must be in a network in which if someone orders a pizza, they make it for him in a different pizzeria, somewhere else, while in the pizzeria where that person is sitting, they're busy making pizzas for people sitting in a pizzeria twelve miles down the coast or else up in the mountains. Therefore, our pizzas were being brought to us from some secret location, and so we had to wait patiently. I explained my theory, but no one laughed. In fact, Selene said:

"It's not like the village here, a couple of customers so they serve you right away. Look around, the place is packed."

She was really being an asshole; I was about to stand up and leave, but just then, the waiter brought our pizzas. They had each ordered a classic Margherita pizza, and I had ordered a sausage pizza. What the waiter brought was one Margherita, two vegetable pizzas, and two seafood pizzas. The fact that there was an extra pizza wasn't a problem, Ettore was a sure bet. I ate one of the vegetable pizzas; I was so hungry I would gladly have eaten a kerosene pizza.

The last ordeal of the day was the Bluemoon Disco. We got there at eleven, the time for slow dancing, what we call the tile dance, cause you dance on a single tile, which creates ideal conditions for conquests and affirmations. A little combo was playing on a stage under the pine trees. It was almost dark; we made our way through a labyrinth of chairs and necking couples, overturning bottles of Campari as we advanced. We did not go Vanes's table, but instead to the table of someone named Ninni, a charming if imbecilic twenty-year-old boy wearing a phosphorescent shirt. There were boys and girls, all slightly sunburnt and none of them with a decent, normal first name—they were all Ninni and Fede and Cris and Ghigo and Marcy—and all of them were talking at the same time. Selene started chatting animatedly with Marcy, making sure to leave me with no one to talk to. I thought, "I'm going to get up and leave," for the second time. Just then, Vanes walked by and said: "Look who's here, the little blonde from the raft. Wanna dance?"

Selene said, "No, I promised this dance to my steady," and pointed at me.

Vanes glared at me scornfully, hooked up with a German girl, and before ten minutes were up he had completely bathed one of her ears in saliva. Selene, on the other hand, didn't dance with her steady, i.e., me, but with Ninni, and so I asked Cris to dance. Then she danced with Ghigo and I danced with Marcy, and so on, and I was just starting to think about walking out for the third time when the emcee stepped up to the mike and started emceeing. He looked like Vanes's dad, with a toupee on his head that looked like a dead alley cat. He said:

"Ladies and gentlemen, this evening's big event is a dance contest; we will have three separate categories, and a grand total of nine prizes. The prizes are provided by Rivabella's Top Dollar Boutique, and for each of the three categories they will consist of a first prize of a plush doll, a second prize of an assortment of perfumes, and a third prize of a bottle of spumante."

And he pointed to three toy bunnies, as tall as basketball players, three gold-wrapped packages, and three gleaming spumante bottles.

"Oh yes, I want the big bunny, let's win the big bunny," said Selene. Her small-town chromosomes were starting to show.

"Oh, that's disgusting!" said Giusi.

"I want that bunny," said Selene. "Timeskipper, heaven help you if we lose."

That was easy for her to say. All the contestants were expert dancers, they hullygullied and fruged like grasshoppers; everyone knew how to dance, even the Germans.

The emcee announced the three contest categories. They were beat dance, which meant dance however the hell you wanted, cha-cha-cha, and waltz. Hope sprang back to life.

"Selene, do you remember, we used to do the waltz in the village square when we were kids, you were a great waltzer, and I wasn't half bad."

"But the waltz is a dance for old people," said Selene.

"If you want the big bunny, you're going to have to dance the waltz," I said.

She resigned herself to the waltz. The first round was for beat dance. The combo—Max and His Vocalists—started playing a song that I suddenly realized, about halfway through, might or might not be "Get Off of My Cloud" (R. Stones). The dancers weren't very good, but there were a few women who shook their asses more than the rest, and Vanes mimed midair penetrations with his wad. He came in first, second place went to a young double-jointed couple, and Giusi and Ninni came in third.

Second contest: cha-cha-cha. The song was "Patricia" (P. Prado). This time, there were two pairs of professional dancers who completely outclassed the rest of the field, coming in first and second. Bringing up the rear with third prize was a mother-and-son team.

Last contest: the waltz. They weren't all old folks. There were two pairs of Germans, with one of the German couples weighing in at 510 pounds, taken together. There were a few local couples in their thirties, two little kids, and us.

"Shit," I thought. "People love little kids."

The combo started playing the waltz, "Diavoletto" (S. Belloni). At first we were a little stiff, then we started to move with some flair. The little girl tripped and was forced off the dance floor, limping as she went. One down, I thought ruthlessly. I immediately saw that the local couples were unimpressive, except for a guy and a gal dressed in black, who moved so fast and so smooth that they seemed to be running on greased rails. Then there was a surprise. The two Kraut Panzers swooped and hovered like a pair of butterflies, and when they pirouetted they set up a tornado effect that practically swept everyone else off the dance floor. They were good, but we were relying on the glamour factor. I was a little stiff, but elegant—ten years of dancing in the village square give you a certain posture, if nothing else. Selene had studied dance, and it showed, she knew how to swing her hair as she turned and I noticed that, as she spun around, her skirt flew up and her legs were on display.

"Faster," I said.

"But my panties are showing."

"You want the big bunny?" I asked, and with those magic words she started spinning like a top. There was a burst of applause, and, covered with perspiration, we took our bows before the jury, which consisted of the musicians in the combo.

The verdict was a travesty of justice.

First prize went to the German Panzers, who were so likable.

Second prize went to us, for the panties.

Third prize went to the couple dressed in black, who were far and away the best, but they took it in good spirits and accepted the bottle of spumante.

"It was because I'm having my period," explained the woman.

Selene was gleaming with perspiration and a little out of sorts, but fortune smiled upon us. The male Panzer came over and said: "Mein vife zez dat she likes Italian parfuma, if you are villing ve vill exchange our punny for your pox of profuma, nein?"

Ve vere very villing to take punny und giff pox of profuma to Choiman vife, all vere very happy und Italien-Deutschland friendship vass reschtored.

*

"What a nice evening," Selene said to me in the street outside my pensione.

"It really was," I whispered back, snaking my arm around her waist.

"Well, see you tomorrow, on the beach," she said, wriggling out of my grasp and planting a kiss on my cheek. She walked off, the big bunny slung over her shoulder the way a hunter carries a dead warthog.

When I threw myself down on the bed in my room, my eyes were filled with tears. I said to myself, "This time I'm leaving for real, all she wants is to take her revenge, and I fell for it like an idiot. Fuck them and fuck Rivamarina. I came close to drowning, I spent two thousand dollars on gelato, I ate a cold pizza with Brussel sprouts, I danced in a dance contest and she kept the big bunny, but that's it, I'm done, tomorrow I'm taking the train and going home, I'm done with Italian women, from now on nothing but French girls and German women that weigh over 220 pounds."

I packed my bags immediately and, of course, couldn't get to sleep until five in the morning.

The next morning I slept until ten. But I didn't go right out and catch the next train. I thought that I wanted to see her just one last time. "She's been nasty and cruel, but I've been mean to her, too, and I don't want false pride getting in the way. I'm going to go say good-bye to her. I'll say, 'Fine, you've taken your revenge, I'm leaving, but please, don't turn into the kind of girl who behaves like this all the time, love is more than blackmail and vendetta, it's not a contest. No matter what, I'll always love you, even if you've been a little bit of a shit, actually, a huge turd.'"

I was saying all this aloud as I walked along toward the beach, and people looked at me as I went by as if I were insane. I looked for Selene's beach umbrella, but I couldn't find it. Finally I heard her voice, and she came running toward me.

Her face was radiant. What had happened to her last night? Had she made love with the big bunny?

"Why are you dressed like that? Come on, let's get a rowboat and go for an outing."

"And who's going with us? You and me and Giusi and Pappi and Cris and Vanes and the Virgin Mary?"

"No, just you and me, alone."

Luckily, I was wearing my swimming suit under my clothes; I had forgotten to bring a spare pair of underwear, another sign of destiny. I rowed as hard as I could, I wasn't much of an oarsman. She had stretched out on the stern of the rowboat, which was something like a big tanning table, and she said to me as I rowed: "You sure have developed some muscles, look at those shoulders," and then she took off her top.

I thought, if she still wants revenge, let her go ahead and take it, but they'll find her body a week from now, if the current is favorable. But then she said:

"I've been a little bit awful to you. I really put you to the test, didn't I? But I wanted to see if you're still as damned stubborn and proud as you used to be, and especially if you still cared. I care about you, I really do."

I stopped rowing. The sun was hot, and, in accordance with the elementary laws of physics, so was her skin. We started kissing, and we just couldn't stop. I could feel her back growing hotter and hotter, she was turning red as a crayfish, but we kept kissing. "Let's take a swim," she said, I answered no, and I kept kissing. Finally, we heard a dull thud, and we both looked up.

The current had driven us ninety hotels down the beach, and just twenty yards from the shore. We had drifted against another rowboat, with an astonished father, mother, and three children aboard.

"You should watch where you're going," said the father, in a paternal tone of voice.

I jumped to my feet and said:

"Sorry, one of our oars is broken."

Three huge embarrassments at one fell swoop.

First, the oars were intact and in full view.

Second, Selene's top was all lopsided.

Third, just as I leapt to my feet I realized that I'd had an erection for three hours, and even if I wasn't the size of Vanes, there was an obvious pyramidal effect in my Speedos.

The father did his best to paddle away from us, and one of the children asked:

"Daddy, does that man have a tail?"

That night, we had our first sado-maso sexual encounter; we were burnt like a pair of lobsters and every time we touched, our skin smarted.

"There'll be plenty of time to do it better," said Selene.

"That's right," I said. "Fifteen years, you promised."

When I went back to the village, my nose was peeling off in patches. The news wasn't good. Gancio had collapsed again, he'd recovered, but now he was in the city, in a clinic. Uncle Nevio was battling like a lion to thwart Fefelli, who wanted to build a new road, cutting through the chestnut grove and the Fanara, so that he could build still higher up, in the middle of the forest. There was even talk of using dynamite to clear away a few inconvenient rock spurs. There were small horrors in our village, great horrors around the world. In Prague, the Russians had invaded, and at the Casa del Popolo, there was deep and angry disagreement. Fistfights had broken out. People were calling Baruch a Fascist because he had said, "I've seen tanks before, and these aren't exactly the same, but they do resemble the ones I've seen."

My father said, sadly:

"As far as I'm concerned, there's no such place as Russia anymore. I'm just sorry for Karamazov." He said it as if Karamazov were still alive.

"And what do you think?" he asked me.

"The same as you, Dad," I said.

"For once, we agree on politics—it's going to snow in August," he said. He seemed to have aged, he had lost a lot of hair, and he moved slowly now, as if he were always afraid of falling. But when he worked, it seemed to rejuvenate him, and wood shavings flew in all directions, like so many falling stars. Still, I couldn't manage to feel sad in those late-summer days.

I walked out onto the meadow, looked up at the stars, and thought: "Those stars exist because I love Selene. If I didn't love her, they would disappear."

Even Verdolin would have hesitated to utter that one.

Rufus came running, tail wagging. He had a more responsible demeanor now that he was the proud father of eleven puppies. Selene and I will have the same number, I thought, though maybe not all at once.

4.

My last year of high school began, only to be rudely interrupted by the first sit-in—in fact, a double sit-in. Riccardo's group had occupied the second floor of the school, in open defiance of scholastic and paternal authoritarianism, to hold a student-run seminar on new forms of resistance philosophy. Tamara's group had occupied the third floor, in open defiance of scholastic and paternal authoritarianism, to hold student-run lessons on new forms of labor protest.

Fred, Baco, and the Perfect Lovers took an opportunistic stance as Tamarists with anarchist overtones or anarchists with a background of retro-Tamarism. Lussu formed a group unto himself.

Those were days that changed a great many people; days that many others chose to forget as soon as they could. Days of a fever that swept through the population, to the benefit of one and all, even those who hated that year of 1968. Days of occupations and desecrations, days for which stern buildings still secretly yearn, deep in their architectural cores. Days of arguing and mimeographing, days of hastily assembled meals and late-night guitar serenades, days of verbal fumes, Jamaican fumes, the fumes of tear gas. Days of sudden bursts of housewifely zeal, when occupying students mopped every floor in their occupied schoolrooms, or incomprehensible guerrilla rages, when every faucet in the building was unscrewed—a subversive technique of which no trace can be found in the writings of the great Che

Guevara. And all of these things unfolded amidst a multicolored proliferation of graffiti: messages of love and political
denunciations, sketches by Verdolin, and hastily executed cocks
that the feminists underlined with cryptic graffiti, or else femi-
nist slogans underscored by anonymous cocks, because we
males kept quiet in political rallies, but in private we unleashed
jeremiads and accusations of lesbo-Catholico-cut-me-off-ism.

And when night came, it took the edge off the polemics and
evened out the ideologies. In the jury-rigged alcoves and in the
profusion of sleeping bags, couplings flourished of all and
every sort, including tricuspid lovemaking, with turnover, huge
scenes of liberation, and dramas of jealousy, with floods of
tears and lacerating doubts, as we were all torn between the
call of the personal and the collective.

Like the time that Mina, the girl with Indian-style braids,
asked one evening whether it would be okay for her boyfriend
to sleep in the school, even though he was apolitical?

The women said yes, because your sexuality forms part of
your militancy but is not subordinate to it, as long as he's not a
complete Fascist.

The men said no, because we're here, readily available, and
we don't see why you would need to dip into the cauldron of
the outside world's apathetic sexuality when there's so much
revolutionary cock available here in the building.

One guy went so far as to put it this way: it would be like
saying, I'm in Che Guevara's bedroom, and I decide to open the
door to . . . I don't know, a Christian Democrat like Fanfani.

We tossed him out of the school before the women had a
chance to beat him up.

In the end, we reached a decision: "Let's see how your
boyfriend behaves." The boyfriend, a sly dog, was transformed
into a militant comrade by week's end, and worked his way
into the pants of a German girl doing an internship in Italian
extremism.

Selene often came to the school to pick me up, dressed in what she considered occupation style, wearing a poncho and beat-up tennis shoes; all she needed was a lunch box and a submachine gun. I told her, I don't want you to feel obliged to become all political, I want you to feel independent. Oh, I'm independent, I'm independent, she said, you're so careful to keep me independent. Carpaccio cross-examined her and in the end pigeonholed her as a social democrat in the bourgeois-Scandinavian-*solidarista* tradition, which meant that she occupied the last slot available on the right in our revolutionary coalition. I heaved a sigh of relief. We made love frequently, not in a sleeping bag, but in an unforgettable sandwich of Scottish plaid blankets that reeked of mothballs, so that in the middle of lovemaking she would cry out: "Kiss me, Eega Beeva."

Then Selene had to study for some crucial tests, and she told me, "I won't be able to see you for a little while."

A lot happened during that little while.

There was a scorching-hot political meeting. Tamara declared that the Riccardian faction had no relationship with the working class, and were locked in an embrace with the well-to-do privileged avant-garde intellectual elite. Riccardo shot back that the Tamarian faction was saddled with a naïve and mythical conception of the working class but had no real understanding of it, and that the Tamarians feared the intellectuals for their critical intelligence—adding that, in the final analysis, intellectuals are the working class of the mind.

There followed a number of fine debating points, such as a chair over Giap's head, and a lively mixture of heterosexual and homosexual slaps and punches.

The debate was cut short when the police burst into the hall, clubbing freely, and clearing the school of its occupiers. Paolo Lingua suffered a fracture to one pinky finger.

The following day, we reoccupied.

The Riccardians made a low and cunning move in their

quest for overall leadership. They called a political meeting with two genuine blue-collar workers from a machine-tool shop in attendance; one of them was actually dressed in factory over-alls. All that was missing was a sign saying FACTORY WORKER and an acetylene tank and blowtorch. They placed the factory workers in the middle of the rally, and they were a little awk-ward and shy at first. Then one student with a Venetian accent spoke up, and the factory worker wearing overalls said, "Oh, you sound as if you're from Treviso; so am I," and the tension broke and they started talking about small-scale factories and the exploitation of labor. It was a spectacular success, the stu-dents did everything short of asking the factory workers for their autographs—just think, two real factory workers, I even touched one. Riccardo was walking on clouds.

"We know how to talk to intellectuals, but also to the pro-letariat," he proudly announced. "And you don't."

So Fred and I prepared our countermove. The following day, a flyer appeared on the announcement board: Room Seven, second floor, the Bateau Ivre Collective presents a dis-cussion with the French philosopher Jean-Baptiste Paponnard, from the University of Narbonne, author of the books *The Pre-tence of Liberty* and *Toward a Communism of Ambiguity: From Karl Marx to David Bowie*. His books are forthcoming in Italy from the new publishing house, Fanara Press.

It was a response to the Riccardians' mobilization of the two factory workers. When Riccardo was asked about Paponnard, he grudgingly allowed that he was a lesser disci-ple of Foucault, in any case an interesting if unexceptional figure. So the school room filled with the members of both groups.

Paponnard entered the room: he had a full head of wild white hair, he was wearing a seedy, tattered overcoat that stretched to his ankles, and he was unmistakably sozzled. He immediately grabbed one of La Schiassi's breasts, and came close to being stabbed with one of Verdolin's pastels, specifically a pale indigo. Then he asked for a beer, belched, and began to speak.

I translated.

He said that living *dans la rue* (in the street) is the sole truth, because it is there and there alone that you can see people and truly understand the direction in which history is moving, and that fucking, smoking, and drinking are the only things that make life tolerable. But one day the Sirians will land their spaceships on the planet Earth, and they will judge who has behaved well and who has been evil. They will load all the good people onto the spaceships and take them to Sirius One, a place filled with sunshine, fruit trees, and dogs. The bad people, on the other hand, will be sent to Sirius Two, a place not unlike hell, except that instead of fire there are showers, ice-cold showers all day, every blessed day, and you can forget about trying to get out of taking them.

It was a distinctly metaphorical discourse, and I did my best to render it more accessible. But everyone in the audience understood that it contained a profound grain of truth.

Riccardo concurred that living in the street, that is to say, amidst the chaos of the revolution, is helpful in understanding the true needs of the people, and he was in general agreement on the issue of the spaceship, because new ideas cannot issue from that which we already know, but must come from an elsewhere, from a heterotypy, to use Foucault's phrase, an *ailleurs* that we must be capable of recognizing, when it comes.

"C'est ça," Paponnard answered.

Paolo Lingua said that this image of hell as a continual shower is a strong incitement to action, because we are filthy with our revisionism and our sense of guilt, which only justifies a degree of violence that can be variously calibrated according to the specific circumstances, because a clean conscience is not always a peaceful conscience.

"C'est ça," said Paponnard.

A redhead, with a mane of hair like a Molotov cocktail, said that she wasn't clear as to whether the Sirians in question were the ones from Damascus, in the sense of the revolutionary potential of Islam, or whether he had a different reference in mind.

Paponnard said that he was talking about Sirius, the star in the sky, and that she had asked a first-rate question. In reality, he had said that she, the redhead, had a first-rate pair of tits, but I had left that detail out of my translation.

"What differences are there between the French movement and the Italian movement?" asked Tamara.

"In France," said Paponnard, "it is easier to find food, there are lots of places that provide free food and charity, while on the other hand, in Italy the food stores are less careful about shoplifting, so that evens it out; moreover, in Italy they often do the street cleaning at night, but in France you're more likely to catch a beating."

This was an exceedingly abstruse metaphor. Giap was the only one to understand it.

"Comrade Paponnard means to say that in France, the political platform is often handed out as a form of charity by false leaders, while in Italy it is necessary to rise up in rebellion and wrestle the political line from reality on a daily basis. With respect to the question of violence, in Italy people try to cleanse it, in hiding and with great hypocrisy, while in France, police-state repression is not concealed, and hence it is less treacherous."

"C'est ça," said Paponnard.

Lussu stood up. He had figured out the ruse.

"Professor Paponnard," he asked, "do you by chance have a dog?"

Paponnard broke down in tears and said that he used to have a dog, but they had taken the dog away from him. One night, when it was really freezing out, the police had forcibly taken him in to give him a shower and wash his clothing; they wouldn't let dogs into the police station, and when he got out, his Boulboul was gone.

I translated in a confused manner, but this time there was a long and appalled silence. Fred rose to his feet and spoke:

"Clearly, in any political activity, there is someone at your side, and you must take care to maintain that bond: this is a clear invocation to preserve the movement's unity."

Paponnard vomited, and we all applauded.

Paponnard was the sole topic of discussion for three days, until Riccardo happened to see him panhandling at the street corner by the church, and was suddenly forced to admit what many had understood from the very beginning. We had palmed off as a *philosophe* a French bum who had been begging and sleeping in the street for the past few months.

"It was a childish and fascistic fraud," said the Riccardistas; "it was a creative way to cultivate self-deprecating irony," we responded. "Paponnard was a true philosopher," one attendee added, and he even went to a bookshop to ask for a copy of *Marx to Bowie*. In short, Jean-Baptiste Paponnard lived on in our collective imagination. The only serious repercussion was that Paolo Lingua punched Fred and busted his lip, saying: "You scum, you're mocking the revolution." But the next day, a television news crew came to interview the students occupying the school, and Lingua managed to ensure that he alone was interviewed. That coup marked the beginning of his gradual drift toward conservativism, rolling rightward at the rate of one party per year.

A month later, I found a place to live, a cramped hovel that reeked like a latrine, but through the window I could see an apricot tree, and exceedingly amiable cats liked to enter my room, stepping daintily over the windowsill. I hung up a poster of Lake Ontario, a photograph of Selene, a Che Guevara, a Lee Evans (the black American sprinter who took gold at the Mexico City Olympics), a Gramsci, a Poe, and various Beatles; it struck me as a nice little room. For some time now I had been making regular visits to the clinic where Gancio was recuperating, but they always responded that he was still on the mend and that it was too early for him to see anyone. Finally, one day, they said, "Okay, you can go in, but don't get him worked up."

Gancio was sitting in front of the window, watching as the sparrows flew past, swiveling his head like a cat. Perhaps he was dreaming about his old blowgun. His hair was shaven to a stubble, and he was skinny as a wall spider. I wrapped my arms around him; it felt like he was made of glass.

He lay back on his bed, and crossed his arms over his chest. There was an infinite weariness and a great dignity in his expression.

"I did it all to myself, Timeskipper," he said. "Do you remember, down at the river, when we swam out to the end of the water hole, where the water rushed toward the bridge, and there were all those whirlpools? We used to see who could swim closest, who could hold out longest as the current grew stronger and stronger. I always won, I'd swim to shore just a second before the current swept me away, and you guys always swam to shore first. That's how it's always been for me: I like it best where the current sweeps fastest, where the danger is greatest. And now the current has swept me away, and I'm lying on the riverbed."

"If you can just make it through the rapids, then you'll be in smooth water again, and it flows eventually to the sea, in the distance," I said.

"Right, the sea," he said, half closing his Amazon Indian eyes. "I was happy at the beach with Nora, then they came to see me. They tracked me down, they brought the shit to me, right to my house, they gave it to me free of charge."

"Who are they?"

"Aw, that doesn't matter. How is Selene?"

"She's good. She's studying hard."

"Are you two together? Is the London playboy still dogging her?"

"I'll never be able to thank you enough for what you said that day at the party. You really helped me out."

"Really? I didn't even notice. You have a cigarette?"

"I don't smoke, Gancio, don't you remember?"

"Got anything strong to drink?"

"Next time I come to see you, I'll try to smuggle in a bottle of Guatayaba firewater. I promise."

"The next time, then," Gancio laughed.

A nurse walked into the room, picked up his skinny arm, gave him an injection, and left without a word.

"They keep me calm, real calm, dead calm," he said, with a bitter smile.

"Hang tight, Gancio," I said. "Uncle Nevio is waiting for you to get out. He says he has a real job for you."

Gancio turned a cadaverous shade of white, his fingers knotted around the sheets. I got scared, and I was about to call a doctor, but he stopped me with a wave of his arm.

"It's nothing. Just this junk they inject me with, it makes me puke. The doctor says that I have the liver of a ninety-year-old man. Not bad, right? It was better when the beer made me puke."

"You'll live to vomit again with us."

"I don't know about that, Timeskipper," said Gancio between tiny sips of water. "The average Guatayaba lifespan is twenty-eight years, I used to think that I could make it to twenty-eight, but now I'm not so sure. But I need you to promise me something. Two things, actually."

"Whatever you want."

"First thing, when you go back to the village, tell Uncle

Nevio that you saw me, and that I'm fine, relaxed, recovering, blooming like a rose. And if the axe does finally fall, I mean, if I wind up with a Guatayaba dart in my back, tell him that I was always grateful for what he did, even though I might not have ever thanked him enough."

"Stop talking like a dead man."

"They're things you say once in your life, then never again," said Gancio. Who had I heard say something like that before? Then he added, his voice suddenly hoarse:

"And second thing, take revenge for me."

"On who?"

"On the Pastori brothers and their friends. Timeskipper, is it possible that no one ever wondered where the heroin was coming from? And it wasn't just at the disco, it was in town, at the Mephisto Bar, and in plenty of other places. I think lots of people knew it was circulating and pretended not to see. How do you think those bastards bought those fast new cars—with the money that Fefelli paid them? They were supplying the whole area, working with some slime-buckets from the city. It's my own fault that what happened happened, but I'm pay- ing, and they're not. One time, the police caught them dealing outside the disco, and arrested them. Fefelli intervened, ordered them set free, posted bail for them. They've stopped dealing now, but it's not like the shit they sold can be recalled, it's still there, in my blood. Take revenge for me, Timeskipper. I know that it's a nasty sharp knife I'm putting in your hand, but you're the only one that I sometimes felt was at least a lit- tle bit like me."

"I don't know about that, Gancio," I said. I couldn't look him in the face. "Now, you try to get better, then we'll talk about the other things."

"Bastards," he said again, with his eyes closed. The dragon that was tattooed on his arm seemed to have faded. I was afraid that it would fly away, along with his fading strength.

"But if the Pastori brothers stopped dealing," I asked, "who sold you the junk after they stopped?"

"I'd better not say," said Gancio. "Please, don't ask me."

"Are you afraid?"

"I'm not afraid of anyone," he said. "After them, there were young kids on Vespas, who sold it from town to town. Maybe the Pastori brothers still wholesale it to them, I don't know. And then . . ."

"And then?"

"And then, sometimes, Osso sold it to me."

That day, a great many things changed. I understood that the Shadow covering the village and was much bigger and more dangerous than I thought. I was almost afraid to go back. I studied day and night and kept my head down. With Selene, I was silent; she understood that something serious had happened, but she didn't ask about it. I could tell that in some way I was moving away from her. Gancio's words had thrust into me like a knife: you're like me, he had said. A shared fury united us. I had swum away from the icy current before him, but maybe one day I would let it pull me all the way, I would challenge it in full. "Don't follow me, Selene," I said one day, when I was drunk. "There's a hard road ahead of me."

"If you want to leave me, tell me that you're in love with a movie star—that I can get worried about. But what you're telling me, right now, that's not enough to scare me," she said calmly.

"I'm having two affairs: one with Brigitte Bardot and one with Cary Grant."

"Hand over Cary, and keep the little French whore for yourself."

Selene had learned to joke again, and that made me happy. But I was afraid for her and for me. One day, I read these lines by Apollinaire:

I was waiting for the end of the world, and my own death came howling like a hurricane.

I went back to the village for the Christmas holidays. The legendary year of 1968 was almost over. The village was covered with snow when I got there, the train had to stop half a mile outside of town, and I walked the rest of the way. And the scars left by the hurricane were already visible.

My dad told me that there had been a murder the night before, the first murder in the village since the end of the war. Favilla the blacksmith had lost his mind. He'd murdered his wife with a shotgun blast, and then he'd put the barrel of the shotgun in his mouth and killed himself. There was no motive, people said, but it wasn't true. The loan sharks had ruined him. He had borrowed money to open a hardware store, and he couldn't meet the payments.

"Who are the loan sharks?" I asked. "Who's selling drugs in the town?"

"I'll tell you when I know for sure," said my dad. "The only thing I do know is that money has changed. It's no longer something you have in your pocket to buy something you need. Now money is a boulder, it falls on people's heads, it knocks them unconscious. Now nobody says they're doing all right, everybody's dissatisfied, there's never enough money."

"Just like in the city."

"I don't know what it's like in the city," he said, shaking his head. "Here they've pitted us all one against another."

On Christmas Eve, there was an Antarctic chill in the air. Regina was making a stuffed goose, and it looked as if she were readying the mummy of Ramses the Great. She said, "Get the hell out from underfoot, boy." So I went to wish Balduino a merry Christmas. Sashay had left to set up housekeeping with the orchestra musician, and there were two new pinball machines; one of them was called Pirates. Balduino said that he wanted to sell the bar—there were three other bars in the village now; the only people who still frequented his were the still temporarily alive old people. "I'll keep coming here," I said. "Oh, come on," he said, "the young girls all go to the Mephisto Bar or the other new bar next to the bank. Plus they make hamburgers now—that's twenty lire of bread, 180 lire of ground meat, and 1,800 lire of American name. If I sold a buttered roll and called it Nebraska Snow, how much do you think I could charge? You know what Baruch says? That under Fascism, we had to ask the Germans what we could and couldn't do, and now we have to do the same with the Americans. History turns like a merry-go-round."

We were walking along with our hands in our pockets and our faces tucked into our raised coat lapels, when we heard a sound from the bell tower, and a gust of wind blew snow into our faces. But we were well supplied with a flask of vodka; a couple of quick shots and we continued walking. They were still working on the fountain. The mysterious masterpiece lay hidden beneath a snow-covered sheet of canvas; it looked like an iceberg in the middle of the piazza. The clock in the bell tower struck eight.

For a moment, I saw the fountain glittering in the sunlight, a carousel of pikefish and dolphins. Then, high up on the bell tower, I saw a pair of short legs in red tights, jutting out into the void. It was the Violin-Playing Devil, and he was playing the theme music from *Alfred Hitchcock Presents* (A. Gounod).

"The little devil of minor disasters," said Balduino.

But another gust of wind nearly knocked us to the ground. Flying in the midst of the sleet, we saw the Shadow cover the piazza and pass overhead, with a shrill birdlike caw. It climbed up the bell tower, painting it black, and enveloped the little devil. The imp suddenly stopped playing and plunged into the void. We hurried to the spot where we'd seen it fall, the way a hunting dog does when he sees a pheasant drop. There was nothing to be seen, only the mark of a tiny body in the snow, and a splatter of something red that looked a little like candle wax.

The next day, I went up to the woods, to look for unusually shaped branches. My dad wanted to make a big centerpiece for a dinner at the Casa del Popolo; they were going to celebrate Baruch's sixtieth birthday. I climbed up all the way to the Fanara. The basin was frozen solid and icy daggers dangled from the trees; I felt as if I were in an enchanted grotto. The snow-covered ground was embroidered with tiny animal tracks. I saw other, bigger tracks, made by a big, booted foot.

"Oh, gnome," I said loudly, "come skate on the ice."

There was no answer.

"Gnome, you damned trouble-making boletus, come out, it's Christmas, I have a gift for you."

It was the truth. I had brought a pocket knife.

The forest was silent. I followed the gnome's footprints. They got closer and closer together, which was a sign that he was growing tired, then they vanished into a hollow tree. I stuck my head into the hole.

"Come out," I said.

Then I looked a little closer. The tree was twisted and it had huge roots. It looked as if it had arms and legs, but most important, high up it had a pair of branches, loaded with snow, that looked just like a white mustache. The hole was the mouth, and two knots in the wood were the eyes.

My gnome was resting, in an eternal sleep. One by one, the forest was losing its creatures.

Unexpectedly, the sun came out. By New Year's Eve, nearly all the snow and ice had melted away. Water came singing down from the trees and ran through crevices and crannies, forming rivulets and little cascades, spreading out across the meadows and giving a shining coat to the roads.

"It's pretty," I said, as I helped my father saw a small log.

"It would have been better if it had stayed frozen," he grumbled.

The fate of the village was teetering between Uncle Nevio's stubborn determination and the vast power of Fefelli and the developer Arcari, a power that was spreading its tentacles throughout the region. Uncle Nevio had succeeded in putting a halt to the construction of the road up to Mount Mario, and the courts had backed him up. But recently, there had been a reshuffling of the coalition government and Fefè, who had managed to recalibrate his political alliances perfectly, had been named undersecretary of public works. Now he had ten times as much pull. On New Year's Eve, there were fireworks, and we were all out in the street. On the television set in Balduino's bar, we watched the celebrations going on all over the world. People were drinking toasts just like we were, in New York, in Moscow, in Rio de Janeiro. I called Selene, who was vacationing in the mountains, and told her that I was thinking about her. "I'm thinking about you even more," she said. "Is Brigitte Bardot there with you?" "Yes, but she's hooked up with Baco," I said, "and now Cary Grant's with Fred, so you're out of luck."

"There's skiing up here," she said, and I answered, "Here, too." It was true. Caprone had pulled out his tractor and tied a rope to it, and he was serving as a ski lift. He pulled all the townspeople up the slope to the soccer field, and then we'd ski back down. I had found an old pair of bamboo skis, Baco had found a badly dented pair of Rossignols. Roda was trying to be a hot dog with a new pair of skis; he might have been a good soccer player, but on skis it looked as if he had three legs, and they just kept getting tangled up.

Balduino and Carburo were drunk; they took a sled and announced:

"Now Team Italy will defeat the hated German team of Löwenbräu-Jägermeister."

They started down the hill, and then shot into the under-brush at something approximating the speed of light. The God of Drunken Old Guys saved them; they just scratched up their faces pretty good.

On the second day of the new year, the hurricane burst upon us at dawn. I heard a line of trucks grinding up the hill in low gear, but I was too tired to wonder why they were work-ing at dawn. They climbed up to the Roselle subdivision, along the damaged road. They removed the barrier that blocked the way and continued uphill toward the slopes of Mount Mario. There they stopped at the two big rock spurs that prevented them from going any further.

It started raining. It was eight o'clock in the morning; I woke up when I heard the sound of Uncle Nevio's Vespa pick-up. He was upset, on the verge of tears.

He held out a piece of paper.

It was a ministerial decree that accorded permission to undertake work for the purpose tourist development on the unfinished road running from Roselle to Mount Mario, four miles in length, dated 2 January, overriding all other regula-tions in this matter.

"I can't bring myself to tell your father. Can you wake him up?"

There was no need. The explosion did it for us. Thunder-ous and deafening, as if all the fireworks and firecrackers of New Year's Eve had gone off at once. Followed by the noise of a hail of rocks.

"God damn them to hell," shouted Uncle Nevio. "That was dynamite!"

My father appeared, dressed in an undershirt and a pair of heavy woolen underpants. He looked up, toward the woods, where a cloud of dust was rising into the air.

"They blew up the first rock spur, the one with all the

quartz. They've done it now." We went out into the road, there were lots of people outside their houses, which is what saved their lives. Because a minute later, we felt the earth shaking, and an avalanche roaring toward us with a noise unlike anything I had ever heard, louder even than when the river flooded.

"Dad," I shouted, "what's happening?!" It sounded to me as if I had the voice of a six-year-old.

"Bastards!" said my father, and burst into tears of rage, his tears an accompaniment to the disaster. A wall of earth thundered down onto the town, hitting the northern end. When I think back on it, it seems like an enormous human body collapsing, wounded in its rocky heart, the trees like so many crumbling bones, the uptorn roots the sinews, the grass the skin, the groundwater the blood, and all of it was screaming with pain. The swollen, downrushing river of muddy soil swept over a dozen or so houses, and then moved on, devastating gardens and vineyards and orchards, tumbling down into the valley, toward the river, with a sad dull rumbling, as if asking forgiveness.

"Carburo's house," shouted my father. "Him, his wife, his children!" And he set off at a run, in his absurd clothing. It was like an old silent movie.

"Wait," said Uncle Nevio, "let's call somebody."

"Wait my ass, run and get shovels."

Around the curve, Regina appeared, riding her bicycle, with a pair of spades over her shoulders. She was followed by Luis on his tractor and Caprone on his, and lots of other people, all heading toward the landslide. When we got there, there was nothing but dirt, with a few chimney pots and a roof, torn open. Two children were sobbing in the middle of the road. They were Carburo's youngest sons, he had lowered them out the window.

We started digging, it went on raining, I was digging with my hands, and I cut myself on a bottle, a bottle of walnut liqueur;

we were directly above Carburo's dining room. Carburo's wife was pulled out of the rubble with nothing worse than a broken arm. Luis managed to tear apart the wall of earth with his tractor: an opening, between two ceiling beams. My father lowered himself inside and pulled out Carburo; the beams collapsed, and they were both trapped, their heads outside, their legs crushed—half saved, half dead. I opened my mouth to scream, but nothing came out. A few minutes later, they had both been extracted. Carburo was dead, my father was still breathing. An ambulance took him away just as the firefighters arrived.

Six people died that day. Carburo and his son Taddeo, and a married couple that worked at the cement plant, along with their three-year-old son, who had the same name as me. Slim the Magnificent died, too, trapped in his hut filled with canaries in cages. With him died all his bird imitations. There were others who narrowly escaped death. If the avalanche hadn't turned aside, if the Fanara and the chestnut grove and the Tree Gnome hadn't pushed its fury aside, half the town would have been destroyed.

I spent that night in the hospital with Regina, while they operated on my father. A courteous nurse told me: "If you're interested in watching television, they're talking about your village."

"Thanks, but I don't feel like it," I said.

It was a good thing I didn't watch. An army of journalists had descended on the town, even Milio in a camouflage combat jacket. The television news crew had interviewed Uncle Nevio; he had expressed his opinion pretty forcefully, but in the end only this was broadcast:

"We're hurt, but we'll rebuild."

All the rest had been edited out.

Then there was a brief section with a geologist, and an interview with Fefelli.

"Work wasn't supposed to start yet, and that rock spur

wasn't scheduled to be blown up," he declared. "The decree ordered that a permit was issued for work to 'begin' today, but before moving forward in any substantial way, of course, the expert opinions of the regional planning commission and staff geologists had to be received and taken into consideration. Someone is at seriously at fault here, and we will investigate thoroughly to ensure that nothing like this happens again."

There was no mention of Arcari's company; in fact, Arcari had completely vanished from the entire matter and had been erased somehow from all the documents. The only people under investigation were two nameless engineers, and a certain Fattorini, an explosives technician, who emigrated to Argentina where he could train talented young men to produce explosions that would prove politically more productive.

My father was still in the hospital, with a reserved prognosis of internal bleeding. For those killed in the avalanche, there was an impressive funeral; the mayors of every village and town in the valleys attended. Fefelli at least had the decency to skip the ceremony, with the excuse that he was ill. It seemed like a wound that would never heal, the mark of a slow, cruel crime that would haunt us for the rest of our lives.

The bulldozers were already at work. As they frantically wheeled and turned, delving and flattening, eradicating stones and earth, tiles and wood and shreds of lost lives, they seemed to be saying to the village and to the country at large: this is one of the first things that you will be asked to forget.

5

We would never forget; how could we forget? That's what I was thinking as I sat in the train hurtling toward the Bigcity, the age-old capital of our region, carrying my father's black notebook. I had been in the Bigcity only a few times, once to see a soccer match and two or three times to go to the library. I never spent time there, though. One whiff and I'd turn tail. I hated the traffic and the luxury shops, I hated the decrepit atmosphere, the stucco figures with broken noses, and a certain countrified air that I saw in the inhabitants, an air that they tried to cover up, with evident embarrassment, concealing it beneath expensive clothing and English-made shoes. In the train, I read the notebook and discovered that my father hadn't been the only one to write in it. I saw Carburo's handwriting, as well as Uncle Nevio's and Baruch's. My dad wrote about the illegal excavation of the river, the undermining of the mountain, and about men going up to fell trees under cover of night; he had recorded the license-plate numbers and the model of trucks that carried the logs away. Carburo wrote about nighttime meetings at the Villa Meringue, with carabinieri squad cars escorting official limousines. He noted the names of the Pastori brothers' friends and recorded their arrest for dealing drugs. Baruch wrote about loan sharking, mentioning the name of Ossobuco and a certain Signore C. Uncle Nevio had inserted photocopies of official documents into the notebook, with evidence of the malfeasance that he had uncovered in the Fefelli administration. This was not the journal of a gang of vindictive, rage-ridden eccentrics. Rather, this was a short book recounting the civic resistance of a group of friends, perhaps a sectarian and slightly naïve text, but good-hearted and sincere. The message was this: It's up to us to defend all of this, it is our legacy, the treasure and the toil of all those who are dear to us; we want things to change, and we continue to hope that they will. That was the message that I was going to deliver in the Bigcity; I was going to deliver it to an honest man, to an institution, or to a party, hoping that the message would not be lost in the shuffle, and I felt that I had been entrusted with an important mission, so important that I couldn't think of any comparison, such as, just to mention something off the top of my head, Jules Verne's Michael Strogoff or Pecos Bill riding to summon the cavalry to relieve the fort under Indian attack or Grey Eagle hurrying to ask the Seminoles for help against the blue-coat soldiers or the final runner in a team of angry black Americans in the 4x100 relay race at the Olympics—yes, that was the best comparison, even though, as I said, I was so deeply moved that it was almost impossible to think of any comparisons, such as White Fang pulling a sled with his wounded master from one end of the Yukon to the other, or, more modestly, Moses with the tablets . . . well, okay, anyway, that's enough.

I had an appointment in a law office; the address was Piazza della Giustizia 2/b. There was a thick, soupy fog in the city, and I had a hard time finding the right bus; once I did, I got off at the wrong stop. I found myself in a huge boulevard lined with tall buildings and full of cars with their headlights on. I ran across the wide road, through a hail of honking horns and revving engines, then I turned into a side street with an abundance of brightly lit shops packed with clothing, food, and bric-a-brac of all sorts. Finally I entered a piazza with a church, but it wasn't the piazza that I was looking for. It was harder than finding my way in the forest. In the middle of the piazza was a fountain, like the basin of the Fanara. In the basin, a lonely and depressed goldfish swam to and fro. A jet of water splished and splashed in the middle. If I had been high up on the mountain, surrounded by my trees, I would have started my duoclock and the gnome or my mother or the Cheerful God would have been able to show me the way, but in the city I knew no being, whether human or imaginary.

As I walked along, turning these laments over in my head, I noticed a girl in a sky-blue scarf hurrying past; she was walking as fast as all the other city dwellers, but when she saw me she slowed down and cried:

"Timeskipper!"

"Venerelli!" I replied.

It was really her, my first official partner in kissing. She hadn't changed for the better: she'd gained weight and her features were rendered vulgar by heavily applied makeup. But her tits were the same as ever, maybe even a little more so. She told me that she worked as a waitress in a bar nearby; she took me to see it and treated me to an espresso with whipped cream.

She had wrapped a white barman's apron around her waist, and she stood looking out the big plate-glass window.

"Life was better in the village, even the fog was different. Here the fog sort of sticks to you, it dirties your clothes, it soaks through to your skin. Say, do you remember the field trip in the big blue bus?"

"I'll say I remember."

"You're much cuter now," she said.

"So are you," I lied.

"Tell me what's happened in the village. Does Fangio still drive his bus?"

"Yes," I answered, and I still don't know why I said it. I can't imagine what sort of life she led; probably she hadn't even heard about the avalanche. But I didn't feel like telling her about it. The story of the village was locked up in the duo-clock, and it would have taken many drops of water and at least a century of normal time to tell her everything. Maybe it was better for her just to remember things the way they used to be. I asked her to tell me how to get to the Piazza della Giustizia, I promised that I'd come back to her bar, and I left. Farewell, Venerelli of the beautiful nipples that made me suffer such pangs.

The courtyard of the lawyers' office building was antique, stern, and covered with dog droppings. I looked at the nameplates next to the buzzers; there must have been three dozen. They looked like the medals on a general's chest. It was an office building with decorations for Juridical Valor. All the building's occupants were lawyers or accountants; every one of them had at least two postgraduate degrees and two dogs, each with two assholes. The man I was coming to see was named Speri, but I couldn't find him. Then I finally made out his name at the bottom of an oval plaque. On the plaque was written, Avvocato Cannavale, Esq. in large letters, Avvocato D'Intesa in medium-size letters, and Avvocato Speri in small letters.

I rang the bell, and a very attractive secretary buzzed me in; she was probably the office manager. She introduced me to a somewhat less attractive secretary, who in turn took me to see a fat, dumpy girl—she was Speri's secretary.

Speri had been waiting for me. He was young, with a neatly trimmed mustache; he looked like a very homely version of Clark Gable. Sitting near him in his office was a portly and distinguished-looking gentleman, with a mustard-colored waistcoat, who was puffing at a pipe stuffed with Prince Albert tobacco, not that I could tell from the aroma—the package was sticking out of one of his pockets. This, evidently, was the Avvocato D'Intesa.

Speri told me that he had spoken by phone with Uncle Nevio, and he had been informed that we intended to lodge one or more criminal complaints as civil plaintiffs. I handed him the notebook. He opened it and immediately showed it to D'Intesa, who seemed to find it interesting. D'Intesa leafed through it, wrinkling his brow and taking deep, princely puffs on his pipe.

"Certainly," said Speri, "that avalanche was a disaster caused by criminal negligence, but then they managed to bury all the evidence a second time. We hope that we can succeed in bringing this to trial, but the people involved have highly placed protection, especially this Arcari. Arcari is slippery as an eel, he works only with foreign money, he never shows up in the documentation, and he launders money for a very powerful Masonic lodge that—"

"That detail is of no interest to this boy," D'Intesa interrupted him brusquely.

"As for your former mayor, Fefelli, this is a time of political misfortune for him. He has made a series of mistakes, but he remains enormously powerful. I assure you that I will do everything possible for your father; I have heard what an admirable and courageous man he is. Our party is battling on numerous fronts, these are very tough times, but we need to fight for minor issues like this as well."

"We don't think of this as a minor issue," I said.

"You have to understand, my boy," said D'Intesa, taking a seat—and I didn't like the tone of that "you have to understand, my boy" one bit —"it's a minor issue in comparison with everything else that's happening. There are dark interests at work behind that avalanche, but if you only knew about all the huge and dark mysteries that we see. Do you know what the abbreviations SID, SIFAR, and CIA mean? They are preparing a war against us, against decent, honest people, like your father and your uncle, who vote for this party, just as you will vote for us one day. But we can't just run headlong into battle, we have to employ strategy because they've held the reins of power for

such a long time. We have to learn from them how to be slippery and patient, how to make our move at the right time. This
notebook is filled with interesting things, though none of them
are new. We know that a great many people gather at Villa
Meringue, including men from the armed services. The Pastori
brothers are notorious neo-Fascists, and then there's Arcari,
who is a member of a lodge, that is, how to put it? a group of
opportunistic businessmen working in concert—when you're a
grown-up you'll understand better. They are already so powerful that they can blackmail Fefelli. But we, let me say it again,
my dear boy, will employ cunning and strategy, it will take time
and patience, but you'll see, we'll succeed. In the meanwhile,
we'll take good care of this notebook."

I wanted to say, "I'd prefer to leave it with Speri."

"In any case, we'll call your uncle, and we'll let you know
how things develop."

"Excuse me, D'Intesa," said Speri, "perhaps we should give
him a written receipt of some kind. Acknowledging the fact
that we have received from him a notebook with a number of
informal accusations or complaints . . ."

"That won't be necessary," said D'Intesa, aiming the pipe at
him as if it were a pistol. "If the notebook becomes juridically
significant, then we'll put everything in writing. If not, we'll
simply return it to him. Are you satisfied, dear boy?"

"This is hardly a time when I can feel satisfied about anything," I replied.

"I understand that the way we talk can be somewhat
obscure," said D'Intesa. "But you see, my boy, although juridical
expertise may seem distant and chilly, in the end it attains what
we want."

"Or what we don't want," added Speri.

This time it was the little puffs of smoke that rose from his
pipe, one after the other, that triggered the duoclock. I saw Speri
with a future as a striptease artist: one by one they stripped away

all of his political investigations until he was left with only a theft of Cuban lobsters from the Festival dell'Unità, the Communist political assembly. He left the party and continued to bust people's balls in a small prefecture in southern Italy. D'Intesa, on the other hand, enjoyed a flourishing career. He became a member of a parliamentary commission of inquiry that would go down in history for its countless plea bargains and acquittals. He finally became a popular guest on talk shows. He moved away from the red party to another party, this one shocking pink, then he ricocheted back to the first party, then I couldn't see a thing, it was like trying to follow the trajectory of the ball in a pinball machine. I wondered what would become of Cannavale.

The door swung open, and my question was answered. A rotund, well-dressed man with the face of Dracula appeared, only instead of blood, he slurped down plate after plate of spaghetti all'amatriciana.

"It's the editor in chief of that newspaper, for the lawsuit," he said. "I want you all in my office immediately."

"This is the boy I was telling you about; he's from the village of the avalanche of Fefelli and Arcari," said D'Intesa. "The notebook that he brought is . . . reasonably well documented."

"Good," said Cannavale, and he meant bad. I didn't need a duoclock. That man would have acquitted someone who had devoured a nursery school full of children.

"We'll be there in a minute," said Speri.

"No, come immediately. And as for you, D'Intesa, an avalanche is made of soil and mud, not the two names you so recklessly mentioned."

"I swear I won't say a word," I felt like saying, perhaps in a Sicilian accent, even though I believe that the phrase can be uttered in any of the countless accents of the world. D'Intesa and Speri left the office with me, tails dragging. It seemed as if they were three huge fish: Speri an honest barbel, D'Intesa a pikefish ready to swallow him whole, and Cannavale, a giant Wels catfish with a mouth big enough to swallow both of the smaller fish and a whole courtroom filled with jurors.

As soon as I stepped out into the courtyard, slaloming through the dogshit, I was back in the dank, grey city. I should have noticed that the Piazza della Giustizia—the Plaza of Justice—was filled with a dense bank of fog and that this condition might well have proved prophetic. But when all was said and done, I still relied upon my Uncle Nevio's words: "Cannavale is a swine, but Speri and D'Intesa are on our side; they'll help us out."

I strolled along beneath a portico. Above me were snickering gryphons and aristocratic escutcheons; I peered at them in search of my own: Timeskipper de Forrest and Gnomus Boletus ap Rivers. My crest features two clocks on a green field, with a Latin motto: *Time Is on My Side*.

Then I noticed that the young city honeys all looked identical at the age of eighteen, with pageboy hairstyles, short carcoats with astrakhan collars, miniskirts and ankle boots. The boys wore high-necked sweaters, even the boys who had short necks, and desert boots. I looked down at my own shoes— they looked like a pair of thoroughly masticated licorice drops, while my turtleneck had more than the usual number of air intakes. Normally, I didn't care about style, in fact, nonstyle *was* my style, but surrounded by all those shops, I suddenly had a ravenous hunger for fashion. And then I spied Chelsea Clothing, the biggest shop I'd ever seen. Seven plate-glass display windows filled with clothing, one just for the sweaters, made of cashmere, angora, and merino wool; my mouth watered the way Verdolin's did when he saw an art-supply store. There was one sweater with a price tag that read: *20,000 lire*. It was a V-neck, a beautiful shade of green, that went perfectly with my big, lustrous eyes. In that sweater, I would wow Selene, I might even wow Brigitte Bardot. I had a small wad of bills that Regina had taken from my father's biscuit tin; Regina told me, "He would have given you this money; use it on your trip to the city." I thought of Luciana's slogan for her female clientele: "When everything is going wrong, buy a dress that's not too long." What would the slogan be for a man? I decided that I would either come up with a slogan or I'd give up the idea of buying that sweater, so I stood there in front of the display window, shifting from one foot to another, until I finally laid the following egg: "Every man, richer or poorer, should own at least one sweater made of angora . . ."

Okay, it sucked, but it cleared the bar I had set for myself, so I walked into the store. I was immediately enveloped in an aroma of expensive wools and shorn sheep. The shop clerk, unquestionably a count working incognito, gazed at me with chilly nobility.

I planned to make a strong impression with one of the three following phrases:

My Rolls-Royce is late picking me up; it must be all this terrible fog. While I wait, I'd like to be shown some of your finest garments, a little something that's warm and light, and that a girl would be tempted to nuzzle.

Or else: Would you happen to have something that would go with a safety-orange tuxedo?

Or else: I am the son of the Avvocato Cannavale. I'd like something as a gift for my father, but two sizes smaller, because he likes a snug fit.

Instead, I used a more concise opening line:

"Could I see that sweater in the window, the one for twenty thousand lire?"

"Signore," he replied, "actually, it's priced at two hundred thousand lire."

"I can't believe it," I blurted out.

"By all means, don't believe it," he sighed, "but that's the price."

It was true, I had miscounted the zeroes. I was about to walk out of the store in a wave of embarrassment when I notice a tall customer picking out jackets, with two clerks serving him haughtily. I look again and think to myself, this can't be. It's the second blast-from-the-past of the day: it's the Troll. Now, he has definitely changed for the better, at least in terms of outward appearance. He is still hunchbacked and clumsy, but his pimples are gone, he is elegantly dressed in a dark-blue blazer with solid-gold cufflinks jutting from his shirt sleeves, he is nicely coiffed, and he seems supremely confident. It's him, the one who loved chickins, the one who took nine years to finish elementary school. The ugliest duckling of them all has become a handsome pheasant.

"Troll!" I call.

"Timeskipper! It's been years!" He reaches out to shake my hand and smiles. His teeth are still snaggly: it's him, no doubt about it.

We walk out of the shop; he's loaded down with two bags filled with fashion. He treats me to an aperitif and tells me his story. At the battery farm, he had carefully examined the logistics and, working with a colleague, he invented a way of plucking the chickins clean of feathers at the speed of sound. Dead chickins, of course. He even patented it in Japan, and now he's selling and installing it in all the chickin farms in Italy, as well as Austria and Germany, and if he can just sell it to the chickin farmers of the Eastern Bloc, his fortune will be made. At age twenty-two, he is already a millionaire, he's married to a woman from Padua, and he lives up in the hills, in a house with a garden. In that garden, he's installed cages with sixty chickins, and he's working on a new invention that he hopes to patent, a chickin feed to develop a chickin twice the size of normal chickins, with thighs like the winner of the Tour de France.

"But what's that good for?"

"People have plumped up nicely, they have more money, and they want to eat more. The chickin sector is drifting toward the minicockerel, I'm moving against the stream, toward the super-mega-chickin. And I'll be successful. Timeskipper, who'd have ever guessed it, that I, the biggest donkey in the class, would become wealthy?"

"You were never the biggest donkey, you were always neck and neck with Marcella."

"C'mon, tell me about the village," he says. "I heard the terrible news about the avalanche."

"Yes. My father is in terrible shape, but he may recover. Gancio's sick, too. There's also some good news, but I can't think of it right now. Anyway, you shouldn't feel too sad about things."

The Troll, unexpectedly, stands silently weeping, big salty tears plopping onto the mixed nuts. It's as if he has hurtled ten years back in time, as if his confidence and money and the Godzilla chickins have all vanished, and he's just a little hunchback sitting at a desk in the back row again, staring out the window at a strange, incomprehensible world.

"I should never have left," he says.

I don't know what to say to him, I can't tell what's happening inside the head of that overgrown boy, maybe it's just like what happens with so many people: half of him is still back in the reeking battery farm and half is here, in the dark-blue blazer with golden cufflinks. Maybe he isn't as happy as he seems, and I say to him:

"Why don't you come back to the village once in a while? It might do you good."

"When a chickin leaves a henhouse," he says, "it's heading for the frying pan."

Nicely put. Good-bye, Troll.

I walk through the hospital corridors. They've changed the flowers, and now it really does smell like a graveyard; the smell of medicine was easier to take. My father is in his room, which he shares with an old man with a fractured skull: the old man jumped off his balcony, out of loneliness.

My father is locked in a plaster suit of armor, asleep. I wait for him to wake up. On the bedside table is a newspaper that he hasn't unfolded, a bottle of water, and his watch, with a strap that's been repaired three or four times. He opens his eyes.

"I took the notebook to the lawyers," I say. "They were very pleased and said that there's a lot they can do with it."

"Good," says my father. "You see, it was a good thing to write for all these years."

It seems to me that he's doing a little better, but I'm afraid to say so. He drops off again. I take his hand, and I touch his calluses one by one. There are no calluses on my hand. There's a hundred years between my childhood and his. We both lived through a period of rapid change, the most rapid of the twentieth century, perhaps of any century. And yet we've always been so close.

On the train returning home, I'm reading a book: *Martin Eden*. I'm on the closing scene, when he leaps into the ocean and kills himself. I can't go on. I close the book, and at that instant I sense that my father is dead.

The day of the funeral, I went into the woods; I wanted to talk with my father one last time. I waited for the dew drops to fall from a hazel tree and I saw him, sitting on the stone bench on the hillock, with his dogs.

"You'll see," I said, "your notebook will bring some big changes."

"No, nothing will change at all," he replied, petting Fox. "We believed in change, our lives were a litany of filthy misfortunes and grim necessities, but every so often the trumpet sounded and we all leapt to our places, ready to fight and help one another out. We believed it was possible to be free, to prevent the return of those twenty years of Blackshirts. But the trumpet call is dying out, now. They sold us out, one by one. They sold our unfortunate lives and our personal histories, to make history together with the others, a false history, without even a happy ending, a story that just ends in indifference for everything and everyone. If it helps them win a few votes, they'll gladly insult us, too.

"But Dad," I said, "they'll remember you fondly as a good, strong man. A little hot tempered, perhaps, but that was the fuel you ran on."

"I wanted to do more. I worked and worked and thought about politics, about my anger, and maybe I overlooked what was happening to you, to Regina, to my brother Nevio. I carved and cut and hammered enough wood to build Noah's ark, and then there was no one to put on board."

"Don't worry about it, Dad. When I came home and heard you hacking away all night with your hatchet, I thought: 'What a dad! It would have been better just to name me Pinocchio.' And I never came to say hello to you in the woodshop, because I didn't want to smell the reek of wine on your breath and listen to your rambling rants. We loved each other because we never pretended things were different than they were, we both looked our unhappiness right in the face. You may not have been a perfect father, and I wasn't an ideal son, and Regina wasn't my mother, but our house was a home, I spent happy hours there, and now it will seem empty. That's enough though; like you taught me, you say certain things once in a lifetime. When I saw you crawl into that hole in the rubble, I knew it might be the end but also that you had won, once and for all."

"Keep an eye on Rufus," my father said, "and on Regina."

"I'll make sure to give both of them bowls of mush," I replied.

*

The parish priest was drunk, completely sloshed, and he delivered a sermon that even Fidel Castro, pissed off and suffering from hemorrhoids, wouldn't have dared to give. He thundered against sinners; in fact, he said, these words: "The filthy sinners who are destroying our forest, who think about nothing but money, and who have killed seven of our fellow villagers." With every word, he was risking immediate transfer to the parish of Maracalagonis. "Our town carpenter," he added, "never showed his face in church, but I know that deep in his heart he was a religious man. If I had asked him to build a crucifix, he would have done it." No one objected, and for that matter, who knew everything about my father? Perhaps not even I did. Baruch said a few simple words, then the parish priest was lured away with a glass of Gewürztraminer as bait, and everyone sang a chorus of the Internationale in quiet voices. The graveyard was a spectacular sight, with broom plants and red handkerchiefs.

When my father was lowered into the grave, we heard a thunderous voice: "What a shitty casket this is!"

We all started: it was straight out of a story by Poe. Could it be the voice of my father, complaining from the tomb? No, it was Balduino, as full of liquor as a wedding pastry.

"He never liked mahogany. He always used to say walnut is a nice wood, I want to be buried in a walnut coffin."

And then something unusual happened. The ceremony came to a halt. The coffin maker and Balduino the barman hopped in the car and sped off to a neighboring town. Don Brusco asked what was happening.

"We forgot that we need a permit from the provincial interment commission," said Baruch.

"There might be an underground water table," I said.

"There might be a truffle field," said Caprone.

"Or maybe an ancient amphora," said Luciana.

The parish priest, further plied with Gewürztraminer, fell

asleep on a tombstone. A short while later, the new coffin, this time made of walnut, arrived. Four of us hid behind a hedge and transferred the body. We woke up the priest, the new coffin was lowered into the grave, and Uncle Nevio came running up, a shoe in one hand.

"We forgot this," he said.

We all thought: if he's in heaven, there are clouds, and he won't need shoes. If he's in hell, you burn with or without shoes. In the Happy Hunting Grounds, everyone rides a horse. In Muslim paradise, you take off your shoes before entering. Buddha famously went barefoot. And if, in the afterlife, there is nothing, then it's a safe bet he won't be walking.

When I returned home, I found Selene at the front door. She had just arrived, her train was late. I'm so sorry I missed the funeral, she said. I kissed her, I wanted to make love, funerals make you horny, it may be blasphemous to say so, but that's the way it is; it's what my father always said, and this seemed like a good time to take his advice.

"I know that you're a little distant right now, Timeskipper," she said. "But I'll wait for you. I don't feel like making love right now, though."

We slept together for two nights, I officially introduced her to Uncle Nevio, and for those few days I didn't feel lonely. Every morning, Regina came to water the flowers, and Rufus and Baruch came by, and once even Arturo Hundred-and-One, step by step, with his cane.

"You know who made the bed I sleep in?" he said to me.

"My father," I replied.

"No, your grandfather," he said, and step by step, he crept away.

That afternoon, I took Selene to the train station. Then I collapsed, I stood crying like a baby in the middle of the street, and Rufus howled in accompaniment.

My uncle said that no one had phoned from the law office. Two days later, I returned to the Bigcity and went to Piazza della Giustizia 2/b. Speri wasn't there. I was given a letter from D'Intesa that read:

"My Dear Boy: the notebook is quite interesting as a document of the life of a courageous man; perhaps with some editing it could become an encouraging book for the militants. But what it says is not sufficient to warrant a new trial, a few license-plate numbers and a few photocopied documents just aren't enough, it would take a hundred times that. If you need help, please feel free to contact us. With cordial regards."

I saw, however, that there were four pages missing from the notebook. I lost my temper and took it out on the secretary; she was typing busily and telling me, "There's nothing I can do about it."

I said, "I don't believe no one is here. I'll just wait for them," and I sat down on the sofa by the door. I waited until late that evening, and then I realized there was nothing to be done.

"You know, miss," I said, "it finally dawned on me why you have your law offices here. Piazza della Giustizia 2/b means Plaza of Justice, *to be*. Someday, but not now."

The secretary smothered a giggle. Perhaps laughing was one of the worst crimes that you could commit in that office. That was my first lesson in the official administration of justice.

While I was in the city, the door of Uncle Nevio's shop opened, and a carabinieri colonel, tall and dignified, walked in. He was known as l'Americano, because he had gone to the United States to study for three years in a special school for special policemen. With him was Licio Pastori.

"I am really very sorry about your brother," said Licio. My uncle took the extended hand and shook it mechanically. Then Pastori said: "Let me introduce you to Colonel Maluschi, the new chief of the investigations division."

"It's a pleasure to meet you," said the colonel. "You are a good mayor, and you are well loved. Of course, there are those who hate you, too. But it's just like in my own line of work: you can't make everyone happy." He browsed through the store, looking at everything with interest. "And I see that you have some magnificent hunting rifles. Is that a Browning? Mind if I take a look?"

My uncle took the rifle out of the display case. The colonel ran his fingers over it lovingly; he clicked a cartridge into place.

"How beautiful guns are. When they aren't being fired, of course. Or, at the very most, when they're being fired at a pheasant, for instance."

"Right," said Uncle Nevio, who felt suddenly uneasy, as if he had a long tail with brightly colored feathers.

"You see, Mister Mayor," said l'Americano, aiming the Browning at the wall and taking a bead on an imaginary pheasant, possibly a subversive pheasant, impossible to say with any certainty, "the investigation into the avalanche has identified the guilty parties. It was the overhasty and culpable initiative of two engineers, a pair of reckless good-for-nothings, one of them had a record of involvement in illegal construction. Then there was the explosives technician who fled the country. Let's hope they catch him, but the odds are against it. Now it's important that the town return to business as usual. I see that you're rebuilding. It's time to forget about old accusations, old wounds."

"If there've been any misunderstandings," said Pastori, "we need to put them behind us. Fefelli himself is tired of dealing with lawyers and the courts."

They seemed to work in perfect coordination, a pair of actors who had rehearsed their lines. A select elite of respectable soldiers, Fascists, and politicians, working together to create the country they wanted. You really had to be paranoid to think that they might want a country different from the one we lived in.

"We know that there other charges waiting to be brought," said Maluschi. "We know that a notebook your brother wrote is circulating, that your nephew has been to see certain lawyers. Young boys shouldn't be involved in matters of such importance."

Uncle Nevio was suddenly afraid. He looked out the window into the piazza, to see if anyone was walking past. There was only a jeep, parked, with a pair of carabinieri sitting inside.

"And so," continued the colonel, "I am here to ask you to calm this town down. Signore Ossobuco told me yesterday that he's afraid to come home, that he is being accused of loan-sharking. That's a heavy accusation; it's up to you to get to the bottom of this. You are the mayor of all the citizens of this town, not just a faction."

"I think that before we calm things down, we need to uncover the truth. I don't know if the term you're looking for is calm down. Maybe it's cover up, defuse—you pick the verb you think works best."

"All right, then, the term I choose is to bring order," said the colonel in a harsh tone of voice. "That is my first responsibility, and yours as well: to maintain order. Otherwise, I have to assume that you're the wrong mayor for this little town."

"You really shouldn't keep so much gunpowder in your shop," said Pastori, who was wandering from counter to counter. "Just a spark is all it would take to blow everything up."

"Out of here, both of you!" said Uncle Nevio.

"Oh, we'll leave if we've made ourselves clear," said Maluschi.

"Perfectly clear," said Uncle Nevio.

They left the shop, climbed into the jeep, and drove off to carry out further missions. But before they returned to the heat of battle, they stopped by Chicco's restaurant to eat a couple of quails.

I learned about all this from Uncle Nevio, but only many years later. From that day on he became moody and laconic. "The mayor is tired," people started saying. He kept to himself the fear of having that conversation; he never even discussed it with Baruch. And that was too bad, because it gnawed at his heart.

In the last three months of high school, I studied day and night, alone or with Fred and Tamara, drugged to the gills on quarts of cold espresso. Our average heart rate was four hundred, at rest. Baco was taking a pharmaceutical called Plegine, it really gave you a charge, but it had side effects: three hours of intensely concentrated study, followed by an hour on the toilet, then back to the books.

I can't remember much about exam day. Our exam board was considered to be about average in terms of malice and sadism. I remember one teacher, a Sicilian, who asked me to talk about Pirandello, and then went on talking and never let me get a word in edgewise. There was a tiny female math teacher who reminded me of the Forest Gnome; she had unpredictable mood swings, but she was harder on girls than on boys. I had studied hard, so I managed to survive an equation designed to prove the singularity of the Holy Trinity. Then it was time to face the teacher of ancient Greek. He had a terrifying reputation and he looked just awful: he was bald as a billiard ball, he had heavy eyebrows and a huge, unkempt black beard. He looked like the villain in a Chaplin movie.

"*Odyssey*," he thundered. "Book sixteen, from this verse, read, translate, provide commentary."

I started reading. It was the meeting of Telemachus and Ulysses: as I read I saw each word, every image, the room vanished, Ithaca surrounded me with its olive groves, I saw the sea of Cesenatico (never having laid eyes on the actual Greek sea). I felt as tired as Ulysses, as overjoyed as Telemachus.

"Now translate?" I asked.

"No," he replied, "the way you read it tells me all I need to know."

And there was a huge smile plastered across his huge ogre's face. I thought, "School is boredom, torture, and other things that vanish the day you leave, but there are others that emerge only over time, and others you'll never forget, and one of them is this moment of genuine understanding with a huge old man I've known only for a few minutes and whom I'll never see again in my life."

The evening they posted the results. I went out with Selene to celebrate our graduation; her results were almost as satisfactory as mine. She told me that she was leaving for England, with the highly improbable explanation that she wanted to study English. She would be gone for three long months. I was dismayed, but I had learned that the happiness of a couple is the sum of the happiness of each individual composing that couple. Her happiness went up by two points, mine dropped by one: the result was a net increase. It is a mathematical principle, and is therefore abstract and difficult to apply. But, for once, I managed.

"Where exactly will you be going?" I asked.

"I'll be staying in a boarding school, in a town called Coventry."

"Why, what a remarkable coincidence," I said. "I happen to own a castle in Coventry, but I never go there. Could you drop by twice a week to feed the cat?"

"The cat eats only twice a week?"

"It's a ghost cat. There are nothing but ghosts in the castle. There is the headless phantom, the thyroidless ghost, and then there's Signor Waldemar, Van Maxel, and Karamazov . . ."

"Karamazov?"

"Yes, he's there, too. And there's also the phantom drummer, who plays all night long. Perhaps that's why I go there so seldom. And then, of course, there's the phantom priest."

"What does he do?"

"He kisses you when you expect it least."

And I kissed her. That night we made love like a pair of alley cats. I couldn't remember the last time it had been so intense. She even did a striptease for me, to the tune of "Fever." "Fabulous," I told her. "I want to become your manager."

The next morning I took her to the train station.

"I'll think about you lots," I said, "and you know how much I can think. If you meet Brian, say hi for me."

"Don't be a dope. I love only you."

"I trust you. Anyway, you might be interested to know that in ten or fifteen years, Brian is going to become two hundred and twenty pounds of lard with an ascot around his neck; it may already have come to be. It just so happens that I know how to skip forward in time."

"I know that. It's why I'm leaving. You live in three or four different times, and there's room for me in only one of them. And since you're such a sorcerer, what will you become?"

"A serial killer," I said, "or else a member of parliament, and you will either be a respected physician or a tremendously well-preserved piece of ass, the kept lover of a shitty little local manufacturer."

"Any other alternate futures for me?"

"You might be a stripper at the Crazy Horse. Or possibly my wife," I said.

She left, and I kissed her right up to the minute the train pulled out. When the train faded into the distance, I realized that I was alone and I would be alone for the days that followed, days that would be decisive for the rest of my life. The duoclock had four hands. Two of those hands told me that I was still part of the forest, and that it was about to bloom anew, that I would see Selene again, and that I would discover my true talents: I would act in a theatrical production of the *Odyssey*, I would play Edgar Allan Poe in a movie, I would write a book titled *The Memoirs of a Young Right Winger*, and I would become the mayor of Maracaibo.

The other two hands of the duoclock told me: you will kill

Fefelli. The anger of Gancio, your father, and all those who fought up on the mountain will flow into you at one time, and a sacrifice will be required of you.

Before going back to the village, I said good-bye to everyone, even Riccardo and Giap, and I told them come up and see me, while thinking to myself, let's hope they don't. I kissed Tamara good-bye, considered screwing Tremolina, then changed my mind, and got drunk with Fred and Baco, who were no longer a couple. I bought a green sweater, this time for exactly twenty thousand lire, and I bought a Totò record for Regina. I got drunk again, and this time listened to Thelonious Monk all night long. The next morning, before it was time to catch the train, I went to see Gancio. They told me that he wasn't there anymore. He had been released. The doctors were against it, but he had left for South America.

The Guatayabas had a new chief.

6

I went back to the village. It would be a long summer, and I would have to decide what to do when it was over. Should I attend university, or leave for Cuba, or kill myself, or found a rock band and then kill myself on tour, or set up a left-wing fruit and vegetable stand, or assassinate a tyrant? Life lay spread out before me, I was free, and freedom is dangerous, you can't know in advance if there is a whirlpool in your river, ready to suffocate you, whether the road around the curve continues uphill or ends suddenly in a ravine, whether what awaits you is a welcoming tavern or the Sheriff of Nottingham. "Liberty," Baruch used to say, "is a mushroom that you have to taste; you can't know in advance if it will poison you or not." And I didn't know which of my two clocks would tick louder. I didn't even know anymore if I was young or old. A young man who is going to die at age twenty is already old at eighteen. But if Uncle Nevio had another forty years to live, he might be younger than me.

The same thing was true of the village, it was suspended between two ages. There were still lots of old houses with vegetable patches, woodpiles, and wells, Caprone's sheep wandering across the road, the piazza with its bar and people sitting out front, the sound of the cowbells on cattle along the edge of the road, bicycles with dim lights moving slowly through the fog. There was the forest, the Fanara, the hidden farmhouses, the river with its fishermen, the silence of Mount Mario. After that there was the highway, already a little old, with potholes in

the asphalt, the cement plant, increasingly smoky with the passing years, the old wound on the mountainside, the Roselle subdivision with half the houses uninhabited, the new stores with
their neon signs already flickering, but everything flowed, and
the village continued to transform itself. A new gas station with
an automatic carwash, a thousand new television antennas on
the roofs, horrible new row villas halfway up the mountainside.

And the new fountain, scheduled for unveiling in August.

They had told me that there were major changes even at Balduino's bar—a bigger television set and a jukebox. The jukebox
had only a dozen slightly out-of-date songs. "Romantica," "Non
ho l'età," and "Piove." Then it had a polka, a mazurka, and a
franksinatra. There was "White Christmas" by Bing Crosby, but
if you wanted to hear it you had to push the button for "Zin-
gara." Turning to the more modern tastes, there were the Beach
Boys, "Satisfaction," and a single—of which only a single copy
existed—"Tu che sei la vita mia" by Arturo and the Dreamboys.
It was the most popular song. When the jukebox appeared in
the bar, it made quite an impression, and caused a great deal of
annoyance, especially among the tressette players, who, as is
well known, need their concentration. Maria Casinò said: if you
play "White Christmas" I get all emotional, I feel like crying,
and I can't play anymore. Breadlocks the baker said: every time
I hear that song that bombards me in the nuts (he was talking
about "Satisfaction"), I am certain to play my hand wrong. Well,
you'd better get ready for far more invasive forms of technology,
said Baco, in America they're already preparing a hybrid of pinball, television, and jukebox—it's called a video game.

"As long as that's all that arrives from America," said
Baruch, "I'm not too worried. As long as they don't send us
anything that explodes."

Baruch, sadly, was always right.

Aside from the big-screen TV and jukebox, though, the bar
was the same as ever, with the pool table, as threadbare as an

old collar, and the display case for the fishing trophies. The Mephisto Bar and the Acapulco Bar and the New Bar had tarted themselves up with counters made of jasper and alabaster, and you could sit on ottomans upholstered with hippopotamus scrotum or else in the little triclinium, where you could stretch out on a chaise longue, and when you bought an aperitif, they offered olives and pickled onions free of charge. "I mean, that's clearly unfair competition," said Balduino.

"Well," I said, "you could offer little cubes of mortadella."

"It wouldn't work," he replied. "If Caprone comes in, he'll eat them all."

"You just tell him that he has to leave some for the others."

"You try telling him," answered Balduino.

So we set out two trays with signs. One read: FOR CAPRONE. The other read: FOR THE OTHER CUSTOMERS. Caprone got so mad that one afternoon he walked in with a thirty-pound mortadella under one arm, threw it behind the counter, and said: "There: now we're even, you *ghittoni*."

Ghittoni meant: miserly, tight-fisted wretches.

In the evenings, everyone still gathered in the piazza, at the same little tables, and talked about my father. They said that before he died, he had finished the final prototype of the fountain, and that he would have been happy to see it in action. I noticed that Baruch wasn't there. They said that he was moving house. He had sold his home, a farmhouse surrounded by cherry trees, and would go to live in an ugly apartment house behind the church.

"Why?" I asked Baruch later.

"Maybe you're old enough to understand," he said. He told me that he had cosigned a loan for a friend, he wouldn't tell me his name, who had gotten deep in debt to loan sharks and the bank. His friend had been unable to dig himself out of his plight, and Baruch had paid his debts, but he'd had to sell his house to do it.

"That's not right, Baruch. They are dishonest hoodlums, you didn't owe them a cent."

"When you give your word, you've given your word. And I have gout, so my feet are killing me; I was tired of walking all the way to the piazza. Now I live closer in."

My uncle told me the rest of the story. Ossobuco and Osso were no longer the local loan sharks; they had made their money, and they were buying real estate and farmland. Now it was Chicco, the restaurateur, who was lending money.

"But he's a comrade, a fellow Communist," I said.

"I'm not sure he's a comrade anymore. He's a loan shark, and I told him that if he doesn't cut it out, I'll have the police on his case."

I walked by the restaurant. Chicco happened to be out front, seated at a table, doing his accounts.

"Timeskipper, what are you doing here? Are you ready to order your wedding banquet?"

I couldn't say a word to him. I shot him a glance of such cold fury, though, that he stood up and went inside. He had understood perfectly. Perhaps that look scorched him more than any insult could have done. Or perhaps it was just a gnat bite in his new and remorseless existence.

At the end of June, Uncle Nevio and I started going down to the river again, and we started fishing again, as well. We went upstream now, where the water was still clean. One time, we took Fred and the perfect couple with us. La Schiassi immediately shrieked, "No, those poor little worms, no," so we had two options: either to bait our hooks with bread and polenta, but in that stretch of river there weren't any carp, which like that sort of bait, or else we had to send La Schiassi away. Instead my uncle patiently explained the laws of nature to her, the fact that in the river, fish eat flies and dragonflies and everything else that happens to come into contact with the surface of the water. Sparrows eat worms, whales eat plankton, which is a cloud of tiny creatures, the praying mantis chews her husband's head off, lions eat antelopes, and we humans eat half the species that live on the face of the earth. And if we're really looking for a cosmic meaning to it all, the worm has his revenge in the end, because he devours the fisherman, nicely tenderized in his grave.

Within minutes, we watched as La Schiassi impaled earthworms on fishing hooks with unexpected sadism, muttering "Hold still, you nasty little creature." Verdolin looked on lovingly. He loved her just as much in her bloodthirsty mode.

After that, La Schiassi caught her first fish, and the law of nature took its inevitable course.

Fred fished with his hands. I had taught him the rockbanger trick. My uncle and I each caught two big barbels, which we threw back in the water, and lots of midsized fish, which we kept. We built a fire and fried the fish in a pan. We looked like cowboys in a bivouac, if you retouch the picture to add in olive oil, salt, Coca-Cola, bread, celery, napkins, and plastic trash bags.

Uncle Nevio chose this opportunity to tell us:

"Kids, you're the first ones to know. Before the height of the August holidays, there's going to be a big party for the inauguration of the fountain. But in October, I won't be running for mayor again. I'm going to retire from politics and go live with Luciana."

I was disappointed. I didn't know anything about the threats. But that's not why he was giving up; he was giving up because he wanted to live well during the last years remaining to him. He'd had a heart attack but was keeping that a secret. He would always be the mayor, to us.

"Promise me not to breathe a word to anyone," he said. We told everyone we met, and that was exactly what he wanted.

There were people who said, he's making a mistake. There

were others—most of them women—who said, he's doing the right thing, he just wants to enjoy a peaceful old age with Luciana. Many of the townspeople were worried about the upcoming elections. Giglio Arduini, who had become the most important local party leader, suggested Dr. Carabelli as a candidate. Oh, no you don't, said others, we don't want a fag mayor. But Carabelli was by this point a village institution, and a beloved one. Day and night, he rode out on his Lambretta making house calls, on mountaintops and at the lowest points in the valleys, in summer heat and winter chill. Moreover, the pharmacist had left him for an aerosol-spray salesman. After lengthy debate, it was decided that Carabelli would run for mayor, and we could finally say that sexual liberation had conquered even my little town.

The other faction, the people from Villa Meringue, now held their meetings in a hotel-qua-bordello, the Hotel Lara, owned by the Pastori brothers. They decided on a candidate of their own: Boccoli, the president of the bank. And they announced that they, too, would hold a celebration to present the mayor-in-waiting, and to present a magnificent piece of news.

They had succeeded in obtaining permits to build the Millerose Residential Complex, located above the Roselle subdivision, just a short distance before the rock spur that had caused the disaster. There would be eighty apartments, a swimming pool, tennis courts, and a hotel with a conference hall. There would be work and money for everyone, but especially for the developer Arcari. This time everything was done openly, without hiding behind shell companies. They had treacherously scheduled their party for the same day that the fountain was to be inaugurated. Among those addressing the crowd would be Arcari, Fefelli, Minister Anguilla, and a number of generals. There would be a big open-air banquet on the grounds of Villa Meringue. The guest of honor was to be the famous actress Gina Jocesò. Last of all, a concert by the tenor, Malavasi, backfromhisacclaimedworldtour, and fireworks. "Dark suits would be appreciated," it said at the bottom of the invitation.

Even if it was just on a provincial scale, it was a first example of the military-industrial-political complex with a cultural pretext and a light dusting of pussy. All the PVSWs, or Protagonists of the Village's Social Whirl, would be attending. Only later would we start calling them VIPs.

Since nobody in town was talking about anything else, we went to see my uncle and we told him: they're holding a big party to overshadow your event, and we will respond: eye for an eye, buffet for buffet, fireworks for fireworks, and sex bomb for sex bomb. We will celebrate your farewell and the new fountain with a party that'll make their party look like a bingo game at the parish church, no disrespect intended for Don Brusco.

Uncle Nevio said, "What do I know about parties? What can we do besides grilled sausages and a polka combo?"

We met in a special emergency session. The party committee consisted of me, Baruch, Giglio Arduini, Fred, and a guy named Cavadori, who was the impresario of the Chestnut Festival and the Miss Provincial Best-Legs Pageant, as well as a personal friend of Italian pop idol Fred Bongusto. At the end of the session, we had planned the following events.

At noon, grilled sausages for everyone in the piazza. In the afternoon, games and polka dancing with the musical group Camilla and Her Corsairs. In the evening, at the Casa del Popolo, at six P.M. sharp, a documentary on the Italian Resistance movement would be shown, and in the piazzetta outside the bank, a marionette show featuring *Fagiolino medico della mutua* ("Greenbean, the socialized-health-care provider"). At nine o'clock, a runway presentation of lingerie from Luciana Moda Bella. At about nine-thirty, the inauguration of the fountain, followed by a spectacular show of the pyrotechnician's finest creations, by the maestros of fireworks, the Brothers

Pipitone. At ten, the biggest British rock concert ever held in the region.

"That all sounds wonderful," said my uncle, "but there's just one thing I don't understand. How much will all this cost, and where are we going to find the world-famous British rock band?"

We explained that while we hadn't calculated exactly how much money it would cost, we were all willing to work for free, and even to put in money of our own, and then there would be the cash from the raffle, as well as money that might be contributed by sponsors, if we could find any. The party had been planned to appeal to every generation, from kids to rock 'n' rollers, from militants to retirees who loved to dance, from foodies to people who loved loud bangs and bright flashes. We had it all: lingerie, culture, cholesterol. No question about it, it'd be a huge hit.

"That's fine," said Uncle Nevio. "But let's be clear about one thing. I have some extra money, because I sold a share in my store. I want to put in at least two million lire of my own money. I want to see those pieces of shit squirming with envy."

At least in theory, it seemed like we had everything in place, but now came the hard part. First of all, we needed a major rock band. Fred said, "Let's call up the Rolling Stones, maybe they feel like coming to Italy, what does it cost to ask?" I called Information and asked, "Could you find me a London phone number? The name is Rolling Stones, *r* as in Romeo, *o* as in Oscar . . .

A voice replied, sweetly: "Are you pulling my leg?"

"Couldn't you just see if there is a Mick Jagger in the London phone book?" I begged. The line went dead. We read through the trade papers: the Beatles were on tour, the Nomadi would be playing in Mestre on that day. I was about to call Information again and ask for Tom Jones's phone number when Cavadori showed up and said: "Kids, we're in luck. We can get the Scrapers."

"Who the fuck are they?" we all said at the same time.

"You don't know anything. Nobody's heard of them in Italy yet, but soon they're going to be famous. In Belgium, Germany, Switzerland—they're the band everyone's listening to." And he showed us a Belgian music magazine; they had a hit song, ranked twentieth on the charts: "Wild Night." He also had a German newspaper with a photograph, four guys with phosphorescent jackets, and heads of hair that surpassed anything achievable with cow urine; they must have used artichoke fertilizer to get those hairdos. Each of them had a different kind of plant on their head. The drummer had a palm tree, the guitarist had a weeping willow, the bass player had a cactus, and the lead singer had a brilliantined banana shape, like a toucan's beak. And Scraper, it seemed, was their twisted translation of bulldozer, meaning they bulldozed away any outdated musical preconceptions; but it was also a name that suited our tradition of labor in the fields and construction yards.

Uncle Nevio looked at the photograph and said: "I'll bet my ass and my few remaining shreds of reputation on this group."

We split into two teams: one was official, the other was secret. The official team was responsible for organizing the festival; the secret team, consisting of me, Fred, and Grillomartino, was in charge of sabotaging the enemy events.

Plus we had unexpected help. Gancio had come home. He had a tan, a mustache, and a new dragon tattoo. Even before welcoming him home, we said: tell us everything.

"It's too much, guys, there's just too many things. But one thing in particular I can tell you: the Guatayabas exist, and I saw them. They smoke herbs in their pipes and afterward they see one god apiece, each one of them has his own personal god to talk to. The women have kinda droopy tits, but they're a lot of fun and they never say no. They eat manioc and crocodile chops, the *Gazzetta dello Sport* comes two days late, but it always comes. I'm going to stay here for a couple of months, put together some money, and head back. Down there you can live on pennies."

That river of half-truths and tall tales reassured us that it was good old Gancio; he hadn't changed.

It was the best gift Uncle Nevio could have had; his quasi-son, as he called him, had come home and was doing fine. I was the only one—because I knew every detail of Gancio by heart—who could see that something good had happened to him, but a black shadow was still there in his alien head.

Finally, it was the day before the party. At Villa Meringue there were more policemen than you'd see at a protest march. They were searching and inspecting everything in sight. They even came into town, a three-man squad, commanded by one pudgy cop whom we immediately dubbed Garcia, after Sergeant Garcia, from *Zorro*. They walked into the bar and started sniffing around, eyeing everybody.

"If you're looking for Che Guevara, he's having a piss," said Balduino.

They didn't like that. They asked everyone sitting outside for their ID. Then they made the mistake of asking Caprone. He lost his temper, and happened to have a scythe with him; we barely managed to stop him. Uncle Nevio showed up and said to the three cops: "Boys, there's going to be a festival tomorrow, not a war. I don't understand why you're acting like this. I'm the mayor of this town, and I'd like to ask you to show a little respect while you're here."

He said it in such a powerful tone of voice that Sergeant Garcia almost snapped to attention. They searched a few hedges along the road, and then left.

We prepared our sabotage plans. What we would need was a truck and a bomb. Breadlocks the baker lent us the truck. The bomb would be provided by Dolcino, who worked for the dairy products cooperative. He delivered it to us the night before, saying, "This is like a nuclear weapon." We were ready.

Our party started at noon. A huge sausage barbecue, a fog of sausage, a cloud of pure pork in angelic form. The smoke signals and the aroma spread out over the entire valley. The Cherokees of Scaricalasino, the Apaches of Monfalco, and the Comanches from Polverino all phoned in: message received, we are on our way, with demijohns of wine. The grilling raised the temperature from seventy-eight degrees to ninety-six degrees. It became necessary to drink heavily, but no one complained.

Then it was time for the games and the raffle. Among the prizes, I saw a giant bunny just like the one from the waltz contest, and my heart split down the middle. However, the festival was roaring along merrily. There was bingo, a tressette tournament, and last of all, an arm-wrestling competition.

From Tuscany had come Garzellini, the sledgehammer of Barberino. He had an arm, Luciana told us, that required a sleeve like other men's trousers. He beat everyone he arm wrestled with ridiculous ease. Until he came up against Caprone. They locked hands, their wrists came together, their gazes met, and then Caprone opened his mouth in his usual three-toothed grin. That, according to some observers, was when, psychologically, Garzellini first began to waver. The emcee called for the match to begin, and Garzellini, the Sledgehammer of Barberino, immediately went on the attack, but Caprone, the Billy Goat of the Vignabassa, gave not an inch, not even a thirty-second of an inch. Garzellini started looking under the table to see if his opponent were nailed down somewhere, or if he was held up by a pneumatic jack, or maybe had some mechanical parts, like Terminator, because the harder he pushed, the more his adversary laughed and acted indifferent. It was as if forty men had added their strength to Caprone's arm. Then there was a sound as if someone had stepped on an Easter basket; it was Garzellini's metatarsal arch collapsing, and then Caprone shouted "*Alé*," and Garzellini's arm flopped over onto the table.

Not very many people came to see the film on the Italian Resistance movement, and some members of the audience even snored loudly, but Baruch comforted Giglio by telling him that, knowing what an afternoon we'd just had, the souls of the partisans would understand and forgive. While the stage was being set up and, under the canvas, people were busily polishing the fountain for its inauguration, Gancio, Fred, and I set off to scout out the situation at Villa Meringue, disguised as young bakers. The bomb was concealed beneath a canvas. The first official automobiles and early guests started to arrive. The carabinieri were keeping watch at the gate, and there was even an officer perched high up in a horse chestnut tree, looking like a crow. I saw Osso, big and fat, rocking to and fro on his heels, dressed in a tuxedo. He looked like a stuffed penguin. Gancio couldn't resist, and shouted: "Be careful, Osso, you'd better not fart tonight." Osso turned around, saw us, and stood there, openmouthed, overweight, ridiculous, and penguinified. Then he slapped his left fist into the crook of his arm, wordlessly telling us to go fuck ourselves. A carabiniere walked over, droning: "Move along, move along." I wanted to say, "How far?"—drive two feet forward and then say—"Is this far enough?" but we had to avoid being noticed. The attack was based on the fact that we had a mole in the villa staff, specifically Veleno, one of the waiters from the Foglia d'Oro restaurant, who had been hired to wait tables during the party. He was a trusted comrade and party member, and he hated Fefelli; Veleno's mother had once been Fefelli's cook, and Fefelli had fired and insulted her. We got out of the truck and scurried down to the meadow below the house, silent as a

Guatayaba war party. Veleno was waiting for us behind the villa, where the tool shed was located. The shed had a little door that opened directly into a hole in the privet hedge. We handed through the device.

But while they were celebrating, unaware of the impending explosion of Dolcino's bomb, we had problems of our own: there was no sign of the Scrapers, and they had been scheduled to arrive at seven that morning. It was now only a short while until the inauguration of the fountain, and we were very tense. Most worrisome of all, the lingerie runway presentation, which was supposed to be held at the Casa del Popolo, had been delayed. There were already 200 people waiting outside, and the auditorium could hold only a hundred. A daring decision was made: there would be only three models, one per generation, and on stage outdoors in the village piazza. "Sodom and Gomorrah," said Don Brusco. "White wine or red?" asked Balduino, arriving in the nick of time, with a bottle in each hand. "After all," sighed Don Brusco, as he sipped and then gulped, "it's hot out, women would be walking around half-naked in any case." And he gave his approval for the lingerie show in the piazza.

When the bell tower sounded nine, this was the way matters stood.

At Villa Meringue, everyone was seated at a giant horseshoe-shaped table, decorated with flowers. At the part of the horseshoe that pointed toward the horse's ass, sat all the most important attendees: Arcari, with a big smile on his face; Fefelli, in something of a daze; three very warlike generals, Minister Anguilla, hunched over, sucking on a breadstick. Then there was the mayoral candidate Boccoli, in a dark-blue blazer, and Gina Jocesò in gold lamé, with a risqué décolletage and a profusion of necklaces. Seated further out along the table was an assortment of mayors from other towns, the CEO of the cement plant, with his wife; the editor in chief of the city gazette and *his* wife; a cardinal without Mrs.; a count, with corresponding contessa. Along the curving sides of the horse-shoe were the LIPs, or less important people, such as Osso, Ossobuco, Rondelli the grocer, and various deputy mayors, etc. Colonel Maluschi, the head of the security detail, strode back and forth, angry as a wasp, because not enough napalm—that is, mosquito coils—had been used, and the mosquitoes were pestering civilians and soldiers alike. Everyone was starving, but to say so was taboo. Finally, twelve waiters in white jackets arrived with groaning trays, and smoked-salmoned and caviared the guests. The count immediately began choking on a piece of bruschetta, and a wave of horror swept through the party. Maluschi stood ready to perform an emergency tracheotomy with a bayonette. One matron poured butter down her plunging neckline. But there were no other mishaps, and the party groaned onward. The Pastori brothers ate standing up, ready for action. The fireworks were set off, along with a few firecrackers. Everyone ate and drank, and drank and ate.

In the piazza, a ululating howl arose from the crowd, signaling the lingerie runway show had begun. We formed a cordon, afraid the crowd might go wild. Luciana Moda Bella appeared and announced: "This evening you will see three lovely pieces of lingerie, each for a different age, because women are beautiful at any age, at twenty, thirty, and forty, and after forty, they are still forty, forever."

Thunderous applause.

"Our first masterpiece in lingerie," said Luciana, "is a two-piece in black lace, with hand-embroidered panties and bra, ideal for the younger set, and modeled by our lovely little Sicilian girl, Nuccia Riggio."

From the piazza came a bloodcurdling shriek: Nuccia's father. No one had thought to warn him. But once Nuccia appeared, in all her Latin loveliness, Mamma Riggio said happily: "Oh, after this evening's show, I can marry her off in no more than a week," and Poppa Riggio began to calm down.

"And now," said Luciana, "for the age whose beauty is ripe as October grapes, a nuptial baby-doll, in Scottish silk, modeled by Gina la Postina, our mail lady."

And Gina hand delivered to the eager crowd all her beauty, registered and special delivery; everyone clapped furiously except for Caprone, who stood weeping, appreciating the sight in his own special way.

"Last of all," concluded Luciana, "for us overforties—and whoever just said 'per leg' can go fuck themselves, excuse me—here is a floor-length nightgown, a Paris Pigalle selection, as modeled by Zoraide."

Zoraide showed off the satiny loveliness of her years, and when she opened her nightgown to show off her black fishnet stockings, it took four of us to hold Caprone back.

In a thunderstorm of hormonal sensations, the audience surged from the stage to the middle of the piazza. There Uncle Nevio waited for everyone to settle down, and then waved one hand. Twelve men, working together, lifted off the canvas that covered the fountain.

There it was, the long-awaited apparition. And for once, it was better than what we had dreamed of.

I had never seen anything so beautiful, even in Paris, or at least that's what emotion made me believe. The fountain was illuminated from within, the water was still, and bright blue, the jets of water were not yet spraying. In the middle of the basin stood a Venus, covering herself with her hands in all the right places. Around her stood four mermen, each holding a giant seashell, and a spiraling assortment of dolphins, pikefish, tunas, and leaping frogs, some in copper, others in marble. But the most beautiful pieces were four pikefish made of enameled Canadian pine. I remembered seeing the fish heads in the woodshop, as my father carved the scales. Now all those hours of work shrank to an instant, but they were worth it, all the same.

My uncle stood looking up at the Venus, who returned his gaze with some interest. He was clearly a little drunk. With one hand on his hip and the other holding the megaphone, he said:

"We could easily have had a famous architect or sculptor build this fountain, but we chose not to, because here in our village, we have equally talented people, and with their work we have built a fountain that, quite modestly, can claim to ass fuck lots of fountains in other big cities.

"We could have built a monument to the Resistance, but I know that we don't need monuments to remember our brothers and fathers and grandfathers; the true monument is inside us. It is our liberty.

"We could have dedicated it to an illustrious man from this town, but here we are all illustrious and important.

"We could have built a modern fountain with a giant cockroach of cement and steel, but everyone around here seems to be busy building giant cockroaches.

"We could have sculpted a fully clothed Venus, but we have nothing to hide, I can even tell you who the model was for the statue, the factory worker Cee-cee, pardon me, Marina Roda, newlywed.

"Last of all, somebody asked me, but why is it a sea-themed fountain? First of all, in tribute to our river, which we all love so much and which, like all self-respecting rivers, flows into the sea. And then there's our general desire for clean water, to wash away all the filth that we have seen and hope never to see again. But first and foremost, we would like to have the sea here, we'd like to be able to get up in the morning and go sailing in a boat, but if we can't then let's dream it, because, thanks be to God, in this village we are still all crazy and we imagine things, and that's why we built the fountain that we all dreamed of, and if anybody has any objections, then let them object to this. One, two, three, and let her rip."

And out of a hundred different apertures jets of water began to burble and spray. Venus and the tritons were weeping, the pikefish and tunas were pissing, and the frog was spitting. There was a roaring cascade of applause.

"That's gonna be some water bill," said Balduino, but he was on the verge of tears, like everyone else.

At that very moment, up at the villa, Veleno opened the canvas containing the bomb. Inside was a hermetically sealed container. Veleno put a handkerchief to his mouth and lifted the lid.

Inside were four wheels of a cheese known as Puzzone di Fossa (literally, "tomb stinker") a blend of spoiled cheese rennet and ricotta curds, ripened for two days in the hot sunlight. It was as if he had ripped the underpants off Lucifer's ass, or ripped open a cemetery, or unbridled all of the gorgonzolas in Christendom. As the lid of the container was pulled back, it freed a horde of swampy spirits and malodorous phantoms, flicking phosphorescent marsh gases and vapors that spread with clammy greed toward the elegant dinner table. When the smell—smell, though, is so inadequate to describe it—reached the assembled guests, every fork froze suddenly in midair, Arcari's smile went out like a match in high wind, and Gina Jocesò's tits were vitrified on the spot. A carabiniere standing at attention keeled over without a word.

"I believe I detect a certain unseemly scent," said Fefelli.

"Men," Colonel Maluschi commanded, "seek the source!"

"What source?" asked Sergeant Garcia.

"The source of this smell, a sewer main or something like that. Just find it!" shrilled Fefelli.

When the box containing the stench of Satan's asshole was finally located, they had to dig a pit two yards deep to bury it. They tried a three-foot-deep hole, but the smell was still powerful and pungent. The domestic help were questioned and re-questioned, but nobody knew anything about it. Maybe it was left over from some long-ago party, and it had just been forgotten there, in the bushes.

Then the cake with a model of the new residential complex was brought to the table, complete with a profusion of tiny spun-sugar houses, a gelatine swimming-pool, and a hotel made of chocolate shavings. With a triumphal air, Arcari served out slices of his creation. But no one was hungry anymore, and there were eighty pounds of leftover cake, out of the original ninety-pound confection.

Then Fefè rose to his feet, raised a toast, and announced: "And now, the moment of musical artistry that we've all been waiting for: the tenor Malavasi, backfromhisacclaimedworld-tour, will sing operatic arias, accompanied on the pianoforte by Maestro Stradivari."

"That's Stramicioli," the maestro corrected him.

And Malavasi let loose with "La donna è mobile" (G. Verdi).

They might have been cheese-stenched to death, but we on the other hand were in deep deep shit. The famous rock band hadn't shown up, and the piazza was crowded with people—people sitting on chairs, on the ground, and in the balconies, as well as a few perched on the branches of the trees. The spotlights were illuminating the stage, where Roland amplifiers and microphones towered in preparation for the show. Food and drink had been provided, or as they say in the world of rock, the backstage had been catered. There were fifty bottles of cold beer and just as many panini with prosciutto awaiting The Scrapers in their dressing rooms (in civilian life, the sacristy of the village church). Even though Don Brusco had received an invitation to Villa Meringue, he had opted for our festival for three reasons.

In primis, to use the ecclesiastical phrase, he was not a very worldly priest, and the notation at the bottom of the invitation—"*Dark suits would be appreciated*"—had struck him as offensive. "What are they worried about, that I'll show up in a hot-pink cassock?" he muttered.

In secundis, someone had told him that in English, The Scrapers means "archangels."

In tertiis, our wine was much, much better than theirs.

It was already ten thirty and catcalls and derisive whistles were starting to rise from the audience. In addition to the throng of locals, all of the young rock fans and hoodlums from down in the valley were there. The Scrapers were a big attraction, even for those who had never heard of them—the photos on the posters made them look like a group of real delinquents.

"Hey," shouted one of the young punks, "when's the concert going to start, midnight?"

"You've got to give us time," said Maghino, the electrician, newly promoted to lighting technician. "The Scrapers ain't just your ordinary group of farts."

It might not have been the kind of announcement you'd hear at the festival of San Remo, but it quieted the audience, at least for the moment.

But a few minutes later, a bottle sailed into the air and shattered on the stage, and mutterings of unrest again started to fill the piazza. The bell in the campanile rang, eight, nine, and ten loud clangs. On the eleventh clang, I finally saw Gancio giving me the thumbs up. A red van with a Union Jack came tearing up the hill, swerving to a halt. Inside were The Scrapers, their instruments, the manager Cavadori, and two girls they'd picked up hitchhiking.

"There was a carabinieri check point, and since two of the band members don't have any identity papers, we had to take a detour on the mountain road," explained Cavadori.

The Scrapers stepped out of the van. In person, they weren't as tall as we'd expected, but their clothing was dazzling. And the longer I looked at them, the longer the singer—the one with a superbanana hairstyle—looked vaguely familiar.

"Hey," I said in English, "are you the singer?"

"Yes," he said.

"And what's your name?"

"John Malcolm, aka Gino Domineddio, you idiot. Don't you remember me?"

It really was him. He had emigrated to Belgium to work as a pizza chef, and he was returning home as a rock star.

"What are you anyway, English?" I asked, after the conventional hugs and greetings.

"We're an emigrant rock group," he explained. "Two Sicilians, an Abruzzese, and a Sardinian, but we've worked in every pizzeria in Europe, first as waiters, and later as musicians. We all speak English. No one will suspect a thing."

But there was another problem. The Scrapers needed to rehearse and do sound checks for at least fifteen minutes. And that's when Uncle Nevio had a brilliant idea.

He asked the Pipitone brothers to move up their fireworks show. At the first explosion, everyone turned toward the soccer field, where the fireworks were being set off. Behind them, on the stage, the Scrapers started rehearsing. Sound and light, all together.

The Pipitones were masters at aerial embroidery, using gunpowder and various secret ingredients. Their show completely outshone the four colored farts that Villa Meringue had let off. In the dark-blue sky overhead, there appeared white dahlias, red geraniums, and dandelions that scattered down in silver cascades. Missiles hissed straight up, emitting multicolored sneezes and volcanic splurts, and there were Chinese boxes of flame, one color tucked inside the next, a dark-blue jellyfish that gave birth to a bigger jellyfish and then an even bigger green jellyfish that covered them all, and just when you were certain it was over, **BAM!**, the biggest golden jellyfish of them all—it took up the whole sky. To the accompaniment of the guitar riffs of Billy Bachisio Puddu, there was a procession of green Martians, flying dragons, and in a final spectacular crescendo, a snapping crackling popping pyroscintillation that seemed like the landings in Normandy, three solid minutes of explosions. When the fireworks show was finally over, not only did we applaud but, according to the news reports, so did all of Villa Meringue, including the carabinieri, with Colonel Maluschi angrily shouting, "That's enough, that's enough, stand down, men," but the men just looked up into the sky and kept clapping.

"Those fireworks were a bonus," said Fefelli, in an attempt to pass them off as his own doing, but few if any believed him. Malavasi, who had been forced to break off his arias because of the din, said, with a tone of irritation:

"May I begin again now?"

"Certainly," said Minister Anguilla himself.

Malavasi began to perform the aria "Bella figlia dell'amore" from *Rigoletto*, and as just as he was singing the second line, "*sui vezzi tuoi*," the searing guitar notes of Billy Bachisio Puddu overwhelmed his voice by about a hundred decibels. Villa Meringue was downwind from the band, and for Fefelli's guests it was like having the Scrapers standing in the middle of the dinner table. Malavasi backfromhisacclaimedworldtour swore loudly and stomped off into the night.

The concert was a rush of pure adrenaline. Domineddio was a real concert animal, he was covered with sweat before he even got on the stage, and when the band hit the first notes of "Tutti Frutti," he drenched the first three rows of seats. He wore a pair of tight-fitting purple satin trousers and moved his pelvis in a way that many of the ladies present found unseemly but strangely interesting. The drummer pounded away like the charge of a cavalry brigade, the bass player stood motionless, moving only his fingers, the lead guitarist had stuck his smoking cigarette between two frets, which was so cool that Armando the accordion player said, "I want to try that." In fact, the next evening he tried it himself, and set his accordion on fire.

John Malcolm Domineddio alternated hits by Iggy Pop, the Rolling Stones, and Elvis Presley with songs he had written himself, such as "You Dirty Woman" (*puttanazza*) and "I Love My Bike" (*amo la mia moto*), and then he shifted to a romantic ballad, "Midnight in London," which he had actually written in a pizzeria in Bellinzona after being dumped by his Swiss girl-friend. There were lots of curtain calls, a "Ventiquattromila baci," which he sang in a fake English accent. Then in response to a request, he sang "Nessuno mi può giudicare", and for the band's finale, they did the Beatles' "I Wanna Hold Your Hand," and that was the apotheosis because a girl, who had read about someone doing this in a magazine, slipped off her bra and threw it onto the stage, and immediately Luciana thought: "Well, this must be the proper thing to do," and from under her blouse she extracted her 38D black-lace brassiere and swung it around her head and let fly, and Zoraide immedi-ately followed suit, tossing a 40C bra with batten reinforce-ments, and then half of the women in town imitated them. The stage was covered with lace and trimmings and cotton, and Domineddio gathered them up and kissed them, and it was a good thing that the parish priest was already completely sloshed and was paying no attention to the concert at all.

In the surging crowd, Balduino edged over to me and asked: "Um, it's not like us guys are supposed to throw our underpants up there, right?"

"No," I said, "we get a free pass on this one."

The concert ended with a "Thank you, what a great audi-ence you've been." Luciana gave Domineddio a big kiss, and then started handing bras back to their rightful owners. Every so often, she'd say: "You didn't buy this one from me, though, did you?" There was only one minor incident. Schillaci and the bass player Jerry Melodia took one look at one another and threw their arms around each other, weeping. They were cousins, and hadn't seen each other in twenty years. Of course, that was their secret. We had won the battle of the festivals eleven times over. The village deserved a night like this.

The next morning when we woke up, everything looked much better. The Scrapers left for a multiconcert Ticino Valley tour; we embraced and exchanged addresses.

By that evening, we were already a little bored.

Three days later, everything went back to its usual colors.

In September, Gancio disappeared again.

In October, Carabelli won the mayoral election by a small margin, and the walls were immediately covered with graffiti attacking him and mocking his sexual preferences.

In November, I decided that I might not go back to university; maybe I'd look for a job instead. Selene would be back from England for Christmas; we wrote each other long letters, but I wasn't sure that I still loved her. It felt as if we had gone back to our two separate worlds. I could feel the forest calling to me, but I couldn't find my way back to it. Everything was going by slowly and in a blur, like a line of cars returning to the city in the night. The memory of this wonderful August party had placated my fury. I wondered: What if I decided to spend the rest of my life here in the village? What if I became a carpenter, like my father, or tried to become a correspondent for the *La Gazzetta delle Valli*, taking Testuggine's place? I could live quietly and write a book that they'd discover only after I died, the literary find of the century, a carpenter who wrote the masterpiece, *Woodchips*, the manuscript discovered in the case of a grandfather clock. What if I became the political leader of the valley's left wing? What if I got married to a nice young girl? What if I got married to Fred? What if I left for the Caribbean? My plans were as clear as a bottle of Barolo.

One day in December, the twelfth to be exact, began with a chill in the air. I woke up and suddenly remembered what my father had said about the key in the nail box and the cabinet in the woodshop. I looked in the nail box and found the key immediately. Before walking into the woodshop, I turned on the radio.

The announcer reported that a bomb had gone off in Milan, in Piazza Fontana.

7

I don't know how many of us there were, thirty thousand according to the television, eighty thousand according to the organizers. I had never seen so many people in one place in my life. The main square of the Bigcity was full, and so were all the streets leading into it. People kept arriving from the train station, it was like when a river finds a new channel, and it fills up the water holes and spreads out into the canebrake, and where there used to be sand, now a torrent is rushing, or a rivulet. Excited, and scared I was one drop in that river. Sad, with too many different feelings all at once: hope and despair, anger and the joy of being together with so many others like me. I noticed the big things, the stage with the speakers, the hundreds of banners, the tight groups of factory workers, the university students shouting slogans, overlapping and interrupting, in a warlike, baying chorus. But it was the little things that really struck me. Maybe it was because I needed to pick out something I could focus on in that huge self-propelling canvas, like when you look at a painting of an enormous battle, and it dazes you, so that you have to find a detail and look at it: a horse's head, a fallen soldier, a tree in the background.

I remember a group of factory workers standing silent amidst all the noise and shouting, and an old man wearing factory overalls holding a sign with a photograph of one of the dead. I remember Baruch walking next to me, trying to match the pace of the marchers, but limping from his gout, so that

Fred and I, from time to time, would hold his arm to support him, and he objected.

"When I was in the mountains," he said, "I let my partisan friends carry me, but I had been shot in the leg. I can walk under my own steam today."

I remember two women wearing yellow overalls, pushing a cart full of thermoses of coffee and tea and offering cups to the marchers—it was a cold day. I remember looking at the Christmas presents in the shop windows and thinking to myself that I still needed to buy a gift for Selene.

Then the crowd swayed uncertainly, a frightened voice called out, "The police are charging at us," and someone from the organizing committee announced over a megaphone: "Stay calm, don't worry, there are so many of us here today that it would be easier for us to charge at them." I remember Loris and Tamara, who had met again, after their brief interlude; they were walking arm in arm. There was a mother with a little boy, she was hurrying him away, as if he were in danger, and a young marcher shouted, "You don't need to be afraid of us, ma'am." Then there was a guy who stepped out of an expensive bar and shot us a Fascist salute; members of the organizing committee dragged back two marchers who were running to pummel him. A plate-glass window shattered into a thousand pieces, and there were a few marchers stealing shoes and other marchers saying angrily: "What does that have to do with the dead?"

I remember a beautiful girl, wearing a red coat; our eyes met, and hers were filled with tears. The chilly sensation I felt as I glimpsed the Avvocato D'Intesa on the stage. And when I closed my eyes, all that noise turned into a waterfall in a gorge. I saw the deserted piazza at night, filled with empty tin cans and crumpled paper, as if after any other political rally or giant concert. "Where did you go, all you people who were there that day?" I wondered. "Would you do it again? Were you different then, did you believe other things, or did someone tell you to believe and you were just doing what you were told? Could you have imagined, that day, that there would be justice for no one, that instead the injustices that followed would grow one upon the other, like mold on a dead tree?"

I saw in my duoclock how the city changed so suddenly and profoundly, and I thought: "That day the city must have taken fright; even cities need peace and tranquility. It swallowed up our rage and fury and buried it deep, imprisoning our anger in its subterranean chambers, and now it lets its shops and display windows glitter, to keep us from remembering where that anger lies buried. 'Just forget about it, please,' the city says to us. 'I'm an old city, I've seen medieval wars and outbreaks of the plague and single combat and enemy invasions and gunfire in the streets and tanks—please, just let me grow old in peace.'"

And when I opened my eyes, an orator was delivering a speech, but I couldn't understand a word he was saying; behind me a group of marchers was shouting ferocious slogans. My Uncle Nevio caught up with me, he was breathing heavily, he had stuffed himself with heart pills like a racehorse. I saw Verdolin, he was panting, he said that he had met Selene at the far end of the portico. She told him to say that she'd wait for me in front of the bookshop, after the demonstration.

She'd caught the first plane back. "I didn't do it for you," she said. "I did it for those poor, dead men, but also for you." She told me that the news analyst on British television had said "A hard situation and a dark future for Italy," and he had really seemed worried. We kissed as the piazza emptied out. Maybe it was inappropriate, but we couldn't do anything else. I held her by the arm, and I wouldn't let her go even when we said good-bye to our friends.

"You want some rope to tie her up?" asked Fred.

Selene spent Christmas Eve with her family, but she said that she wanted to come up to the village for Christmas Day. My uncle commanded: "I want to meet her, let's invite her to dinner at Luciana's house." "No," I said, "that's too big a commitment." "No one ever got pregnant by eating a lasagna dinner," he shot back. "All right," I said, "but don't embarrass her, she's very shy." At the beginning of the meal, my uncle and Luciana pretended to be even more shy than Selene; they talked with their parking brakes pulled tight. Uncle Nevio cleared his throat and said, "So tell me, tell me, young lady, how do you like the medical profession?" And Selene replied: "I'm still in my first year of medical school; I've just started studying anatomy." And Luciana observed, "Well, anatomy is a wonderful thing." I couldn't tell if she was talking about Selene's anatomy, her own, or just anatomy in general. Then, noticing that Selene was enjoying both the food and the wine, they began to relax. My uncle said, "You should study hard, miss. If you need a guinea pig, you can practice on me, I've got every disease and condition in the book, and I really need a doctor." "What you need isn't a doctor," said Luciana, "what you need is Santa Tirella."

"Who is Santa Tirella?" asked Selene.

I would have had some explaining to do. I'd have had to say, "She is the saint of the Blessed Lacy Corset, the saint who restores a healthy sexual harmony to couples, there are even poetically rhyming songs about her." But I said nothing.

Then things started to heat up. My uncle told us about the time that Dr. Carabelli had been summoned to a farmhouse far out in the countryside and the peasant had told him, in a serious tone of voice, "Come into the bedroom, Marisa is very ill." The doctor had pulled out his thermometer and said, "I'll wash my hands, you take her temperature, just slip this under her tongue." The farmer came back and said, "Doctor, she swallowed it." "That's impossible," said Carabelli, "let me take a look." The doctor walked into the bedroom and there, on the floor, lay a cow.

"I brought her inside so she won't get lonely," explained the peasant.

Selene laughed hysterically; the wine had made her pink-faced and countrified. Luciana started to pinch my arm and whisper into my ear, "She's so pretty, oh how pretty she is, if you let her get away you're a fool." After she pinched me for the fourth time, I said, "Luciana, I understand," and she whispered back, "With you men, it's best to drive the point home."

Then my uncle told us in considerable detail about his attacks of renal colic and started to talk about medicinal herbs. He was so expert and had such a wealth of knowledge that Selene stopped him and said, "Do you mind if I take some notes?" and she got out a notepad and started writing as if she were in a classroom.

I was proud of my uncle. The dinner had gone off beautifully. As we were at the door, saying goodnight, Luciana said to me, "Wait, I have something to give you."

It was a baby-doll nightgown for Selene.

"If you let her get away," she repeated, and chopped the air with her hand in a mock threatening gesture.

For New Year's, La Schiassi's parents went to the Maldives; this marked the beginning of the painful emigration of the Italians toward those distant islands. And so we were free to spend New Year's in their mountain house in the Dolomites. "These are nice mountains, but ours are nicer," I said, but it wasn't true. When the sun turned the mountains red, it was like being on another planet, and the woods looked like they probably held an assortment of first-class gnomes. There was a great deal of Dolomitic snow, though it tasted exactly like the Apenninic snow we had back home. We went skiing. Selene skied like an agile squirrel, while I approximated a warthog with a pair or ironing boards strapped to its feet. There were three couples. Me and Selene, the Perfect Couple, and Fred with a German girl he knew.

"I just want a quiet vacation," he explained. "I'm not rethinking my attitudes."

At night we heard the squeaking of springs from the nuptial bed on which Verdolin was screwing La Schiassi, though they tried to keep it quiet because they were embarrassed, every so often you could hear a quiet grunt of pleasure. Selene, in contrast, shrieked like a bacchante, and we knocked things off the dresser in our frenzies.

One night, I started shouting:

"Where is my Spiderman costume? Where did you put it, you know I can't get an erection without my Spiderman costume!"

After I pestered her repeatedly and to point of exasperation, Selene finally agreed to reprise the striptease she had performed for me. We had a little transistor radio with terrible reception; we searched through the stations, looking for suitable music. In the end, she undressed for me to the tune of "Quarantaquattro gatti" (forty-four pussycats), a song from the children's song festival, the Zecchino d'Oro. Despite the music, the end result was more than satisfactory.

One morning we woke up early; the forest was a pinball machine of darting squirrels. Selene ran ahead of me, I chased after her, but I lost my way in a clearing. In the middle of the clearing was a rock jutting up out of the snow, like a reef in the sea. I thought she might be hiding behind it, because there were tracks in the snow. Instead, it was a gnome, much older than the Boletus Gnome; this gnome was smoking a pipe made out of a pinecone. He was taking a piss.

"Pardon me if I disturbed you, sir," I said.

"Not a bit, son," he replied, "be my guest. Have a piss yourself."

I peed for a minute, then buttoned up my trousers; he was still pissing.

"Do you, by any chance, know a gnome from the lower woods, near Mount Mario?" I asked.

"That's my great-grandson," he answered. "Why?"

"I don't like being the one to bring bad news, but . . ."

"Oh, has he been treed again? It happens, especially if something gives him a fright. He'll be treed for twenty years or so, then he'll regain his gnomic form."

"And does the same thing happen to you?"

"I'm too old," said the gnome, pissing away contentedly all the while—indeed, the stream seemed to be growing in strength. "If I turned into a tree, I'd never manage to turn back into a gnome. I'd rather just die and get it over with."

"When does that happen?"

"Well, for us Dolomitic gnomes, it's enough to speak with a human being once and we die immediately."

"Oh, no!" I shouted. I had killed him!

"You dummy, you fell for it," said the gnome, then he peed on my head and disappeared into the forest with a loud laugh that echoed seven times.

"Timeskipper, what are you doing standing there in a trance, in the middle of all that snow?" said Selene, and threw an icy snowball right at the back of my neck.

"You damned cat," I yelled, and I ran over and grabbed her. I managed to get to her, even through three layers of sweaters.

As we were kissing, we saw Fred and his little German friend walking arm in arm. He stopped and kissed her passionately.

Our paths intersected and I stared at him in amazement.

"Hey," he said, "don't ruin my reputation."

"Or mine," added the fräulein.

I went back to the city, and the merry-go-round of uneasiness began turning again. Selene had enrolled in medical school, she attended all the classes, in the evening she studied beautifully illustrated books featuring chancres, pimples, and burns of varying degrees of severity; I saw very little of her. I wandered through the university, collecting curriculum packages and syllabuses, but I couldn't settle on a subject. I was wavering between literature, philosophy, and botany. I had bought a counterfeit student ID and I was eating my meals at the university cafeteria because I had no money. My father had left me a small sum, and I didn't want to sell his beautiful wooden creations, his cuckoo clocks, and the two antique grandfather clocks he had restored. Uncle Nevio insisted: "I'll take care of you, you and Gancio." But Gancio was far away. He hadn't left for South America after all. He had phoned from Paris to say: "I'm working in a restaurant where the menu features 'Tortellini à la Hemingway,' but aside from that, everything is going well."

I went to a political meeting in the department of literature: the speeches were more or less the same as the ones we'd heard in high school, the beards were a little longer and there were more quotes from revolutionary authors. I saw Riccardo, who barely said hello, and Lussu, who was thrilled to see me.

"We're doing it for real this time, Timeskipper," he said. "When the time comes, I want to talk to you about something. You, I trust."

Two days later they arrested him for the first time. They searched his apartment, but all they found were some leaflets. In prison, they beat him. I saw him again in a bar.

"Get ready, Timeskipper," he said. "*Appompiadi a bastusu*: get ready for a fight."

One evening Selene and I had planned to go out, but on the phone she told me that she was exhausted: she'd spent five hours in class that day. And she scolded me for failing to enroll in any specific subject. The deadline was just fifteen days away. "That's my business," I said. "Do what you want," she replied, and hung up the phone.

I went to the cafeteria. I ran into a brunette there that I talked to sometimes. I chatted her up, suggested we go see a movie, and we did. Then, up to her apartment. For two hours, my dick refused to cooperate in any way; at any moment I expected it to run yelping under the bed. Then it finally came to life, allowing me to screw the brunette as quickly and as unsatisfactorily as a bunny, and while she went to the bathroom, I fled the apartment. How excruciatingly embarrassing. I took the train back up to the village. I wanted to talk to Baruch. I was well and truly confused.

As soon as I got home, I remembered the key. I opened the cabinet in the woodshop, and there I saw my father's secret.

There were twenty-seven carved wooden statuettes; each one stood about eight inches tall. It was a secular crèche scene, but without a manger and a Christ child. There was Baruch with his walking stick, Karamazov with the bandanna around his neck, Caprone with a wooden lamb on a pedestal, Regina with a newspaper, Luciana showing off a pair of roomy underpants. There was my uncle with a hunting rifle and Rufus at his side. There was Lavamèl, sitting with his cat in his lap, Slim with a turtledove perched on one shoulder, Balduino with a demijohn of wine, Bortolini with a fishing rod, and Carburo, Zoraide, Favilla the blacksmith, and Breadlocks the baker, as well as three or four others I didn't recognize; maybe they had died when I was still little. And on the pedestal, there were the six of us, the river rats, at the age of seven or eight. Me, Gancio, Osso, Selene, the Troll, and Fulisca. All together, just as we were back then, even if one or two had wandered away from the pedestal to walk about on their own, and we hadn't all gone in the same direction. And then my father had done a self-portrait, holding a hatchet in one hand, like a Sioux brave, and below it was the legend: *Me*.

I called Uncle Nevio to come see, and he started clapping his hands with joy, like a little child.

"Everyone has to see them," he said. "Let's take them to the Casa del Popolo right away, or let's set up a kiosk in the piazza."

"Leave them here for another day," I said, "I want to look at them a little longer."

"All right," said Uncle Nevio. "But this is a wonderful thing. It's a consolation for the other two pieces of bad news we got today."

"Gancio?" I said, immediately.

"Yes, Gancio," he sighed. "He's back, but he doesn't dare show his face. Someone said that they'd seen him at the Hotel Lara, hanging out with the Pastori brothers, along with some lowlifes and hoodlums."

"I'll see if I can track him down. What's the other piece of bad news?"

"The other piece of news is not so much bad as it is annoying. On Saturday, Fefelli and Arcari, with their entourage of creeps, are coming back to the village; they're laying the cornerstone of the residential complex, and there's going to be a ceremony. Carabelli doesn't know if he should attend or not. They invited him, but every night they scrawl on the walls that he's a pederast. I've seen him rubbing out the graffiti himself, to keep from squandering tax money on it. Poor guy, I don't know how much longer he can take it."

My uncle pedaled away slowly on his bicycle, his collar raised against the cold. Rufus barked somewhere behind the house, I looked up toward the mountain and I saw the Shadow. "Get out of here, you bloodthirsty monster, I'm sick of you. Which of the statuettes do you want to take now? Why don't you go to the city, there's lots of people there." But the Shadow slid along the forest, like a snake, and then turned down toward the river.

I couldn't get to sleep. The grandfather clock was striking

the hours. I heard a voice calling my name. It was Gancio. He stood motionless in the middle of the meadow, his hands in his pockets.

"What are you doing here so late?" I asked.

"What do you mean, late?" asked Gancio.

I realized it was almost dawn. In my mind, it was barely midnight.

"It's no one's fault," he said, in a weary voice.

"What isn't?"

"What I said to you, to take revenge for me, I don't believe that anymore, so don't do it. It's not Osso's fault, or Fefelli's or the Pastori brothers' fault, or because society was hard on me. It's fate that gives you a shove and you wind up in the water. But you yourself have to decide whether to get back up on the bank or swim with the current until you find a whirlpool that's stronger than your own will to live—and if you do that, so long, catbird."

"Gancio, don't start doing yourself damage again. Remember that evening the Scrapers played, and we set off the cheese bomb at Villa Meringue, and John Domineddio came back. And your Guatayaba friends."

"You want the truth, Timeskipper?" said Gancio. "You know what I saw in South America? Poverty, lots of poverty and misery and exploitation and people who would cut each other's throat for a pair of shoes. And when I finally got up to the Indio village, half of them were dead or in the hospital, they're poisoning their water to drive them out, so they can clear-cut the jungle. I took fistfuls of weird mushrooms to keep from seeing it, but that only made me see it more clearly."

"The Indians are fighting," I said, "and they will keep on fighting, just like us."

"Their river is bigger, the current is more powerful," said Gancio. "Their lives are short, compared to us they have the lifespan of a butterfly. As for me, what does it matter?"

"Didn't you once say to me: these are things that we say only once in a lifetime?"

"In a lifetime, friend, in a lifetime," he said, sadly. The dawning light cut out abruptly, the darkness fell again, and Gancio was gone. In the sky, I saw a dark cloud in the shape of a dragon. Then I remembered where the Shadow had been heading. I grabbed my bicycle and pedaled as fast as I could down to the river. I climbed down to the bed of rocks, but it was too dark to see. I turned on the light on the handlebars, and to keep it lit I pedaled around in circles. I pointed the beam of light down toward the water hole, and on the sandy bank I saw Gancio, hunched over, as if he were asleep.

I sat down next to him.

I threw a rock into the water.

"Sixteen skips," I said, "in your honor, Gancio."

Then I went to tell my uncle.

He hadn't died of a drug overdose after all. It might have been the result of mixing alcohol and pills, perfectly legal drugs. The direct cause was cardiac arrest. He would have turned twenty in just a few months. My uncle was shattered. Dr. Carabelli ordered him not to go to the funeral, but Uncle Nevio was there, in the front row. Everyone was there, even Osso.

Osso came over to me and stood there, waiting for anything, a fist in the nose, a phrase.

"I'm sorry," he said.

"How can you be such a hypocrite?" I asked him. "You sold him a dose of death yourself, and you know it."

"It's true, I did—but I didn't realize what I was doing. I'm sorry," said Osso.

What abject poverty there must have been in his mind, if he had been unable to see what he was doing for a fistful of money. And now, how could he fail to see that he no longer belonged with us, that he had chosen a new place, a seat at the banquet table of Arcari? I couldn't speak, I was paralyzed. I felt sorry for him, and he disgusted me. At last, Regina took him by the arm and spoke to him: "Go away, go away, if you have any respect for the dead boy and for Nevio, leave here." Osso left, practically breaking into a run.

After the funeral I returned home. I arranged the statuettes on the table. Almost without realizing what I was doing, I set the living to one side and the dead to the other. Only we kids were still together, on the pedestal of our childhood, when we were still friends.

And suddenly I saw everything clearly. Those statuettes and the precious life they contained. My father's painstaking labor to bring out their faces in the wood he had taken from the forest, linking every face with these places forever. He had constructed them and hidden them from the greed and fury of the outside world in order to preserve some essence of those people, to keep the avalanche of the passing years from sweeping them away. Those statuettes were men and women, and now they were looking up at me. Somebody had played with their lives, someone had sold them, corrupted them, bent them to his will. Now that someone had to pay. Perhaps Fefelli was old and tired now, but he had been the one who'd helped the Shadow to find its way into our village, it was he who had nurtured within his own cadaverous body the Pastori brothers, Ossobuco, and Arcari. Just as I had nurtured in my anger that very thought which had tormented me ever since I was small.

I picked up the statuette of Baruch: it seemed as if it had begun to glow, and its features grew more and more lifelike. The ticking of the minute hand split the silence in two. The duoclock enveloped me, it tore me away from the table and sent me flying out the window, high over the woods, all the way up to the stone basin. It was chilly, and I was shivering. Baruch's statuette vibrated and then spoke:

"Put me down on the ground, I'm tired."

I set it down on the moss, and it sent out tiny roots, then small branches, and before my eyes it grew, aged, and turned into a tree, a great spreading oak, and high atop the further-most branch dangled Baruch's jacket.

"Do you remember," the tree said to me, "when you found out that the partisans had murdered Fulisca's grandfather, and you came to talk to me about it, to sort out your confusion? Do you remember what I told you then?"

"Yes, Oak-Baruch," I answered. "You told me: just be grateful for every day of your life that you can wake up in peace, without having to divide the world into friends and enemies."

"And what else did I say?"

"I don't remember . . ."

"Then I told you: it's been the fate of many to wake up that day, the day they have to go and fight. It's not a good awakening; it's a grievous, painful, cruel awakening. When that day comes, don't ask others who you are—your friends will say you're a hero, others will say you're a murderer. You alone can know, and you'll pay every hour for the rest of your life for your decision. Only many years later will you be able to say whether you brought additional pain to the world, or whether you helped it to heal—whether you nourished more life than you stamped out. That is the nature of responsibility."

"It's all too much for me to think about," I said, shivering in the cold. "You are an aged tree, Baruch, I don't have all your years of life, your lymph, your solid trunk—tell me something that can help me."

The tree's canopy seemed to heave a sigh, and black and white magpies flew off.

"Remember this, Timeskipper, my little sapling. When that day comes, you'll feel as if you're alone, but you're not. And remember something else, even more important. Look at those who surround the tyrant you hate, and you will see a thousand servants, a thousand accomplices. Look at those who surround the servants and yes-men, and you will see thousands and thousands more. Were they born yesterday? To fight them before that day, means to fight them on that day."

"Your words are unclear," I said.

"I'm an oracle, I'm not the damned weather report," Oak-Baruch responded with a tone of indignation; he shook his canopy of leaves and inundated me with a shower of fuzzy caterpillars.

I found myself back in my house, in the dark; a caterpillar was creeping across the table. I thought I had understood. My turn had come. I was neither sad nor angry, I clearly sensed that every act I would perform from now on would have a special importance because afterward there would be nothing left for me to do. I would never again put on my heavy jacket and wrap my scarf around my neck, I'd never close the door behind me and pat Rufus and start off down the road to town. Never again the village, never again the forest and the mountains, the basin and the Cheerful God. Never again Selene. Never again blood, after this day.

I stopped in front of Uncle Nevio's shop. I had a key; he'd given me a copy in case he ever lost his. He trusted me. I opened the door; I knew how to turn off the alarm system. I knew that the key to the safe was hidden in the mouth of the mounted pikefish and that in the safe there were two pistols and plenty of bullets. I took the Beretta 9 mm—my uncle had let me shoot it a few times. He couldn't accept that I was the first member of the family who didn't want to become a hunter. I locked up the shop and went home. I went back to bed and fell asleep.

Into the room came Selene, in tears: she was as tiny as a statuette and she glowed in the darkness. She perched on the edge of the bed, like Tinker Bell.

"I heard about Gancio, I'm coming up tomorrow on the first train. Please, I beg of you, I tried calling your uncle over and over, but the line is always busy. Maybe he took the phone off the hook so he could sleep in. I feel that something awful is going to happen. Did you really understand what Oak-Baruch told you? Please wait until I get there."

"I won't do anything strange," I said, "and I'm tired of talking with shadows."

"You're right, Timeskipper, we've been far apart lately, but I believe in the work I'm doing. I want to become a good doctor, I know that I've abandoned you lately, but how many times have you left me by myself? Please, listen to me, don't throw yourself into the stream, Gancio couldn't fight the current, and you can't fight it either. I love you, listen to me."

I stepped outside, she scampered after me, leaping like a squirrel.

"I can't hear you," I lied. "I can't hear what you're saying."

The clocks were twisting, skirmishing, biting one another, clawing and snatching, perhaps only one of them would survive.

"Listen," said Selene in a frail, breaking voice. A cloud covered the light of the moon, and she vanished.

The next morning, I dressed in a sweater and a pair of my father's trousers that hung loosely on me and had roomy pockets. There was a warm sun, a break in the chilly weather. I walked up toward the Roselle subdivision and I saw the dark-blue official limousines parked at the entrance of the street leading up to the future residential complex. The limousine engines were turned off, no one was moving. "Maybe I'm early," I thought, "or else they're waiting for someone."

The pistol was a bulge in my trouser pocket, I pulled down the sweater to cover it. As I was walking, a carabinieri Alfa Romeo squad car honked at me; the policemen inside yelled:

"Hey, kid, don't walk in the middle of the road!"

I got even closer to the dark-blue official limousines. From a distance I could see Arcari and Colonel Maluschi. They both seemed morose; maybe not enough people had showed up. I cut through the meadow and behind the apple orchard. "I know the lay of the land around here a lot better than you guys do," I thought to myself. I emerged from the hedge enclosing a vineyard, about ten feet away from them. They were all within easy range. "Look at those who surround the tyrant, and you will see a thousand servants, a thousand accomplices." I closed my eyes, I steadied my respiration, and I took two steps forward, my fingers wrapped around the handle of the pistol. I opened my eyes.

Fefelli wasn't there. Don Brusco was there and so was my uncle and Dr. Carabelli the mayor, who was removing his ceremonial mayoral sash. The Pastori brothers looked at me in astonishment.

"Everything's been called off, Timeskipper," said my uncle. "Fefelli died this morning. A massive heart attack while he was getting ready to come up here."

"If you ask me," said Arcari with thinly concealed anger, "we could have held the inauguration ceremonies all the same. There are plenty of journalists here. Fefelli would have wanted it that way."

"Please," said the parish priest, "show a little respect for the dead."

Something welled up from the bottom of my throat: it might have been vomit, or a belly laugh. The Pastori brothers shoved past me. Nerio said:

"Fucking old man could have died in his sleep. Then we wouldn't have gone to all this trouble today."

"Yeah, anyway he was already history, he had no power anymore," said Licio, and they got into their car, a mayonnaise-colored Mercedes, the most beautiful automobile I'd ever seen.

Gancio always used to say: "Someday I'm going to steal a car like that."

I walked back through the fields, I ate a nice, big bunch of black grapes, I felt life coursing through every vein and artery in my body, every pore in my skin.

"And so," I thought, "I missed my big opportunity to go down in the history of my little village and all of Italy. Certainly, Arcari will take Fefelli's place, and one day someone will take Arcari's place. But I've done my duty, I faced the challenge that had been awaiting me all these years. Now I'm almost a free man."

Before I could be completely free, I still had a few things to do.

First of all, that night I put the pistol back into the safe; no one had noticed it was missing. I slipped it back into its black velvet case. I closed the lid. "O heartstopper, iron-mouth, equalizer," I said to it, "Queen of my tin soldiers, rest in peace for a thousand years, or even for a shorter period of time, much shorter. What I have learned, what I now carry inside me, in my own red velvet, is worth a hundred pistols."

Second thing: I went home, got all the statuettes, and took them to Regina. Her face lit up when she saw them.

"Your uncle told me they were wonderful, but I couldn't have imagined how beautiful they really are. He never would let me see them. We'll put them in the piazza or somewhere everyone can see them and recognize themselves."

"Perfect," I said. The last item of business was to phone Selene, but at her house they told me that she had already caught the train to come up to see me.

That wasn't good. Selene couldn't know what I was about to do. I left a note on the front door: "I'm going to the city, back late tonight." I hid in the woods and waited for darkness to fall. I walked down through the meadows, skirting the road. I knew exactly where the road was, curve by curve, even if I couldn't see it. I knew that there was a row of cypress trees on the hill above the Hotel Lara, and from there I would have to cut straight down until I reached the parking area where the hotel's clients left their cars.

The Mercedes was there, between two trees. The sounds of music and laughter drifted down from the hotel; at this time of the evening, everyone was drinking and playing poker. I waited for the right moment, when the noise was loudest. I smashed the window open with a rock; I pulled the driver's side door open. Jimmying it open would have taken too long. I waited: nobody was coming out of the hotel. A truck went by, I hunkered down in the shadow of the car. Now came the hard part. I had done this with Gancio lots and lots of times, but never with a car like this one. I felt as if he were there with me, guiding my hands. I took a screwdriver and pulled the wires out from under the dashboard, twisted them together, and started the engine. I still didn't have a driver's license, but I'd driven cars a few times before. I took the Strada della Strega, an old mountain road that had been there even before they built the state road. By now it was virtually abandoned, it led only to a few farmhouses, it was unpaved and full of twists and turns; some stretches were very rocky. Once you went past the last house, it became even narrower and rougher, and it climbed up to what the locals called Inferno Point, and then it entered a giant crack in the cliff, continuing precariously over a dizzyingly deep gorge. There were no guardrails, no one had used it for years, except for the occasional hunter on foot. I was creeping along, driving carefully; I had managed to turn the headlights on, but the road was twisty: the light filtered out onto the rock walls and down into the darkness of the abyss. I knew that the tires were just inches away from the edge of the road. "You're swimming in the strongest current, out in the middle of the river," I thought to myself. "What else did you expect?" I drove under a black, jutting boulder; a stream of water was issuing from beneath it, and at this point the road turned muddy and narrowed even more. Finally, the headlights shone upon a rockslide that blocked the narrow road entirely. I braked, the rubber of the right tire was halfway over the edge of the precipice. I got out and looked down. Far below me, in the black ravine, the wind was making the leaves rustle; it sounded like the breathing of some immense animal. Down there, enclosed between two rock walls, was the ancient heart of the mountain. A million years ago, a river ran along there, and perhaps in its depths lived monsters and creatures that even my own imagination could never grasp.

"O car," I said, stroking its hood, "I have nothing against you, you are sleek and beautiful, you've brought good things into this world. If only you had remained what you are, an overgrown go-cart with a well-engineered motor, not the empress of every road and every city. You are an emblem on the banner of those who have destroyed all that was full of life and generosity in my town. There are millions of cars just like you, hurtling along the highway, smashing into one another, turning into carcasses of twisted steel, and in cars like you people die, fat and, if not happy, at least resigned, and more and more of them are dying every day. You are a car that belongs to two bastards, it's not your fault, but now you have to leap into the void, now you have to experience what it means to take the last breath of your life. I hope you understand, because there are certain people who no longer know what it means."

I put the Mercedes in neutral, put my shoulder against it, and gave a push. It started off, its rear shimmying like a cow's. The mountain opened its maw, and I heard the succession of bangs and crashes, one after the other, as if giant jaws were gnawing at the metal body, and then a final dull thud swallowed the car up for good.

Immediately afterward, it started raining. I had no clear idea of how far I had traveled in the car. I ran downhill for what seemed like hours, until I was panting too hard to go on. I stopped to catch my breath and then set off at a dead run again. I finally got home at three in the morning; Selene was sitting on the front step, weeping. Regina was at her side. She handed me a mug of hot broth and punched me hard on the back.

"You're alive," said Selene, drying my hair. "I was so afraid."

"Yes," I said, "so was I."

8

The Pastori brothers had so many enemies that they didn't even try to find who had taken their car; they had so much money that they could buy another mayonnaise-colored Mercedes whenever they felt like it. But they were furious about it, just furious. The mountain gorge swallowed up the car, covered it with thorns and bracken, and transformed it into a happy vegetomineral, monster. Let it rest in peace.

After Selene went back to the city to take her first final exam and receive her first A plus, Verdolin came up to see me. Since he showed up missing his better half, that is, without La Schiassi, I realized that it had to be about something important. He told me that a magazine that published underground comics was holding a competition for a story by new artists and writers; he had already sketched out main characters, what he needed now was a story, and I was the only one he knew who could do it.

"I don't know if I could do a very good job," I told him. I started working on it, and I wrote the whole story in a single night. The next morning I handed it to Verdolin; as he was reading it, I walked away, embarrassed. I heard him laughing as he read.

"Timeskipper," he said, "this is great stuff. You're going to be a star." We submitted our story: "Mickey Marx Versus the Killer Jukebox." A week later, a letter arrived from the editor in chief of the comic magazine. It said: "You didn't win. But you're really pretty good, and you should keep working. Keep it up, and send us more stories."

Verdolin was disappointed, but I didn't let it get me down. The duoclock told me that, in a few years, another magical letter would drop into our postbox, and this time our story would be published.

Anything could happen. After all, everything had changed in the course of a week: I had thought I was just a step away from the abyss, then I took that step and found myself walking across an invisible bridge, a bridge that took me from where I was to a land of subtle and laborious delights. I decided that I would go back to the city and work with Verdolin on a lengthy graphic novel, and I would also be able to write some short stories, and maybe my first novel, as well; it would be six hundred pages long, and it would narrate the battle between the deities of good and the deities of evil in a mountain village at the turn of the eighteenth century. Set against this background would be a love story between two young people, with a local feudal lord who is interfering in their affair, keeping them apart, while he carries on a series of bloody battles in a larger war with a foreign country where a solitary hero lives in a castle on the banks of a mist-shrouded lake and where a fairy confides to him a strange prophecy according to which the hero decides to set out to kill the feudal warlord who has, in the meantime, decided to have his way with the young woman and he sends two bravoes to kidnap her and at that moment out of the woods marches an army of gnomes, and the young woman asks, "Are you good gnomes or evil gnomes?" and that is the end of the first chapter.

Before leaving the village and returning to town, I felt that I needed to go back into the forest. It was as if they had turned it upside down. Everything was jumbled from the avalanche, but nature was covering up the scars as the plants grew and spread. The canopies of the big trees were still visible, the huge chestnut trees and the oak tree where the owls lived helped me navigate, like constellations, but I had to make an uphill detour. I took a trail I'd never seen before; I thought it would take me back down to the Fanara, but instead it kept on climbing, sections of it were really steep, practically sheer, and I had to grab branches to keep climbing, there were enormous hollow stumps that I had never seen before, and centuries-old oaks, and beech trees, and then, unexpectedly, the pine trees began. A soft carpet of pine needles spread out beneath my feet, and I came out into the open in an unfamiliar place. I was right at the foot of the sheer wall of Mount Mario. A waterfall was thundering down, from a fissure in the cliffside. The noise was deafening and enchanting.

I walked over to the base of the waterfall. Before running down the hill, the water pooled, forming a basin of crystalline water; perhaps that was the water source that fed the Fanara. There was a cross that must have been erected in memory of someone and, hung up on a rock peg, a drinking ladle. I looked down into the water and saw a reflection of the mountain top. Then I heard footsteps behind me—a man with a black cape was climbing up the trail I had taken, and he had a big bag slung over his shoulder. I was suddenly afraid. Then I saw that he had a snakeskin tied around his belt. It was Celsus: everyone assumed he had died long ago, but he was alive, he'd never left the mountainside, he had survived avalanches and devastation.

"Celsus," I said when he was close enough to touch. "Do you remember me?"

He looked at me calmly.

"You gave me two cigarettes," he said.

"Where do you live?"

He pointed downward. I saw something that looked like a tiny hut concealed among the tree trunks.

To my surprise, I heard the roar of an engine. I remembered that higher up somewhere there was a mule track that the partisans used to get to the caverns where they hid. People said it was still pocked with land mines. A green jeep came revving through the bushes and came to a halt above us. A man wearing rock-climbing boots and holding a climbing stick came down toward us.

"Hello," he said with a smile. "This part of the mountain is becoming popular." And then, speaking to Celsus: "So, did you catch anything?"

Celsus held out the bag to him. It was full of royal agaric and porcini mushrooms. The biggest mushrooms were wrapped in newspaper. I looked at the date: it was a paper from 1948.

"Good," said the man. "Here's something for you." And he gave Celsus two packs of cigarettes and a bundle—perhaps it was something to eat.

I was about to say, "Isn't two packs of cigarettes worth a lot less than that huge bag of fresh mushrooms?" But then it dawned on me that way up there the laws of the market meant little if anything, and it meant nothing to try to explain to Celsus what "worth less" or "worth more" meant. He lived with next to nothing.

Celsus strode off briskly. But the mushroom trader felt like chatting. He told me that he was from Lucino, on the far side of the mountain. There was an old and extremely rough road that ran around the mountain; long ago it was the only road linking the two valleys. Nowadays, though, with his all-terrain eight-gear all-wheel-drive jeep he could get up there without particular problems; automotive technology was amazing, wasn't it? And Fiat was an incredible car maker. The mushroom trader was a restaurateur, he owned a little trattoria called the Cavallo Bianco, I said that I'd eaten there before, but it wasn't true. One day, he had driven up there in his jeep and he'd spied this strange troglodyte creature with a basket of very fine mushrooms; he bought the whole basket, and ever since then, once a week, come rain or shine, the two men met to swap mushrooms for cigarettes and food—call it trading, call it barter, it worked for both of them.

"I don't know how that man does it," said the restaurateur. "He doesn't have a clock or a watch, but he's always on time."

"Maybe he has a duoclock inside him," I wanted to say, or else tell him that you only need to take a look at the shadows on the mountain face.

"He lives in a clapboard hut. He came down to the village only once, to pick up a demijohn of wine. It really is incredible that in modern times someone could live in such total isolation. Who can live like that?" he said.

"Celsus can live like that," I thought, as the jeep roared off into the distance. All of the destruction our modern society had visited upon the mountain had done nothing to harm that old man. He'd moved a little way along the slope, he'd found his woods and its age-old laws waiting for him. His tenacious grip on life was stronger than anything else, it was the same force that made the forest grow back after a disaster. Years ago, it had seemed like a miserable life to me. Instead, I now saw, it was a hidden and mysterious life.

The waterfall roared and splashed. Blinding sunlight illuminated everything, the mountain top glittered with snow. I saw my mother and my father down on the trail below; on their backs they carried wicker shoulder baskets filled with firewood, my mother waved to me, while my father wiped the sweat from his brow. From my lofty vantage point I saw the entire valley of the future, more factories and houses scattered everywhere, a lava flow of cement, and my village shrinking smaller and smaller, until it was just a dovecote, with the wooden statuettes arranged inside it. I saw Arcari enjoying a successful and highly dishonest career, and Baruch, now ancient, reading the newspaper and saying: "This one is just like that other one, millions of dollars instead of billy clubs and Blackshirts." I saw one of the Pastori brothers shot down in

cold blood, right in front of the Hotel Lara. I saw Colonel
Maluschi standing trial on charges of mass murder in a terror
attack, unfazed and scornful. I saw an endless procession of
betrayals and triumphs, and twenty years later, the fountain in
the piazza, even more beautiful than before. I saw Osso, puffy
and swollen from drinking, and Baco hunched before a flickering blue screen. I saw La Schiassi and Verdolin with their
children, and Lussu in his prison cell. I saw Fred aboard a sail-
boat in the South Seas, and I saw Tamara die in a burning car
wreck, one day when she was happy and was coming home
from the beach. I saw myself, old and angry, climbing up that
mountain and telling someone, "Of course I know the trail,"
but in fact I had lost my way. I saw Selene in a white smock in
a hospital room, leaning over Uncle Nevio's bed, listening to
his heart through a stethoscope, and looking over at me.

Then I heard a sound of branches being trampled, someone
singing in a baritone voice, and the Cheerful God arrived. He
was just the way I remembered him, colossal, with long, tangled hair, filthy and dirt covered. His sky-blue eyes stood out
in his bearded face the way that shiny glass eyes do in a teddy
bear. He reminded me of a certain big bunny.

"Timeskipper!" he said. "Well, well, well, look who's still
alive. Your fellow villagers are really stinking things up, they
have more cars than wishes, and instead of stopping to think
about what they're doing, they keep digging and pouring
cement, and the mountain is coming down again. Half of the
hillside came down on top of me in this last avalanche. I'm
going to take a nice bath now."

He stripped off his clothes and walked into the water hole,
gesturing for me to follow him in.

"But it's ice cold," I said.

"Get in the water, city slicker."

Shivering, I shucked off my clothing and waded in. The
water was icy, but I was standing it pretty well.

"You've gotten stronger, Timeskipper. You're not as strong as a whole forest, maybe, but you're as strong as a young tree, anyway, say a ten-year-old hazel tree. If you don't completely run to seed living in the city, maybe one day you'll grow up to be a fine pear tree."

"One day by which clock?"

The God burst into laughter, and made the water boil with his gusto.

"Come on," he said, "let's take a little excursion."

"Where?"

"Dive in and follow me."

He vanished in a half somersault. The water hole was only a few yards from bank to bank, not much more than a yard deep, and the water was crystal clear, but he was gone, I couldn't fig-ure out where. I dipped my face under the water and felt a whirlpool sucking me down. I tried to relax and give in to the suction, allowing the current to pull me along, the way I'd been taught. Suddenly I was surging along in a subterranean river that was rushing down a rock tunnel, I was plunging downward at a terrific rate. Then the tunnel roof dropped, and I was forced to plunge under the water. I was running out of oxygen when I saw light at the end of the tunnel and surfaced. I gulped air into my lungs. I was bobbing in the basin of the Fanara, and the Cheerful God was washing his armpits while two frogs shampooed his hair. I realized that nothing would astonish me after that.

"Enjoy your swim, boy?" he snickered.

"How can this be?" I asked. "Is the water hole linked to the Fanara underground?"

"That's right. People think that if you want to go from point A to point B there is always just one route, the one you can see on the map or the path that other people show you. If people only knew how many hidden passageways there are in the world and in their minds. We invent machinery to join things that are already united. We line up our cars along the highway, and all around us there are roads through the fields and under the dirt and beneath the water in the river. Close to your house, for instance, there is a passageway that runs directly to Maracaibo."

"Where?" I shouted in my excitement.

"At the travel agency, just go and buy a ticket." He burst into wheezy laughter, and the frogs laughed along with him.

"You sure are a funny guy. But could you take it easy with the underwater shortcuts? I came that close to drowning."

"You'll learn." And he turned and dove back into the water. This time I followed immediately, into a greenish water filled with filamentous algae, where newts and emerald-green frogs swam, then I was caught up in a tepid current that dragged me along faster and faster, tumbling me as it swept me forward. Every so often I managed to pull my head out of the water, and I saw light in the distance, and I thought to myself: "Hold on, Timeskipper, you can do it," and the current swept along more and more powerfully and then hurtled me down a waterfall that went down and down and down, until I finally thudded to a halt on something hard but wobbly.

I was on the raft in Rivamarina, the domain of Vanes. All around was sea, little sailboats, and hotels, just the way I remembered it, except that now there were ten times as many hotels and ten times as many people on the sand. The Cheerful God, dressed in a frog-green pair of bermuda shorts, was on the raft, flirting with a couple of German tourists in bikinis.

"Maybe we got lost along the way," he said when he saw me, "but this ain't bad, what do you say?"

"What now?

"Back in the water, on the double," he said.

"Let me catch my breath," I implored. But he ignored me.

"Watch this one, girls," he shouted. He did a triple twist in midair with four somersaults and then a back flip, surged back out of the water, beating his arms like wings, and then plunged headfirst into the water like a cormorant. The German girls weren't sure whether they should clap or summon an exorcist. I jumped into the water feetfirst. I saw the god on the seabed, swimming in the middle of a pod of whales. I caught up with him; by now I had learned to breathe underwater. Everywhere I looked I saw coral and sea anemones and wonderful fish, first tropical fish, then Mediterranean fish, then goldfish, and I recognized the morose goldfish from the basin of the fountain in the Bigcity and waved to him as I passed, then we began to pass schools of mullet, a sign that we were getting closer to fresh water, and then I saw the pikefish—my old friends the pikefish with their hook piercings and their battered snouts, damaged in their war against the fishermen. They greeted me by slapping the water with their tails. But from the seabed a big menacing fish swam up, ten times as big as the others. It was a bearded Wels catfish, with a face that was a hybrid of Stalin, the Avvocato Cannavale, and Fefelli. It swam straight at me and as it opened its gaping maw, I shot to one side, out of reach, and wriggled to the surface.

Now we were lolling in the fountain, amidst the silvery pikefish and the alabaster newts. The piazza was empty, and a big, round, yellow moon hung in the sky. A jet of water was spraying lightly on my head. I looked up, and there was Venus with an odd expression on her face.

She was beautiful and motionless, but her expression was clearly one of vexation, and after a few minutes she opened one side of her mouth and whispered to my companion:

"If you've come to apologize, save your breath."

"I've been busy," stammered the god, "meetings, theophanies, apparitions. Even a palace coup. Please, honey, forgive me."

"Get lost," said the irate beauty, with a wave of her marble hand, "or I'll let the pikewolves loose on you."

With the noise of a metal trap, one of my father's creations snapped its jaws shut, in a very disquieting manner.

"Goddesses . . ." sighed the god, and signaled me to dive back into the water without delay.

This time, the journey was a short one; we slipped down a long, smooth, light-blue subterranean tunnel that looked like a bobsled piste; after describing a parabolic curve, I found myself head-over-heels in the air only to plunge back into the water. It wasn't very deep, I reached the surface in just two strokes.

And this time I was in the water hole, our old hangout on the river.

The Cheerful God dipped a finger into the current and when he pulled it out, a fat grouper was dangling from it.

"No fair, that's not a local fish."

He lit a fire and set the fish on a spit to roast over the flames.

"*Aquae ad unum marem conveniunt*," he said, "and after all, I'm hungry and I'm a deity. I can do more or less what I want."

"You're insane and you're self-important," I said. I was badly dinged up and chilled to the bone.

"You're the one who's self-important," said the God. "You just want everything to turn normal when it suits you? You thought you knew everything about how time and space and their opposites worked. You had fun leaping from one clock to another. But then it didn't work the way you thought it would. You want to know why? Because you don't place enough faith in the world. You thought that you could control the hands of the clock yourself, didn't you, deluded one, little bird lost in the tempest, baby fish caught in the rapids! You wanted to use up something as precious as your determination to fight in the space of an instant, instead of using that force every day. You thought that your fate was sealed, that you had foreseen every-thing: drama, tragedy, and revolver shots, but instead, as you can see, now you're here, right where everything began and will always begin again."

"Then what's happened, if I haven't understood a thing?"

The Cheerful God bit into the grouper, and he never even offered me a taste.

"What's happened? Good question. I imagine that you are not referring to the beginning of the universe, only to your own little piece of history. Well, in the meanwhile, you've lived, and this is already a considerable achievement. If you're interested in knowing, there's already been a meeting and a vote in the forest, to determine your future. It was quite an assembly—you've got some imagination, kid. On one side were the Shadow, the little devil with the violin, the Sacra Pilla, goddess of money, the dark elves, the Strega Berega, the Boletus Gnome, Saturn, the math teacher, and two anomalous Harpies, two tremendous babes with wings. On the other side there was me, the Edible Gnome, Oak-Baruch, Santa Putilla, the water elves, Dionysus—whom you met previously at your final high school exams, in the person of the Greek teacher— as well as a representative of the left-wing parties from Sirius, and finally a gentleman with a mustache and a cape named, I believe, Edgar Allan Puck."

"The last name's Poe," I said.

"Um-hmm. Right. He said that it might be his fault that from time to time you imagine fairly dystopian futures, but that you are basically a good kid."

"Here's what the Shadow said: 'He says he's afraid of me, but he never seems to get tired of challenging me. I'm sick of him, and now I'm going to fix his little red wagon for good.' So I replied to the Shadow, 'Don't you think that you've done enough harm in this valley?' 'I just obey the orders I receive,' he answered, 'loyal through the centuries. She's the one,' and the Shadow pointed to the Sacra Pilla, 'she can never get enough, and she pushes men to the brink of ruin and to rack.

If it were up to me, I'd just do piecework for the Confederation of Bacilli, they've got more than enough work to keep me busy. Look on this order sheet: today alone, I have fifty cases of pneumonia, and the zone I cover is three times the regulation size. I asked for a substitute, but they won't help. And does he help? No, he sits around and plays the violin.'

"'I stick to small misfortunes,' answered the little devil. 'I don't really like getting involved in killing, I'm not much of a sword-swinging archangel, personally.'

"'Watch what you're saying,' said Santa Putilla."

"And what finally happened?" I asked.

"So then everyone, the various proponents and opponents, had a chance to speak their mind. Saturn said: 'He's on my team, he's hot tempered and egocentric, he has mood swings, and then he has this thing about being unique and special, but he's still just a woodsman.'

"'He's good at reading the *Odyssey*,' said Dionysus.

"'He's good at reading *Playboy*, too. He does nothing but jack off all day long, and he's a chauvinist pig,' the Harpies objected.

"'He's so sincere that he bleeds,' said the Sirian. 'On our planet he would be at the very least a third-category Alkazar, and what's more, the points that Saturn makes are profoundly right-wing.'

"In other words, it was a very heated political rally. The two gnomes started banging on each other's whiskers with crowbars, a blond elf told the Strega Berega: 'Either you vote in favor or you get no more sex from me,' and in the end I had to say: 'That's enough, there is obviously no consensus here, so we're going to have to toss the dice.'"

"Toss the dice!?" I exclaimed, profoundly offended. "You have a full quorum of deities and assorted myths and legends, and you wind up tossing the dice? That's a nice example of irresponsibility!"

"No, I'm the one who tosses the dice, sweetheart, that's where the skill comes in. I tossed the dice and I said: 'Hmmm, that's odd. According to the dice, fate has chosen Fefelli.'

"'You cheater!' said the Shadow. I took a swing at him, but it doesn't really matter, the Shadow never feels a thing. He left, saying, 'Well, maybe it's a good thing after all; all I'll need to take him down is a snap of the fingers.' He was referring to the Honorable Fefelli."

"So you play for our lives with a toss of the dice."

"The way you do in the stock exchange? No, no, it's not like that at all. We took into account your courage and the recommendations you received and the fact that you're one of the few idiots alive who still believe in us. You're free to select one of your sixteen potential futures but I can't tell you which one to choose, only that in one of the futures you become Pope. Oh, don't make that face, I'm only kidding. All I ask is that you promise to preserve the clocks as an important and precious heritage, and that you won't betray either of them. The clock of everyday toil and the clock of possible worlds, the clock that counts your steps here on earth and the clock that measures your dreams. The clock that flows and the clock that turns. The clock that steals the people you love most and the clock that brings them back to you. The clock that kills your enemies and the clock that lets you imagine all the different ways you would kill them yourself. The clock that makes you love and the clock that allows you to be loved—do you follow the allusive assonance?"

"And I'm going to have these clocks forever?"

"If you can tell me what the word 'forever' means, then I'll answer the question," said the Cheerful God. "And now let's see who can make their stone skip the highest number of skips."

"Well, you be careful, because I'm really good at this game."

"Then you go first."

I took a *giarella*, or skipping stone, that seemed to have been hand polished, and I swung it with all my strength and let fly. It skipped twenty-six times. That was my personal record, at least as far as I could remember.

"Look at that!" I shouted triumphantly. "I'd really like to see how you're going to do better than that. You may be a god, but twenty-six is outstanding!"

"You're right, I'm really going to have to try my hardest," he said thoughtfully.

He picked up a giant stone, as long and broad as an ironing board.

I hadn't thought of that.

He roared, launched it flat out across the surface of the water, and as he launched it, he hopped on top. The stone and the god went sailing along the river together, upstream. That wasn't stone-skipping, that was flying across the water. I mean, you could invent a sport like that.

"Not bad, eh?" said the god from downriver, hopping over the lock without slowing down, and dwindling away in the distance.

"So long," I said, waving the fish skeleton in a gesture of farewell.

"I'm going back to the source," he yelled. "We'll see each other again, Timeskipper. In exactly six turns of the duoclock."

"I understand perfectly," I said.

Evening was falling, and I was starting to feel a chill. I saw a little boy coming toward me from the little waterfall, balancing on the stepping stones. He looked exactly like me, or almost exactly like me, his hair was a little lighter, he was wearing a windbreaker that looked like a fireman's jacket, and he had on a pair of strange shoes with big rubber soles and a welter of laces, fire-engine red.

"Must be a new model of gnome shoes," I thought.

The boy sat down next to me and said:

"Dad, when I go near the waterfall and listen to the noise, it's like I fall asleep, and then I see the strangest things."

"Really?" I said.

At dawn the next day, I left for the city, with a bigger suitcase than ever before. The train pulled out a little behind schedule, and I had enough time to recognize and call by name all of the Monti Alti, one by one. Then the engineer blew the whistle, announcing the train's departure. I remembered something that Baruch once said, the day that Fefelli was elected mayor and we were all down in the dumps: "There are people who say that they want to fight, then they confuse the whistle starting the match for the whistle that ends the match, and they go home and have dinner." I looked out the window at the passing scenery. The countryside was shrouded in morning mist, the sun was starting to peek through. I imagined people waking up, others already at work, others sleeping in or luxuriating under the blankets, midway between the colors of their dreams and the sunlight pouring in their bedroom windows. I closed my eyes, and the river poured in.

TRANSLATOR'S NOTE

There is a cast of bizarre and alarming characters in *Timeskipper*, portrayed in a disquieting, almost surreal light.

We're not talking about the gods and talking dogs, the mushroom gnomes and sentient trees. Those are straightforward, realistic portraits of the inhabitants of a young boy's imagination in a small mountain town in postwar Italy.

No, it is the mayors and lawyers and journalists and real-estate developers who seem to be teeming across the landscape in the sooty light of a "black" sketch by Goya.

It is, I think, in keeping with the odd sequential logic of *Timeskipper* (*Saltatempo* in the original Italian) that a translator's note comes at the end. A few of the points raised in this essay might have been useful to the reader earlier, but then again, there are some plot spoilers in here as well.

As a reader, you have the Timeskipper option of rerunning time itself—you may want to read the book again. If you do, this is a fast-forward exploration of some of the motifs and themes that are woven into the story, visible, as if in filigree, to an Italian reader, and close to invisible in the English version of the book.

There are all sorts of untranslatables in this book, having to do with sports, pop culture, food, music, and village life. But politics is perhaps the most overarching theme obscured in translation.

To begin with, on page 62, Timeskipper alludes to the boom time (a reference to Italy's postwar "economic miracle," also described in Italian as "il boom") following Fefelli's election; he then ironically echoes himself: "boom, boom, boom."

An Italian reader knows, subconsciously, that "boom"—or those booms—describes economic growth, but that it also refers to a wave of terrorist bombings that bloodied Italy beginning in the late 1960s. The Italian reader knows that as instinctively as an American reader knows that Kennedy was assassinated in 1963, with all that followed.

There was one specific bombing that began what the Italians call the "Years of Lead," a wave of terrorism that almost tipped Italy into civil war. It is known as the Piazza Fontana bombing, after the central Milan square where it occurred.

The foreshadowing of that bombing is present throughout *Timeskipper*. The new fountain! In the town square! Everyone in the book is looking forward, with a mixture of anticipation and foreboding, to the new fountain in the piazza: the Fontana in the Piazza. And on page 349, a full 90 percent of the way through the book, we discover what Fontana Piazza/Piazza Fontana really is.

There were sixteen dead that day. It was a Friday afternoon, and the bank—the Banca Nazionale dell'Agricoltura—was crowded with farmers, in Milan for the weekly market. A famous photograph of the aftermath of the bombing shows dusty, tattered hats—clearly hats worn by Italian farmers—piled on a rubble-strewn bank counter.

Throughout the book, that number recurs. Sixteen rooms in Chicco's new inn, sixteen Ballantyne argyle sweaters that Timeskipper claims to possess, Timeskipper is told to read from book sixteen of the *Odyssey*, he skips a stone sixteen times in honor of Gancio, and the god tells him that he has sixteen potential futures—the same number of futures that were obliterated by the bomb.

When the time comes to bury Libero, Timeskipper's father, on page 318, Uncle Nevio comes hurrying up, a shoe in one hand. This is perhaps the subtlest and most poignant reference to Piazza Fontana, the death of the anarchist, Giuseppe Pinelli. His fall from a fifth-story window is memorialized in Nobel laureate Dario Fo's play, *Accidental Death of an Anarchist*. Pinelli was arrested in connection with the bombing and, three days later, fell, or was pushed, out of the office of a police detective during questioning.

The official story was that he jumped, and one of the policemen present, trying to prevent his fall, grabbed his foot, and was left holding one of Pinelli's shoes.

The problem with that story, of course, is that the body was found in the courtyard below, with both shoes.

The huge demonstration in the Bigcity, on page 350, is a reference to a famous demonstration that occurred days after the bombing.

The president of the Italian parliament, or chamber of deputies, Sandro Pertini, spoke to the crowd that day. Pertini, a Socialist, was—like Baruch—a Resistance leader, and to the mind of the youth of Italy in those explosive years, one of the few reputable members of the country's leadership.

Pertini did another memorable thing on that visit to Milan. He refused to shake the hand of the city's police chief, Marcello Guida. Understandable: when Pertini was a prisoner in a Fascist penal colony under Mussolini, the warden of that colony was none other than Marcello Guida. This is the kind of politician Stefano Benni is trying to portray, and that an Italian reader can easily imagine, in the character of Fefelli.

Last of all, the Pastori brothers' Mercedes. It is hard to say just what Timeskipper is casting into the abyss with that car. Suffice it to say, however, that there is a small town just outside of Naples that is widely considered to be the center of the Neapolitan organized crime system, the Camorra. Even before a new model of Mercedes becomes available in Stuttgart showrooms, it appears in the streets of that small town. So it is safe to say that to an Italian reader, the Mercedes represents a certain Mafioso mentality.

There are other references to noted—in some cases, despised—Italian figures. When Timeskipper says that Fefelli would someday be looked upon as a guru by others, on page 232, he is clearly alluding to Silvio Berlusconi, prime minister of Italy, real-estate developer, and media monopolist, whose brushes with the law are legend. Villa Meringue would seem to be a reference to Villa Wanda, the headquarters of the notorious Italian schemer and head of the P2 Masonic lodge, Licio Gelli (whose name appears as one of the odious Pastori brothers). And Minister Anguilla is a pretty unmistakable stand-in for Giulio Andreotti, seven times prime minister of Italy, twice tried and twice acquitted for collaborating with the Mafia, jocularly dubbed "Beelzebub" by the Italian left.

There are other references that are not quite translatable: the lawyers Timeskipper goes to see in the Bigcity, Speri and D'Intesa, have names that depict their roles. The naïve Speri's name might translate as "hope and dream," while the lurid D'Intesa's name reads to an Italian as "connivance, cahoots, nudge nudge, wink wink."

There are other less portentous names that remain untranslated: the bluff farmer Caprone is a "ram" or "he-goat." The deaf farmer Cipolla is "onions." The pessimist Lavamèl is "it'll go badly." And the ethereal Selene Lunini is a lunar virgin goddess, an evanescent deity of the moon.

If you really know the Italy that Timeskipper grew up with and, tragically, foretold, you understand why the author—and his Italian readers—would be so fond of the sprites, elves, and water nymphs that fill its pages. So many of the real people were stranger—and grimmer—than fiction.

ABOUT THE AUTHOR

Stefano Benni is widely considered one of Italy's foremost novelists. His trademark mix of biting social satire and magical realism has turned each of his books into a national bestseller. His many novels include: *Bar Sport*, *The Company of the Celestini*, *The Cafe Beneath the Sea*, and the remarkably successful *Margherita Dolce Vita*, published by Europa Editions in 2006. Benni is also the author of several volumes of essays and poetry and many collections of short stories.

The Days of Abandonment
Elena Ferrante
Fiction - 192 pp - $14.95 - isbn 978-1-933372-00-6

"Stunning . . . The raging, torrential voice of the author
is something rare."—*The New York Times*

"I could not put this novel down. Elena Ferrante will blow you
away."—ALICE SEBOLD, author of *The Almost Moon*

This gripping story tells of a woman's descent into devastating
emptiness after being abandoned by her husband with two young
children to care for.

Troubling Love
Elena Ferrante
Fiction - 144 pp - $14.95 - isbn 978-1-933372-16-7

"In tactile, beautifully restrained prose, Ferrante makes
the domestic violence that tore [the protagonist's] household apart
evident."—*Publishers Weekly*

"Ferrante has written the 'Great Neapolitan Novel.'"
—*Corriere della Sera*

Delia takes a voyage of discovery through the chaotic streets and
claustrophobic sitting rooms of contemporary Naples in search of
the truth about her mother's untimely death.

Cooking with Fernet Branca
James Hamilton-Paterson
Fiction - 288 pp - $14.95 - isbn 978-1-933372-01-3

"Provokes the sort of indecorous involuntary laughter that has
more in common with sneezing than chuckling. Imagine a British
John Waters crossed with David Sedaris."—*The New York Times*

Gerald Samper has his own private Tuscan hilltop, where he whiles
away his time working as a ghostwriter for celebrities and inventing
wholly original culinary concoctions. His idyll is shattered by the
arrival of Marta. A series of hilarious misunderstandings brings this
odd couple into ever-closer proximity.

Old Filth
Jane Gardam
Fiction - 256 pp - $14.95 - isbn 978-1-933372-13-6

"This remarkable novel [...] will bring immense pleasure to readers
who treasure fiction that is intelligent, witty, sophisticated and—
a quality encountered all too rarely in contemporary culture—
adult."—*The Washington Post*

The engrossing and moving account of the life of Sir Edward
Feathers; from birth in colonial Malaya to Wales, where he is sent
as a "Raj orphan," to Oxford, his career and marriage parallels
much of the twentieth century's dramatic history.

Total Chaos
Jean-Claude Izzo
Fiction/Noir - 256 pp - $14.95 - isbn 978-1-933372-04-4

"Rich, ambitious and passionate . . . his sad, loving portrait of his native city is amazing."—*The Washington Post*

"Full of fascinating characters, tersely brought to life in a prose style that is (thanks to Howard Curtis's shrewd translation) traditionally dark and completely original."—*The Chicago Tribune*

The first installment in the Marseilles Trilogy.

Chourmo
Jean-Claude Izzo
Fiction/Noir - 256 pp - $14.95 - isbn 978-1-933372-17-4

"Like the best noir writers—and he is among the best—Izzo not only has a keen eye for detail but also digs deep into what makes men weep."—*Time Out New York*

Fabio Montale is dragged back into the mean streets of a violent, crime-infested Marseilles after the disappearance of his long-lost cousin's teenage son.

Book two in the Marseilles Trilogy.

The Goodbye Kiss
Massimo Carlotto
Fiction/Noir - 192 pp - $14.95 - isbn 978-1-933372-05-1

"A nasty, explosive little tome warmly recommended to fans of James M. Cain for its casual amorality and truly astonishing speed."—*Kirkus Reviews*

An unscrupulous womanizer, as devoid of morals now as he once was full of idealistic fervor, returns to Italy, where he is wanted for a series of crimes. To avoid prison he sells out his old friends, turns his back on his former ideals and cuts deals with crooked cops. To earn himself the semblance of respectability he is willing to go even further, maybe even as far as murder.

Death's Dark Abyss
Massimo Carlotto
Fiction/Noir - 192 pp - $14.95 - isbn 978-1-933372-18-1

"A narrative voice that in Lawrence Venuti's translation is cold and heartless—but, in a creepy way, fascinating."—*The New York Times*

A riveting drama of guilt, revenge, and justice, Massimo Carlotto's *Death's Dark Abyss* tells the story of two men and the savage crime that binds them. During a robbery, Raffaello Beggiato takes a young woman and her child hostage and later murders them. Beggiato is arrested, tried, and sentenced to life. The victims' father and husband, Silvano, plunges into a deepening abyss until the day the murderer seeks his pardon and he begins to plot his revenge.

Hangover Square
Patrick Hamilton
Fiction/Noir - 280 pp - $14.95 - isbn 978-1-933372-06-8

"Hamilton is a sort of urban Thomas Hardy: always a pleasure to read, and as social historian he is unparalleled."—NICK HORNBY

Adrift in the grimy pubs of London at the outbreak of World War II, George Harvey Bone is hopelessly infatuated with Netta, a cold, contemptuous small-time actress. George also suffers from occasional blackouts. During these moments one thing is horribly clear: he must murder Netta.

Boot Tracks
Matthew F. Jones
Fiction/Noir - 208 pp - $14.95 - isbn 978-1-933372-11-2

"More than just a very good crime thriller, this dark but illuminating novel shows us the psychopathology of the criminal mind . . . A nightmare thriller with the power to haunt."
—*Kirkus Reviews* (starred)

A commanding, stylishly written novel that tells the harrowing story of an assassination gone terribly wrong and the man and woman who are taking their last chance to find a safe place in a hostile world.

Love Burns
Edna Mazya
Fiction - 192 pp - $14.95 - isbn 978-1-933372-08-2

"This book, which has Woody Allen overtones, should be of great
interest to readers of black humor and psychological thrillers."
—*Library Journal* (starred)

Ilan, a middle-aged professor of astrophysics, discovers that his
young wife is having an affair. Terrified of losing her, he decides to
confront her lover instead. Their meeting ends in the latter's
murder—the unlikely murder weapon being Ilan's pipe—and in
desperation, Ilan disposes of the body in the fresh grave of his
kindergarten teacher. But when the body is discovered,
the mayhem begins.

Departure Lounge
Chad Taylor
Fiction - 176 pp - $14.95 - isbn 978-1-933372-09-9

"Smart, original, surprising and just about as cool as a novel can
get . . . Taylor can flat out write."—*The Washington Post*

A young woman mysteriously disappears. The lives of those she has
left behind—family, acquaintances, and strangers intrigued by her
disappearance—intersect to form a captivating latticework of coin-
cidences and surprising twists of fate. Urban noir at its stylish and
intelligent best.

Carte Blanche
Carlo Lucarelli
Fiction/Noir - 120 pp - $14.95 - isbn 978-1-933372-15-0

"This is Alan Furst country, to be sure."—*Booklist*

The house of cards built by Mussolini in the last months of World War II is collapsing, and Commissario De Luca faces a world mired in sadistic sex, dirty money, drugs and murder.

The first installment in the De Luca Trilogy.

Dog Day
Alicia Giménez-Bartlett
Fiction/Noir - 208 pp - $14.95 - isbn 978-1-933372-14-3

"In Nicholas Caistor's smooth translation from the Spanish, Giménez-Bartlett evokes pity, horror and laughter with equal adeptness. No wonder she won the Femenino Lumen prize in 1997 as the best female writer in Spain."—*The Washington Post*

Delicado and her maladroit sidekick, Garzón, investigate the murder of a tramp whose only friend is a mongrel dog named Freaky.

The Big Question
Wolf Erlbruch
Children's Illustrated Fiction - 52 pp - $14.95 - isbn 978-1-933372-03-7

Named Best Book at the 2004 Children's Book Fair in Bologna.

"[*The Big Question*] offers more open-ended answers than the likes of Shel Silverstein's *Giving Tree* (1964) and is certain to leave even younger readers in a reflective mood."—*Kirkus Reviews*

A stunningly beautiful and poetic illustrated book for children that poses the biggest of all big questions: Why am I here?

The Butterfly Workshop
Wolf Erlbruch and Gioconda Belli
Children's Illustrated Fiction - 40 pp - $14.95 - isbn 978-1-933372-12-9

Illustrated by the winner of the 2006 Hans Christian Andersen Award.

For children and adults alike: Odair, one of the Designers of All Things and grandson of the esteemed inventor of the rainbow, has been banished to the insect laboratory as punishment for his over-active imagination. But he still dreams of one day creating a cross between a bird and a flower.